MATTHEW HATTERSLEY

A BULLET FOR THE PAST

Vinci Books

vinci-books.com

Published by Vinci Books Ltd in 2025

1

Copyright © 2024 Matthew Hattersley

The author has asserted their moral right to be identified as the author of this work in accordance with the Copyright, Designs and Patents Act 1988. This work is a work of fiction. Names, characters, places and incidents are the product of the author's imagination or are used fictitiously. Any resemblance to actual persons, living or dead, places and incidents is entirely coincidental.
All rights reserved. No part of this publication may be copied, reproduced, distributed, stored in any retrieval system, or transmitted in any form or by any means, including photocopying, recording, or other electronic or mechanical methods, nor used as a source for any form of machine learning including AI datasets, without the prior written permission of the publisher.
The publisher and the author have made every effort to obtain permissions for any third party material used in this book and to comply with copyright law. Any queries in this respect should be brought to the attention of the publisher and any omissions will be corrected in future editions.
A CIP catalogue record for this book is available from the British Library.
Paperback ISBN: 9781036700850

The EU GPSR authorised representative is Logos Europe, 9 rue Nicolas Poussion, 17000 La Rochelle, France
contact@logoseurope.eu

By Matthew Hattersley

The John Beckett Series

Darkness On The Edge Of Town
When The Kingdom Comes
A World of Sun and Violence
A Bullet For The Past
A Line in the Sand

Chapter One

When you had nothing to do but wait by a window, Stuttgart was the same as any other European city – cold, impersonal, soulless; a sprawling panorama of concrete and neon stretching out to the horizon.

It was late afternoon here in the Swabian metropolis, and the air creeping in through the gap in the window was cold against the man's skin. He adjusted his position, just enough to stave off the creeping muscle cramp in his right shoulder and keep his blood moving.

Wearing short sleeves in the fall, especially in Germany, had been an oversight on his part, but he appreciated the ease of movement the simple t-shirt provided. He preferred that over comfort. Tonight's shirt was black, though he sometimes wore dark navy. He had three of each colour in the holdall by his feet, along with a change of underwear and a leather bag containing essential toiletries.

He waited.

The room behind him was silent, devoid of the usual signs of habitation. No ticking clock, no hum of appliances, just the faint rustle of the curtains in the evening breeze. The only furniture was a wooden table and two mismatched chairs, one of which he'd been sitting on for the last two hours. The walls were bare except for a single faded print of a landscape that could have been anywhere. The carpet was threadbare, the walls a dull beige. The view, however, couldn't have been better, providing him with a clear sightline of Wolframstrasse and the modern Hampton by Hilton hotel.

Like always, he'd spent days meticulously researching the location, down to the smallest detail. He knew the Hampton's layout, its entrances and exits, and the timing of the employees' shifts. He knew the delivery schedules and the patterns of pedestrian traffic. Knew too that this specific apartment he'd chosen was ideal for its position and privacy. He'd found it on the rental market and, after a couple of phone calls, discovered the broker was on holiday and the owner lived in Berlin. It was perfect – no one would disturb him, no one would come knocking. And he would be gone in an hour, maybe less.

He glanced at his watch before returning his gaze to the street, resuming his statue-like stillness.

He observed the flow of people and cars with unwavering patience.

He watched the driver of a white van unloading crates of alcohol into the back room of a local bar before driving away.

He waited.

His was a solitary existence, but he preferred it that way. Even if he wasn't doing this, there would be no close relationships in his life. He enjoyed his own company and the silence that came with it. Years in the US military and then as a specialised skills officer for the CIA's Special Activities

Center had honed his ability to wait for hours, even days if necessary. It was all part of the job.

Waiting. Watching.

Staying ready.

He adjusted his grip on the cold metal of the high-powered sniper rifle in front of him. The Mk 13 was a masterpiece of lethal engineering, but tonight it was an extension of himself. The scope, a Schmidt & Bender PM II, offered unparalleled clarity, allowing him to observe his target with precision detail. He leaned closer and adjusted the focus until the crosshairs were sharp. Up here he was a silent force, a godlike presence in the sky, ready to cast down his judgement on the depraved and avaricious mortals below. He rested his finger on the trigger, his focus narrowing as he slowly swept the area.

He knew his mark was inside the hotel, involved in a clandestine meeting with a high-ranking member of the Hessen Bruderschaft – one of the most powerful organised crime groups in the world. But he also knew the meeting wouldn't last long. Because what the mark had for sale was too expensive, even for the Hessen Bruderschaft.

He exhaled slowly, consciously, keeping his heartbeat steady. Down below, a flicker of movement caught his eye. He leaned into the sight as the front door of the hotel opened and three large men emerged, scanning the area with stern expressions. Bodyguards, professional and alert, but not his concern. His focus shifted to the smaller man following them.

Dressed in a sharp charcoal suit with a pale blue shirt open at the collar, the man had neatly styled short black hair, and aviator glasses with photochromatic lenses reflecting the streetlights. He looked important. He didn't look like a scientist, but they never did in his experience.

Especially not the ones sitting on an invention worth millions of dollars to the right people – or the wrong ones.

Through the scope he tracked the man as the bodyguards herded him towards a waiting car, a sleek black sedan with the engine already running. He had seconds. Maybe less. He tightened his grip on the trigger, releasing his breath in a measured flow.

One... two...

He paused as a man in a light grey suit stepped forward, placing a hand on the mark's chest to stop his movement. The man in grey glanced across the busy road towards the apartment block, his gaze sweeping directly past the open window where he was holding his position.

But there was no way he could see him from that distance.

He couldn't know.

His finger hovered over the trigger as he watched through the scope, realigning the crosshairs with the mark's head. Except now his instincts were tingling. Something was off. It was almost as if someone wanted him to...

Wait...

He adjusted the focus, but he'd seen it correctly. A trickle of black sweat at the mark's hairline. Hair dye. It wasn't him. It was a decoy.

As the realisation hit, a floorboard creaked behind him.

Someone was in the apartment.

He swiftly moved away from the window, reaching for the pistol he'd placed on the table. But before he could grab it, a large figure dressed in black burst through the door, knocking the gun from his hand and sending it skittering across the floor. He twisted away but the intruder followed, offering him no choice but to fight. They collided with a heavy thud, fists and elbows blurring in a desperate struggle for dominance. The big man was fast, and wearing tactical gear designed for combat. He was also a mean-looking sonofabitch, with a shaved head and a scar running across one clouded, milky eye.

With a grunt, the intruder shoved him away and swung a fist at his head. He ducked and retaliated with a sharp elbow to the jaw – a solid blow that would have floored most men – but the big man recovered quickly and lurched forward, grabbing him in a bear hug around his chest, squeezing the air from his lungs.

Teeth clenched, he karate-chopped the man's neck, desperate to break free. When that didn't work, he shoved his thumbs into the man's eyes, pressing them into the sockets. The man yelled out in German, stumbling forward but still holding on tight. With the big lump off balance, he was able to use the momentum to drive them both to the ground. They collided with the table, tipping it over as they crashed to the floor.

Stars exploded in his vision as the air was forced from his lungs. He tried to get up, but a crushing weight pinned him down, the man's knee digging into his chest as large hands gripped his throat. Desperate, he drove his knee into the attacker's groin, making the man yell out once more and loosen his grip. Seizing the chance, he twisted free, throwing his attacker once again off balance.

They rolled across the floor, fists and knees flailing. Spotting his gun, he reached for it, fingertips brushing the barrel until he could coax it into his grip. Just as he got hold of it, the big man yanked him back and they grappled for the weapon, the cold metal slipping in their sweaty hands. They gritted their teeth with the effort, sweat pouring off them, both focused solely on the next ten seconds. The gun barrel jerked left and right as they fought for their lives. The intruder's face was inches from his, close enough to see the brutal determination in his one good eye, close enough to feel the rancid heat of his breath. A fist slammed into his ribs, but he barely registered the pain. Writhing, he twisted the gun barrel upwards, but the bigger man jerked out of the way, using his weight to push it back down. It was a battle of wills, and only one would walk away.

With his muscles screaming in protest, he fought to keep the gun pointed away from him. Summoning every last ounce of strength, he shoved the barrel under the intruder's chin. The man's eyes widened in realisation, but by then it was too late. He pulled the trigger, the gunshot deafening in the confined space. Blood and brain matter splattered across the wall and ceiling. The big man stiffened momentarily, before collapsing into a lifeless heap. Done.

For a moment he lay there, chest heaving, the dead weight of his adversary pressing down on him, ears ringing from the blast. Then he shoved the body away and got to his feet.

Moving back to the window, he grabbed his holdall but left the rifle where it was. It couldn't be traced back to him and it was too bulky to carry. The mission had gone sideways, but he couldn't dwell on it. He had to get away before anyone else arrived.

In the bathroom he swiftly tidied himself up, flattening his hair and tucking his t-shirt into the waistband of his pants. Then he exited the apartment and raced down the fire escape into the night. He needed a rethink. A new plan. His mission wasn't over, not by a long shot.

But for now he had to disappear.

Chapter Two

It was early evening in Costa Rica, and the Casa Selva hotel nestled in the lush greenery of Manuel Antonio was an oasis of tranquillity. Palm trees swayed gently in the warm October breeze, their fronds rustling softly, and the scent of tropical flowers mixed with the salty tang of the ocean. In front of the hotel's outdoor dining space, the now vacant pool sparkled under the setting sun.

At a table on the edge of the dining area, John Beckett was finishing his meal, savouring the last bite of grilled mahi-mahi. The fish was tender, perfectly seasoned with lime and garlic and with a nice hint of smokiness lingering from the grill. He washed it down with a gulp of cold beer, the crispness refreshing in the dying heat.

He'd been working at the hotel near Espadilla Beach for the last two months, fixing leaks, repairing shutters, and handling other handyman jobs. It was simple work, but honest. He liked the routine, the physicality of it. Unlike the complexities of the career he'd left behind, his tasks here were straightforward, with a clear start and finish. He liked that.

He wiped his mouth with a napkin and balled it up before leaning back with his bottle of beer, letting the atmosphere wash over him. His fellow diners were mostly tourists, their conversations a blend of English, Spanish, and other languages. The air was filled with laughter and chatter, interspersed with the scrape of cutlery on plates and the bubbling gurgle from the pool's filters. There was an underlying peace here that he felt he'd been searching for his entire life, a slice of heaven tucked away from the chaos of the world.

He sat up as Isabella, one of the serving staff, approached his table. She was petite, with dark hair pulled back into a neat ponytail and a warm smile that always reached her brown eyes no matter who she was talking to.

"*¿Terminaste?*" she asked, gesturing at his plate.

"*Sí, gracias,*" he replied. His Spanish was good, having had plenty of practice these last eighteen months – first Spain and Portugal, then an extensive tour of South America, and now here, but he didn't say much if he could help it. Mainly he just enjoyed kicking back and being part of the scenery. He could see himself staying here a while.

Isabella pointed at his nearly empty bottle of beer. "*¿Quieres otra?*"

He shook his head. "*No, gracias.*"

She smiled and took the plate away. He watched her go, then picked up his beer and took a final swig. The cold liquid was refreshing, but one was plenty these days, particularly on a week night. He liked to stay sober, even if he didn't need to be alert like he once did.

For a man like Beckett, who didn't need much to get by, life here at Casa Selva was ideal. His pay was modest but it came in cash. He had a room to sleep in and meals at the hotel each day. He enjoyed working outside, the fresh air and physical labour providing a welcome distraction. It was enough; he had no need for more. If he leaned back in his chair he could see the beach and the ocean, waves gently lapping at the shore. Over to the west, the setting sun cast a golden sheen over the landscape.

But as he enjoyed the view he felt a familiar prickle run up the back of his neck. Years of training had sharpened his instincts to a razor's edge and he knew straight away – he was being watched. The laughter and chatter of the tourists faded into the background as he became hyperaware of his surroundings. He stretched, subtly scanning the area, letting his gaze wander over the hotel grounds. The pool, the outbuildings, the trees.

He spotted them on the far side of the complex, near the beach huts: two local men in their early twenties, standing out in their cheap, flashy clothes. One had a shaved head and was wearing a multicoloured tracksuit, a cigarette dangling from his lips. The other sported a sleeveless denim jacket over an oversized t-shirt, a red baseball cap twisted backwards on his head. He had a patchy beard and twitchy, nervous energy.

Beckett recognised the one with the cap. Jace. A cocky kid, full of ego and greed. Two days earlier, he'd caught him trying to extort protection money from the hotel owner and taught him a harsh lesson in manners. They were angry young thugs, trying to establish themselves as an organised crime gang, but they were full of bluster and lacked resources. Just pests. But pests that needed crushing before they grew wings.

Jace and his friend were looking in his direction and gesticulating to one another. Clearly they were back to cause more trouble. His muscles tensed, but he kept his expression relaxed and didn't look directly at them. As Isabella stepped out of the restaurant she noticed the pair. Her eyes met his, wide with caution. He smiled and raised his hand.

"*Está bien*," he said softly. *It's fine.*

Isabella hesitated, then nodded and went back inside. Beckett set his beer bottle down and got to his feet, taking all the time in the world. As he brushed himself down, he caught his reflection in the restaurant window. He avoided mirrors as much as possible these days, so it was always a bit of a shock to see himself looking so laid-back and civilian-like. He was wearing thin linen trousers, no socks, and the same tattered loafers he'd bought in Venezuela. His linen shirt had the sleeves rolled up, revealing hard, sinewy forearms. He was fitter than he had been in a while, his muscles honed from manual labour and a punishing morning exercise routine. His hair was short and wavy, lightened by the sunlight and chlorine from the pool.

He moved slowly, watching Jace and his friend out of the corner of his eye, making sure they saw him leaving. Taking the long way around the dining area, he then cut across the courtyard, steering Jace and his friend away from the hotel guests.

He walked through the car park to a patch of grass on the east side of the complex. A painted white sign declaring the name of the hotel in elaborate red lettering stuck up out of a colourful flowerbed on one side of the lawn, while a large rockery on the other side was illuminated by a string of lamps hanging between two trees. He stopped there.

Jace appeared in less than a minute, swaggering over with an air of misplaced confidence. His baseball cap was pulled low, his eyes narrow. The guy with the shaved head walked beside him, hands in his pockets, a sneer on his face.

"Hey, old man," Jace called out, stopping six feet away. "Remember me?"

Beckett didn't reply.

Jace smirked. "We're gonna teach you a lesson this time."

He nodded. "Come on then."

Jace came in low and fast, aiming a sloppy kick at Beckett's shin. He shifted, easily avoiding the strike. As Jace stumbled forward off balance, Beckett grabbed his arm, twisted it behind his back, and kicked him in the lower back, sending him sprawling to the ground like a discarded rag doll.

His buddy was quicker and more aggressive, swinging his fists wildly. Beckett stepped away, dodging each blow with ease. Then dipping under a right hook, he grabbed the guy's wrist, pulled him forward, and delivered a sharp elbow to his ribs. The man gasped, doubling over in pain and Beckett finished with another elbow to the back of his neck, sending him to the ground.

Jace, not learning his lesson, scrambled to his feet, his surprise turning to fury. He charged again, head down like a bull. Beckett met him with a straight punch to the nose, feeling the crunch of cartilage beneath his knuckles. Blood spurted, splattering Jace's shirt as he staggered back, hands clutching his face.

Beckett dropped his guard, assuming his work was done. But the friend recovered faster than expected and pulled a telescopic baton from his pocket, snapping it open with a menacing flick.

"Fuck you, English," he snarled.

He swung wildly with the baton, making a strange whooping sound like he was mimicking a character from an old kung fu movie. Beckett jumped back as he advanced, narrowly avoiding the first strike. Seeing the next swing coming, he stepped inside and grabbed the guy's wrist, squeezing and twisting at the same time. He felt the bones give, the ligaments tear under the pressure. The man screamed in agony and released his grip. As the baton clattered to the ground, Beckett kicked it away before a swift elbow to the side of the head dropped the man like a stone.

Jace, blood streaming from his nose, launched one last desperate attack. But he was all bluster and no technique. As he lunged, Beckett grabbed him by the jacket and flipped him over his hip. He hit the ground with a thud and Beckett was on him in a nanosecond, pressing his forearm against the guy's throat.

"Enough?"

Jace nodded frantically, eyes wide.

Beckett held him there for a moment to make sure the message was clear, then got up. "Get your friend and get out of here," he said, stepping back. "And if I see you around here again, I won't be so gentle."

Jace grudgingly got to his feet and helped his friend up. They both staggered off, supporting each other as they staggered down the road. Beckett watched them go. He'd gone easy on them, but he doubted they'd be back. He took a deep breath, the adrenaline still coursing through his veins, then turned and headed back to his room. He wanted to distance himself from the scene, wary of any guests who might have heard the commotion. But as he walked away, he noticed a blonde woman standing near the hotel's entrance, watching him from afar. A guest, no doubt.

Damn it.

Back in his room he shut the door and leaned against it. He didn't regret his actions, but he wished it didn't have to be this way. He had come here to escape, to find peace. Yet no matter how far he ran or how much he tried to blend in, trouble always seemed to find him. He ran a hand through his hair, felt the tension in his muscles.

A knock on the door jolted him alert. He turned and opened it a half inch. Isabella stood there, worry sharpening her fine features.

"*¿Todo bien?*" she asked. *Everything okay?*

Beckett forced a smile. "*Sí, todo bien. Gracias, Isabella.*"

She nodded, but still seemed unsure. "*Si necesitas algo, avísame.*" *If you need anything, let me know.*

"*Por supuesto. Buenas noches,*" he replied, closing the door as she walked away. He appreciated her concern but didn't want to drag her into his problems.

He lay on the bed and stared at the ceiling, scanning his body for injury. His knuckles ached from where he'd punched Jace, but other than that he was fine. He closed his eyes, letting exhaustion wash over him. As sleep came, his last thought was of the woman he'd seen watching him. There had been something in her expression that bothered him, something he couldn't quite put his finger on. He hoped she wouldn't cause any trouble for him.

Hell, he'd had his fair share of trouble already.

Chapter Three

Beckett woke early, no alarm needed, and was dressed and at work before any guests had surfaced. The morning was still, the buzz of insects the only noise. After a simple breakfast of bread rolls, jam, two bananas and coffee, he headed out to the splash pool, net in hand. The sun was already making its presence known, the air warming as he dipped the net into the water, skimming the surface to catch the bugs and debris that had collected overnight. It had become the part of his morning routine he appreciated most. The motion of the net gliding through the water was almost meditative, each sweep bringing clarity to the water.

The splash pool was a tranquil, albeit man-made, oasis enclosed almost entirely by tropical foliage. Palm trees swayed above, casting dappled shadows on the water, whilst the scents of blooming hibiscus and frangipani mingled with a hint of ocean salt. The pool's surface reflected the vibrant plants and brilliant blue sky above it like a painting, disturbed only by the occasional ripple from a darting dragonfly or a fallen leaf.

Life was a lot like this pool, Beckett thought. No matter how clean you tried to keep it, something unpleasant always crept in that you had to deal with. But as long as you kept at it, and didn't let the crap build up, you could maintain some semblance of order. He caught a beetle in his net and watched it struggle for a moment before flicking it away. Small victories.

His thoughts wandered as he worked, the repetitive action causing his mind to drift. Yet being who he was his instincts remained sharp, a constant hum beneath the surface, and his daydream shattered as he sensed he was no longer alone. He looked up. The woman from last night emerged from the hotel entrance on the other side of the pool. She walked slowly, almost hesitant. She was dressed for the climate in a pair of short white shorts that highlighted her shapely legs. A pastel blue blouse was tucked so tightly into her waistband he couldn't help but notice her curves. Pale blonde hair peeked out from under a sun hat, the wide brim barely concealing the sharpness in her eyes.

"Good morning," she said, squinting against the early morning light as she got closer. She was American, with a slight southern lilt to her accent.

"Morning," Beckett replied, the way he might to any other person staying at the hotel. He continued working, but his awareness remained on her.

She walked a little way around the pool towards him, her sandals crunching softly on the gravel path. "I'm Erica," she offered with a warm smile, extending a hand. "Erica Reed."

"Michael," Beckett said, giving the cover name he'd been using for almost two years. He shook her hand. Her grip was firm and confident, her skin soft and a little silky, possibly recently moisturised.

She stood, watching him work. "You're up and at it very early," she said. "I'm always impressed how much work happens behind the scenes in places like this. All the effort that goes into making our stay so easy and relaxed. People like you are the unseen heroes."

Beckett offered a half-smile but remained silent. He wasn't sure he agreed with her and he was wondering what she wanted. He continued skimming the pool.

"I saw what you did last night," she continued, leaning in and lowering her voice.

Beckett nodded, noncommittal. "Okay."

"You weren't scared of those two men?"

He shrugged, dipping the net back into the water. "They're just kids. But they've been causing trouble for the owner of the hotel. I'd already told them to leave him alone. Last night was just me reiterating that point."

Erica scoffed but seemed impressed. A little excited, even. "Well, you certainly did that."

Beckett raised his head to glance at her, trying to get a read. Her eyes were clear blue and sparkled with intelligence, her full lips were set in a determined line. She wasn't wearing much make-up but had a natural beauty that some people might call understated. Her athletic build suggested she was used to physical activity.

"How long have you been working here?" she asked.

"A couple of months," he replied, scooping another leaf from the water. He flicked it to the side, not breaking his rhythm.

"And before that? Your accent tells me you're a long way from home."

He straightened his back, reminding himself of their roles here. Him as a hotel employee and her as a valued guest.

"Travelling around," he said. "Finding work where I can."

"I see." Erica tilted her head playfully "A nomad."

"I wouldn't go that far."

She looked him up and down, making no secret of it. "You've always done this kind of work?"

"No. I'm from London originally and worked in insurance," he said. "But two years ago I received a surprise inheritance. I decided to leave the rat race behind and see the world."

Erica nodded, seemingly convinced by his story. But why wouldn't she be? He'd given her no reason to doubt him. He'd been relaying a similar version of what he'd just told her to anyone who asked for the last eighteen months – ever since he fled from his old life as part of Sigma Unit, an elite, off-the-books division of the British Secret Service. His cover story was simple and believable, keeping people from asking too many questions. But Erica's sharp eyes made him uneasy.

"Interesting," she said, studying him. "I just thought there might be more to it. You handled those guys pretty well for someone who worked in insurance."

"Like I said, they were just cocky kids who needed to be taught some manners. I got lucky." He leaned on the net, observing her more closely. Her skin was pale, almost untouched by the tropical sun, and her nails were neatly manicured. She couldn't have been out here for more than a few days at most.

She smiled, though to him it looked forced. "Well, it's good to know someone like you is around. Makes me feel safer."

Beckett nodded but remained guarded. Erica seemed

nice enough, but he knew better than to trust appearances. "Glad to hear it," he said, returning to his work.

The silence that followed was filled with morning birdsong and the clatter of breakfast carts. Beckett rinsed his net in the pool, keenly aware of Erica's presence, and the fact she seemed desperate to say something.

"Actually, I wonder if you could help me," she whispered. "I'm not sure who else to ask."

Her gaze darted across the pool towards the hotel's open glass doors, beyond which the first guests were arriving at their tables for breakfast. Beckett noted how delicate yet strong her jaw was in profile despite the flutter of concern creasing her features.

"What do you need?" he asked her.

She turned back, hesitating for a moment. Then it poured out of her. "Well, it's just... you seem kind... and perhaps understanding too. I'm a girl travelling alone, ya know, and it's a lovely hotel here but... I don't know, I've started to feel unsafe. Last night I think someone tried to get into my room. And I have this feeling... like someone might have put cameras in there."

Beckett studied her for a moment. His instincts told him to be cautious, but the fear he recognised in her eyes wasn't something a person could fake. "I don't think you have anything to worry about," he said. "The hotel owner is a good man and wouldn't allow such things to happen."

"Right. Yes." She fidgeted with the buttons on her blouse. "I just... I'd feel better if someone could take a look. Maybe check the locks, too?"

Beckett caught how her hand shook a little as she raised it to wipe a bead of sweat from her neck. "All right," he said. "I'll take a look."

Erica released a long breath. "Thank you so much. I'm in room 214. Maybe we could go there now?"

Beckett set the net down. He was all but finished here anyway. "Sure, why not."

He gestured for her to lead the way, then followed, maintaining a respectful distance and nodding hello to the morning staff as they passed. Erica moved quickly, forcing him to quicken his pace to keep up. He noticed the stiffness in her shoulders, the way she clenched and unclenched her fists, knuckles white with tension. Something was bothering her, but it wasn't the story about cameras in her room. That was all made up.

They climbed the stairs to the second-level landing, which was open to the elements and looked out over the hotel gardens. Reaching her room Erica paused, fumbling the keycard out of her pocket and almost dropping it. She was self-conscious. Nervous, even. Beckett watched her take a deep breath to steady herself before sliding the card through the reader and opening the door.

"Here we are," she said, stepping aside to let him enter first. "Thank you so much for this. I appreciate it."

The room was standard for the hotel – clean, comfortable, with a queen-sized bed, a large white lacquered dresser and a flatscreen TV on the wall facing the bed. A cream and gold bathroom was visible through an open doorway, and French doors led out onto a balcony overlooking the main pool. The net curtains were drawn, and the room was lit by a single bedside lamp.

Beckett moved into the room, methodically checking the obvious places first – the vents, the mirrors, the picture frames. He even examined inside the lamp fixtures and took down the fire alarm to check inside. He knew he wasn't going to find anything, but Erica seemed reassured by his thoroughness. Pulling back the curtains, he checked the balcony. Everything seemed in order. Finally, he crouched to check under the bed. Dust bunnies clung to the corners, but there were no signs of any hidden electronics.

He got to his feet. "There's nothing here," he said, turning to Erica. "Was there anything specific that made you worry?"

Her face fell. "Not really. Only a feeling of unease." She sat on the edge of the bed and slumped her shoulders, looking around the room as if expecting something to jump out at her.

Beckett cleared his throat, one eye on the exit. "Look, if it'll put your mind at ease, I'll keep an eye on your room. But is there something else the matter?"

She shook her head. "Can you sit for a minute?" she asked, patting the bed beside her. "I just… I just need to feel safe."

Beckett hesitated. He didn't like where this was going. She was a fine-looking woman, but he was happy working here and there was no way he was going to jeopardise that by fooling around with one of the guests.

"Please, Michael." She patted the bed more insistently. "I just want to talk."

"What about?"

"Just sit."

He perched on the edge of the bed, as far away from her as he could without it being awkward. "What's going on, Erica?"

She bit her lower lip. "It's just… I don't know who to trust." Her voice was barely audible, and he had to lean in to catch her words. "But I suppose that's true for everyone."

Up to that point she'd looked jumpy and panicked, but now he saw a flash of something else cross her eyes. Something he didn't like. He leaned back, and immediately felt a hard cold press of metal at the back of his neck. He tensed as a male voice snarled in his ear.

"Hands where I can see them."

Beckett's instincts flared, but he did as instructed. "What the hell is this?"

The woman who claimed to be Erica Reed stared at him but didn't speak, her eyebrows knitting together as if contemplating an impossible conundrum. Beckett stared back, trying to figure out if she was complicit or coerced, but he couldn't tell. And what was this anyway? A mugging? Some kind of payback? His mind raced with possibilities, none of them good.

"Don't move," the voice behind him instructed. "I mean it. I will kill you."

The man was kneeling on the bed behind him, so close Beckett could feel his breath on his neck. He visualised their positions, considered how he could turn the situation in his favour. A sharp pivot to the left, driving his elbow into the man's solar plexus while grabbing the gun with his left hand. He'd have the guy gasping for breath and disarmed in less than a second. He tensed. It was risky, but it was his best shot at walking out of here unscathed…

Right until the moment Erica reached under the duvet, pulled out a gun, and aimed it at his head.

"Don't be stupid," she warned, as if reading his thoughts. Her grip on the pistol was impressively firm. Gone was the frightened woman, now replaced by someone cold and calculating.

"What's going on?" he asked, searching for a tell in her hard blue eyes that she hadn't just played him so easily.

"I'm sorry," she said, without sounding it. "But you're coming with us."

Before he could react, a bag was yanked over his head, plunging him into darkness. The coarse fabric scratched against his face, blocking out all light and muffling sound. He braced himself just as a heavy object struck the back of his head, sending a jolt of agony through his skull. The world tilted violently. He fought to stay conscious, but it was too much. Another sharp blow to the side of his head rattled his brain further. Pain exploded behind his eyes. He collapsed onto the bed, straining to make sense of what was happening. But there was only confusion. A white light burst across his vision. Then there was darkness again. Then there was nothing.

Chapter Four

Beckett's head throbbed, his thoughts were sluggish. Every effort to rouse himself was met with a wave of disorienting fog clouding his mind. A dull pain in the back of his skull thumped in time with his heartbeat, but the memory of what caused it was hiding on the edge of his awareness. He blinked himself awake, the simple act of opening his eyes requiring more effort than he'd expected.

His vision was blurred and unfocused, shapes and shadows dancing around him. He took a deep breath and tried to recall what had happened. Then he remembered: Erica, the woman from the hotel. The cold press of a gun on his neck. The bag over his head. He forced his eyes wide, willing them into focus.

Gradually the room took shape around him. He was sitting on a steel chair, the backrest hard against his shoulder blades. The dim light from a single overhead bulb cast a pale glow on the table in front of him and illuminated dust particles floating in the air. Handcuffs on his wrists were shackled to a steel ring embedded in the table's surface. The cold metal dug into his skin as he tested the restraints, tugging lightly at first, then harder, but they held firm.

Apart from the table and chair, the room was empty – a plain, utilitarian space with no windows and not even a camera watching him from the corner. That was probably a bad sign. Facing him was a single metal door with no window.

He took a deep breath, the act of inhaling sending a sharp pain through his head. His muscles felt heavy and unresponsive, like they were filled with lead. He licked his lips, the dry, bitter taste in his mouth confirming his suspicion – he'd been knocked out and then sedated. Whoever Erica was working for clearly didn't want him waking up too soon. His tongue felt thick, his throat parched.

As he gathered his bearings he heard footsteps approaching. A moment later the door creaked open, and a large man with thick white hair entered the room.

Beckett sat upright. "I should have guessed."

"Howdy, John." Xander Templeton grinned. "Fancy seeing you again."

Templeton stepped through the doorway, allowing the door to shut behind him. Beckett had almost forgotten how physically imposing the CIA section chief was. Tall and broad, he had a wide chiselled jaw and piercing blue-grey eyes that held an intensity no one could ignore. Today he was wearing grey chinos and a dark green sweater with a short zip at the collar. Like he'd just stepped off the fairway.

Beckett remained silent as Templeton approached the table, regarding him with a smirk. "Look at you, you look like a damn hippy," he snarled from the corner of his mouth. "Too long on the lam, living like a fugitive, I expect."

"I've not been tried for anything," Beckett replied. "I did nothing wrong."

"Yet you've been a pain in my ass ever since you screwed over your unit and jumped ship."

"I didn't screw anyone over. I had no choice but to go dark."

"Semantics, Mr Beckett. You say tomato…"

"What the hell is this, Templeton?" The pain in his head did nothing for his patience.

Templeton sauntered around the table. "Just a little reunion. It's been too long."

"Cut the crap. Why am I here?"

The American stopped directly in front of him, leaning in. "You really have to ask me that?"

Beckett took a deep breath, focusing on slowing his heart rate. Staying calm was crucial. He knew he wasn't a threat to anyone's national security but he also knew Templeton saw it differently. To him, Beckett remained a loose cannon and a liability. He had a head full of classified information and knew too much about the British Secret Service and their numerous joint missions with the CIA. People in high places couldn't afford that risk.

"I'm no traitor," he said. "I'm not going to cause you – or anyone – any problems. I'm out."

"I'm afraid that's not for you to decide, son," Templeton replied. "The problem is, you have the potential to create a big old shitstorm for a lot of people. Makes me kind of nervous, ya know?"

"So what's the plan? You kill me?" Beckett looked around the bare room. "I'm assuming this is a black site somewhere?"

Templeton raised an eyebrow, a fresh smirk playing at the corners of his mouth. "Something like that. We're actually in the hull of a US naval vessel moored a few miles off the coast of Belize. But you are correct that if anything were to happen to you here, no one would ever know."

Beckett felt a surge of frustration. He hated feeling trapped, cornered. But he couldn't let Templeton see that. He had to stay strong and keep his wits about him.

"Do I have options?" he asked.

Templeton grinned. "Now we're talking. You see, I knew you were a sharp guy, John." He leaned against the wall, acting nonchalant, good cop and bad cop all rolled into one. "I had a very revealing chat with a mutual friend of ours recently. Vanessa Adler. She spoke very highly of you."

Beckett's jaw tightened. Adler had promised to keep his identity to herself. But he said nothing, letting Templeton talk.

"It sounds as if you were quite the hero down in Venezuela," he continued. "Ms Adler said in her report that you saved her life. I suppose we have to thank you for that."

"It was nothing," Beckett said. "What else did Adler tell you?"

"Calm down, son. She didn't give me anything I didn't already know. See, you were already on my radar. Although I'll admit, you are a hard man to find."

"I did hope to keep it that way."

"No one stays hidden forever, Beckett."

"Clearly." He leaned back, the metal chair inflexible beneath him. "So what am I doing here? I don't imagine you've brought me here to shake my hand and send me on my way with a retirement gift."

"No, I'm afraid I'm all out of watches."

"I've got nothing to tell you. Nothing to trade. If you want me dead you'll have to get on with it."

Templeton held his hands out and mimicked weighing up his options. "It's not important what I want, John. But what if I told you there was a way out?"

The tension was broken by the click of heels outside the room. The door opened and the woman from the hotel stepped inside. She looked very different from the meek, approachable woman Beckett had met by the splash pool. She was now wearing a sharp trouser suit, the fitted jacket fastened over a white shirt buttoned to the collar. Her blonde hair was pinned up in a tight bun, giving her a hard, professional edge. In her hands she held a cardboard file.

"I believe you've met," Templeton said.

Beckett caught her gaze. "Erica is it?"

She walked over to stand beside Templeton. Her expression was impassive, but her eyes betrayed a flicker of something else.

"Actually it is." Her voice was deeper and more refined than Beckett remembered. "Erica Reed is my real name. We didn't think it mattered telling you, especially as—"

"You were about to double-cross me and bring me here?" Beckett cut in.

Her lips twitched. "I was going to say – especially as we *might* be working together."

"Oh?" His attention flicked back to Templeton.

"It's a possibility," he said. "But that all depends on what happens in the next couple of minutes."

Beckett looked from one to the other, then down at his handcuffed wrists. Funny; he didn't get the impression there'd be room for negotiation. He dragged his gaze back up to Templeton. "I'm listening."

Templeton stepped up to the table and leaned on it with his fists. "I need you to do something for me. A job."

"What sort of job?"

"One that's high stakes. Extremely dangerous. One that requires absolute secrecy and flawless execution."

Beckett nodded. "I see. And if I refuse?"

Templeton chuckled. "Well, John. Then you'll never leave this room."

Chapter Five

Beckett stared at Templeton, his bleary mind spinning, trying to find a way out of this mess. He knew he couldn't trust Templeton, but he also knew the man was dangerous and egotistical, always looking out for his own interests first. Whether any of this would be useful, he wasn't sure. He clenched and unclenched his fists, feeling the bite of the handcuffs against his wrists.

"What's the job?" he asked at last, knowing that once he was given the details, there'd be no turning back.

Templeton straightened and gestured to Erica, who stepped forward, holding out the card folder she was carrying. Beckett observed her closely, noting the slight hesitation before she placed the file in front of him. Their eyes met briefly. There was a flicker of something unspoken – remorse, perhaps – before she looked away.

"We need you to take out a rogue agent," Templeton said. "Nothing you haven't done before."

Beckett flipped open the folder and leafed through the documents. Not so easy with hands cuffed and chained to the table. Inside the file were photos, surveillance reports, the kind of material he'd seen hundreds of times in his old career.

"Who is this person?" he asked.

"He goes by many aliases, but his real name is Saul Turner," Reed said. "He's a specialised skills officer at the SAC."

Beckett nodded. He knew the SAC – Special Activities Center – well. It was the CIA division most similar to Sigma Unit, involved with deep cover, covert ops, paramilitary tactics, the whole nine yards.

"Turner's been in the thick of some of our most classified missions," Templeton continued. "He was a good officer. But now he's dirty. A liability."

Beckett scoffed. This was starting to sound familiar. He imagined Templeton had said those same words about him. He looked up. "Why not deploy one of your assets? And why isn't SAC handling this internally?"

Templeton sighed. "The agency's a complex beast, Beckett, you know that. Layers upon layers of bureaucracy." He paced, rubbing at his granite chin. "This needs to be off the books, completely deniable. We can't risk internal leaks or cross-departmental blowback. SAC is aware, but they want it handled with absolute discretion. No fingerprints."

Beckett's eyes narrowed. "What's Turner done?"

Templeton stopped pacing and fixed him with a hard stare. "He disappeared from his latest assignment in Eastern Europe six months ago. Since then he's been off the grid. No contact, no intel. We've intercepted chatter indicating he's been in touch with Russian operatives and other hostile actors, raising red flags and blood pressure all over Langley and Washington. We have credible intel suggesting he's planning to sell classified information – names of assets, operational details, locations of covert facilities. If this intel gets into enemy hands, it's a national security disaster."

"Turner was one of our best, but now he's a threat," Reed added, as Beckett flipped through the file. "We need to find and eliminate him before he sells to the Russians and compromises more assets. This isn't just neutralising the threat. It's about preventing any fallout."

Beckett raised his head, taking them both in. "Why me?"

"Because you're one of the best operatives I've ever encountered," Templeton said.

Beckett smiled. "Okay, now tell me the real reason."

Templeton's expression softened slightly, though his eyes remained cold. "We need to keep this mission off the books to ensure the president has full deniability. The SAC is behind this decision, and they tasked me with bringing you on board." His voice lowered. "We have reliable intel that Turner's now operating stateside, in New York City. We can't use our people for obvious reasons — can't risk being seen operating on home soil. We need an external asset, someone with your skillset who's off the radar. That's where you come in. You're perfect for this kind of black bag job."

"You want me to go to New York?" Beckett asked.

"Correct. We'll provide you with a new passport and alias. Everything will be taken care of. Find Turner and take him out, clean and quiet, and I'll forget I ever heard the name John Beckett. You'll be free to go wherever you want."

"I'd be a ghost," Beckett said.

Templeton smirked. "You already are. No difference. Except you won't have to watch over your shoulder for the rest of your life."

"How do you want it done?"

"Any way that gets results," Templeton replied. "We'll sort the clean-up once it's over."

"Then I'll need equipment. Guns."

"Of course. You got a wish list?"

"No reason to overthink it," Beckett said. "A sniper rifle, something like an H&K PSG1. Two or three pistols, preferably Glocks. Plus silencers and plenty of ammo."

Templeton nodded towards his companion. "Reed will get everything you need and manage the gear until it's required."

"So she's coming too?"

Reed tipped her chin up but otherwise her features remained impassive. "You have an issue with that?"

"Not at all. It'll be nice to have some company." He leaned back, assessing first Reed and then Templeton. Something felt off. "How good is this guy?"

"A top-tier operative," Reed said. "This is high stakes, high risk. But from what I've heard, you're the man for the job."

"You've heard about me?" Beckett gave her a half-smile, testing the waters.

She didn't bite. "Turner is dangerous and has intel that could blow the lid off many of our operations," she said, her tone clipped.

"And his presence in New York means the clock is ticking," Templeton added. "We need this done within the next three days. We'll provide you with everything you require. After that, you're off the grid for good."

Beckett took a deep breath, rattled his chain. "It doesn't appear I've got much choice."

"Good man." Templeton thumped his fist against the table triumphantly. "Reed will escort you to New York and support you with whatever you need."

"Support me?" He glanced at Reed, who remained stoic. "You mean babysit me."

Templeton clamped his hand down on Reed's shoulder. "Reed is one of my best operatives and Turner is dangerous. You're going to need her help."

Beckett glanced down at his handcuffed wrists. "Fine. I guess we're going to New York."

Templeton grinned. "Welcome back to the game, son."

"Yeah, thanks." Beckett shook his head. "Some days it feels like I never left."

Chapter Six

Inwood, Manhattan was a neighbourhood of contrasts. Aged apartment buildings and small, worn-down businesses lined the streets, their exteriors telling tales of long-standing neglect. Yet amidst the weathered bricks and greasy storefront windows, patches of greenery offered a surprising counterpoint. Trees lined the sidewalks, their leaves rustling in the light breeze that provided a cooling respite from the urban hustle and bustle. The faint aroma of hotdogs drifted from a vendor down the street, while the constant hum of traffic filled the air.

At the corner of Cooper and West 207th Street, Saul Turner hid behind a row of spruce trees, eyes locked on the apartment building across the street. Typical of the area, the exterior was drab and run-down, allowing it to blend into the background, unnoticed. The perfect hideaway for someone keen on staying under the radar. He shifted, adjusting his position for a better view while remaining concealed. His apartment was on the top floor of the low-rent building and he had similar places in Washington, Los

Angeles and London – always in the worst neighbourhoods, always leased under a different alias.

Turner had been scoping out the building for the past hour, watching, waiting. He had no reason to believe anyone else knew about this apartment, but he couldn't be too careful now they were on to him. Further down the street a group of kids played ball, their laughter almost out of place in the grey, fatigued setting. He watched them briefly, a twinge of something close to regret, or perhaps even jealousy, surfacing for a second before being pushed aside by his indomitable focus. He returned his attention to the apartment building.

The front door opened and a woman stepped out. She was middle-aged, with a weary expression and a heavy bag slung over her shoulder. She looked around briefly, scanning the street with a hint of caution, before heading down the block. Turner watched her until she was out of sight. The coast looked clear but he remained where he was, assessing the building and surrounding streets for signs of surveillance or unexpected company. He clocked a man walking his dog, a couple arguing on a nearby corner, a delivery truck idling a few blocks away. But nothing out of place.

Satisfied, he picked up his holdall and emerged from behind the trees. He crossed the road, keeping his head down as he walked, just another faceless soul among the many. At the building entrance, he paused to glance up and down the street before opening the door and slipping inside.

The hallway smelled faintly of mildew, a constant presence. The walls were painted a dingy beige, peeling in places. It wasn't the nicest place, by any stretch of the imagination, but Turner didn't care. He wasn't trying to start a life here. Or anywhere. For a man like him, homes were just tools to help him in his work much like his gun, or his encrypted laptop with custom-built software, or the people he encountered.

He took the stairs rather than the elevator, preferring to move his body wherever possible. As he ascended, his senses were attuned to every nuance – the creak of a floorboard, the distant hum of an appliance, the faint echo of voices through thin walls. His footsteps barely made a sound on the worn linoleum.

His apartment was on the fourth floor, room 4E. He pulled the key from his pocket, double-checked he was alone in the corridor, then opened the door with a quiet click. He stepped inside, closing the door softly behind him. The apartment was sparse and practical, designed for functionality rather than comfort. A small couch, a desk and a single chair furnished the living room. The kitchen area had basic appliances, all spotless and arranged with military precision. Turner locked the door and set the chain before moving through to the bedroom. Here too the room was devoid of personal touches. No photographs, no mementoes, just the bare essentials – a bed, a small closet, a nightstand. If Turner engaged in any kind of media that wasn't relevant to his job he might have called himself a modern stoic, or even a minimalist, but he didn't go for labels. He was just his next mission. A blank canvas. Another tool to be used.

He placed the holdall on the bed and unzipped it, unpacking with care. On top were neatly folded clothes: dark jeans, and dark-coloured t-shirts. Beneath these, an encrypted tablet and one of his passports. He stowed the empty holdall in the closet and pulled out an almost identical bag. This one was heavier, packed with equipment he might need while in town. He laid the items on the bed – digital lock picks capable of bypassing electronic security systems, a coin-sized micro-listening device, an encrypted smartphone, augmented reality glasses with facial recognition and data overlay features, a small EMP device for disabling electronics, and two SIG P320 modular handguns.

He checked each item in turn, ensuring everything was in perfect working order, then undressed completely, placing his worn clothes in a metal laundry box in the hallway before moving to the bathroom. The space was small and functional, just like the rest of the apartment. He turned on the shower, the water gushing out in a sharp, steady stream. He adjusted the knob to make it ice cold, then moved to the mirror.

It had been three weeks since he'd last looked at his reflection. His thin lips were set in a line of determination, his strong jaw covered with dark stubble. He would remove that shortly. His hair was short and neat, styled for ease and anonymity. A white scar ran from his temple to his jawline, a memento from a knife fight in Caracas. Another faint line across his forehead told the story of a close call with shrapnel in Kandahar. His nose, slightly crooked, had been broken more times than he cared to remember.

He stared at his reflection for a moment longer, undeterred by the hard, dispassionate look in his eyes, then stepped into the shower. The icy water hit his skin like tiny needles, but Turner welcomed the discomfort, letting it sharpen his senses and clear his mind. He washed himself, his hands gliding over his lithe, muscular frame, a mere thirteen percent body fat. He traced his right index finger down the long scar on his left arm, the receipt from a machete attack in the Philippines. A circular burn mark on his right shoulder came from an interrogation gone wrong in Syria. Turner liked his scars. He saw his body as a canvas of his life's work, each welt and disfigurement a brushstroke of violence and survival.

He stood under the freezing jets, his breathing steady and controlled. The water washed away the sweat and grime, but it also served a deeper purpose. It was a ritual of purification, a moment to prepare for the task ahead. His muscles tightened under the relentless cold, but he remained still, embracing the discomfort as he prepared himself for what awaited him.

After several minutes he got out and dried himself off, ensuring no moisture remained, then folded the towel neatly and placed it back on the radiator rail. Dressing in a fresh pair of black canvas pants and a black t-shirt from his closet, he picked up the encrypted tablet and moved into the front room.

He sat at the desk, his back straight, and powered on the tablet. The screen flashed to life, its brightness slicing through the dim room like a blade. He navigated to the documents folder and opened the files he had saved, examining the surveillance images and facial recognition hits. The mark was now in New York. He was close. But Turner had to step carefully. They were coming for him, and there was no room for error, no tolerance for failure.

He rolled his head from side to side, his C4 through C7 vertebrae clicking as he did. It felt good. He was ready. Bader might have dodged him in Germany, but he wouldn't get away this time.

Chapter Seven

Beckett sat in the cramped airplane seat, the hum of the engines a constant backdrop to his thoughts. The steady drone was almost hypnotic, but did little to soothe his concern. He was forty thousand feet above the North Atlantic, possibly nearing Florida, but without a window seat he couldn't verify their location. Around him, his fellow passengers slept or chattered softly.

He glanced at Reed beside him. She was asleep. Or at least her eyes were closed and features relaxed, her chest rising and falling with each breath. She looked peaceful and undeniably attractive when not viewed as a mendacious abductor. It was clear why Templeton had sent her to trap him. However, he wasn't pleased with himself for succumbing so easily to her damsel-in-distress routine.

He shifted in his seat, feeling the stiffness in his muscles from the long hours of travel. The seat cushion offered little comfort. He sat back, his legs jiggling with unspent energy. Like any good soldier he grabbed sleep when he could and had slept for the first hour on the plane, but they were only two hours into their flight from Belize City to New York, with another two and a half to go until they touched down at JFK, and he was restless.

The journey had started with a helicopter ride from the floating black site to the mainland, followed by the first commercial flight out of South America. Both he and Reed were travelling incognito and Beckett's new passport was in the name of Simon Rivers. It had a decent enough ring to it.

He glanced at Reed as she stirred, mumbling something he didn't catch. A second later she was wide awake, confusion turning to vigilance as she looked around.

"How long was I asleep?" she asked.

"About an hour, maybe more. Don't worry, you didn't snore."

She looked at him as if he'd said something obscene. "I never snore."

"Okay. Just saying."

He rolled his shoulders back. So far he hadn't spoken much with Reed beyond formalities, their conversations focused on the mission and logistics. His first impression of her was that she was rather brittle and reserved, but he knew he needed to understand her better if they were going to work effectively together. Shifting in his seat, he consciously adopted a persona of empathy and intrigue, much like he would when recruiting or interrogating an asset.

"So... Reed," he began, keeping his tone light. "How did you end up working for Xander Templeton?"

She gave him a sidelong glance. "I've not been with the agency long. In fact, this is my first post," she said, her voice low to avoid being heard by those close by. "I was in the Marine Corps before this. There was a time not long ago when I thought I would quit the military altogether, maybe open a bookstore or something. But then someone from the agency approached me. They had all the right words, you know? Promised me the world."

Beckett nodded. "Marine Corps. Impressive. What unit were you with?"

"3rd Battalion, 8th Marines," she replied. "I was deployed to Afghanistan, and did a couple of tours there. Helmand Province mostly."

"Helmand. That was no picnic. What was your role?"

"I flew UH-1Ys on my first tour before realising I wanted to focus on intelligence. It was hard work, transitioning, but I went through SIGINT training and then worked in counterinsurgency, analysing communications and intercepting enemy signals. Eventually I moved on to more specialised missions – embedding with local units, gathering intel firsthand, that sort of thing."

Beckett smiled. He remembered the work well. "Why did you leave?"

She shrugged, her eyes flicking away momentarily as if recalling memories she preferred to keep buried. "Just felt like it was time for a change. The Corps was… it was good, taught me a lot, but I needed something different. I was getting restless, felt like I was going through the motions. I wanted something more challenging, something that would push me further."

"And the agency promised that?" Beckett asked, watching her closely. Her jaw had tightened at the mention of her old work. There was something there.

"They sold me on making a real difference," she said. "Being on the front lines of national security, dealing with threats before they become crises. Plus, the perks aren't bad.

Better pay, more autonomy, and the kind of work that's never boring."

"Oh, it's never boring." He smiled, trying to put her at ease. "Sounds like a good deal. Where'd you grow up?"

"Maryland. I'm the youngest of three. I have two older brothers, so I was always a bit of a tomboy, I guess. It wasn't a bad childhood. My dad was a cop, and my mom stayed at home to care for us kids. Pretty standard, nothing too dramatic. I joined the Marines right out of high school. Figured it was a good way to get out and see the world."

Her answers were brief and felt rehearsed, her eyes not quite meeting his.

"Maryland's nice," he said. "And now you're working for Xander Templeton. What's your experience with the man?"

Reed gave him a look that suggested he needed to try harder. "I think he's my commanding officer and a great man," she replied coldly. "His approach might be a little… unconventional, but the results speak for themselves. And he's very well-respected."

"I'll take your word for that."

"You should."

"And what are your orders for this mission?"

Reed glared at him. "I'm here to assist, make sure the mission goes smoothly. Templeton thought I'd be a good fit."

"Assist how?"

"Logistics, support, whatever's needed," she said, her tone growing colder.

Beckett nodded, aware he was pushing too hard, but his restlessness and the weight of the last twenty-four hours were getting to him.

"To assist in anything, we need to know what's going

on." He leaned across the armrest between them and whispered, "You still haven't told me what the deal is with the rogue agent. All I know is he's become a liability and I have to do something about that."

"It's a little more than being a liability," Reed hissed.

He shrugged. "Semantics."

She shifted uneasily in her seat, looking for personal space their close proximity didn't offer. "What more do you want to know?"

He dropped back a little, glancing past her out the window as the plane banked right. "A lot more. Who is he? What's his story? What was he working on before he went rogue? Why's he in New York?"

"Most of that we don't know. The rest is on a need-to-know basis."

"And I need to know."

Reed hesitated for a long moment before reaching into her bag and pulling out a small tablet. "For your eyes only." She handed it to him with a serious look.

He took the tablet and powered it on. The desktop was empty except for a single folder labelled *Summer 2023*. Beckett tapped it and a secure login prompt appeared. Reed leaned over and entered the credentials, her fingers moving swiftly over the electronic keyboard.

The app opened to a series of heavily redacted documents and he began to read. There was a list of aliases, previous deployment coordinates with timestamps and geotags, as well as summaries of past missions. However, most of the critical intel was redacted, leaving only fragments. It offered nothing new. Beckett memorised the four aliases Turner had used in the past two years and returned the tablet to Reed as the clink of glass signalled the arrival of the drinks trolley. A moment later a female flight attendant appeared over the seat in front, prompting Reed to stash the tablet in her bag.

"Can I get you anything?" the attendant asked with a cheerful smile.

"No, thank you," Reed answered for the both of them.

"Actually, I am a little thirsty." Beckett flashed the attendant a broad grin. "I'll have a club soda, if you'd be so kind."

Beside him Reed sighed. "Fine. I'll have the same."

The flight attendant had short dark hair and smelled of vanilla. She cracked open two small cans of club soda and set up a pair of plastic glasses, placing a cube of ice in each. As she leaned over to set the first drink on Reed's tray, Beckett discreetly grabbed a napkin and pen from the trolley. He scribbled down Turner's aliases and stuffed the napkin into his pocket. Reed, busy pouring her soda, didn't notice.

With his drink in hand and the trolley moving down the aisle, he leaned back, attempting a different approach. "Why do you think Templeton's acting independently from the agency?" he asked.

Reed's eyes flicked to him, showing a hint of irritation. "He's not. Not really."

Beckett sipped his drink. He knew the US Secret Service was a many-headed beast, with countless secret divisions. Templeton's explanation about his role in the mission was sort of plausible but Beckett wasn't buying it. There was always the possibility Templeton was setting him up, but that didn't seem likely. If he wanted him dead, why hadn't he taken the chance when he had it?

"There's nothing you can tell me about Turner's whereabouts, or what his plans are?" he asked.

All you need to know is how to complete the job you've been given."

He leaned in closer. "I know that, Erica. But understanding how he operates would help. And frankly, I'm still in the dark about why I'm involved at all. To get us to this point you've already burned through a lot of resources. Who's bankrolling this off-the-books mission?"

"If we knew those things we wouldn't need you. This would have been taken care of weeks ago."

"Yes." Beckett glared at her. "That's why I'm so confused. Why don't you know these things?"

Reed's jaw tightened as she looked away. When she met his gaze again a moment later her eyes were steely and tone immovable. "Turner's a threat to national security. That's all we need to know."

Beckett felt his frustration rise but kept his mouth shut. He wouldn't get anything more out of her right now. *Patience.*

"Templeton knows what he's doing," she added, almost to herself.

Beckett drummed his fingers on the armrest. Yes, Xander Templeton knew exactly what he was doing.

And that's what worried him.

Chapter Eight

Beckett sat on the edge of the hotel bed, massaging the back of his neck. The Grand Regency's polished marble lobby had promised more luxury than the room delivered, but it was adequate, typical of any mid-range establishment near Times Square. The walls were adorned with bland modern art prints, and the thin carpet's geometric pattern blurred if he stared at it too long. The bedspread was pale blue, standard issue, no frills, and it was the same story with the curtains. A small desk with a cheap chair, a wall-mounted flatscreen TV and a mini fridge completed the setup.

Reed had booked the room and the one next to it on agency funds, which was fortunate since Beckett currently had no money, no phone, and just the clothes on his back. He'd have to fix that soon, but for now he needed to ground himself and recalibrate.

He lay back on the bed and closed his eyes, but a knock at the door adjacent to the bathroom pulled him from his thoughts. It wasn't the main door, but looked to be a connecting door to the next room. He hadn't noticed it until now. That was sloppy. He could blame the flight and the knock on the head but neither was good enough, he needed to focus.

He rose off the bed as the door opened and Reed stepped into the room, a wry smile twitching at the corners of her mouth. "It's for ease of movement and privacy," she said, catching his surprise. "Don't get any ideas."

Beckett raised an eyebrow, momentarily thrown by her flirtatious tone. Not that he was a prude, or a monk, but the comment felt contrived and didn't quite land, what with that wall of steel she'd been projecting since she walked him into a trap back at Casa Selva. He brushed it aside, focusing on his real priority – getting out of the hotel and digging for answers, preferably alone. His trust in Templeton and Reed was shaky at best, and he needed to understand his true purpose in New York City. Even if killing Turner got Templeton off his back for good, that wouldn't be enough. He needed to know why he was the one chosen to do it. The agency had hundreds of people on their books who could take out a rogue operative without leaving a trail as to who gave the order.

He feigned a yawn. "You know, I could use some sleep."

Reed leaned against the wall, arms crossed. "Didn't you sleep on the plane?"

"Barely. I just dozed. I need a shower, too." Stretching his arms he caught a waft of himself and knew that wasn't a lie. "I haven't washed since you threw a bag over my head."

"I guess we could both use some rest." Reed glanced at her watch. "You go first. Best one of us stays awake just in case."

"In case of what?" he asked, barely able to hide his frustration. This wasn't going how he wanted.

"In case we get a call. I've got an encrypted phone Templeton can use to reach us."

"Right. I also need new clothes and a toothbrush," he added, gesturing down at the now grubby and sweat-stained shirt and light trousers he'd put on for work that morning. "You didn't exactly give me time to pack."

She pushed herself off from the wall. "Fine. You want to go now? I'll come with you."

He snorted at the insinuation. "Come on, Reed. You don't need to be my shadow the entire time. Despite what Templeton told you, you can trust me. And for this mission to succeed, we have to trust each other. You're running things here, right? Well, you're going to have to let me out of your sight on occasion. You've got my passport. I won't be able to get far. I can't leave the country."

What she didn't know was that he'd had a passport and enough money for a plane ticket stashed in a safe deposit locker at JFK for the past ten years. But he wasn't planning on doing a runner. If this was his path to freedom, he'd do what was needed. Finish the job, get Templeton off his back. Then he could collect his niece Amber from where she was hiding in Spain, and start a new life somewhere sunny. A real future for both of them.

Reed studied him for a long moment. She was still wearing the buttoned-up shirt and sharp suit from earlier, her hair scraped back off her face and pinned at the back of her head. It was unnerving how different it made her seem from the woman who'd approached him at the pool that morning. He wondered which Erica was the real one, or whether neither of them were. But then her features caved a little and she reached into her jacket, pulled out a credit card. "Use this."

He took it, glancing at the name, Ms Erica Reed. "Really?"

"Yeah, buy yourself something pretty," she quipped.

"I won't be long." He pocketed the card along with the room key and headed towards the door, feeling Reed's eyes on him the whole time.

Stepping out onto the street, the city's energy hit him like a wave. But that was New York for you. He took a moment to find his bearings then turned right, walking briskly down West 42nd Street. Except he wasn't heading for the shopping district. He needed information, and there was one place he hoped to get it.

As he crossed 6th Avenue, the Bryant Park Winter Village loomed ahead, and beyond it the white stone and Corinthian columns of the New York Public Library. Beckett passed between the huge stone lions flanking the broad steps and hurried up towards the entrance where he pushed through the heavy bronze doors.

In contrast to the chaos of the streets outside, the library was a haven of stillness and quiet contemplation. Beckett paused in the entrance hall, scanning the signs and information points before moving into the Rose Main Reading Room. A vast space stretched out before him, filled with rows of long wooden tables, green-shaded lamps, and high arched windows letting in streams of natural light.

He made his way to the computer terminals at the far end of the room, the soles of his loafers tapping loudly in the tranquil space. At an empty chair he sat and twisted the screen towards him. Leaning over the keyboard, he started with a simple Google search: *Saul Turner, USA Military.* The results were predictably vague, consisting mostly of public records and unremarkable mentions in obscure articles. Turner was a decorated soldier, recipient of the Distinguished Service Cross, and had risen to Major. But none of it explained why he was a target. Beckett's fingers drummed on the keyboard. He needed more.

Next he tried accessing the SIS database with his old login, but a red warning flashed on the screen: ACCESS DENIED. He cursed under his breath. It had been a long shot, but no such luck.

He leaned back in his chair. Time to think. Beaumont was his next best bet, but a quick assessment of time zones told him his old friend in London would be asleep. Beckett hadn't been in contact with him for some time as he didn't want to risk exposing his whereabouts. But since he was now working for Templeton, he had a bit more room to manoeuvre.

Five minutes later he'd created a new email account in the name of David Garland. It was an old alias of his, but he hoped it would still resonate with Beaumont when the name appeared in his inbox. Opening a new message window, he typed out a semi-coded message.

Subject: Old Friend in Need of Help

Hey Jacob

Long time no see. I hope you and Martha are doing well and you don't mind me contacting you out of the blue like this.

I don't suppose you know the whereabouts of our mutual friend Saul Turner, specifically in New York City?

I'm currently in New York myself and need to catch up with him. Most urgently.

A Bullet For The Past

Any light you can throw on the matter would be most helpful. Use the four names on the attached document as a starting point.

Your old friend.

He attached a separate note file containing the four aliases he'd jotted down on the plane, then hit send. He closed the browser window and deleted all cookies, browsing history and site data – removing his digital footprint as best as he could under the circumstances.

With the message sent, Beckett turned his attention back to his research. Namely, what was Turner doing in New York? Google and other mainstream sites would be a dead end but he had other sources, other options. He navigated to 4chan and spent the next half hour diving into the murky depths of its conspiracy theory threads. It was tedious work filtering through the noise, but he knew these forums well from his Sigma Unit days. Amongst the sea of weirdos and conspiracy nuts, he'd occasionally stumbled upon a hint of a whisper of a lead. Today, however, there was nothing useful. Undeterred, he switched to Reddit, delving into the various sub-forums dedicated to espionage, underground activities, and conspiracy theories. He combed through countless posts, hunting for any clue that might steer him in the right direction. But again he came up empty. No cigar.

Frustrated but not beaten, he changed tactics, moving to the darker and grimier corners of the internet, onto the unlisted sites, Inside Job and Black Sheep. These forums existed in hidden layers of the world wide web, shielded by complex encryption and obscure access points. They thrived in the shadows, catering to a niche audience of intelligence veterans, hackers and hardened conspiracy theorists. To the general public these sites were invisible, their existence known only through whispers in underground circles.

It was on the Black Sheep forum where something caught Beckett's eye – a thread regarding the infamous Rosenwald Committee and a meeting due to take place this weekend in upstate New York. He clicked on the first post and began to read, his interest sharpening. The Rosenwald Committee was a name he knew well. Though a relatively new addition to the shadowy world of elite influence, they already wielded considerable power. They styled themselves as a modern, more progressive take on the Bohemian Grove set – a secretive cabal with deep pockets and a focus on technology and innovation. Comprised of crypto billionaires, AI developers, cyber warfare specialists, venture capitalists, and tech moguls obsessed with life extension and doomsday scenarios, they were the Bilderberg Group, if all the conspiracy theories were true. The sheer amount of wealth and influence they commanded had intelligence agencies on both sides of the Atlantic on edge.

The post revealed they were meeting this weekend, near Pharaoh Lake, a few miles north of Albany. An area of forestry, lakes and wilderness. Not a convention centre in sight. A shiver ran down Beckett's spine. If Turner was involved with the Rosenwald Committee, the implications were troubling. The more he read, the more unsettled he became. The committee's clandestine gatherings were attended by high-profile figures with unlimited resources, all of them hungry for an edge – making it the perfect venue for Turner to peddle sensitive intel. The post went on to explain how this year's agenda focused on biomedical innovation and advancements in military technology.

Beckett paused, his instincts suddenly on high alert. He glanced around the library, unable to shake the feeling he was being watched. To his left, an elderly man with a thick moustache and wire-rimmed glasses was absorbed in a book about World War II. Four tables down, a young woman with bright red hair and oversized headphones typed furiously on her laptop, her face set in concentration. Neither seemed to take notice of him, but Beckett had survived this long by trusting his gut. He wiped his data and search history once more, then logged off the terminal.

Walking out of the library, he hurried down the stone steps and blended with the flow of pedestrians on 42nd Street. He kept his head down and his senses sharp but didn't look back until he reached the corner. There he glanced over his shoulder, but the dense crowd made it impossible to detect anyone following him without drawing attention.

Perhaps he was being paranoid. And that for Beckett was nearly as unsettling as being tailed. What he needed was a clear head, unbiased thought, and a balanced perspective. Then he could figure out how to find Turner while staying ahead of whatever game Templeton was playing.

One thing was clear, though. He was getting closer to the truth, and that was all the motivation he needed to keep pushing forward.

Chapter Nine

Beckett quickened his pace, losing himself in the crowd as he had done countless times before. It was easy here. The vibrant energy of New York City surrounded him – the blaring taxis, the relentless wail of sirens, the murmur of voices. He kept his head down, blending in as just another passerby, a nobody, yet his thoughts remained sharp and focused, his mind racing with the implications of what he'd uncovered.

The Rosenwald Committee meeting at Pharaoh Lake was a potential lead, but he needed more information, and fast. If Turner was planning to sell intel to these people, the stakes were higher than ever.

Navigating through the throngs of tourists and locals, Beckett's senses remained on high alert. He weaved around commuters and sidestepped tourists, avoiding eye contact as he mulled over possible scenarios and next steps. There was a lot to consider, but first he needed sleep. He also couldn't return to the hotel empty-handed. He was supposed to be out buying clothes and supplies.

He ducked into the next department store he came to, moving swiftly through the aisles. There had been a time when Beckett cared about style, but right now he'd take functionality, comfort and ease. Without much thought beyond choosing the right sizes, he grabbed a three-pack of white boxer shorts, black socks, two pairs of dark blue jeans, and two beige linen shirts. He tossed them into his basket, then picked up a toothbrush and toothpaste. The hotel provided these, along with soap and shampoo, but he liked having his own. In Beckett's world, small comforts made a difference. He carried the items to the counter, barely acknowledging the cashier as he beeped Reed's credit card, then headed back out.

His head was spinning as he walked down West 42nd Street, but he knew the importance of rest and recuperation. No point pushing himself over the edge so early in the mission. But as he turned the corner and spotted The Grand Regency across the street he stopped dead. Reed was coming out of the main entrance.

She paused on the roadside, glancing left and right, but didn't see him. He retraced his steps and ducked behind a newsstand on the corner to watch her. She'd changed clothes. Gone were the formal garments, replaced by a fitted leather jacket, dark jeans, and beige running shoes. Her hair was no longer in a bun but in a sleek ponytail and she was wearing dark sunglasses.

Damn, Reed.
Could you look any more suspicious?

He hung back, observing her with growing curiosity. Before he left there was something about her that seemed odd, the way her tone shifted. Now his instincts told him she wasn't out for a casual stroll.

She set off from the hotel with a sense of urgency, her

steps brisk and assured. Beckett emerged from behind the newsstand and followed her, maintaining a safe distance on the opposite side of the street but keeping her in view. She turned onto West 42nd Street, then took a right on 8th Avenue, heading towards Chelsea. Beckett adjusted his path, blending into the flow of pedestrians as he tailed her.

Reed continued straight down 8th Avenue, walking past a long row of diners and upscale restaurants. The rich aroma of food filled the air, reminding Beckett he hadn't eaten since the flight. As he followed, the bustling restaurant and theatre district gave way to residential streets, neon signs replaced by family homes and the occasional storefront.

It was clear Reed had a specific destination in mind. She moved with purpose, scanning her surroundings with focused intent, unlike the leisurely pace of a casual walker. Beckett stayed back, using the busy streets as cover.

At 23rd Street, Reed turned right, heading west. Beckett quickened his pace, weaving through the thinning crowd as they entered Chelsea. The area was quieter, making concealment more challenging. He briefly blended with a family pushing a stroller, before crossing the street as Reed turned left onto 9th Avenue, heading south. Traffic was even lighter here, and there were fewer people on the sidewalks. Beckett maintained a greater distance, his focus entirely on Reed.

At the next corner, she stopped and pulled out her phone to answer a call. Beckett ducked behind the outdoor display of a small souvenir shop, pretending to browse. He picked up a miniature Statue of Liberty, turning it over in his hands while keeping an eye on her. She looked agitated, speaking in a staccato rhythm to whoever was on the other end. After thirty seconds, she ended the call and resumed walking, her pace quickening.

Beckett replaced the ornament and continued his tail. They were near Chelsea Market now. The streets buzzed once again with activity, offering ample cover, but he held back as Reed's vigilance intensified. She paused frequently, scrutinising her surroundings with increased attention. Beckett mirrored her actions, using trees, parked cars, and storefronts to maintain cover.

Where the hell are you going, Reed?

As they neared the entrance to the High Line, Reed abruptly veered left into a side street. Beckett hesitated for a moment, then followed. The street was narrow and lined with small eateries and a sea of outdoor diners. The high walls on either side muffled the city's hum, replacing the sounds of traffic with clinking dishes and murmured conversations.

Reed reached the entrance to an alley and Beckett ducked into a doorway as she stopped and glanced around. He waited. Had she seen him? Risking a peek around the edge of the brickwork, he caught her entering the alley. All good. After a beat, he slipped out from his cover and approached cautiously.

The alley was narrow and dim in the evening light, with two industrial dumpsters along one side and a fire escape ladder bolted to the building opposite. Beckett positioned himself at the corner, near the first dumpster, peering around to see Reed halfway down the stretch of alley, talking to a man he didn't recognise. He was of average height with no real distinguishing features, and wore a plain grey suit, his light brown hair cut short and neat. He looked like a typical spook – bland, unremarkable, but with an air of alertness. For a moment Beckett wondered if this was

Turner in disguise, but dismissed the idea. Turner was listed as six-one in his file – the same height as Beckett – while this man was about three inches shorter. A person could cut and dye their hair, they could even wear lifts in their shoes, but what they couldn't do was make themselves shorter.

Reed and the man exchanged words, their conversation too quiet for Beckett to overhear. He edged along the wall, using the dumpster for cover.

What are you up to, Reed?

The man handed her a small package no larger than a paperback book, which she slipped into her jacket pocket. Then they exchanged a nod and the man turned to leave. Beckett ducked down behind the dumpster, pressing himself against the cool brick wall at his back. He held his breath as the man walked past him, ready to act if necessary. A second later he heard Reed's footsteps approach the mouth of the alley.

He waited until she was a safe distance ahead before resuming his pursuit. Reed appeared to be heading back the way they'd come, but her demeanour and pace were less intense than before. She'd completed her task and seemed satisfied with herself.

Beckett stayed back as they navigated the crowded streets, but as Reed neared the hotel he quickened his pace. He anticipated she'd check on him when she got upstairs and he'd rather her think he'd returned to his room than been out this whole time. As Reed entered the hotel, he raced up the steps behind her, reaching the lobby in time to see her heading for the elevator on the far side.

His eyes darted to the staircase on his right. It would be tight. Rushing through the door, he grabbed the handrail and hauled himself up, taking the stairs two at a time. It took him seven seconds to reach the first-floor landing. As he sped around the corner to the next flight he glanced down the corridor, gauging the distance between floors and the elevator's speed. The lights showed Reed hadn't yet reached the first floor. He could work with that.

As he climbed the stairwell he kept track of the floors and calculated his remaining time. Once he reached his floor he was out of breath, but saw no sign of Reed. He rounded the corner by the elevator and checked the display. She was close. He hurried down the hallway to his room, spurred on by the ping announcing her arrival on the sixth. Behind him he heard the soft whoosh of the doors opening. She was just a few steps away.

He reached his door, swiped his keycard, and slipped inside, closing the door with a soft click behind him. He kicked off his shoes while upending the shopping bag, tipping his purchases onto the surface of the desk. Throwing the bag to one side, he yanked off his shirt and trousers, tossed them to the floor, then launched onto the mattress, pulling up the covers and adjusting his position to appear as natural as possible.

He heard Reed's door open and close, followed by her footsteps approaching the connecting door. He closed his eyes, letting his breathing slow and his muscles relax. The door creaked open and he felt her eyes on him. He lay still, breathing evenly, twitching his eyelids a touch to mimic REM sleep. After a long moment the door clicked shut and he heard her moving around in her room. He considered getting up to shower, but it had been a long brutal day, and the bed was cool and comfortable. Despite the nagging thoughts and half-formed theories spinning in his mind, he knew he'd get nowhere with them tonight. Tomorrow would bring its own challenges, but just now, with the room growing dark as the evening wore on, the weight of sleep was already pulling him under.

Chapter Ten

It was late evening in New York's Meatpacking District. The cobblestone streets, slick with wear, reflected the streetlamps, casting shifting shadows as revellers and stray cats moved through the area. The air was thick with the stench of garbage and diesel, mingling with traces of cologne and amyl nitrate. Warehouses lined the streets, with many converted into upscale restaurants and exclusive nightclubs. Yet on the outskirts, some remained vacant, their brick facades scarred by years of neglect. Windows were boarded up or broken, leaving only darkness visible inside.

Among these buildings stood an old warehouse, set back from the street. Once a cigar factory, it now lay empty and forgotten. Graffiti covered its external walls, with tags and murals telling stories of rival gangs. Inside was a vast empty space, the smell of rust and decay strong, an occasional drip of water from a leaky pipe the only noise. A broken conveyor belt and an old set of industrial weighing scales were stacked against one of the walls, all covered in many years' worth of dust. It was the sort of building that was so far gone it would take a wrecking ball to fix. Yet being so abandoned and unnoticed by the world, it was ideal for activities requiring its inherent darkness and isolation.

The narrow staircase to the basement was lit only by a basic lamp, hanging from a hook and powered by a small generator that hummed with electricity. At the bottom, a heavy steel door stood as a barrier to the room beyond.

In the centre of this stale windowless room, a man was bound to a chair. His head hung low, his reddish hair matted with blood, some of it fresh, some dried. His face was swollen and bruised; one eye nearly closed. A deep gash ran across his cheek, still bleeding, and his lips were split and puffy. His clothes, once neat and businesslike, were torn and stained with blood. His suit jacket lay crumpled on the floor and white shirt had turned a shade of pink. His hands were tied tightly behind him, the ropes cutting into his flesh as he struggled in vain to free himself.

Turner moved closer to the man in the chair, leaning down to look him in the eyes. "Now are you ready to talk?"

The man glared defiantly. "Fuck you!"

Turner punched him in the nose. The man's head snapped back, a strangled cry escaping his lips as blood spurted from his nostrils. Turner had felt the cartilage break, the sickening crunch just a finality. The man writhed in the chair, but the ropes held him fast, tightening with every twist. The Arbor knot was doing its job. He coughed and sputtered blood as Turner watched with cold detachment.

"Let me know when you're ready," Turner said, flexing his fingers, the thick latex gloves squeaking as he did. He hated getting blood on his clothes, so he wore full protective gear, including a hair net and goggles. The plastic sheeting covering the floor and walls added to the psychological impact and ensured no evidence was left behind. It made whoever was in the chair think it was the last room they'd ever see. And for this guy, that might be true. It all depended on how talkative he got in the next five minutes.

Turner stepped back, the plastic crinkling underfoot. He didn't take his eyes off his captive, noting the fresh wave of pain crossing the man's features. He was close to breaking. But they weren't there yet.

And Turner wasn't ready to stop.

The man in the chair was a bloated pig of a man, his face bearing the perpetually smug expression of someone who had never faced real adversity. He reminded Turner of a guy he'd grown up with in Madison, Wisconsin; a typical spoiled rich kid who felt it was his God-given right to abuse and torment the young Saul Turner at will. Back then, Turner had been a quiet, peculiar child, an easy target for bullies who thrived on making others feel small. The humiliation he'd endured had left deep scars, but those same scars had shaped him into something formidable.

As an adult, Turner hadn't shed his eccentric, introverted nature, but he had turned his weaknesses into strengths. His loner personality, once a source of ridicule, became a cornerstone of his work. His meticulous memory and fastidious attention to detail, traits that had once marked him as an oddball, were now invaluable assets.

His life took a pivotal turn at the University of Maryland when he was approached by Stephen Majors – the man who would become his mentor in his early days at the CIA. Majors saw potential in Turner where others had seen only quirks. Under his guidance, Turner developed a fierce reputation for recalling minute details others overlooked, and planning operations with an almost obsessive level of precision. That timid boy from Madison had evolved into a hardened operative, driven by a desire never to feel small again.

He glanced around the dark room and then focused back on his captive. "I get it, you're a tough guy," he said. "But we both know how this ends. You tell me what I want to know, and maybe you'll get out of here alive." He leaned closer. "Or, we can continue. Your choice."

The man in the chair wheezed, spitting blood. "I… I don't know anything!" His eyes darted around the room, searching for an escape that wasn't there. "Please. I can't say."

Turner shook his head slowly. "Wrong answer."

He grabbed the man's hair, jerking his head back to meet his gaze. The man's eyes were wide, his pupils dilated with fear.

"I know you're involved in this. So tell me. Will he be there?" Turner's grip tightened, shaking the man's head to punctuate his demand. "Tell me."

The man grimaced but stayed silent. Turner released him, stepping back to pull a pair of pliers from his pocket. The polished metal glinted under the light as he held them up.

The man gasped. "No. Please. No."

"Let's try this again." Turner moved around the back of the chair and grabbed the man's hand, prying his fingers apart. The man struggled weakly, but Turner was far stronger. He positioned the pliers around one of the man's fingernails and began to pull. The room echoed with the man's screams, but Turner didn't flinch, his focus unbroken until the nail was ripped free. Blood flowed freely from the wound, and the man sagged in his chair, sobbing.

"You think this is the worst I can do?" Turner's voice was soft, almost gentle. "Sir, I haven't even started."

"Okay! Okay!" the man pleaded, his voice barely audible as Turner moved around to face him. "Please, stop. I'll tell you... I'll tell you everything." He convulsed with sobs, the pain consuming him. His eyes met Turner's, wide with terror. "Just... please... no more."

Turner gave a curt nod. There was no smile, no sense of accomplishment filling him. But why would it? He knew this would be the outcome before he even started.

"Good," he said, slipping the pliers into his pocket. "Now, start talking."

Chapter Eleven

Beckett's eyes snapped open. The room was pitch black, but his instincts screamed at him – something was wrong. He lay still, his breathing steady, ears straining for the faintest sound. Someone else was in the room. He didn't move, waiting for his eyes to adjust, forcing them to catch any hint of movement. After a tense moment he discerned a faint silhouette near the door.

A floorboard creaked. Beckett's pulse quickened. Remaining motionless, he watched them edge closer. Then, in one fluid motion, he sprang from the bed, catching them off guard. There was a thud and the sound of fabric tearing as they both hit the floor, grappling in the darkness, limbs and fists twisting, each seeking the advantage.

Beckett's hand found the intruder's wrist, twisting it sharply. They let out a muffled gasp before a knee jabbed into his ribs. He shifted his weight, throwing the intruder off balance, and wrenched their arm behind their back. Pressing down with his weight, he felt their struggle weaken beneath him.

The intruder grunted and growled, thrashing in an attempt to break free, but Beckett maintained control, one knee driving into their back as his free hand fumbled for the lamp on the nightstand.

The room flooded with light. Beckett leaned back to see Reed sprawled beneath him, eyes blazing with rage. "What the hell are you doing?" she hissed.

Beckett's grip tightened. "I could ask you the same thing. What are you doing in my room?"

"Get the hell off of me," she snarled.

He released her and rocked back on his heels. Reed sat up, rubbing her wrist, her face flushed with anger, or was it embarrassment? Her hair was tousled, and her scant attire – a vest and panties – left little to the imagination. Beckett himself was only wearing boxers, and for a brief moment he sensed a mutual discomfort. But he brushed those feelings aside, still furious and needing answers.

Standing, he held out his hand to her. She ignored it, pulling her legs up to her chest and touching her lip tentatively with her left hand. Unusual for a right-handed person.

"Don't worry, you're fine," Beckett said, watching her intently.

"Yeah?"

"What the hell were you doing in here?" he asked, stepping back and sitting on the edge of the bed.

"I don't know. I got the wrong door, I guess. I thought this was the bathroom."

Beckett held her gaze. He smirked. She'd have to learn to lie better if she was going to make it in this game.

"What's in your hand?" he asked, nodding at her right fist, which had been clenched since he switched the light on.

She hesitated, her eyes darting away. "Nothing."

"Open it then."

Reed looked as if she was about to bolt. He leaned forward and his expression hardened. A silent threat.

"Fine. Shit." She unfurled her fingers, revealing what looked like a tiny surveillance camera nestled in her palm.

"I see. And, what? You were going to plant this in my room somewhere?" He tilted his head, watching her as she stared at the carpet. "I know this job can be lonely, Reed, but you only had to ask if you wanted to see me naked."

She didn't laugh. Neither did he.

He got up and held his hand out. She stared at it for a moment, then handed him the camera with a face like a teenager who's been caught raiding her old man's drinks cabinet. He examined it briefly before tossing it into the wastebasket.

"Tell me why the hell I should trust you," he said, surprised when she lifted her eyes to meet his gaze directly.

"Because I'm on your side," she replied. "I'm here to help you, I swear."

Her rage of a moment ago seemed to have subsided, and for a second she looked on the verge of tears.

Beckett moved closer and helped her to her feet. "I'm afraid I'm going to need more than that." He stepped aside and gestured to the bed. "Go on. Talk. Fast."

Reed lowered herself onto the edge of the mattress, crossing her legs and then her arms. "Templeton was worried you might skip town at the first opportunity. He wanted me to keep an eye on you, which I thought would be straightforward. I quickly realised I was wrong."

"So you are here to chaperone me?"

"No," she spat. "But we're risking a lot on this mission. It's not been... *completely* authorised, and if it goes south... it's bad for everyone. We're just erring on the side of caution."

Beckett nodded. Not authorised. Templeton hadn't stated it outright but it was what Beckett had suspected. At least now he knew where he stood.

"Did you think spying on me would do any good?" he asked.

Her arms tightened across her chest. "I just follow the orders, Beckett. I don't make them."

"Who do you think I am?" he continued, not believing for a second that she didn't have a mind of her own. "If I was going to pull something and jeopardise the deal with Templeton, a camera wouldn't stop me. But I'm not going to do that. Because I stick to my word. Unlike some people."

Reed didn't respond. Though she was clearly trying to hide it, she looked a little shaken. Beckett walked into the bathroom and filled a glass with water, handing it to her on his return. He watched her for a moment. The fact they were both in their underwear was awkward, but he wasn't done with the questions yet.

"Who were you meeting?" he demanded.

She looked up, confused. "What?"

"Stop that," he told her. "I followed you before. I could have jumped ship while you were meeting your contact in the alley; I could be anywhere by now, but I'm here. So who was he?"

Reed rubbed her neck, but he was starting to lose patience.

"Come on, Reed. Are we on the same side here or not?"

She looked down into the half-empty glass. "Cooper. One of Templeton's guys."

"What did he give you, the camera?"

She nodded.

"Anything else?"

"No."

He didn't take his eyes off her. She was hiding something, but he decided not to push it. "Just doing your job."

She lifted her head. Her eyes were guarded and tired, and only now was he noticing how pale her skin was without the make-up she'd been wearing earlier. "Yup," she said, her tone oddly flat. "Just following orders and all that jazz."

Beckett nodded. "All right. Fine. I think we both need to get some sleep."

Reed agreed, getting up off the bed and heading towards the door. As she reached it, she hesitated with her back to him, as if about to speak. But Beckett beat her to it, remembering something.

"Hey, wait a moment. I don't suppose you know anything about the Rosenwald Committee meeting this weekend?"

She turned to face him. "No. I don't," she said, but he saw a flicker of something cross her eyes. He'd never met anyone like her before. She was impossible to read – almost vacant on the surface, though hell knows what going on beneath.

He picked up his trousers from the floor, pulled her credit card from the pocket and crossed the room to where she stood at the door.

"Okay then. Goodnight," he said, holding the card out to her.

She gave him a weak smile as she took it, then left. Beckett stared at the door as it clicked shut. Something was off but he couldn't pin it down. He sank down onto the bed and lay back, his thoughts no clearer than they were before. He had to find out what was going on and who he could trust. The clock was ticking, and he couldn't afford any more surprises.

Chapter Twelve

Back in her room Reed leaned against the door, battling a swirl of conflicting emotions – frustration, shame, self-hatred, all the usual suspects. The mission felt like it was slipping through her fingers, the once clear objective now murky. Was this what always happened when other people got involved? Was it something she just had to deal with? Or was it... him?

She glanced around her bedroom. The bed seemed to mock her with its promise of rest – she was too wired to sleep, especially with all this adrenaline coursing through her veins. She walked across the room and into the relative cool of the en-suite bathroom, the porcelain floor tiles cold and clammy beneath her bare feet. She caught a glimpse of herself in the mirror and stepped closer, drawn to the reflection staring back at her.

Jesus, Erica.

She barely recognised herself. Her hair was a tangled mess, and dark circles underlined her eyes. She looked as exhausted as she felt. Without further inspection, she stripped off her underwear and dropped them in a heap on the floor.

She turned on the shower, adjusting the water until it was almost scalding, and then stepped under the stream. The hot water stung, but she welcomed the sensation. Grabbing a bar of soap, she scrubbed her skin with a ferocity that bordered on self-punishment. She worked methodically, washing each part of her body as if she could scrub away her dismay and anger. It never worked out that way, but she had to try. When she was done, she closed her eyes and let the jets wash away the suds and grime.

With her head under the water, her mind drifted back over the last twenty-four hours, and then jumped forward again to the next twenty-four. She replayed events in her head, visualising a timeline where everything worked out just as she needed it to. She was confident it would be fine. Just as long as she stuck to the plan.

But with her eyes closed other images flashed through her mind, troubling and painful. The more she tried to stop them, the more her thoughts slipped into darker territory. She closed her eyes tighter as if she could block out the memories, but they came anyway – sharp, intrusive reminders of the past. Memories she'd buried deep that always resurfaced at times like this, when she was feeling stressed or filled with self-loathing.

She could still feel the fingers digging into her flesh, holding her down. The cold, hard ground beneath her, the weight pressing her into it.

Distorted, leering faces. Mocking voices, cruel laughter. Then breath, hot and sour against her neck. Hands, where they had no right to be.

No. Stop.

She forced the images away, opening her eyes and staring at the tiled wall, disgusted by the memories. The hot water pounding against her skin was now just an annoyance. She shut off the shower, stepped out, and wrapped herself in a towel.

The bathroom mirror was fogged, so she wiped it clear, staring at her reflection again. Drops of water clung to her skin and her hair hung limp around her face. For a moment the person staring back wasn't the hardened operative she'd become, but the broken girl she once was. A fresh wave of anger blossomed within her; it was a familiar and comforting sensation. She spat into the sink, trying to expel the bitterness from her soul. Those bastards had tried to break her but they failed. She was stronger now, different. She wasn't that person anymore. She'd rebuilt herself, piece by piece.

After drying off quickly she moved into the bedroom, dressing in a fresh pair of underwear and a large t-shirt for sleeping in. Standing in front of the mirror by the dresser, she met her gaze with steely determination. What was it about mirrors tonight? Maybe if she'd paid more attention in her psychology classes she'd know. Perhaps they represented the truth you couldn't hide from yourself, the unfiltered reality of life.

At least now she could see some fire in her eyes, a spark that refused to be extinguished.

"You can do this," she whispered to herself, her voice firm and steady. "You can."

She thought back to all the people who had let her down when she needed them most, the ones who stood by and did nothing. The dismissive medics, the general who'd pressured her to retract her complaint. They were the reason she was here, doing what she did.

"You're not that person anymore, Erica," she told herself. "You've got this."

The past still clawed at her, but she'd learned to live with the scars. She had a mission to complete, and she couldn't let her past dictate her future. With one last glance in the mirror, she walked to the bed and lay down.

This mission was uncharted territory for her, but she had to remember she was doing the right thing. Everything was going to work out as it should.

She just needed to have faith.

Chapter Thirteen

The new day's sun had barely pierced the dense cloud cover over London as Jacob Beaumont pulled into his designated parking space beside Nightingale House. He switched off the engine, adjusted his tie, and checked his watch. It was a few minutes to six, but he'd been awake since four. Maybe he *was* getting too old for this lark – he could hear Martha's voice in his head, telling him as much. But he liked the early mornings. He enjoyed the sense of pride that his work still brought him.

Besides, today was Friday and only his second day in the office this week. Over the last eighteen months, his schedule had been reduced from full-time, to four days a week, to three, and now just two. Martha wanted him to retire completely, arguing he had every right to enjoy a peaceful life after losing two fingers and sustaining nerve damage on his last mission with Beckett. He had a good pension and, technically, he deserved the rest. But, for Beaumont, work was his lifeblood. Even on part-time hours, and now bound to a desk, he remained an active member of Sigma Unit. His country still needed him.

He locked the car and walked to the entrance. In the early morning light, Nightingale House looked more run-down and neglected than usual. Nestled on the fringes of Soho, and surrounded by modern developments, its once stately facade was now crumbling, making it appear more conspicuous rather than less.

Swiping his keycard, he entered the foyer and called the lift, hearing the familiar groan of machinery as it descended to the ground floor. The scent of old metal and mildew greeted him as he stepped inside, but it was a familiar smell he didn't mind at all. Nightingale House was an anachronism, and Beaumont appreciated its quirks. He pressed the button for the third floor, the ancient pully system jolting to life with a reluctant hum, and leaned back against the wall. The ride up was slow, but it gave him a chance to prepare himself mentally for whatever trials and tribulations lay ahead. It was the week's end for most, but for Sigma Unit just another day in the unending cycle of covert missions and intelligence gathering.

The lift shuddered to a halt and the doors parted to reveal a low-lit corridor. He made his way to his office, its door marked simply with his name and the title *Head Analyst*. Although he wasn't the head – not anymore; Andrew Miles ran things up on third these days – he'd been allowed to keep the title as a show of respect. Either that or they were so busy, no one had got around to scraping it off his door.

He unlocked the office and stepped inside. The room was just as he'd left it: a clutter of classified documents, battered filing cabinets and obsolete tech. Yellowing blinds shut out the weak morning light, giving the room an almost claustrophobic feel. It always amused him how disorganised and ramshackle his office appeared compared to the analyst station down the corridor – a modern Faraday cage filled with blinking server racks, advanced intrusion detection systems, and high-security, multi-monitor workstations.

Beaumont settled into his chair and spent the next few minutes logging onto his laptop and then the encrypted server where most of his day-to-day work was stored. Once inside, he leaned back, scanning the array of emails waiting in his inbox. As always, it was mainly automated updates and routine reports. He began sorting through, highlighting the messages he could deal with later and flagging the urgent ones. One email in particular grabbed his attention, the subject line standing out amongst the usual bureaucratic noise.

"What the...?"

The hairs on the back of his neck stood up as he recognised the name in the sender's column. Leaning closer, he squinted at the subject line. *Old Friend in Need of Help*.

"No... Beckett?"

Beaumont and Beckett had met in 2008 at Northwood during a high-stakes mission to rescue British scientists held hostage in Libya. Beaumont, then with Counter-Terrorism Warfare, and Beckett, an SAS lieutenant, had forged a firm bond after Beckett had saved Beaumont's life during an ambush and they'd remained close ever since. Their performance on that mission, amongst others, led to their induction into Sigma Unit around the same time.

Beaumont clicked on the email, his heart pounding with anticipation as he read. It was a brief and rather cryptic message, but he understood the intent immediately. He could almost hear Beckett's voice, urgent and intense, as he read. Beckett had also attached a document containing four names – aliases of this Saul Turner person, no doubt.

Hitting print, he pushed back from his desk, the chair groaning under the shift of his weight. As he headed for the door, he grabbed the sheet of paper out of his old, yellowing printer on the way.

He moved down the corridor and entered the main workspace, which was already buzzing with activity. Analysts worked around the clock, but this morning the place seemed particularly busy. Most were glued to their screens, absorbed faces illuminated by the data in front of them. Across the floor he spotted Tom Grossman, one of their top analysts at Sigma Unit. The young man was hunched over his desk, engrossed in whatever was displayed on his dual monitors.

Grossman looked up as Beaumont approached. His dark brown eyes were a little glassy, a little bloodshot, but otherwise he looked alert as always.

"Morning, Grossman," Beaumont growled.

"Sir."

"Working on anything important?"

The young man bristled as if he was being tested. "Always, sir."

"Can it wait an hour or so?" Beaumont asked, glancing around. "I need your help with something urgent."

"Of course." Grossman sat up. "What do you need?"

Beaumont handed him the printout. "I need you to dig into these names and cross-reference each of them with the name Saul Turner and New York. It shouldn't take you long but I need you to drop everything and focus on this."

Grossman nodded. "Got it."

"I want background, current location, known associates, anything you can find." Beaumont leaned in closer, lowering his voice. "But let's keep this between us for now. Understood?"

Grossman twisted around in his seat so they were face to face. "Right. I see. It's just…"

"Don't worry about Miles," Beaumont reassured him with a smile. "If he has an issue I'll deal with him. But I do need your help with this."

"Understood, sir." Grossman turned back to his screens, fingers flying over the keyboard as he glanced down the list of names.

Beaumont watched for a moment, then walked slowly back to his office. He had a feeling this was just the beginning of something much larger, and he could already feel his stomach ulcer flaring up. If Andrew Miles or Victoria Harwood got wind of this, he might be taking his retirement sooner than expected. Yet he knew better than to take John Beckett's request for help lightly. They might not have spoken for a while, but Beckett was a friend and a good man. If he needed help, then Jacob Beaumont was damned if he wasn't going to oblige.

Chapter Fourteen

The next day Beckett was up early. He rolled out of bed and immediately began his morning routine of push-ups and sit-ups. He kept his movements silent, stifling gasps as he put his muscles through their paces. When he was done, he walked to the bathroom with great care, conscious of every creak in the floorboards.

Opting for a sink wash over a shower, he turned the taps just enough to produce a trickle of water. With only a thin door separating his room from Reed's, the merest sound could wake her and he didn't want to do that. She'd looked exhausted last night and he figured she'd be sleeping late today. It had been around half past two when he caught her in his room, and she'd probably stayed awake until then to ensure he was sound asleep.

After drying himself off he dressed in the new clothes he'd bought the day before. The jeans were a little tight around the crotch, but they'd give, and the shirt was lightweight and allowed ease of movement. He rolled up the sleeves and pulled on his old shoes, listening for any signs of movement from the room next door. With any luck, he'd be back before Reed woke. He cast one last glance at the door separating their rooms, then made his way out.

Down on the street the early morning air was cool and crisp. The billboards in Times Square flashed their advertisements, but the crowds were thin. Delivery trucks rumbled down the streets and a few early risers were out for their morning jogs, but that was all. Beckett headed along West 42nd Street. The library was closed at this hour, so he took a right down 5th Avenue and soon found an internet café tucked away on a side street.

Inside was stuffy and there was an unpleasant odour in the air, but he didn't plan on staying long. He scanned the room. It was busy for this time of morning and most of the computers were occupied. Only…

Damn it.

He patted his pockets, confirming what he already knew. No money.

He glanced at the counter, where a pale-faced young man lounged in a battered leather chair, eyes glued to his phone.

Beckett waited. Patience was key.

Most of the customers looked to be foreign students, but a few older Americans and a couple of tourists were dotted around. He assessed each one for possibilities. After a few minutes, an old man in a suit stood and shuffled towards the restroom in the corner.

Perfect.

Not wasting any time, Beckett slipped into the vacant seat, the man's warmth still lingering on the chair. He rolled the mouse. Checked the login. No timeout. He was in.

Navigating to the email provider with whom he'd set up an account the day before, he typed in his login details and hit enter, conscious of the clock ticking. The old man would probably be two or three minutes doing his business, but not much longer. The computer was old and frustratingly slow. He tried to stay calm but it was tricky; he needed information, something concrete to allow him to move forward. After what felt like an eternity, the screen flickered to life, revealing his inbox and one new email. The one he was hoping for. He opened it and read.

Not entirely sure what you're up to, but it's good to hear from you.

I managed to run some brief checks on the names and criteria you provided. Not much, but there are a couple of hits worth noting.

One of the names, Christopher Wilson, is currently renting an apartment in New York. The rent is paid up to the end of November. I've attached the relevant details and the address.

Be careful and good luck.

Beckett felt a surge of gratitude. His old friend had come through for him once more. He noted the address and committed it to memory.

Good man, Beaumont.

He logged out of the email provider, cleared the browser history, and got to his feet. Moments later the old man returned, none the wiser, and resumed his place in front of the screen. As Beckett made for the door, the guy on the counter glanced up and their eyes met briefly.

Beckett gave him a casual nod of acknowledgement before stepping out onto the street.

The quiet of the early morning was now giving way to the bustling energy of New York City. He paused to get his bearings. He was on East 38th Street. Turner's last known address was in Inwood, over three hours away on foot, and he still had no money.

He chewed on his lip. Without a passport, ID or money, he felt exposed. He had the safe deposit box at JFK, and substantial savings accounts in the Cayman Islands and Switzerland, but for now immediate cash was still a problem he needed to solve.

He walked to the end of the street. The nearest station was Grand Central, a few minutes away. He'd have to take a risk. The last thing he wanted was to draw unnecessary attention but walking wasn't an option.

Keeping his head down, he entered the station and hurried down the steps, disappearing into the flow of commuters. Reaching the lower level he hesitated, eyeing the barrier up ahead. He waited until the guard's back was turned, then vaulted over it. He cleared the turnstile with ease, but the guard turned at the wrong moment and shouted after him.

Beckett kept walking, not breaking stride. This was New York, and he trusted the guard had better things to do than chase down a fare jumper, especially one who moved with the confidence of someone who knew exactly what they were doing.

The guard's shouts faded as Beckett raced down the next flight of steps, merging with the crowd on the platform. Down here, it smelled of damp concrete with a hint of something burning. Rush hour was on the horizon and the platform was packed, but no one noticed Beckett as he weaved his way to the far end. Most people were lost in their own worlds, absorbed in their phones or tuned into whatever was playing on their headphones. Those engaged in hushed conversations had them suddenly drowned out by the rumble of an approaching train.

A second later there was a rush of wind and the train roared into the station. The doors slid open with a mechanical hiss and Beckett stepped inside, finding a place to stand next to the door, his back to the wall. The car quickly filled and he grabbed a pole, the cool metal grounding him as the train lurched forward.

The ride was uneventful, thirty-six minutes of stops and starts. Faces came and went, none memorable. Finally the train pulled into 207th Street station and Beckett exited, the familiar white noise of a working city greeting him as he emerged from the underground.

He walked briskly through the morning streets, heading north. The city was alive, the sidewalks busy with people on their way to work and street vendors setting up their carts. It took him ten minutes to locate the address Beaumont had provided and once there he slowed his pace, taking in Turner's building and the surrounding area. A nondescript building in a typical neighbourhood – unassuming, unremarkable. The sort of place he himself would often rent when working in the field.

Beckett crossed over the road and stood close to the main entrance, doing his best impression of a nonchalant local just passing the time of day. He watched as people came and went, noting the flow of foot traffic and the lack security cameras. Minutes ticked by before, finally, a resident exited the building. Beckett slipped through the door before it closed. It was a classic move but executed flawlessly, and unnoticed in the morning rush.

Inside, he paused to assess the layout. The elevator was to his right, the stairwell to his left. He walked past both, not ready to go upstairs just yet. His focus shifted to a row of mailboxes against the back wall. They were old and battered, some with chipped paint and faded numbers, others with doors that didn't quite close all the way.

He approached the mailboxes, pretending to search for his own. One of the lower boxes had its door hanging open just wide enough for a finger or two. With a glance over his shoulder to ensure no one was watching, he knelt and slid his hand inside. The metal scraped at his knuckles but with a little effort he managed to pry it open, revealing a stack of letters. He sifted through them, spotting a thick envelope at the bottom of the pile. The papers inside the envelope felt to be held together by a sturdy paperclip. That would do. Carefully he opened the envelope, pocketed the paperclip, then placed everything back where he'd found it.

Straightening up, he retraced his steps and opted for the stairs over the elevator. Less risk, more control. He jogged up them, reaching the fourth floor in no time at all. Apartment 4E was at the end of a short corridor, directly facing the stairwell. He approached and crouched by the door, bending the paperclip into a makeshift lockpick. The door was old, and so was the lock. He inserted the pick, closing his eyes and letting his other senses take over as he felt for the tumblers. Years of practice guided his movements, and within seconds the lock clicked. He stood and eased open the door.

To say Turner's apartment was sparse would be an understatement. The furniture and fittings looked brand new, as if they'd never been used. The space had a cold, clinical feel, like an upscale showroom – everything pristine but devoid of personality. The air carried a hint of antiseptic. Beckett moved through the rooms systematically: the living area, the kitchen. In each he found only the bare minimum. No personal touches, no clutter.

And, more dishearteningly, no leads.

His frustration grew as he entered the bedroom. The bed was crisply made, the closet held a few neatly hung clothes, the dresser drawers were empty. It was aggravating, but he held his focus. If there was information here, where would it be? If he lived here, where would he stash it?

In the bathroom he lifted the heavy porcelain lid off the cistern. Empty.

Damn it.

He walked out into the corridor, rubbing his fingers against the stubble on his jaw. He was about to leave when he looked up and saw a small hatch in the ceiling between the bedroom and the bathroom. Fetching a chair from the living room, he climbed up, pushed the panel aside, and eased his head and shoulders through the gap. It was a tight squeeze and the space was dark. He managed to get an arm into the gap and felt around. But apart from a thick layer of dust and a couple of twisted wall plugs, he found nothing.

Just as he was about to give up, he lifted the hatch lid and felt around the back of it. His fingers brushed against two solid objects, taped to the rear. A gun and what felt like a pen drive. He freed them and lowered himself down into the light.

Bingo.

The gun was a Glock 19, the standard sidearm for US special operations forces. The pen drive was about the size of his little finger, with a USB-C connector at one end.

He replaced the hatch and climbed down, slipping the pen drive into his pocket and inspecting the Glock. It had no magazine, but it could still be useful and he'd rather have it than leave it with Turner. He tucked it into the back of his waistband and covered it with his shirt.

As he prepared to leave, he heard a faint creak in the hallway. Someone was there, just beyond the door. His pulse quickened as he moved silently along the corridor, pressing himself against the wall with a view into the living room. A second later the front door began to open – slowly, cautiously. From his position, Beckett could only see their shadow stretching across the floor. But that was enough. Whoever it was, they were coming his way, and the shadow left no doubt.

They had a gun.

Chapter Fifteen

Beckett held his breath, every muscle tensed and ready. His gaze fixed on the doorway as the shadow on the floor grew larger, the outline of the gun clearer. A small handgun, possibly a Glock like the one stuffed in his waistband. Only he had no ammo. He thought about pulling it out and using the handle as a blunt instrument, but decided against it. Too cumbersome. In this tight spot his skills with his hands were a better bet.

As the gun edged around the door, he waited for the right moment. Then with a sudden burst of motion he lunged, grabbing the barrel. He twisted it away, shifting his weight to disarm the intruder and raising his fist to strike.

That's when he saw the face.

"Reed," he hissed, loosening his grip but still holding the gun. The adrenaline surge left him momentarily off balance, his mind scrambling to adjust. "What the hell are you doing here?"

"Right back at ya," she snarled, yanking her arm free. She glared at him. "I woke up and you weren't in your room. Jesus, Beckett. After everything you said last night. I thought we were supposed to be in this together."

He stepped back, regained his composure. "This is Turner's place. By the looks of it, he doesn't use it much. Probably just a temporary stopover."

Reed's expression softened, but only slightly. "How did you find it?"

"I have my ways."

When it was clear she was getting no further information she strode past him, shaking her head as she assessed the apartment. "It's neat and tidy, nothing out of place. No signs of a hasty departure. Looks almost like a show home or a high-end office."

"That's what I thought." Beckett followed her as she moved through the rooms. "Or an advertisement for the colour beige. Either Turner's not using the place as home, or he isn't a fan of home comforts."

Reed nodded, jutting out her bottom lip. "Maybe both are true."

"Maybe. But I don't get it. Who is this guy, and why is Templeton - the CIA section chief for London – leading this op? It doesn't make sense."

They returned to the front room, and Reed faced him without answering his question. "So… what did you find?"

Beckett hesitated, but what could he do? He had no choice but to trust her, for now. "Not much at first but…" He started to pull out the pen drive when he realised something. "Wait, how did you find me?"

Reed pursed her lips. "I have my ways," she said. A hint of mockery.

"Yes. Very good. But come on. Spill."

"I'm a good officer," she replied, serious again. "I can find anyone."

Beckett wasn't convinced. It seemed too convenient. "I take it Templeton has someone watching the hotel? They must have trailed me here."

"No," she snapped. "I told you, I'm good. Now what did you find?"

The woman was infuriating. A brick wall would be more amenable. He reached into his pocket and pulled out the pen drive.

"It was well hidden," he said, flipping it over. "So my guess is it's something important."

Reed raised an eyebrow,. "Wow. Okay." She glanced around the room. "Are there any devices around?"

Beckett followed her gaze. "Not unless they're well hidden too."

"No problem. I have a laptop back at the hotel."

They left the apartment and made their way down the stairs. Beckett sensed the tension between them had eased slightly, but the unspoken questions and unresolved issues still loomed. He followed Reed out of the building, his senses alert as they stepped onto the busy street.

"We can hail a taxi on the corner of the next block," she said, quickening her pace.

But Beckett had one more thing he wanted to do before being holed up in a room with his babysitter for the rest of the afternoon.

"Can you wait for me?" he asked, stopping outside a small diner. "I need to use the bathroom."

Reed shot him a hard look, which was fast becoming her default expression. "No way. You're not running off again."

He raised a hand. "I won't. Scout's honour." When her expression remained unchanged, he lowered his hand and became serious. "I'm not going anywhere. I'm here because

I want my freedom, and that means completing this mission. Just give me two minutes."

She crossed her arms, her eyes searching his for any sign of deception. "Be quick."

A wave of heat and food smells hit him as he pushed open the door to the diner. It wasn't the nicest of establishments – the kind of place where grease and desperation clung to every surface. The peeling vinyl booths were a faded red, dulled from years of use. The linoleum floor, once patterned with black and white checks, was now two shades of grey and mottled with stains that no amount of mopping could ever hope to remove.

It was sparsely populated, just a few grizzled souls hunched over their plates and a couple chatting over coffee in one of the booths. A woman in her fifties with a tight ponytail and dark circles under her eyes wiped down a table with mechanical indifference. She gave Beckett a cursory glance as he walked past, but that was all.

Veering away from the counter, where a middle-aged man in a greasy apron was flipping pancakes, Beckett headed for the rear. There were two doors, one with an M hastily scrawled on the front in black Sharpie and the other an F. Good enough.

He pushed open the M door, the smell hitting him before he'd even stepped inside – stale urine masked unsuccessfully by industrial cleaner. The tiled floor was chipped and the grout darkened with grime. He made a beeline for one of the two stalls, locking the door behind him.

After closing the toilet lid he sat down and took off his shoes, examining each one. They were scuffed and worn, a pair he'd meant to replace months ago. Under the insole of his left shoe he found it – a small tracking device, no bigger than a fingernail.

Damn it.

He was angry at himself for the oversight. But they were old shoes, and he'd been so eager to leave before Reed woke he didn't think to check. Not a mistake he'd make again. He tipped the device into his palm, pocketed it, then replaced the insole and put his shoes back on. After leaving the stall, he washed his hands quickly and exited the restroom. On his way out he spotted a half-drunk cup of coffee on a table near the door. Without breaking stride, he dropped the device into the murky brown liquid.

Reed was waiting by the kerb. She looked troubled. "Can we go now?" she asked as he approached.

"All set." He smiled his best smile. "Fresh as a daisy."

She flagged down a cab and they climbed in the rear, Reed giving the driver the address of the hotel. The ride back was silent, with both of them lost in their thoughts. Even the driver could have picked up on the tense atmosphere. When they arrived, Reed paid the fare and they made their way to her hotel room. Once there, she locked the door and hauled her suitcase onto the bed while Beckett looked around. Her room was more or less a mirror image of his own, but with a bigger bed, a couple of extra chairs, and the telltale signs of a woman's presence. Hairdryer on the dresser. Make-up scattered across the bathroom counter.

Reed pulled her laptop from her case and set it up on the small desk in the corner, logging into the agency network and plugging in the pen drive. Moments later the icon appeared on the desktop, but clicking on it triggered a red error box.

"It's encrypted," she said, not looking up. "But I can sort it."

"A tech wizard." Beckett stood back. "I knew there was a reason you were here."

She shot him a withering glance. "Calm it down, Beckett. There's an agency app that will do the job."

She turned her attention back to the screen, and after a few minutes the pen drive was unlocked. A Finder window opened containing PDFs and image files. Beckett leaned in, scanning the documents as Reed opened them one by one. Surveillance reports, photographs, pages of detailed notes. It seemed Turner had been covertly monitoring a target named Adram Bader for the past three months. The files outlined Bader's movements, meetings, and encrypted communications.

"Check these out," Reed said, pointing to a series of photographs. "This has to be Bader, right?"

Beckett examined the photos. Black-and-white and grainy, they depicted a man in his late thirties with dark hair and aviator-style glasses. Despite the long-range shots, the images captured the man entering various buildings, the architecture suggesting locations in different countries.

Beckett stepped back, running a hand through his hair. "Bader. Do we know who he is?"

Reed shook her head. "Turner clearly sees him as important. What do you think he wants with him?"

"Maybe they're working together. Or Bader has intel Turner needs. Did Templeton give you any information on Turner that I don't know about that might help?"

He watched Reed closely as she considered this, either thinking hard or doing a good impression of someone doing so. "Not that I recall. You know as much as I do."

But Beckett's senses were tingling. Something about this didn't add up. He grabbed a chair and spent some time sifting through Turner's entire case file on Bader. After a few minutes he realised what was wrong. The information was thorough but there was nothing with any real weight to it. Bader was a scientist, originally from Germany, and had been lecturing part-time at Columbia whilst working at Axiom Bioskills Lab NYC. He'd left both positions four months ago. But there was nothing that told them where he was now, or the reason for Turner's interest.

"It's all very vague," Reed muttered, echoing Beckett's thoughts. "Do you think Turner deleted some of the files? Or maybe there's another drive?"

"Or he's just cautious and didn't want to leave any breadcrumbs." Beckett got to his feet. "Given his apartment, I can believe that."

Reed snorted an ironic laugh, though he hadn't meant it as a joke. Turner was clearly a fastidious and clinical operator. It was likely he had the pertinent information stored where no one could get to it – in his head. Beckett would have done the same. Yet there was at least some semblance of a lead.

"This lab," he said, pointing at the screen. "Where is it?"

Reed ran a search. "Yorkville. Just off East 79th Street."

"Specialises in biochemistry," Beckett added, reading over her shoulder.

"Is that bad?"

"Depends on what Bader was working on."

Reed looked at him. "Should we pay the lab a visit?"

Beckett got up and moved to the door. "Absolutely."

"What, now?" Reed glanced at her watch. Perhaps she was worried about missing the breakfast buffet.

"No time like the present. You can buy us a hotdog on the way." Beckett opened the door. "My guess is if we find Bader, Turner won't be far away."

Chapter Sixteen

Turner leaned against the corner of the alley, eyes locked on the entrance of The Grand Regency hotel. The tall man and the blonde had entered minutes earlier, but now the street outside was clear.

He rolled his neck to ease the stiffness from hours of surveillance. He'd been monitoring his apartment when he saw the man enter, followed four minutes later by the woman. He'd observed their silhouettes moving through each room. After they left, he hailed a taxi and followed them here.

But who were they?

And more importantly, who were they working for?

There were too many possibilities and he had no time to consider them now. He had to keep moving. He slipped out of the alley and blended into the crowd on 42nd Street. A quick turn onto 10th Avenue set him on a westward path towards the waterfront where the polished high-rises of Midtown gradually yielded to the rougher, industrial landscape of Hell's Kitchen. He quickened his pace, passing decaying warehouses and run-down auto repair shops, places that had seen better days.

As he moved away from the bustling heart of the city, the sounds changed. The ceaseless hum of traffic and chatter faded, replaced by the distant cry of seagulls. He sensed the waterfront before he saw it. The air grew colder, filled with the briny tang of the sea and the harsher stench of the river. A handful of rough sleepers huddled in doorways. The streets here were all but deserted. Few people ventured this far west unless they had a specific reason.

Turner turned a corner, the Hudson coming into view. He crossed the West Side Highway, heading for the row of old piers stretching out over the water. These days the docklands were a forgotten corner of the city, once a hub of activity but now silent and abandoned. Regardless, he kept his head down and stuck to the shadows as he approached the derelict hangar where he was due to meet his contact. At one time a thriving warehouse, the building was now a crumbling shell, with broken windows and graffiti-covered walls.

He entered the hangar and paused. The cavernous space was cluttered with old crates and discarded equipment but no one in sight. His contact was late. A surge of unease gripped him.

Shit. Was this a....?

His instincts screamed at him to leave. He turned, ready to flee, when two figures appeared at the entrance of the hangar. The first man was tall and lean, with a hawkish face and sharp, intelligent eyes. His hair was clipped close to the scalp, and he wore a plain dark jacket over a grey shirt, jeans, and sturdy boots. Everything about him radiated efficiency and discipline. He didn't fidget, didn't glance around nervously. He was focused solely on Turner.

The second man was shorter but solidly built, with the physique of a seasoned wrestler. His square jaw and broad shoulders gave him an imposing demeanour without him even trying. He wore a simple black hoodie and dark jeans. There was a calmness to him, a sense of controlled strength as if he knew he didn't need to posture or intimidate, his presence alone was enough.

Turner raised his head, running a real-time assessment. He could take them, but not without injuring himself. He needed information, not broken knuckles. He tensed for a moment, giving the impression he was preparing to fight, then he spun around and sprinted towards the far end of the hangar.

"Get him!"

The two men reacted instantly, charging after him as he burst out of the hangar and raced along the riverbank. His heart pounded, gaze frantically plotting out an escape route.

He ran along the dock, the cool air burning his lungs, and veered through a maze of shipping containers, using their close proximity to his advantage. The men were fast, but Turner was more agile, their shouts and attempts to coordinate their chase spurring him on. He spotted a narrow gap and squeezed through, scraping his shoulders against the rough metal and emerging into a tight alley formed by the stacked containers on either side. At the end was an opening just big enough for him to crawl through. Dropping to his knees, he wriggled his way out to the other side, covered in grime. The space widened into a broader path leading back towards the main docks. Turner kept moving, scanning the area for escape routes or obstacles. He rounded a corner and spotted a ladder leading up to a catwalk.

Damn it.

Without hesitation he grabbed the rungs and hauled himself up. Behind him his pursuers grunted and cursed as they struggled through the gap between the containers and then as they reached the ladder. Their shouts were growing more frustrated but they weren't giving in – no doubt motivated by a hefty payoff from whoever sent them. They began to climb, but Turner was already on the move, running along the elevated walkway.

At the end of the catwalk he glanced down and saw a stack of rotting wooden pallets below. Without a second thought he leapt off the edge, hitting the pallets with a jarring thud and rolling to absorb the impact. Above him the men hesitated, giving him a crucial few seconds to jump to his feet and keep running.

At a nearby warehouse he slipped in through a side door. The interior was dark, the air heavy with dust. He navigated around rows of abandoned equipment, the muffled voices of his pursuers fading as he put more distance between them.

Finding a back exit, he slipped into another alley, this one between two buildings. The lactic acid burned in his sides but he pushed through the pain, determined to escape. At the end of the alley he ran out onto a quiet street, the docks behind him. He slowed to a jog, and then a walk, brushing himself down as he joined the sparse foot traffic. His heart was banging against his ribs, adrenaline coursing through his veins.

At a small café, he ducked in through the doorway, the bell above jingling as he entered. He ordered a coffee, using the moment to catch his breath and gather his thoughts. The waitress fixed him his drink and he settled into a seat by the window, scanning the street outside for signs of trouble. After a few minutes he allowed himself a moment of relief. He'd lost them, but the danger was far from over. Things were spiralling out of control, and that was unacceptable. First the two people who'd trailed him to his apartment, and now these goons. It felt like the net was closing around him.

He sipped his coffee, never feeling more alone than at this moment. Somewhere along the way he'd messed up, but he could fix it. If he was the problem, he could also be the solution. And it wouldn't happen again. His mission wasn't yet done, and he needed to stay one step ahead if he was going to survive.

Chapter Seventeen

Beckett paused as he and Reed emerged from the 72nd Street subway station. He took in the sights and sounds, his eyes constantly moving, alert for anything unusual. It was lunchtime and the smell of street food drifted on the air – savoury, sweet and spicy all at once. His stomach grumbled. He was still waiting for Reed to shout him a hotdog, but food would have to wait. They had a job to do first.

He set off walking, heading for East 79th Street where Reed's agency software had pinpointed the Axiom Bioskills Lab. Reed strode beside him, her face set in a determined frown.

"Do you think we'll find anything?" she asked after a few minutes.

"It's the first lead we've had," Beckett replied. "And we could use a break, given we've got little else to go on."

They walked on in silence, dodging the flow of hurried pedestrians. Beckett had been trying to make conversation on the subway ride over, but talking to Reed was like hitting himself in the head with a rubber mallet. He understood she was new to this world, and likely being overly cautious about revealing too much of herself, but he needed to understand her better if they were going to work together effectively.

"Do you ever regret leaving the military behind?" he asked now, but Reed didn't look his way. Her expression tightened. Pace quickened slightly.

"Not at all."

"You never explained why you decided to jump ship."

"I did." She threw him a glance as they were momentarily split by a group of pedestrians. When they came back together she said, "I told you I felt like it was time for a change."

"Yes, that's right." Beckett sensed the strain in her voice but pressed on. "And you also said you were hoping to open a bookstore. Yet here we are."

"Jesus, Beckett." She hissed a curse as a lanky guy in a suit bumped her shoulder hard and hastily called back an apology. It was Beckett who got the glare though. "Why does it matter so much to you? Did you talk about your past with all your assets and ex-colleagues?"

"No, but—"

"Well then give it a rest, will you?"

A fully grown teenager on a kid's scooter almost took her out, but Beckett reached for her elbow and guided her out of its path. "I'm just curious, that's all," he told her, dropping her elbow, danger averted. "I like to understand why people do what they do."

Reed sighed, looking away as they crossed the street. "Things happened. I needed a change. Okay?"

Now Beckett detected something else in her voice – a hint of deep-held emotion, the raw edges of old wounds. "Fair enough. We all have our reasons."

"That we do."

"Still, Templeton must have seen something in you to put you on this mission so soon after joining the agency." It was a statement designed to appease and perhaps claw back a little goodwill from his new partner, but she just shrugged.

"You think being here with you is some kind of reward?" She snorted a humourless laugh. "Because I've got news for you, buddy. This isn't my idea of fun."

Beckett smiled to himself. "All right. Point taken."

After ten minutes the urban landscape around them began to shift, the gritty, crowded streets giving way to cleaner, more modern architecture. The buildings grew taller, too, their steel and glass facades reflecting the midday sun. Turning the next corner they found the Axiom Bioskills Lab right in front of them – the three-foot-high metal letters on the side of the building leaving them in no doubt.

Beckett approached first and pushed through the revolving doors. Inside, the lobby was brightly lit and sterile, the smell of disinfectant lingering in the air. Everything was white or made of clean pine wood. Polished floors gleamed under fluorescent lights.

The woman on the reception desk raised her head as they walked over. She was Asian, likely Chinese or Korean, with sharp eyes behind round, stylish glasses. Her hair was pulled back into a tight bun, and she wore a crisp white blouse that complemented her surroundings. She smiled politely, but Beckett sensed the suspicion beneath it.

"Can I help you?" she asked, her tone civil but firm.

"I hope so. We need information on a former employee."

"Oh, I see." Her eyes flicked to the security cameras positioned around the room. "I'm afraid I can't give out personal information."

Beckett turned to Reed and gave her a look. "Do you have any ID on you?"

He knew as a CIA officer she had no fancy badge to flash like in the movies, but she might have some kind of federal government ID. Reluctantly, she pulled out a small brown wallet and showed it to the woman.

"I work for the Central Intelligence Agency. We need to speak to someone who worked here at the same time as Adram Bader. It's a matter of national security."

The receptionist's eyes widened. "But you don't have an appointment?" she asked, her voice a touch higher than before.

"No," Reed replied, "but this is urgent. Please get someone who knew Bader. Now."

Beckett nodded, impressed by her assertiveness. The receptionist's eyes darted between the two of them for a moment, assessing the seriousness of their presence.

"One moment, please." She dialled a number, her voice dropping to a hushed tone as she spoke. Her eyes flicked nervously towards them every few seconds as if hoping they might vanish. Beckett heard the words "Bader" and "CIA" and then, "Sir, I don't think they're going to leave."

The woman was trying to maintain her composure, but there was a glimmer of something else. Concern, perhaps. Or fear. Her fingers gripped the phone tightly. After a brief conversation, she hung up and forced a smile.

"Someone will be with you shortly," she said, before busying herself with the computer in front of her, avoiding further eye contact.

Beckett and Reed exchanged a glance and stepped back to wait. Less than a minute later, a man appeared from a side door. He was in his mid-forties, with neatly combed hair and a stern, angular face. His glasses and lab coat made him look every bit the scientist, but there was an air of authority about him that suggested he was more than just a researcher.

"I'm Dr Jonathan Weiss," he said. "One of the lead scientists here at Axiom. Can I help you?"

"My name's Reed and this is my partner, Simon Rivers," Reed said abruptly. "We work for the government."

"We're sorry to bother you, but we're seeking information on Adram Bader," Beckett added, attempting to play the good cop in response to Reed's frostiness. "I understand he worked here."

Weiss didn't flinch. "Bader hasn't been with us for a while. What's this about?"

"He's connected to an ongoing investigation," Reed replied. "We just need to ask you a few questions."

The man's gaze narrowed. He stared at the receptionist, seemingly trying to convey a lot of information with just his eyes. Beckett could almost see the cogs turning in his mind, weighing the pros and cons of compliance. After a moment, he nodded. "Please, follow me."

He led them down a series of sterile corridors, the antiseptic smell growing stronger as they went deeper into the lab. They passed through a set of double doors and the corridor expanded into a larger walkway where glass walls on either side offered glimpses into working labs filled with sophisticated equipment. Scientists in white coats moved between workstations, some peering into microscopes, others manipulating samples with steady hands.

Weiss pointed towards one of the stations as they walked. "This is where we conduct our primary research. We specialise in advanced biochemical studies, particularly in the fields of genetic engineering and synthetic biology.

Our aim is to develop pioneering treatments for a range of diseases."

Beckett nodded, his attention divided between Dr Weiss and the lab. "It sounds impressive. Did Bader fit in well here?"

Weiss hesitated for a moment before responding. "Bader had a brilliant mind, no doubt about that."

"But not anymore?" Beckett prompted, catching a brief flicker of discomfort on Weiss's face.

"What do you mean?"

"You said he *had* a brilliant mind. Past tense."

Weiss looked troubled but didn't respond. Before Beckett could press him, they entered a large lab, bustling with activity. More scientists in white coats sat or stood behind workstations, each equipped with microscopes, centrifuges, and other high-tech apparatus

"Here's where most of the action happens," Weiss said, gesturing around. "You'll have to stay here by the door to avoid contamination. But this is where Bader spent most of his time when he was here."

"I see," Beckett replied, but his attention had shifted to a young technician at the back of the lab. He was stick-thin, with a pale complexion and tousled hair. When Bader was mentioned just now, he seemed to flinch. Beckett kept his eyes on him. His movements were jittery, and he appeared uncomfortable, frequently adjusting his glasses and glancing around the room.

"We focus on several key areas of research here," Weiss continued. "One major project involves the manipulation of genetic material to combat hereditary diseases. We're also developing new antibiotics to fight resistant strains of bacteria."

Reed's eyes moved from Weiss to the bustling lab. "But you and Bader didn't get on?"

Weiss hesitated, then sighed. "I suppose it's safe to say that he and I didn't see eye to eye. He was a genius, but he had his own ideas, very ambitious ones. They didn't always... align with the rest of the team."

"What does that mean?" Beckett asked.

"Dr Bader was passionate about his work, sometimes to the point of obsession," Weiss explained, still choosing his words carefully. "He believed in pushing boundaries, even at the risk of stepping outside conventional methods. Not everyone here was comfortable with that approach."

Beckett continued to observe the young technician. He kept glancing over as if he wanted to say something before quickly looking away.

"Did Bader ever mention a man called Saul Turner?" Beckett asked. "They could have been friends or associates."

Weiss shook his head. "I've never heard that name. Sorry."

"And why did Dr Bader leave?" Reed asked.

Weiss shrugged. "You'll have to ask him that."

"We would if we could find him."

"I'm sorry, Ms Reed, but he didn't leave a forwarding address." Weiss smiled but it was as if a wall had suddenly gone up. "I wish I could be more help."

Beckett was still watching the young technician out of the corner of his eye. They weren't going to get anything else from Weiss, but maybe there was another way. "So what's the usual routine here?" he asked casually. "Lunch hours, shifts, that sort of thing."

Reed shot Beckett a disapproving glance. Weiss looked puzzled by the question but answered. "We operate with staggered shifts to keep the lab running twenty-four-seven.

Each team follows a different schedule to ensure continuity. Lunch breaks vary based on workload."

"Sounds like a well-oiled machine," he said with a smile. "But if that's all you can tell us, we'll leave you in peace. Thanks for your help. And the tour."

"Not a problem." Weiss's relief was clear. "I'll see you out."

They walked back the way they'd come in relative silence. In the lobby Weiss offered his apologies again before disappearing through the doors he'd come from.

"What the hell was that?" Reed hissed.

Beckett nodded towards the exit. "Let's get out of here. We've got all we can."

Outside, the air was crisp, a welcome relief from the sterile environment inside.

"He was hiding something," Reed said, once they'd walked down the street and turned the corner.

"Oh, he most definitely was," Beckett replied. "But we also weren't going to get much more from him in that setting."

"You want to bring him in? Question him properly?"

"Bring him in where? We have no authority here."

"No, but… there's always a way."

Beckett raised an eyebrow. "You know you sound like Templeton? You should be careful of that."

Reed didn't respond, but her expression showed she didn't appreciate the comment. "What now?" she asked.

"Why don't you head back to the hotel and see if you can dig up more on Bader on the agency network, or even on Weiss or the lab itself? We rushed earlier, and there could be something we missed."

Reed dropped her weight to one hip and coldly smirked.

"And what will you be doing while I'm hard at work in front of a screen?"

Beckett looked back up the street. "I'm going to stick around, see if I can talk to that young technician who was listening in to our conversation."

"The guy with the glasses?" she asked. "I saw him too. You think he knows something?"

"Maybe. But I'd like to speak to him alone. Man to man. He looked nervy, and he might find you a little… well, intimidating, shall we say."

He couldn't tell if she was offended, amused, or pissed off by that. But then some of the tension seemed to drop away and he thought she looked almost pensive. Like maybe she was out of her depth.

Beckett lowered his head to make eye contact. "Reed, don't worry. I'm in this for the long haul now. I'm not going to do anything to jeopardise your career."

She didn't seem convinced, but didn't argue the point either.

"I could use some cash, though," he added. "For the subway and maybe a bite to eat.

She rolled her eyes, then pulled three twenties from her pocket and handed them to him. "Here. Don't spend it in a bar and be back within two hours. Three tops."

He watched her walk away, then found a spot across the street from the lab where he could keep an eye on the entrance without drawing attention. An hour or more passed. The sun moved across the sky. At around two, Beckett bought himself a couple of hotdogs from a street vendor to curb his hunger.

Finally, at around four, the young technician emerged from the building. His eyes darted up and down the street, and when he spotted Beckett he froze. Panic flashed across his face as Beckett crossed the road towards him.

"Wait. I just want to talk to you." He held his hands up in a show of appeasement, but as he got closer the young man turned and bolted.

Bugger.

Beckett sprinted after him, weaving through traffic and dodging pedestrians, but the technician was fast and knew the area better. The chase led them through a maze of alleys and side streets, the younger man always a few steps ahead. Beckett's muscles burned but he pushed through the pain. At the end of the next street, the technician glanced back.

"Stop!" Beckett called out. "I'm not going to hurt you."

But it was no use. The fear was evident on the man's face. He wasn't stopping for anyone. If anything, he sped up. Beckett kept pace as the technician disappeared into a narrow alley, but when he got there moments later the man was gone.

He slowed to a walk to get his bearings. The alley ran between two streets and another alley intersected it laterally. Beckett approached the intersection, straining to hear anything that might reveal the technician's location.

"You can come out," he called. "I'm not going to hurt you."

As he reached the entrance to the second alley, two men stepped out and blocked his path. Beckett made to move around them but they sidestepped in front of him, making it clear they were here for trouble. Beckett stopped short, taking them in. They were big, ugly and mean, carrying the unmistakable air of hired muscle. Their postures were rigid, their eyes cold and focused.

He glanced around, quickly weighing his options. The

alley offered little room to manoeuvre. His immediate instinct was to turn and run, but as he glanced back, a third man appeared, effectively sealing off the only exit. A menacing grin spread across the man's face as he cracked his knuckles. "Wrong place, wrong time, pal."

Beckett turned back to face the two men closing in on him. Up close it was clear to him they were professional enforcers rather than street punks. The confident way they moved, and the seriousness of their expressions told him everything he needed to know. This was no random mugging. Someone had sent these men to deal with him. He took a deep breath, his mind sharp, his senses heightened.

He might be outnumbered, but he'd been in this position many times before.

And he wasn't going down without a fight.

Chapter Eighteen

Beckett edged to the side of the alley, pressing his back against the brick wall as the men approached, forcing them to converge around him. From the way the lone man on his left was glancing at the pair on the right, he assumed him to be the leader. He was tall and broad, with slicked-back hair. He wore a well-fitted leather jacket over a tailored shirt and a pair of black denim jeans.

It was the other two who were the muscle. The taller of the two wore a blue shirt with a tattoo peeking out from under the sleeve and had the look of a street brawler. He was almost a foot shorter than Slick, but his fists were almost twice as big, the knuckles thick with scar tissue. The third man was built like a juggernaut. Dressed in an old hoodie and cargoes, he was almost as wide as he was tall, with a thick neck and a vacant look in his eyes. It was clear he was a man built for brute strength and not much else. A tool, not a thinker.

"I take it we can't discuss this?" Beckett said, pushing

off from the wall and into a fighting stance as the men closed in.

Slick grinned. "No way, amigo. You aren't talking your way out of this."

Beckett looked from one man to the other, assessing angles, distances, and potential weaknesses. Slick was clearly the one in charge. He wasn't the biggest or the meanest of the three, but taking him out first would likely disrupt the coordination of the attack. In comparison, the man with the tattoo seemed the most eager for a brawl. He'd also be the most unpredictable, able to adapt quickly in the heat of things. He'd be second. The juggernaut would be a tough guy to handle, but Beckett had encountered men just like him over the years. They relied solely on physical strength, underestimating the importance of strategy. The man's slow, deliberate movements also revealed a lack of quick thinking. He'd be last.

"All right, fellas." Beckett shifted his weight and readied himself. "Let's do this."

He sprang into action as Tattoo lunged forward, swinging a heavy fist aimed at Beckett's head. He deflected the punch with his left arm and countered with a right hook to the man's ribs, sending him staggering. Turning his attention to Slick he feinted a punch, and as he swerved the blow, Beckett's boot connected with his knee instead, bending it back. Slick cried out, and before he could retaliate, Beckett drove a knee into his midsection, followed by a heavy elbow to the back of the head. The impact knocked Slick's brain against his skull and he crumpled to the ground, unconscious.

Beckett shifted his focus to Tattoo, who had recovered and was back on his feet, throwing a quick series of punches. Beckett blocked two, took a glancing blow to the shoulder, then responded with a sharp kick to the back of the man's calf. He stumbled, momentarily off balance. Beckett grabbed his wrist, spinning him around and propelling him into his forearm, breaking his nose. Tattoo cried out, blood spurting as he fell back, clutching his face. A hefty boot to his temple sent him sprawling into a pile of discarded construction debris, unconscious.

Before Beckett could catch his breath, rough hands grabbed his shoulders and a knee ploughed into his lower back. The impact hit like a sledgehammer. He buckled but managed to twist free and spin around to face the juggernaut.

"I'll fucking kill ya," the man snarled, in a broad *Noo Yoik* accent.

Beckett dropped into a fight stance and raised his fists, but facing this street thug felt like performing ballet against a heavyweight.

"Who sent you?" he asked.

"Wouldn't you like to know?"

The juggernaut charged, his massive arms wide, ready to grapple and crush. Beckett braced himself, knowing he couldn't meet the brute's strength head-on. Rocking forward onto the balls of his feet, he twisted sharply at the last second, using the big man's momentum against him and running him into the wall. The juggernaut's head hit the brick with a dull thud, but he shook it off and threw back a heavy elbow, catching Beckett in the ribs and sending him sideways.

He barely managed to regain his footing before the juggernaut charged again. Beckett feinted to the left, then spun right, driving a hard elbow into the side of the brute's head. The juggernaut swayed, dazed but still upright. Seizing the moment, Beckett grabbed the back of the man's neck and smashed his head onto his knee. The juggernaut's nose shattered with a sickening crunch, blood erupting as he collapsed, howling in agony.

With the last goon doubled over, momentarily incapacitated, Beckett stepped back to recalibrate. He gauged his distance and trajectory, then delivered a textbook roundhouse kick to the side of the juggernaut's head. It was a direct hit. The blow would travel through the man's jaw, up his jawbone and to the temples, creating enough of a sudden impact to rattle the brain inside his skull and turn the lights off. His eyes rolled back, and he pitched forward onto the ground, unconscious.

Beckett returned his attention to Slick, who was beginning to stir. He walked over, grabbed the man by his shirt, and hauled him to his feet. The man's eyes were glassy and unfocused, but they quickly sharpened as Beckett shoved him against the wall.

"Who sent you?" Beckett snarled.

"Go to hell," Slick mumbled. "You have no idea who you're dealing with."

"So tell me." Beckett tightened his grip. "Talk."

"Nah, homes. They'll kill me."

"I'll kill you."

Slick sniffed. "Do it then." He grinned, baring two rows of pink teeth. "Whoever you are, you're in over your head. This is bigger than you, me, this whole country."

Beckett knew he'd extracted all he could from him. Still gripping Slick's shirt, he pulled him closer and drove his forehead into the man's nose, feeling the cartilage buckle and crack. Slick screamed and dropped to his knees.

Leaving the man whimpering in agony, Beckett knelt beside Tattoo, flipping him over and rifling through his pockets. In the man's jacket he found a worn leather wallet containing three old fifty-dollar bills but nothing else. No driver's licence, no credit cards, nothing. Just cash. He stuffed the money in his back pocket and moved over to the juggernaut, repeating the process. This guy didn't even have a wallet, just a billfold containing sixty dollars in mixed notes. Pocketing the money, Beckett got to his feet and left the alley without looking back.

Three down, three broken noses, and still no answers. Although, the lack of IDs confirmed his suspicion – these weren't random street thugs, they were more likely professionals, sent with a purpose. As he reached the next street, something suddenly clicked. The pieces finally falling into place.

Of course.

He quickened his pace, heading to the street to find a cab. He had to get back to the hotel. If he was right, this was much bigger than he'd anticipated. But more importantly, whoever sent those men might have sent others after Reed.

He had to reach her. Fast.

Chapter Nineteen

Beckett entered the hotel lobby and paused for a moment. The aftereffects of his recent encounter still lingered and he was on edge. Normally he'd have brushed off such an incident during the cab ride back, but it was clear those men had been after him specifically, and the pressing question now was, were there others?

You're in over your head. This is bigger than you, me, this whole country.

Slick's words echoed in his mind as he moved across the marble floor, logging each face as he passed. A middle-aged couple with German accents were at the reception desk but seemed more interested in getting a room upgrade than in him. Nothing was out of place, but his instincts told him to stay vigilant. He had a little blood spatter on his shirt, but it wasn't noticeable from a distance, and no one was paying attention. He made his way to the far side of the lobby, opting for the stairs instead of the elevator to avoid any unnecessary encounters.

He took the stairs two at a time, pausing on each

landing to listen for anything that seemed out of the ordinary. The silence was both a comfort and a concern. Reaching his floor, Beckett stopped outside the stairwell door, pressing his ear against it. Hearing nothing, he eased the door open and looked both ways down the hallway. It was empty. He proceeded down the corridor towards his room, cautious of every corner and alcove until he reached the door. Once there he paused again, listening for signs of danger.

Satisfied the coast was clear, he slipped inside and closed the door with a soft click. The room was as he'd left it, with nothing out of place but nothing to suggest anyone was staying here either. He stepped over to the shared door between his and Reed's room. He could hear the rumble of a voice. Moving closer, he pressed his ear against the door. It was Reed he could hear. That was a good thing. She sounded as if she was on the phone, her tone low but firm.

"No! That's a bad idea," he heard her say. "I've got it under control."

There was a hint of frustration in her voice. Beckett's gentlemanly instincts urged him to pull away, to respect her privacy, but his SIS training took precedence. Any information was valuable.

"Beckett will do what's needed," Reed continued. "He's useful."

Now he stepped back. She must be speaking with Templeton or one of his lackeys. He wasn't pleased about being the topic of conversation but at least she was fighting his corner. He hesitated, then knocked on the door.

There was a muffled response, a rustling of movement, and a few seconds later Reed opened the door. She was wrapped in a towel, her hair wet, droplets glistening on her flushed skin. She looked different – fresh-faced and innocent

– an unusual departure from the brittle, tightly wound woman he was used to.

"Hey, you're back," she said, all sweetness and light on the surface but with a reservation behind her eyes she couldn't mask. "Did you find out anything?"

"Not much."

"Same here. I found a little more about Bader's past – both parents dead, one sister – but nothing useful, and— Hey, what's wrong?"

She followed him into her room as he hurried past and looked around.

"Have you seen or heard anything unusual?" he asked.

"What the hell are you doing?"

Beckett completed a quick circuit of the room, then returned to the door, closing it firmly. "I was jumped. Three of them. In an alley near Axiom."

"Are you hurt?"

"I'm fine. Can't say the same for the three guys though."

"Jesus. I guess they were right about you." She dropped her hands from her hips, looking at him with a new level of curiosity. "Do you think Weiss had something to do with it?"

"No, I don't think so. But they were professionals. It would have taken too long to get out of them who they were working for." He moved past her, checking the windows, the bathroom, even under the bed.

Reed watched him. "Well, there's no one here but me. Are you sure you're not hurt?"

Beckett finished his inspection, satisfied the room was secure. He turned to face her. "I'm fine. Just making sure you are too."

She nodded, but looked fazed. "Thanks. I appreciate it."

He walked back into the bathroom and checked himself in the mirror. Remarkably, he was unscathed, but his reflection revealed a man on edge, his blue eyes wild and alert. He splashed cold water on his face and washed his hands, grounding himself with that simple act. After drying his hands, he re-entered the bedroom.

"Did you speak to Templeton?" he asked.

Reed shook her head. "Not since we arrived in New York. He's back in London for a few days."

Beckett studied her face, searching for tells – the twitch of an eye, a shift in posture, a change in tone. He was skilled at reading people, picking up on the micro-expressions most people couldn't hide. But Reed remained composed. Either she was telling the truth, or she was very good at hiding it. But if she wasn't lying, who was on the phone just now?

She tilted her head. "Did you manage to speak to the technician?"

"He saw me and ran. Which makes me think he knows something. We'll try him again, but for now I want to check something else."

"What?"

"I've got the germ of an idea."

Reed raised her eyebrows. "That good, huh?"

"I need to look at Turner's case file on Bader," he said, gesturing at the laptop on the desk by the window.

"Be my guest." She walked over, logged onto the computer, and turned it towards him as it powered up. "Give me a minute. I'm going to get dressed."

Beckett sat in front of the screen as she moved over to the dresser on the other side of the room. A second later the sound of a hairdryer filled the space, a white-noise hum that made it hard to concentrate. He took a deep breath and focused on a report detailing Bader's last known activities.

He'd read the entire thing twice without finding

anything of note by the time Reed switched off the hairdryer.

"Don't turn around for a second, okay?" she instructed.

He agreed, but it was hard not to do the thing you're told not to. From the corner of his eye, Beckett saw Reed's reflection in the mirror next to the window. She turned her back, letting the towel fall to the floor as she picked up her underwear from the bed.

Oh…

He froze, the dichotomy between gentleman and spy at play once more, along with – he had to admit – a flash of red-blooded male curiosity. Reed's athletic figure was fully revealed, and he couldn't ignore the fact she had an incredible body. It had been a long time since he'd been this close to a naked woman. Not since Portugal. There had been a spark with Isabella in Costa Rica, but he hadn't pursued it, not when they were both on the hotel's payroll. But seeing Reed's lithe form stirred something in him that wasn't just the shame of looking.

Suddenly she turned, their eyes meeting in the mirror. For a split second she looked terrified, ashamed, angry, all emotions he'd never want to instil in someone unless it was part of his job. Especially someone in such a vulnerable state.

"I'm so sorry," he mumbled. "I didn't… I didn't mean to…"

Reed huffed, yanking on her underwear as Beckett returned his attention to the screen. He continued reading, trying to focus on the job at hand. All he needed was something that might validate his hunch. But the information was insufficient, leaving him with more questions than answers.

"Damn it," he muttered under his breath.

Reed joined him, standing beside him dressed in jeans and a sweatshirt. She looked clean and fresh and smelled of shampoo.

"What are you thinking?" she asked, all business again.

Beckett leaned back. "Not sure. But let's review what we know. Turner is in New York, likely because of Bader. Either they're working together, or Turner's keen to meet with him for a reason we don't fully understand yet. This implies Bader is probably in New York too." He glanced at Reed.

"Makes sense," she said.

"Right, but why is Bader in New York?"

"Because he lives here."

"Maybe, but he hasn't worked at Axiom for months, and these files show he's been in Europe for the last three. And then it hit me before," Beckett continued, leaning forward. "The Rosenwald Committee meeting starts tomorrow in upstate New York."

"The Rosenwald Committee," Reed echoed. "You mentioned them last night. You think there's a link?"

"Yes. I do." Reed stepped aside as he stood and began to pace, needing the movement to help him think. "Because I also remembered the focus for their meeting this year is biomedical innovation. Think about it – Bader is a scientist, a biologist. What if he's attending the meeting or is even part of the committee? That would explain why Turner is in town. Maybe he's planning to meet Bader there."

"Meet him?"

"Or Bader could be introducing Turner to potential buyers. We know Turner is in the market for selling classified information."

Reed nodded. "So you think Bader is part of the Rosenwald Committee and is acting as the go-between?"

Beckett stopped pacing and turned to face her. "I don't know. But my instincts are telling me Bader, Turner, and the Rosenwalds are linked somehow. I want to check it out."

Reed leaned against the desk, her arms crossed. "This seems like quite a leap, Beckett. You want us to crash the annual meeting?"

"Not crash. More like sneak in the back door and take a look around."

Reed shook her head in dismay. "What if Bader isn't a part of it?"

"What if he is? That means Turner will be there too."

"You can't take him out at the Rosenwald meeting."

"Maybe not," he agreed, "but we can get a lead on him, and track him from there. We're spinning our wheels here, so it's worth checking out. And if we miss this, Turner is in the wind and we might never find him."

Reed looked thoughtful. She glanced at the laptop, then back at Beckett.

"Okay," she said finally. "Let's do it."

Chapter Twenty

Reed gripped the steering wheel, her knuckles whitening slightly on the leather. It was Saturday, just after five in the evening, and the late sun cast long shadows across the highway as she navigated out of New York. They were heading north towards Albany, close to the Vermont border. The Ford Taurus – a rental arranged by the hotel that morning – handled well enough, but her mind was anything but controlled. Her eyes flicked to the rearview mirror every few minutes, looking for signs of company. They'd parked the car in the hotel's underground lot all day while they rested, and only surfaced half an hour ago, ensuring no one was around as they drove off. There was no indication anyone was following them, yet she couldn't shake the feeling something was wrong. Every new car that appeared behind them set her nerves on edge. As the city's towering skyscrapers gave way to open roads, and the congestion of Manhattan receded into the distance, rather than feel lighter, the weight of her mission pressed down on her.

Stop this, Erica. You're fine.

You've got this.

But her concerns weren't limited to the mission or the possibility of being followed. She was also preoccupied with the man beside her. Every so often she stole a glance at Beckett in the passenger seat, his presence a constant reminder of the stakes. His calm, almost detached demeanour unsettled her. He was focused, sure, but what was going on in that head of his? Plus, he had his own agenda, and that made her nervous.

If she was honest with herself, she was still angry and upset about what had happened in the room yesterday. Yes, she'd caught him watching her getting dressed, but part of her had wanted him to. Or rather, *they* had wanted it; had asked it of her.

How did they put it? *Use your feminine wiles to make the job go easier.*

The whole idea disgusted her. She hated playing this kind of game and hated them more for demanding it. She hadn't signed up for that – none of it. It was her job and she had to see it through, but some days... sometimes...

Jesus, Erica.

Pull yourself together.

She needed a distraction, a way to break the mounting tension in the car. "Are you certain we're going to find Turner here?" she asked.

"No, I'm not sure at all," Beckett replied. "But we might find something useful. A lead maybe, on either Bader or Turner. If Turner is here, all the better."

"Yeah, all the better..." she repeated, her words trailing off.

The traffic had thinned, brick buildings replaced by stretches of dense woodland and open fields. The highway stretched ahead, a ribbon of blacktop cutting through the vast expanse of green.

"You think you'll be able to do it?" she asked, after they'd been driving in silence for some time.

Beckett turned his head slightly, studying her before answering. "I'll do what I have to, you don't have to worry about that."

She felt his gaze boring into her as she drove. "You've killed before then? In similar situations?"

He sighed through his nose and turned to look out the windshield. The light outside was fading. "Didn't they let you read my file?"

"How do you feel about that? What you've done, I mean."

She glanced from the road when he didn't immediately reply. His arms were folded and his gaze dead ahead didn't waver.

"It's a job," he said, and she thought he was leaving it at that, but then he went on. "You can't afford to see them as people. You have to view them as less than you. They want you dead; you're just protecting yourself. If you don't you start questioning, hesitating. It takes a lot of mental gymnastics, but it's the only way to pull the trigger without losing a piece of yourself each time. You have to focus on the greater good, the mission, what you're doing it for. After a while it becomes second nature."

Reed couldn't quite get her head around that. "So you dehumanise them?"

He turned to her. "Exactly. Surely you were taught the same in the Marine Corps. It's them or you. If you start seeing them as equals, it affects your judgement."

"Do you ever worry that makes you a psychopath?"

"No. I'm a professional. You do what you have to do."

She sensed him staring at her again, like he was analysing her. Then he asked, "Have you killed anyone?"

Her grip on the wheel tightened. "Once. That I know of directly."

The silence that followed seemed to go on forever. He was waiting for more but she shook her head. "I don't want to talk about it."

"But you've been involved in war?"

"Yeah."

And wasn't that the truth? War all the time. It sometimes felt like all she ever knew.

An awkward silence settled between them, the weight of the conversation hanging in the air. Reed checked her mileage, her gas levels, she checked the time on the dashboard and her watch. Then she took a deep breath, trying to steady herself, doing her own mental gymnastics to get back on track.

"We're heading into unknown territory," she said. "Both literally and figuratively. The Rosenwald Committee is powerful, and we have no jurisdiction. If they find us and discover who we are, we'll be in trouble with the agency."

"If they find us it'll be worse than that," Beckett replied. "These aren't the kind of people who play by the rules. If they catch us it won't just be a slap on the wrist from your bosses."

Despite his words, he didn't seem fazed. At all. That unsettled Reed even more. "Great," she muttered. "Just what I needed to hear."

The scenery grew increasingly remote with each passing mile, and she had to rely on the Ford's headlights to show her the way. They left the main highway and the road narrowed as it wound through thick forests, trees closing in on either side and the canopy overhead creating a tunnel of leaves and branches. Reed's eyes flicked to the rearview mirror. The road behind them was empty, but the nearer they got to their destination, the more her nerves frayed.

As they neared Pharaoh Lake, signs of heightened security appeared. Her heart quickened. She'd expected security, but not to this extent. Unmarked vehicles were parked discreetly by the roadside, with men in dark suits standing guard. They were getting close and this was no casual gathering.

As they rounded a bend a makeshift barricade came into view, lit by headlights and manned by armed guards.

"Shit," she muttered under her breath, slowing the car.

Beckett cleared his throat and sat upright. "Stay calm," he said softly. "I'll speak to them."

She brought the car to a stop as Beckett opened the glovebox, carefully stashing the gun he had found at Turner's place, now loaded with ammo from Reed's equipment bag. He did the same with her weapon, his movements deliberate and slow, ensuring the guards wouldn't see what he was doing. Her gun was licensed, his wasn't; but if they asked to see her licence, they'd discover her identity, which was equally problematic. Something told her these people wouldn't want the CIA sniffing around their sinister powwow in the woods.

Fuck. Here they come.

Beckett rolled down the window as the guards approached. One was tall and lean with a chiselled jawline, the other stockier with a buzz cut. With their sunglasses and earpieces, they looked more like spooks than regular security. Both were visibly carrying.

"Evening!" Beckett said, slipping into a perfect New York accent. "Is the road out or something?"

The guards exchanged glances. "You shouldn't have

gotten this far," the taller one said, leaning into the window. "Didn't anyone stop you?"

Beckett feigned confusion. "You gentlemen are the first people we've seen for a while. My wife Laura and I were looking for somewhere to stop over. Been doing a bit of hiking." He reached over and grabbed her left hand, giving it a squeeze. She wondered why he hadn't gone for her right one, it was closer, but then she realised – neither of them was wearing a wedding ring.

He was a sharp guy but she flinched at his touch, her mind flashing to unwelcome memories. She hadn't held a man's hand since before…

No.

She shook the thought away, forcing herself to focus as the guard on her side of the car leaned closer, peering in through the open window with narrowed eyes. "You don't have much gear with you for a hike."

"It's all packed away in the trunk," Beckett replied. "Just boots and waterproofs. We like to travel light."

Reed tensed. It was a bold claim, and if these guys wanted to check, they'd be found out in seconds. But they seemed to buy it.

"Well, I'm afraid you can't go any further," the guard on Beckett's side said. "There's an important event happening down the road this weekend. We can't have civilians wandering in. Turn around, please."

Beckett played dumb, a slight smile on his face. "Aw, come on, guys. We'll keep to ourselves. Just trying to enjoy the outdoors."

The guard's expression hardened. "Turn around. Now!"

Beckett stayed in character, holding his hands up. "All right, all right. We'll head back." When he turned to Reed, his face was relaxed but his eyes communicating so much more. "You want to turn this thing around, honey?"

The guards stepped away as she swung the car in a U-turn and they set off back the way they'd come. She let out a slow breath.

"What now?" she asked, once the roadblock was out of sight.

"I'm thinking," Beckett replied. They drove in silence for another half a mile until he said, "Pull over where you can just here."

"What? Are you serious?" She slowed the car to a stop. "Don't tell me you're thinking of—"

"I'm going in the back way," he said, unclicking his seatbelt. "Once I'm gone, drive another mile or so down the road and park up. Wait for me. I'll find you."

"Wait for how long?"

"Until I find you," he replied with a grin. He opened the glovebox and retrieved his gun, checking the magazine before tucking it into his waistband.

"How are you going to get in?" she asked.

"I'll find a way."

"I should go with you."

"No," he said firmly. "I need you here for a quick getaway. If Turner's inside, I'll do what Templeton wants and get out. It might be messier than I'd like but it'll be done. I'll get my life back. Or what's left of it."

"Okay, well... good luck."

He opened the door and stepped out. "I don't need luck. I just need Turner to be there."

She watched him disappear into the trees, then drove away, her mind already racing with her next move. About a mile down the road, she pulled over and killed the engine. She had a call to make.

Chapter Twenty-One

Beckett moved silently through the dense forest, every rustle of leaves and scurrying critter drawing his attention. The faint hum of music, distant but growing louder, guided him in the right direction. He kept his gait light, careful not to snap twigs or disturb the undergrowth. Not easy when he could barely see two metres in front of his face.

He reached a clearing and paused, finding his bearings. The music was clearer now, an atonal melody in a strange key that grated on his nerves. The air was filled with the scents of pine and damp earth, but there was something else, too – a faint, sickly sweet aroma that didn't fit with the landscape.

He also sensed people nearby. That subtle shift in atmosphere caused by large crowds that made you aware of them before you saw them. He crossed the clearing, navigating through the woodland until the trees thinned. As he neared, the natural sounds of the forest at night were overtaken by the music and deep hum of many voices.

Brushing through a group of fir trees he caught sight of

a man standing guard up ahead, partially hidden by the thick foliage. Beckett dropped into a crouch and moved silently through the undergrowth, circling the area to get a clearer view. The guard was dressed in a black t-shirt and cargo trousers and had the relaxed but alert stance of a professional. He also had a rifle slung over his shoulder and a radio clipped to his belt.

Beckett edged closer, using the foliage as cover. When he was within striking distance he waited for the guard to turn away, then launched himself forward. The guard was over six feet tall and broad-shouldered, but Beckett had the element of surprise. It was all over the second Beckett wrapped his arm around his neck.

The guard fought back, clawing at Beckett's arm, but Beckett's grip remained firm, cutting off blood flow to the brain. The guard couldn't yell, he couldn't get away. All he could do was succumb to oblivion. Beckett held tight until the man's body went limp then eased him to the ground, checking to make sure he was still breathing.

With the guard neutralised, Beckett quickly stripped him of his uniform and slipped into the clothes. Almost a perfect fit. He used zip ties found in the guard's pocket to bind the man's hands and feet, then stuffed one of his socks into his mouth to silence him. After dragging the body into the bushes and concealing it, Beckett adjusted his new attire, concealing his pistol down the back of his waistband and slinging the rifle over his shoulder.

Buoyed by his new disguise, Beckett continued through the woods. The speakers were playing circus music now, the noise booming through the trees and only adding to the surreal and macabre atmosphere.

Up ahead he spotted a natural basin enclosed by a high fence and prominent wooden gate, illuminated by hidden lights. He approached with confidence, convincing himself he belonged here, just another member of the crew.

The gate was made of some type of dark wood, reinforced with polished brass rivets. Intricate twisting patterns and what looked to be occult symbols were carved into each of its beams. Beckett kept his head down, giving a casual nod to the guards stationed on either side. He noticed a turnstile off to the side of the main gate, likely for the guards' use. Moving towards it, he held his breath and slipped through, bracing for a challenge that never came. The guards, absorbed in their own duties, barely spared him a glance. He exhaled and kept walking.

Once inside, Beckett took in the full scope of the event. The Rosenwald Committee meeting was in full swing, the atmosphere charged with a strange, frenetic energy. Hundreds of people, mostly men, wandered about in elaborate costumes, some also wearing sinister masks with elongated features. In front of him a row of mahogany booths lined the pathway, each containing a vintage rotary phone.

Beckett moved deeper into the site, keeping to the edge of the crowd as he absorbed the bizarre sights and sounds before him. There were fire breathers, acrobats performing on tightropes strung between trees, and musicians playing weird medieval instruments. The juxtaposition of the ancient and the modern was all around and rather jarring, creating an atmosphere that was both fascinating and unsettling.

Trams painted a deep forest green, appeared to be ferrying guests from one end of the camp to the other, their gold-leaf insignias gleaming as they trundled along well-worn paths, the soft chime of bells announcing their approach. Nearby, a brass band played jazz standards to a crowd of men drinking heartily from large earthenware steins.

Groups of middle-aged men huddled in intense conversation, while others laughed manically with one another. It was a twisted carnival, a grotesque parody of a festival. Beckett clocked the faces of the unmasked participants as he passed, Reed's mugshots of Turner and Bader fixed in his memory, but he recognised no one.

The circus music had now finished, and the soft strains of a live string quartet drifted through the air. It was infinitely more pleasurable. To his left, the landscape rose into a series of planes where tents were pitched – some nestled into the natural curves of the landscape, others perched on rocky outcrops. Down to his right, huge stone fireplaces roared with life, their heat casting an orange glow that pushed back the ever-darkening night. Immense Persian rugs covered the ground in front of each fire.

Ahead, Beckett spotted a rack of cloaks similar to those worn by many of the attendees. Leaning his rifle against the side of the rack but keeping the pistol in his waistband, he threw one of the large cloaks over his head and shoulders. It smelled musty and was made of heavy, dark crimson fabric, but it provided the perfect cover.

As he moved around the festival, Beckett scanned the area, his instincts alert for any sign of his targets. But there was no sighting of either.

No Turner. No Bader.

No cigar.

He quickened his pace, expanding his search to the perimeter, passing campsites marked by carved wooden signs: 'Valhalla', 'Sphinx', 'Harbinger' and 'Cobra'. Lanterns hung from branches, casting a gentle glow on the ground. The remnants of revelry were everywhere – silver trays containing the half-eaten remains of hors d'oeuvres, bottles of rare vintage wines with only a few swallows left, and piles of plush cushions marred with dubious-looking stains.

Beckett stopped at a message board covered in pinned notes and photographs. The images showed men of all ages dressed in costume, from medieval knights to Renaissance poets. He recognised a few faces; a billionaire investor who'd recently taken over one of the big social networks, a couple of movie stars whose names escaped him, and the head of a space tech company currently making headlines. They were all posing and laughing with an abandon that seemed out of character. Beside the photos, a handwritten notice advertised a symposium on global finance, featuring speakers whose names Beckett also recognised.

While he couldn't have predicted what he'd find in these woods, some of it aligned with his expectations. The Pharaoh Lake retreat was more than a meeting of minds and money – it was a microcosm of power, a place where the world's elite could shed their public personas and reveal their true selves, if only for a few days.

He shook his head. No listings for talks on curing poverty or addressing third-world debt. But why would there be? So much money and influence, and yet these people were only here to serve their own interests and those of their shareholders.

The injustice riled him, but he pushed through it and continued exploring, soon finding himself at the edge of a large lake. The water was still, reflecting the lanterns strung from the trees and the stars above. A pier jutted out over the water, where a few men stood engaged in hushed conversation. As Beckett passed, he overheard mentions of tech warfare and policy shifts – the kind of talk that never reached the general populace.

On the far side of the lake, Beckett came across an amphitheatre guarded by an enormous statue carved from a tree. The figure – a robed woman holding a staff – seemed to be watching over the camp's proceedings. A stone altar in front of her was adorned with offerings of wine and bread, possibly remnants of an earlier ceremony.

As he considered circling the lake to the opposite side, a loud fanfare blared from hidden speakers among the trees, followed by the crackling of a PA system and more circus music. A moment later, the festival erupted into activity as people rushed towards the amphitheatre. Something significant was about to happen, yet Beckett was no closer to finding Bader or Turner.

He grabbed a man rushing past and pulled him aside. "What's going on?"

"Excuse me?" The man glared at him.

"This is my first time here," Beckett said, with a grin. "Help a guy out?"

"Why, it's the Saturday ceremony, of course. The big show." He shook off Beckett's grip and called back as he hurried away. "You should get a move on. This place gets busy and you don't want to miss a second of it."

Chapter Twenty-Two

Pulling the cloak's hood low over his face, Beckett followed the man past the statue and into the amphitheatre. The sky had deepened to a velvety blue, and a sense of anticipation crackled in the air. The amphitheatre, like the rest of the site, was both odd and impressive – a vast, bowl-shaped depression encircled by ancient pines and thick oaks. The ground sloped gently down to a wooden stage at the centre, flanked by two enormous stone pillars. Each pillar was intricately carved with mythical creatures, their eyes, set with gems, seemingly following Beckett as he took a seat on the ground beside a row of trees at the back. He picked a spot that offered a clear view of the stage while keeping him partially concealed.

A large crowd had already gathered – men in their prime mingling with those whose power and influence had not waned with age; though, this was likely due to costly investments in biohacking and rejuvenation tech rather than mere genetics. They were seated in clusters of twenty or thirty on the grass, some lighting cigars, others engaged in quiet conversation. Each wore a robe similar to Beckett's, and many sported masks ranging from simple eye coverings to grotesque, carved devils. Beckett settled against a tree trunk, keeping one eye on the stage whilst casting his gaze around the sea of faces.

As the minutes passed, the amphitheatre filled to capacity. Beckett estimated there must be at least two thousand people. The atmosphere swelled into something approaching hysteria until, abruptly, the sharp notes of a violin cut through the murmur and the crowd fell silent.

A single spotlight illuminated a lone figure on stage. Dressed in purple velvet and gold lamé robes, he held a staff topped with a golden eagle, its wings spread wide and catching the light in a dazzling display.

"Welcome, High Priest," the crowd murmured, men for whom today was not their first ceremony. "Welcome, Halloran."

Halloran's voice echoed around the amphitheatre, amplified by the hidden speakers. "Brothers, we gather tonight to cast off the burdens of our daily lives and renew our fellowship."

A wave of approval rippled through the crowd. Beckett felt a tap on his shoulder and turned to see a large man with glasses offering him a program.

"First-timer?" the man whispered.

"Yes. Thank you." Beckett accepted the program. The cover read, *Death of Yesterday's Man. 133rd Performance. Rosenwald Committee.*

"You're in for a treat," the man said with a knowing smile. "Just wait."

Across the amphitheatre torches flared to life, their flames casting long shadows over the crowd. A procession of robed figures appeared, each carrying a torch and chanting in Latin, though Beckett couldn't make out the words. Their robes were deep crimson like his, with hoods obscuring their faces.

They formed a semi-circle around Halloran, who raised his arms and the chanting stopped. "Tonight, we cast off the chains of our mundane existence and embrace the freedom of our true selves," he boomed. "Bring forth Yesterday's Man!"

Two men in dark robes carried a large straw effigy onto the stage. It was shaped like a human but with grotesque, exaggerated features. Beckett couldn't take his eyes off the stage as Halloran's voice grew more intense. "This pathetic figure represents all that holds us back, all that binds us to the cares of the world. By burning him, we reclaim our power, our freedom!"

The crowd erupted in approval, their cheers echoing. Beckett watched as the effigy was doused in flammable liquid and set alight, the flames consuming it with a vicious ferocity.

The men cheered, but Beckett felt a chill as the flames danced, their shadows darkening the faces of the men around him. His eyes flitted from person to person, Turner's last known likeness flashing in his mind's eye. If he was one of the men wearing a mask it was almost a fool's errand, but he trusted his instincts. Turner had a background similar to Beckett's – military, then special forces, then covert operations. That implied a certain presence, a distinct way of moving and behaving. Beckett hoped he might spot it in Turner's stance or build.

Suddenly a deep, mocking voice boomed from the darkness. "Idiots! Simpletons! When will you learn that I will never die?"

It was the voice of Yesterday's Man, amplified to a

menacing growl. The crowd fell silent, their attention fixed on the stage. Halloran stood before the burning figure. "Be gone!" he cried. "Our fellowship compels you to leave! Our knowledge will set us free!"

"Knowledge will set us free!" the crowd echoed, their voices rising in unison.

The flames leapt higher, and a burst of fireworks exploded in the night sky, showering the scene in brilliant colours. The men around Beckett jumped to their feet, roaring with a primal intensity.

Beckett remained seated, his attention split between the spectacle and the crowd. This was more than a ritual; it was an affirmation of the bonds uniting these men, a display of their untouchability and influence. To say it made him feel uneasy would be an understatement.

His gaze swept across the amphitheatre, scrutinising each participant through the thickening smoke and the acrid scent of burning wood.

Knowledge will set us free!
Knowledge will set us free!

The chants grew louder, reaching a fever pitch as the ceremony neared its climax. Beckett's pulse quickened, the adrenaline honing his focus. He methodically swept his gaze across the rows of people – left to right, down, right to left, down – but the sea of robes and shifting bodies obscured a clear view.

Then a flicker of movement caught his eye: a figure partially hidden behind a tree a few feet back from the top tier. Beckett zeroed in as the figure edged out from behind the branches, revealing a brief glimpse of his face.

It was Saul Turner.

Beckett froze, eyes locked on the man who'd dominated his focus for the past forty-eight hours. Turner was watching the ceremony with a clinical, almost obsessive intensity. His eyes darted from the stage to the crowd, searching for something or someone, but never settling. Every few seconds he retreated behind the tree, attempting to remain hidden, but his attention never wavered. His posture was tense as if ready to pounce or flee at any moment. It was clear to Beckett he wasn't here to participate in the rituals. Or gather intel.

So then why was he here?

Beckett had already suspected this mission was less straightforward than Templeton had led him to believe. He cast his attention around the bustling crowd, searching for Dr Bader, his mind racing with possibilities. Turner's presence here suggested the scientist was nearby, but he couldn't spot him.

He refocused on Turner. He had to be here for Bader.

But why?

Beckett narrowed his eyes, frustration eating at him. All at once he felt like he'd been barking up the wrong tree, but perhaps that was the point. Templeton had sent him to New York with vague instructions and limited information and it was fast becoming evident this was deliberate. Templeton was a master manipulator, and there were more layers to this operation than he'd disclosed.

Was Templeton aware of Bader?

Was Bader the real reason Beckett was here?

Beckett's anger flared as the flames engulfing Yesterday's Man roared higher. Surrounded by this grisly spectacle he felt like he was on the brink of losing his mind. A deluge of information and ideas clashed in his mind, but it was the unknowns that disturbed him most. Everything he'd assumed over the past few days had been turned upside down. For his own sanity, he had to figure out what was happening.

If Turner was here searching for Bader rather than selling information, where was the scientist? And why was Turner so desperate to find him? Also, what was Templeton's stake in all of this? And did Reed know more than she was letting on?

There were too many questions and not enough answers. All Beckett knew for sure was that Templeton hadn't given him the full story – and he needed to find out why.

Chapter Twenty-Three

A sleek black car cut through the pre-dawn mist on the M25, its blacked-out windows reflecting the weak light of early morning. It was 4 a.m. on Sunday, and London's Orbital Motorway was deserted. The sky was turning a lighter shade of grey, but dawn was still a way off. It still felt like night.

The car had already been driving for some time, having left Soho just before 3 a.m. At junction nine, it exited the motorway and headed south, bypassing A-roads as it moved through Effingham Junction and onto East Horsley. Its headlights sliced through the darkness, illuminating the winding road ahead, whilst the fields and hedgerows on either side remained shrouded in the early gloom.

After East Horsley the car veered west, heading for Blackheath. A mile or so outside the town, it slowed and its headlights dipped as it turned off the main road onto a winding lane. It drove steadily for the next ten minutes, until it passed through the gates of a large stately home set back from the road and encircled by rows of tall evergreens.

It was a sprawling estate. The grounds, once well maintained, had long since grown wild, giving the place a run-down, almost forsaken appearance. The house itself was a masterpiece of Gothic architecture, with tall, pointed windows and stone gargoyles leering down from the eaves. A thick wash of ivy covered most of the front of the property, the dark leaves obscuring the windows completely in some places.

The car eased down the driveway and stopped at the steps leading up to the front door. In the backseat, Xander Templeton leaned forward and glanced out the window, letting out a gruff sigh. Being summoned here at this ungodly hour was an inconvenience he did not need or appreciate. By this stage, jetlag and caffeine had wreaked havoc on his body clock, but it wasn't the lack of sleep that irritated him. It was what this summons implied.

Templeton was a man used to being in control and he didn't like being told what to do. By anyone.

He leaned forward, speaking to the driver. "Wait here for me. I won't be long."

The driver nodded, wisely keeping silent, as Templeton stepped out of the car. The cool air bit sharply against his cheeks, but he was dressed for the English weather, his coat buttoned tightly against the chill. His shoes crunched on the gravel as he approached the steps up to the main entrance. Once there, he pressed the steel button by the door. It made no sound.

He stood there, he waited, his irritation growing with each passing second.

"Come on," he growled, his breath forming visible puffs in the cold air.

A minute ticked by. Then another. He clenched and

unclenched his fists by his sides. He hated being made to wait, but showing impatience was a weakness.

Finally a voice crackled over the speaker, one he didn't recognise. "Walk to the end of the corridor. Down the first flight of stairs. Second door on the right."

The voice cut off abruptly, leaving an echo of static. That was it. No acknowledgement of who he was or the effort he'd made getting here. The door clicked open with a mechanical hum and he pushed it open, letting it slam closed behind him with a decisive thud.

He glanced around, trying to make sense of his surroundings. The interior was bizarre, not what he'd expected from the stately home's exterior. Suits of armour lined the walls, but the floor, walls and ceiling were covered in a bright white material that reflected the harsh lights above. It was an unsettling contrast, medieval decor against an almost clinical backdrop. There were mirrors everywhere, reflecting his image a hundred times, and creating a disorienting effect like in a funhouse.

Although, there was nothing fun about this experience, Templeton thought as he moved along the corridor. His reflection followed him, distorted and multiplied.

For Christ's sake.

He had better things to do than navigate some ridiculous hall of mirrors. Like always, he was spinning plates twenty-four-seven, with officers and assets all over the world requiring his attention. He should be working. Failing that, he should be in bed or at least enjoying a drink at the hotel bar. But this, he supposed, was work. In a sense.

He reached the end of the corridor and descended the stairs. The basement was no less strange – brightly lit, with polished steel surfaces and more mirrors, giving it the feel of a sterile operating theatre. He hoped that wasn't an omen. He moved forward, his footsteps echoing off the walls.

The bottom of the stairs opened out into a wide space mercifully free of mirrors. Two doors were set at an angle from the stairwell. He approached the second one as instructed. It was painted black and unremarkable, except it had no handle. He knocked, and the door swung open. Inside, the lights were off, making it impossible to see what awaited him. As he stepped through, the door slammed shut behind him, plunging the room into complete darkness.

Templeton stood still, letting his eyes adjust to the gloom. His shallow breathing was the only sound. A moment later a bright light flickered on, revealing the space. But the illumination barely mattered; he was inside a black box with nothing but a single large mirror on the wall in front of him. His reflection stared back, looking wired and stressed. He rolled his shoulders back and puffed out his chest, putting on a show of confidence.

"Walk up to the mirror."

It was the same voice as before, but there was no one in sight and no visible speakers. Templeton stepped forward, hearing a faint whirring sound as he got closer to the looking glass.

"Eyes open," the voice commanded.

He stared directly into the mirror, his eyes wide and steady. He assumed they were scanning his retina. The technology these people had was state-of-the-art.

"Welcome, Mr Templeton," the voice said, devoid of any warmth.

"Welcome?" he muttered to himself. "Funny way of showing it."

There was no response.

He scowled, the weight of the silence pressing down on

him. "What do you want?" he asked, disliking the sight of his reflection speaking back at him. It was unsettling. Plus his jowls shook, and the tip of his nose twitched with certain sounds. It was an unpleasant reminder of his age.

"We demand an update," the voice said.

Templeton narrowed his eyes, scrutinising his reflection as if it might offer answers. "That's it? That's why you called me all this way?"

There was no response.

But Templeton knew this game well. It was a power play, always the same with these people. He sighed, resigning himself to the fact that the house always won.

"Everything is proceeding as planned," he said.

"Can you be certain?"

He cleared his throat. "Yes. I'm on it," he growled. "Things will be handled just as you wanted. As we discussed."

He leaned in, wondering if it was two-way glass and if someone was watching from the other side. He could place his hand on the glass to check – if his reflection touched then it wasn't a regular mirror – but doing that was a beta move and he refused to give them the satisfaction.

"Once I do this for you," he continued, "I want your assurance that whatever happens next, I'm kept in the loop."

There was no response.

"Do you hear me? I need to be a part of whatever's decided."

He heard a soft chuckle, only adding to his indignation.

"Do not worry, Mr Templeton," the voice said. "If you fulfil your end, our special relationship remains intact. Now, go."

He frowned. "That's it?"

There was no response. A moment later the door behind him clicked open. Templeton turned, muttering under his breath, and exited the room.

All this damn way, just for that.

But he was relieved to leave this freaky ass place. If he never came back here, it'd be too soon. As he walked up to the top level he glanced at his watch, already thinking about his flight back to JFK in a few hours. At least he'd get some sleep on the plane. This was far from over, and something told him he'd need to be well rested for what came next.

Chapter Twenty-Four

Beckett had to move fast. The ceremony was winding down and Turner could leave at any moment. There was still a lot of activity both onstage and among those watching but the crowds were thinning by the minute. Ash from the now-charred Yesterday Man effigy floated into the sky like errant fireflies. Keeping his head low, Beckett navigated around the top of the amphitheatre, skirting clusters of robed figures while keeping Turner in his sights.

At the edge of the natural basin, the path was narrow, flanked by thick trees that provided decent cover but obscured his view of Turner every few steps. He pressed on, the gun against his lower back a constant reminder of his mission.

Not that he was going to use it. Drawing attention to himself as an armed intruder would be disastrous. Besides, he needed a clearer understanding of the situation before executing Templeton's orders.

Beckett had carried out assassinations for Queen and country many times over the years without questioning his order. But this was different. Templeton wasn't his superior officer; he wasn't part of Sigma Unit. He wasn't even someone Beckett trusted. Templeton might have him over a barrel, but for his own peace of mind he had to know what really linked the CIA section chief to Turner and Turner to Bader.

After that, all things being equal, he'd do what he was sent here to do. The mission might be more complicated than he'd realised, but first and foremost it was about gaining his freedom – and Amber's. If he had to put his conscience aside and kill Turner to achieve that, so be it. Turner was an officer, same as him. He existed in the same grey area, in the same grey world, he knew the risks.

But as Beckett reached the area where the American had been standing, he found it empty.

"Bugger." He turned around, peering into the darkness for any sign of the man or clues where he might have gone. Below him, the Yesterday Man was now nothing but a burnt, twisted cinder.

Beckett was about to leave when he felt something press into his back. He spun around and found himself staring down the barrel of his own gun. Turner stood behind it, his face a mask of cold determination.

"Who are you?"

Beckett raised his chin, studying Turner's stance and grip. They were about the same height, but Turner was wiry and more angular. His eyes were so dark that in this light it was impossible to see where the iris ended and the pupil began. It gave him a predatory appearance.

"Take it easy, okay?"

Beckett knew Turner was a shrewd operator – there was no way he'd risk a shot and the resulting commotion. Yet he also knew every second was critical in these situations.

Turner would be assessing him in return, and his decision-making bandwidth would be at its limit.

"Well, the thing is, I'm just—" Mid-sentence Beckett shifted to one side, slapping the gun away while kicking out to sweep Turner's leg. The move should have ended it, but Turner's reflexes were lightning fast. He grabbed Beckett and yanked him down with him.

They hit the ground with a thud. Beckett swung a punch at Turner's jaw, but he deflected it with his forearm. He tried to pin Beckett's arm, but Beckett countered with a knee to his side. Turner grunted, twisting his body and using the force to throw Beckett off balance. He rolled, leveraging the movement to break free and scramble to his feet.

Turner was up just as fast.

"I just want to talk," Beckett gasped.

But Turner had other plans. He feinted left, then launched forward with a rapid barrage of jabs and kicks. Beckett blocked or dodged each blow, before delivering a sharp kick to the back of Turner's knee. He stumbled but regained his footing, lunging forward and tackling Beckett to the ground.

They grappled, each struggling for control. Beckett held his own but Turner was a skilled fighter with a block for every blow. They rolled through twigs and debris, neither gaining the upper hand. Beckett's hand found Turner's throat, but Turner twisted away, slamming his leg into Beckett's stomach. The impact knocked the breath out of him, but he managed to roll onto his back just as Turner lunged. He raised his knees and caught Turner in the side, flipping him over.

Seizing the chance, both men scrambled to their feet and leapt apart, circling each other. "Who sent you?" Turner hissed.

"Why do you think someone sent me?" Beckett shot back. "What are you doing here?"

Turner aimed another punch, but Beckett deflected it and countered with a knee, grazing Turner's hip as he spun away. He jumped back immediately, keeping his guard up.

This guy was good – no denying that.

Turner stepped forward and Beckett moved left aiming a kick at his knee. But Turner saw it coming and caught his leg, yanking him off balance. He crashed to the ground and Turner pounced, pinning him down.

But Beckett wasn't done yet. He bucked his hips, tossing the American aside, and scrambled on top. Leaning his weight forward, he shoved his forearm under Turner's chin and pressed down hard on his throat.

Now he had him.

Turner struggled, his sinewy muscles straining against the pressure.

"I just want to talk," Beckett repeated, through gritted teeth.

"Go to hell."

Beckett pushed down harder, but the wily American smashed a fist into his kidneys, causing him to shift his weight. As he did, Turner twisted sharply, driving his elbow into Beckett's solar plexus. Beckett reeled, and Turner shoved him off.

Annoyance surged as they hauled themselves upright, both fatigued but ready for more. Turner was good. Damn good. Beckett lunged, aiming to catch him before he could recover, but Turner jumped away and started yelling at the top of his lungs.

"Help! Security! Over here!"

Beckett froze. What the hell was this guy playing at? He

dropped his fists just as three large men in black combat fatigues came running over.

"What's going on here?" one of them barked, raising his rifle.

Turner raised his hands. Beckett followed suit. "He had a gun," Turner said.

The guards exchanged glances. "Show your wristbands," one of them said.

"Wristbands, now!" another barked.

Beckett glanced at his wrist. Turner did the same. Both were bare.

The guards saw it too. "Freeze!" They stepped back, two of them aiming their rifles at Beckett and the third at Turner. Beckett kept his hands raised as he met Turner's gaze.

So, here we are smart arse.
What now?

Chapter Twenty-Five

The three surly guards flanked Beckett and Turner as they led them away from the amphitheatre. Beckett noted their rifles, held casually at waist height but with fingers tensed on the triggers, ready for trouble. These weren't show-of-force personnel. They were professionals who knew how to handle a weapon.

The night air was cool, carrying a hint of moisture that suggested rain might be on the horizon, even though the sky was clear and studded with stars. None of them spoke. Beckett kept his head down, peering around for possible escape routes. He assumed Turner was doing the same. As they moved away from the main event space, the sound of the crowds and the crackle of bonfires faded to a distant murmur. All that remained was the crunch of gravel beneath their feet and the rustle of leaves. The tension within the group mounted with every step.

After five minutes of walking, Beckett huddled close to Turner. "What was that?" he whispered.

Turner stared straight ahead, his face set in a mask of stoic indifference, almost machinelike. He didn't reply.

Beckett turned to the nearest guard. "Where are you taking us?"

"You'll see," he growled, out of the corner of his mouth.

The path wound down a steep hillside, uneven and treacherous in the dim light. At the bottom, three large log cabins came into view, each lit by a single halogen bulb hanging above the entrance. Though rustic and made of sturdy wood, the cabins' deliberate construction made them stand out against the natural surroundings.

The guards prodded them forward with the butts of their rifles, rougher now that they were away from the main action, steering them towards the middle cabin. One of the guards unlocked the door with a set of keys, and they were shoved inside, the sharp poke of rifle muzzles urging them on.

Inside, the cabin was unexpectedly spacious, lit by a harsh fluorescent strip light hanging from the rafters, its utilitarian design at odds with the wood. A row of stacked chairs lined one side, along with a metal table cluttered with rifles, a pack of cigarettes, and walkie-talkies. The guards dragged two chairs to the centre of the room, positioning them face to face. Beckett and Turner were shoved into the chairs, and their hands were secured behind their backs with bar handcuffs – the rigid kind used on non-compliant prisoners to maintain control. The cold metal bit into Beckett's wrists but he didn't struggle or try to get free. No point.

One of the guards pulled a small device from his pocket and approached Beckett. It looked like a camera, though he'd never seen one like it. The guard took photos of him, first from the front then in profile, as if taking a police mugshot.

As the guard moved over to photograph Turner, Beckett surveyed the cabin. It was more secure than it appeared at first glance. Steel shutters covered the only window, and the door was reinforced steel. Even without the cuffs, escaping would be difficult. Mugshots complete, the guards huddled by the entrance, muttering amongst themselves before exiting and locking the door behind them.

"What now?" Beckett asked.

Turner stared straight ahead. "I guess we wait."

Beckett studied him. Turner was a peculiar man, both in appearance and manner –quite different from how he appeared in Reed's photos. His hair was cut short and styled neat. Although the file listed him as thirty-three, he looked older, with a few grey strands at his temples marring his otherwise jet-black hair. Even under the bright light, his eyes remained fully black, lacking any distinction between pupil and iris. They were less windows to his soul and more like black holes, pulling you in with their emptiness. Turner continued to stare ahead, unblinking and unreactive, aware of Beckett's scrutiny but seemingly indifferent to it.

"What the hell did you think you were doing back there?" Beckett whispered. "You threw us both under the bus."

Turner finally turned his gaze towards Beckett, but his expression remained unreadable. "Who are you? Who sent you?"

Beckett shifted in his chair, searching for a more comfortable position. "Why should I tell you anything?"

"But you know who I am?"

Beckett relaxed his shoulders and softened his expression, figuring a little rapport was needed. "I don't know what alias you're currently using, but your real name is Saul Turner. A former officer of the Special Activities Center, now gone rogue."

Turner smirked – at least that's what Beckett assumed he was doing, but it looked more like he was trying not to throw up. "A rogue agent. I see."

Beckett leaned back, watching Turner closely. "So, you're not trying to sell information?"

"Who sent you here?" Turner narrowed his eyes.

Beckett narrowed his right back. "Why are you so interested in Dr Adram Bader?"

Turner gave a slight nod as if conceding a point. "I saw you went to my flat. I assume you found my pen drive." He shrugged. "Very good. But it's irrelevant. I made sure not to record anything of value."

Beckett's turn to smirk. "You're telling me."

"But you are an interesting prospect," Turner said, his tone analytical, almost robotic. "Clearly well trained in hand-to-hand combat. British… What are you, ex-MI6-turned-mercenary?"

"Why do you think that?"

"If you've been sent to kill me, I'd say it's a fair guess."

Turner's calm demeanour was as infuriating as it was compelling. Beckett needed answers but had to be careful how much he revealed in return. Every moment of this conversation felt like a high-stakes chess match.

He raised his head, meeting Turner's piercing stare. "I was with the British Secret Intelligence Service, but not anymore," he said, keeping his voice low. "And I'm no mercenary."

Turner didn't react. "But you are here to kill me?"

"There are influential figures in your government who think you've become a liability." He paused, rolling his shoulders as much as the cuffs allowed. "Let's just say I've had my arm twisted by those same people. They needed someone like me to handle the situation."

"A foreigner. Someone they can *throw under the bus* if things go sideways."

Beckett nodded. "Something like that. It's not personal."

"It never is for men like us." Turner swallowed; the first sign of vulnerability Beckett had seen. "Will you tell me who sent you?"

Beckett hesitated, then decided to tell the truth. "Someone from the CIA."

Turner snorted softly. "I am the CIA."

"Oh yeah? Still?"

"Correct."

"And who's Bader to you?" Beckett tried again.

Turner's expression didn't falter. "Why don't you tell me your name? You already know mine."

"Why did you call security back there?"

"I assumed it would be easier to escape their security than deal with you. From what you just told me, I was correct."

"I see." Beckett struggled against the cuffs. "And how's that working out for you?" He offered a thin smile. Turner kept quiet.

"Do you know a man called Xander Templeton?" Beckett asked.

"Never heard of him."

"Why would he want you dead?"

"Why does anyone want anything?"

"You're not an easy person to talk to, you know that?"

Turner did that weird thing with his mouth again.

"You're not the first person to say that. But I'm not paid to talk."

"Me neither."

"So you are being paid."

"No."

Turner lifted his chin. "Then why are you here? What does this Templeton have on you?"

"He's an old acquaintance. That's all."

"Okay. What has he told you about me?"

"He considers you a threat to national security."

Turner looked genuinely puzzled. "Why?"

"You've gone rogue."

"No. I haven't. I've gone dark for the last few months, but I'm no traitor. I'm with the SAC. What's Templeton's role and where is he operating from?"

Beckett felt more confused than ever, unsure of his next move. "Why are you interested in Bader? Is he here tonight?"

"I thought he was. That's why I'm here."

"To meet with him?"

Turner looked away, his eyes distant as he weighed his response. Before he could answer, the door swung open, and the three guards strode in. Earlier they'd been brusque and professional. Now they wore smug, self-assured expressions.

"Looks like we've got ourselves a real prize," one guard said, shaking his head in mock disbelief. "Can't believe you thought it was a good idea to come here tonight."

"So your facial recognition software got a hit?" Turner asked, referring to the photos the guards had taken. Beckett had assumed that was the reason.

The guard grinned, a predatory glint in his eyes. "You could say that." He pointed at Turner, and his colleagues moved in. They uncuffed the American and hauled him to his feet. "Stay back and keep your rifles on him. From what I hear, he's a wildfire."

Beckett watched as Turner allowed himself to be led out in silence, his expression giving nothing away. He didn't look back.

"Where are they taking him?" he asked the remaining guard.

"Don't worry about it. Now get up."

Beckett remained still; his hands still cuffed behind his back. "Where are we going?"

The guard chuckled, a cold, humourless sound. He grabbed Beckett's arm, pulling him to his feet. "You'll see."

Chapter Twenty-Six

The forest was still, its silence broken only by the crack of twigs beneath their boots as the guards nudged Turner forward with their rifles. None of them spoke. There was no need. Some men, lesser officers, might have begged for mercy at this stage, or asked where they were being taken. But Turner didn't need those answers. He already knew. Or at least, he knew what they'd say. Whether their expectations became a reality depended entirely on him.

The night air was damp, somewhere between drizzle and a fine mist. As they moved away from the camp, the trees grew taller and more dense. It was darker here too, almost pitch black, with just the occasional sliver of moonlight cutting through the canopy above. Turner stayed calm, though his senses were on high alert. He took in every detail: the gnarled branches, the uneven ground, the distant hoot of an owl. The rich scent of wet earth and decaying leaves filled his nostrils. He noted the tension in the guards, the tightness in their neck muscles and the rigid way they gripped their weapons. They were professionals, but even they got antsy on occasion. The Rosenwald Committee meeting was a high-security event, tightly controlled and heavily guarded. The guards had no reason to expect trouble tonight, which could work to his advantage. But as they continued, their breathing grew shallow and their steps heavy. They were bracing themselves for something. That was a bad sign.

Turner didn't feel fear. He was beyond that. He was a tool, a machine honed for a single purpose. His mission could be boiled down to simple math – one minus one equals success; there was no point in complicating things by inserting himself into the equation. Yet as they pressed on, he was acutely aware he should never have come here tonight.

He'd fallen prey to bad intel, leading him to believe Bader was attending the Rosenwald Committee meeting this weekend. But this wasn't the rendezvous point for the exchange. Somewhere along the way, his search had turned into a wild goose chase. Bader was probably miles away, the real action happening elsewhere. That was on him, and he'd chastise himself later. For now he had to rectify the situation, and to do that depended entirely on his actions over the next few minutes.

He slowed his pace, forcing the guards to do the same as he tried to gauge their exact intentions. They were now muttering to each other in low voices. He caught snippets of their conversation but they were careful, giving nothing away.

Still, he knew. He could feel it.

As they trudged deeper into the forest, the path they'd been following disappeared into long grass. Turner breathed slowly, in and out, controlling his heart rate, staying present. There was no point in thinking about what-ifs or maybes.

His family, his past – all irrelevant now. The only thing that mattered was this moment and what he had to do to survive.

His finely attuned ears picked up the faint click of a silencer being screwed onto a gun. It would have been hardly perceptible to most, lost to the sound of their boots trampling through the grass, but to someone like Turner it was unmistakable.

He sucked in a deep breath.

It was coming.

They'd been walking for about twenty minutes, and he could no longer hear any sounds from the event. Besides, the wind was blowing steadily from the east; even if the guards weren't using a suppressor, no one would hear the shot. Turner was a student of philosophy and in his downtime enjoyed thought experiments, but he knew one thing for sure: when a man is executed in the forest and no one's around to hear it, the execution still happens.

His thoughts shifted to the Englishman. Their conversation had shattered Turner's initial assumptions. The man was not who he'd thought him to be. But then again, that worked both ways. The Englishman had no idea who he was dealing with.

Turner accepted the claim that someone in the CIA had sent him, and that altered the situation, but not enough to matter. The Englishman was clearly an elite player, but he couldn't be allowed to compromise the mission. If they both survived the night, Turner would have to eliminate him before he became a serious problem. It was the only way.

He was a tool.

A machine.

A minute later they reached a clearing. Turner's senses sharpened. This was it. He spun around to face the two guards standing side by side. They looked identical, except for a height difference of two inches and the fact that the shorter guard was holding a silenced pistol.

"All right, stop," the taller guard barked, as he grabbed Turner's bicep and moved him into the centre of the clearing. "End of the road."

"You don't need to do this," Turner told him.

"Oh, we do. We know who you are. And we've got our orders."

The guard grinned but it was strained, a flicker of trepidation visible in the moonlight. Turner seized on it. Twisting sharply, he broke free from the guard's grip and slammed his elbow into the man's throat. The guard staggered, gasping for air. Turner grabbed him and spun them both, the guard becoming a human shield as his partner pulled the trigger.

The shot rang out, blood splattering onto Turner's face as the man's head snapped to one side. Without hesitation Turner hurled the dead weight at the remaining guard, who was still shocked and disoriented from his error.

The guard sidestepped the body and raised his weapon, but Turner was already closing the gap. He grabbed the guard's wrist, twisting with brutal force until he released his grip on the gun. As it fell to the ground, he drove his knee into the man's stomach, doubling him over. Before he could recover, Turner's elbow crashed down on the back of his neck.

The guard collapsed to the ground and Turner was right there, rolling him onto his back and pressing his knee into his throat.

"Who ordered this?"

"Go to hell," the guard spat, clawing at Turner's leg as

Turner shifted his weight to keep him pinned, pressing down on his windpipe.

"Where's Bader?"

"Fuck you."

Defiance flashed in the guard's eyes. Turner quickly assessed the situation and knew he'd get no answers from this one. Rocking back, he used the momentum to thrust his weight forward, crushing the man's windpipe with a sickening crunch. The guard's eyes bulged, panic overriding his defiance as he choked for breath. His fists pounded the ground beside him, a horrified, gurgling sound escaping his lips. But it was over. They both knew it. Turner remained watching as the guard's eyes glazed and he went limp.

He sniffed and got to his feet. Picking up the fallen pistol, he placed it near the guard's hand, then stepped back to assess the scene. It wouldn't hold up under scrutiny, but he doubted there'd be any forensic team coming. The Rosenwalds would cover this up and settle with the guards' families. After that, he wasn't sure. They might come after him, but he could handle that. Either way he had to move.

He turned and sprinted back the way he'd come, aiming to circle the main event space and escape through a different route. As he ran he was already calculating his next move. The situation was spiralling into chaos, and he had no tolerance for that. It was not how Saul Turner operated.

He was a tool. A machine.

And he needed to end this.

Chapter Twenty-Seven

Across the other side of the forest, Beckett was being hustled unceremoniously along a winding dirt track. The uneven ground made him stumble, but the guard kept a firm grip on his shoulder, occasionally giving him a dig in the ribs to keep him moving. Beckett's hands were still cuffed, but the guard didn't seem concerned that guests might see him with a prisoner. The evening's festivities were now over and the crowd was thinning, the attendees drifting to their chalets for the night. Lanterns and torches that had lit the area were being extinguished, plunging the forest into darkness.

"Where are we going?" Beckett asked, twisting around to make eye contact.

"Shut it," the guard snapped. "You'll see when we get there."

They appeared to be sticking to the main paths, which was a good sign. If they were planning on killing him, they'd likely drag him off into the denser, darker parts of the forest. He steadied his breathing, focusing on the small details: the smell of damp earth, the cool night air against his skin, the distant strum of an acoustic guitar.

As they pressed on, his thoughts drifted to Turner, wondering if he was getting the same treatment. It bothered him they'd been split up. He'd been tailing Turner all this time, yet after being in the same room he was no closer to understanding the situation. If anything, he was more confused. After their conversation he remained wary of the man – and rightly so – but some of Turner's comments troubled him.

Up ahead a large wooden cabin came into view. Though as they drew nearer, it became clear it was more of a grand lodge than a simple cabin. The high timber walls and sloping roof made an imposing silhouette against the night sky. Raised on stilts, it had a wide wooden staircase leading up to a spacious porch and a heavy front door. Tall, narrow windows framed with wrought iron allowed the light from inside to cast a glow that dappled the nearby trees with orange light.

Beckett was bundled up the steps and the guard knocked on the door. They waited. Beckett straightened his spine and rolled his shoulders back, preparing for whatever came next. The guard moved around him and uncuffed his wrists. Another good sign.

"Don't try anything dumb," the guard growled. "I'm a damn good shot, even against moving targets."

"Show-off," Beckett muttered under his breath.

There was a noise from inside the lodge and a moment later the door creaked open. A tall, tanned man with thick salt and pepper hair peered out. He narrowed his eyes at Beckett and then glanced at the guard before opening the door wider and gesturing for them to enter. The guard grabbed Beckett's arm.

"Move."

The interior of the lodge opened into a spacious, ultra-modern reception area with sleek, polished concrete floors and white walls. The windows Beckett had seen from the outside were dummies; there was no view of the outside. A state-of-the-art security system was discreetly embedded in the walls, and recessed LED bulbs cast a steady low light throughout, eliminating all shadows. To the left, a picture fireplace flickered with a clean blue flame. The granite mantle above it was sleek and empty except for a foot-high sculpture of Yesterday's Man. On another wall a large high-resolution digital display cycled through images of modern art and serene landscapes. Minimalist leather chairs were arranged around a glass coffee table on a vast white rug that looked like it was made of ermine. Against the rear wall, a stylish bar made from a single slab of polished black marble showcased an array of premium spirits, with a mirrored wall behind it reflecting the room's modern elegance.

"This way, please." The man led Beckett across the room to a set of opaque doors that became transparent as they approached. The doors slid open to reveal a high-tech conference room dominated by a black glass-topped table. Three men sat on one side of the table, facing the door. They looked up as Beckett entered, their hushed conversation halting as the doors slid shut behind him.

The men, all in their mid-forties, exuded wealth and confidence. These weren't the old-money elite but the new power players who had built their empires from silicon and code. The man in the centre had slicked-back blond hair and wore a tailored navy suit with subtle pinstripes. He was classically handsome, though his jaw was a little over-pronounced, and he appeared to have a nervous twitch. To his left sat a man with dark hair and a neatly trimmed beard, who was tapping his fingers lightly on the table. His deep charcoal grey suit was impeccably tailored to fit his athletic build, and the platinum Rolex peeking from under his shirt cuff was anything but subtle. The third man was clean-shaven, with sandy hair and a pair of orange designer glasses perched on his too-perfect nose. Beckett recognised him from somewhere, but couldn't think of his name.

Two armed guards stood in separate corners of the room behind the men, their rifles held with the casual ease of men who knew how to use them. Beckett noted their presence and turned his attention to the seated men.

The blond man smiled warmly. "Can I ask you what you're doing here?"

Beckett raised his head. He'd been running different scenarios on the journey here, preparing for various outcomes. He decided to play it straight.

"I'm not sure how much I can say," he replied, keeping his tone low and steady. "But I'm no threat to you."

Blondie chuckled. "We aren't worried about that. Yet you were found on our property, without a wristband, causing a bit of a ruckus. That's not what we're about here. This is a weekend of peace and innovation."

Beckett held his gaze. "I understand that. And I apologise."

The men exchanged polite smiles, their demeanour relaxed. The armed guards, however, looked mean enough for all of them.

"You still haven't answered my question." Blondie leaned forward, a practised smile on his face. "Who are you, and why are you trespassing on our property?"

Beckett continued with the truth, or at least a version of it. "My name is Simon Rivers. I can't say too much, but I came here tracking a high-value target. The other man involved in the... *ruckus*."

"You were... tracking him?"

"It's a classified operation. I'm working with the CIA."

"The CIA?" Blondie's eyes widened, his twitch more pronounced. "But you're English."

"It's a long story. Can I ask who I'm speaking with?"

The men's smiles faded. "Of course," Blondie replied. "But before that, we'd like to know why we weren't informed of any dangerous people in the vicinity. Surely the CIA knew what was happening here this weekend?"

Beckett smiled. "Again, my apologies. We hoped to handle this quietly." He glanced at his watch. "My handler is aware of the situation. I need to report back within the hour."

A ripple of tension passed through the group, barely noticeable but telling to someone like Beckett. The man with the glasses rubbed his face. "Do you know the man you were fighting with?"

Beckett nodded. "Yes."

The men tensed some more. Beckett continued. "That man is a rogue agent on the CIA's wanted list. I was sent to neutralise him."

"Neutralise? You mean...?"

"Yes."

The men exchanged uneasy glances, then huddled together, whispering among themselves. Beckett remained still, using the moment to assess their reactions. He was employing a classic tactic – dropping a bit of intel to gauge how much they knew, watching for signs of recognition or alarm.

"How did you know the rogue agent was here?" the man with the dark hair and Rolex asked.

"I'm afraid that's classified," Beckett replied. "However, we believe he was scheduled to meet with a scientist named Adram Bader."

The name drop caused a noticeable shift. The men stiffened, their jaws tightening. They were at least familiar with Bader.

So where did the scientist fit into all this?

Beckett set that thought aside and refocused. "The rogue agent was taken away by two of your guards before I was brought here," Beckett added. "I need to see him and arrange his transfer into CIA custody."

Blondie cleared his throat, then paused and did it again. His twitch had become more pronounced and it was clear to Beckett he was playing for time, trying to get his thoughts in order.

That wasn't a good sign. Something was wrong.

"Our security officers escorted him to a more secure facility to await the authorities," Rolex said. "But we've just had word that he escaped."

Beckett remained still, not taking his eyes off the man. Escaped, or was executed? He couldn't ascertain which from Rolex's expression, but the situation was growing increasingly tense.

"How did you let that happen?" he asked. "I've been trailing him for weeks."

Blondie straightened, his smile now a thin line. "We haven't got all the details as yet. I'll receive a report shortly."

Beckett sighed. "You need to let me go. I need to find him."

"Yes, of course."

He noticed Blondie's shoulders relax, a subtle sign of relief at Beckett's resolve to handle the rogue agent himself. So Turner had escaped then, probably eliminating both guards in the process. The men's jitteriness now made sense.

Rolex narrowed his eyes at Beckett. "What will you do once we release you?"

"Carry out my mission," Beckett replied. "Find the rogue agent. Do what's necessary to ensure he can't achieve his aims."

"Which are...?" Rolex asked.

"We believe he's attempting to sell intelligence." Beckett was almost certain now that this wasn't the case. But the delight behind Blondie's eyes confirmed his suspicions. Clearly, they knew differently and were overjoyed at finding out he didn't.

"I see."

The three men conferred again, their gestures more animated now. Finally, they sat back, their smiles having returned.

"Well we can't obstruct the good old CIA," Blondie announced. "You have our full backing, as always. However, I hope you can also appreciate we can't have you on our property. This is a sacred place, Mr Rivers."

"Understood."

Blondie raised his head, addressing the guard over Beckett's shoulder. "Please escort Agent Rivers back to the main road and ensure he gets away safely."

Beckett smiled. "I have a car waiting for me on the edge of the woods. I can make my way back."

"Even so, we'd prefer to make sure you get there safely," Blondie replied. "I'm sorry we failed to secure the rogue agent, but I have faith the CIA will get their man. Good luck, Mr Rivers."

Blondie gave the guard a sharp nod and seconds later Beckett felt a hand on his shoulder, guiding him out. As the guard escorted him away, he took one last look around the lodge. He still didn't know any names, and the identity of the man with the glasses in particular nagged at him, but the encounter had at least clarified a few things. The way the men had reacted, along with what little he'd gleaned from his conversation with Turner, made one thing crystal clear: Templeton had lied to him.

He was now more determined than ever to uncover Bader's significance and why Turner was so obsessed with him.

As he stepped into the cool night air, Blondie's parting words echoed in his mind.

Good luck...

Yes. Something told him he was going to need it.

Chapter Twenty-Eight

The dashboard clock showed 4:15 a.m. as Beckett slid into the passenger seat beside Reed. She jolted awake, having dozed off with her head against the window.

"Shit, you're here," she muttered, rubbing her eyes and checking the time. "Find anything?"

"Start the car," Beckett said. "We need to move."

He'd left the guard a quarter mile back, having assured him he could be trusted to walk the rest of the way alone. The younger man had been wary at first but eventually gave in. Beckett had worn him down with relentless questions and grating small talk, so by the time they parted ways the guard seemed more than happy to see the back of him.

Reed started the engine and they set off, the car's headlights cutting through the pre-dawn darkness. Beckett buckled up and leaned back in his seat, exhaustion and adrenaline battling for dominance in his system. But for the moment, at least, he allowed himself to relax.

He closed his eyes, attempting to sort through his thoughts while ignoring the tension already simmering in the car. He could feel Reed's impatience as she waited for more details, but he took his time, replaying the events at the lodge, analysing every detail, every reaction. He'd picked his words carefully whilst talking to the three Rosenwald heads, providing them only with what was necessary while gauging their responses. Now he knew two things: Turner was in the wind once more, and those men were terrified at the mere mention of Dr Bader. It seemed the scientist had quite a reputation around here too.

But why?

He was still maddeningly short on answers. Opening his eyes, he caught Reed stealing glances at him as they sped down the deserted roads.

"So…? Are you going to tell me what happened?"

Beckett stared straight ahead. "Turner was there."

"Whoa! Did you…?"

"No. He saw me coming. We fought, but then he called for security. They grabbed us both and dragged me off to some lodge deep in the woods to meet with a group of men."

"Which men?"

"Seemed like high-ups in the committee. The sort of men who can make things happen with a single phone call. I recognised one of them…" He paused, trying to dredge up the memory. Still couldn't get it. "I gave them enough to keep them happy and got a little intel in return."

Reed frowned, her grip on the steering wheel tightening. "Did you tell them who you were?"

"I had to play the CIA card. Up until then they were deciding whether to kill me."

She shot him a wide-eyed glance. "Seriously?"

"I'd bet on it. But don't worry, I was careful with what I

said. I also dropped Bader's name. They claimed they'd never heard of him. But they were lying."

"Where's Turner now?" Reed asked.

"They were planning to have him killed, but from what I gathered he escaped. He's in the wind."

"Shit. You're sure he got away?"

Beckett studied Reed's profile, weighing how much to reveal to Templeton's operative. "Ninety-seven percent sure."

"And the other three percent?"

Beckett shrugged. "I always allow for a margin of error. Despite what you might think, Reed, I'm just a man."

He turned away, his attempt at levity falling flat. Staring out the window, he replayed the last few hours in his head. A few things Turner had said gave him cause for concern. The American had seemed genuinely angry when Beckett suggested he'd gone rogue. The way he'd denied it with real conviction, that wasn't an act.

"Turner confirmed he was there looking for Bader," Beckett said. "But he didn't explain why."

"Why do you think?" Reed asked.

"Not sure." He watched the trees whipping past outside. He had his theories about Turner's motives, but none he was ready to share with her.

"Do you know who the committee men were?" Reed asked.

"They didn't give their names. But they played the part of concerned citizens a little too well. The way they reacted when I mentioned Bader was also telling. They seemed edgy; terrified, almost. They knew more than they let on, but… I don't know…"

He trailed off, fatigue partnering with confusion and making his head spin. It had been one hell of a long day and he needed a break, a chance to look at everything with fresh eyes. They drove on in silence, the early dawn light rising to cast a pale sheen over the landscape. Beckett watched Reed out of the corner of his eye, trying to piece together the fragments of what he'd learned and what still didn't add up. She was focused on the road ahead, but he noticed the tension in her knuckles, white against the steering wheel.

"So what's our next move?" she asked after a few minutes.

Beckett rubbed at his eyes. The truth was, he wasn't sure of anything right now. "Finding Bader is still our best shot at getting close to Turner. He's the key."

Reed nodded, her eyes flicking to him briefly. "Remember your mission, Beckett. You need to kill Turner. That's what Templeton wants. That's what sets you free."

"I know, Reed. I am aware of that."

Beckett studied her, trying to gauge her sincerity. She seemed genuine, but in their line of work appearances were often misleading. Still, she was right about one thing: Turner was his primary target, the key to his freedom. Yet Bader's involvement seemed too significant to overlook, like a crucial piece of a much larger puzzle.

"Have you got anything you want to tell me?" he asked, not taking his eyes off her.

Her gaze flicked to the rearview mirror for a second. "Like what?"

"Anything at all."

She shot him a hard look. "Why would I hold back information?"

He didn't respond, just turned back to the window.

"We should be back in New York by seven" she added. "What then?"

"I want to revisit Bader's old lab," Beckett replied. "But it's Sunday and pretty late – or early, depending on how you look at it – we could both use some sleep first."

Reed nodded, visibly relieved. She looked as exhausted as he felt. "Fine," she agreed, her tone softening. "We'll head back to the hotel, get some rest, and then regroup to figure out our next move."

Beckett closed his eyes, letting the hum of the engine soothe him. There was so much to process, too many loose ends still dangling. But right now he needed to recharge. Tomorrow he would continue his efforts, not stop until he knew Bader's life story inside and out. Then he'd find Saul Turner and do what was needed.

He exhaled slowly, feeling the tension ease a fraction. This wasn't over, not by a long shot. But he had a plan, and for now that was enough.

Chapter Twenty-Nine

Beckett woke just after two to find a note from Reed slipped under his door. She said the lab was closed to visitors on Sundays, and so she'd gone to make some calls and research another case she was working on, but that she trusted him to stay out of trouble. He had money now, but it looked like a trip to Axiom would likely be a waste of time. It would have to wait until tomorrow.

Not knowing what else to do with himself, he took a hot bath, letting the steam and heat work the knots out of his muscles. Afterwards, he dressed in his second set of new clothes and took a stroll around Times Square, where the streets were now bustling with noisy tourists. Finding the crowds a bit too much, he headed to a nearby newsstand, bought several newspapers, and returned to the hotel.

For the next few hours, Beckett scoured each of the newspapers from cover to cover, searching for any thread that might connect to his mission. He wasn't sure what he was looking for; nothing of real significance stood out. Still, the routine of reading helped to centre his thoughts, pulling him back into a civilian mindset. Whether that was a good thing, he wasn't sure. It had been a long time since he'd felt like anything other than a ghost or an outlier.

Later he hit the hotel gym, pushing his body to its limits, savouring the familiar burn in his muscles. But it wasn't long before he found himself back in his room, pacing in front of the open window as he went over everything he knew about Turner and Bader, analysing potential motivations. He also considered Templeton's angles, replaying conversations and recalling what he remembered of him from his time at Sigma Unit.

He ordered room service: two cheeseburgers with fries. He left the fries untouched but enjoyed the meat and toasted bread washed down with a couple of ice-cold beers – all charged to the room on the agency's dime, naturally. After all, there had to be some perks to risking his life on an almost daily basis. By evening he felt both physically and mentally prepared for the challenges ahead. He was restless, eager to get moving, but what could he do? He'd heard Reed return an hour ago but she hadn't come knocking and it was getting late. Besides, there was nothing new to discuss. Knowing he needed to be at best, he reviewed his notes one last time before heading to bed early, determined to get a good night's sleep.

When he woke the next morning it was dead on six, his internal clock sharper than any alarm. He started the new week with a vigorous workout in his room – push-ups, burpees, high-knees, mountain climbers – pushing himself hard and enjoying the familiar rush of endorphins. Afterwards, he showered, brushed his teeth, and even smoothed his hair into a passable side parting before dressing quickly. He'd need new clothes if this dragged on much longer, but for now what he had would suffice.

Once ready, he moved over to the door leading to Reed's room, but it swung open before he could knock. Reed stood there, looking as composed and ready as he felt. Her hair was neatly tied back, and she wore a shirt tucked into a pair of extremely tight jeans that he made a conscious effort not to dwell on. Despite the early hour, she looked alert and eager.

"I heard you moving around," she said, a slight smile playing on her lips. "Ready to hit the lab?"

Beckett stepped back. She was almost unrecognisable from the woman he'd been working with for the last couple of days. Whatever she'd needed to do yesterday had somehow drained the tension from her features and relaxed her shoulders. He didn't know whether he should be worried about that or not. But at least she was on the same page about not hanging around today. Time was not a luxury they could afford – Turner could split at any minute. Or already be gone.

"Yes," he replied, returning the smile. "No time like the present."

They left the hotel and merged with the early morning crowd heading for the subway. Despite the October chill, the air was crisp, with the promise of a bright day ahead. As they descended into the subway station, the familiar smells of the city enveloped them: a mix of stale air, coffee, and the faint scent of cleaning chemicals. The distant sound of a busker's saxophone echoed through the tunnels.

On the train they stood close together, gripping the metal poles as the movement swayed them back and forth. Beckett remained alert, watchful of the other passengers.

Close by, a tired-looking businessman stared bleary-eyed at an eReader. Further along, a young couple whispered and giggled to each other, while an older woman with badly dyed hair was engrossed in a tattered old paperback. It was a typical slice of New York life, nothing to give him any concern.

"Do we have a plan once we get to the lab?" Reed whispered. "That Weiss guy was pretty obstructive last time."

Beckett nodded. "He was likely just protecting his staff and his work. But I don't plan on dealing with him today."

"Oh?" Reed looked up at him, her eyes catching the light. "Why's that?"

"Like you said, he didn't seem very forthcoming. But there's always another way around these things, right?"

She frowned. "What do you mean?"

Beckett didn't answer. He'd learnt a long time ago that under-promising and over-delivering was as effective in his line of work as in business. And there was nothing to be gained in stating he'd do something if he couldn't follow through.

"But you still think Dr Bader is the key to finding Turner?" Reed asked, glancing around the carriage as she spoke.

Beckett followed her gaze, noting a couple of young men in plaid shirts who'd boarded at the last stop. They looked like construction workers. Nothing to worry about.

"I'd say it's the best lead we've got," Beckett replied, keeping his voice low. "Turner is a sharp guy and highly experienced. He wasn't giving anything away when I spoke with him and the pen drive didn't give us much, so all we've got is hunches. The good news is my hunches are usually pretty good."

"Usually?" Reed repeated, with a teasing smile that

under other circumstances he might have thought was flirtatious.

"Mostly."

She nodded. The smile faded. "And what about Templeton?"

Beckett sighed. "I know my orders and I'll carry them out. But finding Bader remains our best shot at getting to Turner. I've got more than a hunch telling me he's still tracking the scientist. So we need to be smart about this."

The train pulled into their station and they made their way up to the street level. They'd arrived after the rush hour, and it didn't take as long this time to navigate their way to East 79th Street and the lab. The building's large glass windows reflected the morning sun.

"Okay then, what are we waiting for?" Reed started to cross the street, but Beckett held her back.

"Hold on. Let's not rush in."

She gave him a puzzled look. "What do you mean? What do you suggest we do?"

"We wait," Beckett replied, eyes locked on the entrance.

"Wait? For how long?"

He raised his chin. "As long as it takes for our man to show up."

"Which man?" Reed asked.

But Beckett remained silent. He just stared at the entrance. Waiting.

Beckett was good at waiting – Reed, not so much it seemed. Time dragged on. It was just after ten and there was minimal foot traffic or things to focus on in this part of town. As the minutes turned to hours, Reed grew more impatient. She shifted her weight from foot to foot, she crossed and uncrossed her arms, she huffed, she checked her watch, she shot frustrated then angry glances at Beckett, her tension returning like a bad rash.

"We can't just stand here all day," she muttered.

"Be patient," he replied, not taking his eyes off the entrance. He knew loitering on a street corner hoping to get lucky was a gamble, but he was also convinced this was their best move.

"You really think Bader's just going to show up here?" Reed sneered. "Weiss was pretty clear he didn't work here anymore. And if Bader is involved in something big and illegal, he's not going to just stroll down the street in broad daylight."

"We're not waiting for Bader."

"Who then? Not that technician guy you chased the other day?"

Beckett kept his eyes on the entrance. "Just wait."

By noon Reed was pacing back and forth, her footsteps quick and sharp on the pavement. "What if the guy is spooked and doesn't come in?" she snapped, narrowing her eyes at him. "What if those guys who jumped you also got to him? We could be waiting here forever."

Beckett smiled. "Patience, Reed. I know you're relatively new to this world, but if you want to make it, you'll have to get used to waiting around. It's a big part of the job."

"Oh yeah?"

"Absolutely. Over the last twenty years I'd say I've spent ten percent of my time catching bad guys, and ninety percent waiting around." He allowed himself a slight grin. He was being facetious, but those numbers weren't far off. So you did whatever you could to pass the time, like teasing your colleague a little.

Reed huffed, running a hand through her hair. She

glanced at her watch again. "It's been two hours. This is pointless."

"It won't be. That man knows something. Trust me."

Reed leaned against a lamppost, tapping her foot. "I hope you're right," she mumbled.

Yeah, me too.

But a few minutes after one, just as Reed seemed poised to reaffirm her annoyance, a man emerged from the building. He was tall and wiry, dressed in a light grey hoodie and dark trousers. Pushing his thick-framed glasses up his nose, he glanced around nervously before hurrying away.

"That's our guy," Beckett said, starting after the technician.

They crossed the street and followed at a discreet distance as the young man led them down East 79th Street and turned left onto 3rd Avenue. He walked erratically, forcing them to duck into doorways every so often as he cast worried glances over his shoulder. He was clearly anxious about something.

After crossing East 77th Street, he entered a deli on the corner of Lexington Avenue. Beckett and Reed followed him over there and waited outside the doorway. The aroma of fresh bread and roasted meat wafted out, making Beckett's stomach growl. He was hungry as hell, and Reed's expression suggested she was too, but he shook his head.

"Later," he whispered.

A few minutes later the technician emerged carrying a lunch bag. As he saw Beckett, his eyes widened in panic.

"Shit." He thrust the lunch bag at Beckett and bolted down the street.

"Damn it. Wait!"

Beckett fumbled with the bag, tossing it into a trash bin in front of the deli before giving chase.

"Come on," he called back to Reed as he ran. "We can't let him get away again. We need to talk to this guy. Today!"

Chapter Thirty

Beckett and Reed sprinted after the technician, weaving through pedestrians and street vendors, dodging traffic as they barrelled down East 77th Street and crossed Park Avenue. The young man was faster and more agile than Beckett had anticipated, but fear was a good coach. They followed him along East 77th, crossing Madison Avenue and 5th Avenue, and closing the gap as he darted into Central Park.

"Wait," Beckett yelled out. "We're not here to hurt you. We just want to talk." But the young man didn't listen, speeding away from them around a group of joggers.

The park's winding paths and dense clusters of trees made the chase more challenging, but Beckett was determined not to lose him a second time. He pushed himself harder, glancing back to confirm Reed was keeping up before locking his sights once more on the fleeing technician. As the young man neared a small lake, he abruptly veered off the path, sprinting across a wide expanse of grass towards a line of trees on the other side.

Rather than follow his trajectory, Beckett anticipated the move and cut across at an angle, aiming to intercept him. He gritted his teeth, quickening his pace as the veins in his thighs pulsed with effort. By the time the technician reached the trees, Beckett was already there, blocking his path. The young man skidded to a halt and stumbled backwards, nearly losing his balance.

"Get lost!"

"Hey. It's okay." Beckett approached slowly with his hands raised.

"Get the hell away from me," the man yelled. "I'll scream. I swear it."

"Please, calm down," Beckett said, his voice steady and soothing. "We're not here to hurt you. We just want to talk." The technician's chest heaved with exertion. He looked like a cornered animal, ready to bolt at any moment. Beckett adjusted his stance, projecting calm. "We're the good guys. I swear to you. But we need your help. Let's sit down, okay?"

The man hesitated, eyes flicking to Reed as she caught up with them.

"Please," she gasped. "I work for the government and we just want to talk. You're safe with us."

"That's what you think." The technician sank to the ground, his body trembling. Beckett waited a moment, then knelt beside him on the grass. Reed joined them and they stayed like that for a few moments. The young man was done, but Beckett waited until his adrenaline had subsided a little more before asking his name.

"Brandon," the man replied, more resigned than scared now, though there was still a trace of trepidation in his voice.

"All right, Brandon," Beckett said, with a reassuring smile. "You can call me John. And just to be clear – I'm not here to hurt you or get you into trouble. But I think you might be able to help us."

Brandon took off his glasses and used the pocket of his hoodie to clean them.

"You work at Axiom Labs, correct?" Beckett continued. "We were there Friday asking about Dr Bader. You remember us."

Brandon slipped his glasses back on and nodded.

"My... partner here believes you might know something," Reed added. "Is he right?"

Brandon's fear bubbled back up. His eyes darted from Beckett to Reed and then around the park, unable to settle on any one spot.

"I don't know much," he whispered. "And I don't even think I should tell you that. I have a wife and a new baby back home. I don't want... I can't..."

The poor guy was terrified. Beckett leaned in slightly, maintaining eye contact. "Why are you so scared, Brandon? You need to tell us. We can help."

"No. You can't."

Beckett glanced at Reed for help and she gave him a nod. "How old is your baby?" she asked.

"What?" Brandon looked up, Reed's question pulling him out of his spiralling thoughts. "Umm... she's nine months."

"A girl, huh? That's awesome. I'd like a girl. One day maybe. If I'm lucky. Can I ask her name?"

Brandon sniffed. "Amelia Joy. Joy was my mom's name."

"Beautiful name," Reed said, letting a few beats pass before going for it. "We just need a little information, Brandon. We're trying to protect people like you and your family."

"She's right," Beckett added. "This is a matter of national security."

Brandon's eyes locked onto Beckett's, and for a brief moment Beckett saw a flicker of resolve in them. "It's worse than that," he said, his voice barely audible, as if speaking the words might summon the very thing he feared. "A lot worse."

"What do you mean?" Beckett asked.

Brandon pulled in a deep breath. "Look, I didn't know Dr Bader well. I sat in on a few trials with him in the early days, but then... well... he was working on something important, something... big. He had his own lab and his own research team. He didn't let any of the regular technicians get close." He puffed out his cheeks and shook his head as if he couldn't believe he was saying these things out loud. Beckett nodded, urging him to continue.

"Bader is a weird dude, even for a scientist – secretive, stern, kind of arrogant. No one liked him much. But he was brilliant, everyone said so, and the board at Axiom liked the fact he was working under their banner, so they didn't question him too much. The fucking idiots." He spat out this last part, his grievance evident. "Then one day Bader's entire lab was shut down. And I mean, overnight. One day he was there, the next day no trace of him. A week or so after that, some people came looking for him. Scary people."

"Did they say where they were from?" Beckett asked.

Brandon shook his head. "No. But they were heavy as shit, and I don't mean in a tough guy, meathead kind of way. These guys were wearing suits. They were threatening in a quiet, unsettling way, like they knew nothing could touch them and they could do whatever they liked. Which they did." His voice dropped to a whisper. "They stripped

Bader's entire lab and took all his files and equipment, anything he hadn't already taken. They made it clear we had to stay quiet. Whatever Bader was working on, they didn't want anyone to know."

"What was he working on?" Reed asked.

"I don't know exactly," Brandon replied. "With him being so secretive there were a ton of rumours among the junior staff. All I know is that it was something dangerous. We were all warned not to talk about it. To anyone. And if we did..." His breathing became more erratic, and he glanced around frantically. "I'm sorry. I have to go." He jumped up, nearly knocking Reed over.

"Hey!" She made to follow but Beckett grabbed her arm.

"Let him go," he said, watching Brandon disappear behind a row of trees. "He did well."

They both got to their feet and stood in silence for a few moments. Reed kicked at a small rock, sending it skittering across the path. Beckett stretched his back. For once he was stumped. He was almost certain Brandon had told them everything he knew.

But it wasn't enough.

Reed turned to him "What now?"

Beckett didn't answer. His mind spun at double-speed as he tried to piece together what they'd just learned to what little they already knew. Bader had been working on something dangerous, something potentially life-threatening.

Brandon's words echoed in his mind.

It could be worse than that.

But those words only led to more questions. Who were the men in suits? What was it that Bader had created? And was this creation what Turner was after?

Beckett shook his head. When he looked up, Reed was still staring at him, waiting for an answer.

"Let's head back to the hotel," he said. "We're missing something, and we need to figure out what it is before it's too late."

Chapter Thirty-One

Beckett and Reed left Central Park and made their way to the 77th Street subway station. It was a short walk, less than five minutes, but Beckett deliberately slowed his pace seeking to slow down his internal processes, knowing a clear mind was a better canvas on which to develop new theories than a busy one. Reed trailed closely behind, her expression defaulting back to its usual mix of frustration and slight irritation. He still couldn't gauge whether it was the job itself or the fact she had to work with him that bothered her. Maybe both.

The underground rumble of an approaching train vibrated underfoot as they descended into the station and the air prickled at the skin. They walked along the first concourse to the ticket booths. Reed bought two single-ride tickets and they proceeded to the turnstiles and down another flight of steps to the platform.

Since leaving the park neither of them had spoken, but as they waited for the train, Beckett noticed Reed kept chewing on her bottom lip and then muttering to herself as if she was trying to puzzle something out. Probably because she was. They both were. There was a lot to unravel. Beckett's immediate goal, however, was to get back to his room – somewhere quiet where he could reassess his approach and get his jumbled theories into some kind of order.

The subway station seemed busy for a Monday afternoon. Fluorescent lights cast a harsh, artificial glare over the people waiting on the platform as Beckett and Reed moved closer to the edge standing side by side. Beckett glanced at the display board, noting the next train would arrive in one minute. Perfect. But as he turned away, his instincts spiked. It was that familiar sense of unease that told him he was being watched. He kept his movements subtle, raising his head slightly as he scanned the faces around him. Beside him, a young woman scrolled through her phone. On the other side of Reed, an elderly man was reading a newspaper. Behind them a group of teenagers were laughing and shoving each other. Nothing screamed "threat", yet the feeling lingered.

A few seconds later the train arrived with a rush of air and noise. It was packed, as expected for a trip to Times Square. They boarded the nearest carriage and squeezed into a spot by the doors. As the train started moving, Beckett rolled his shoulders and stretched his neck, using the motion to continue his surveillance. His intuition was still flashing on red, but he could find no visible threats. He closed his eyes and sucked in a deep breath, instantly regretting it as the stench of cheap perfume, sweat, and city grime filled his nostrils.

"Hey," Reed whispered, nudging him. "What's on your mind?"

"That we should take a cab next time."

She nudged him harder. "Be serious. I'm wondering if it's worth staking out Turner's apartment in case he shows up."

Beckett opened his eyes. "Possibly." But he said it more to placate Reed than out of certainty. Turner was a seasoned operator who'd seen them coming last time. Besides, there was no compelling reason for Turner to return home. The apartment held nothing of value.

"Beckett, we have to find him," Reed added. "*You* have to find him. And soon. I know you think Bader is the key – or the bait, or whatever – but if he's a dead end, then we need to forget about him and find Turner another way."

Beckett glanced around the carriage. Even though they were whispering, he disliked discussing sensitive matters in public. "Let's focus on getting back to the hotel," he replied. "I'd like to use your laptop and agency access, if I may."

"That should be fine," she said, though her tone suggested otherwise. "But I'll need to observe. What are you looking for?"

"I'm not entirely sure. I'm hoping for some inspiration." He flashed her a smile but received only a scowl in return. At least it shut her up for the time being. The last thing he needed was Templeton's lackey constantly on his back to finish the mission. He knew what needed to be done, it was figuring out the *how* and the *why* that troubled him.

They got off at Times Square, the station bustling with activity. As they made their way up the first flight of stairs, Beckett now felt almost certain they were being watched. He slowed his pace, trying to catch signs of trouble in his peripheral vision. He was looking for men on their own or in groups of two or three. He spotted a couple of possibilities but didn't want to stop and give the game away by looking directly at them.

Once they stepped out into the daylight, Beckett walked a few metres and then stopped under the pretence of stretching his back. He waited, watching his fellow passengers as they emerged from the subway and dispersed. It had been raining while they were underground and people were looking to the skies, assessing whether to reach for their umbrellas. Most were tourists, their excited faces and clothing making them easy to spot. But then he saw them – two men of similar height and build to himself. They were trying to blend in, but their stiff posture and alert eyes gave them away. They hadn't expected Beckett and Reed to be standing there, waiting. When they saw them, they froze for a split second before attempting to act casual.

Beckett sized them up. One wore a jean jacket buttoned all the way up, the other a dark Harrington jacket similar to one Beckett used to own. Both had the look of men who knew how to handle themselves. Their eyes were cold and calculating, assessing every detail. The man in the jean jacket had a shaved head and a strong jawline, while the other had short, neatly trimmed hair and a crooked mouth as if he were sucking on a lemon.

Beckett turned to Reed. "Come on," he said. "Let's move."

The last thing he wanted was to lead the men to their hotel. He set off in the opposite direction, intending to take a circuitous route away from the main streets and shake them off.

"Where are we going?" Reed asked, trying to match his pace.

"The scenic route. I could use some fresh air."

He navigated through the centre of Times Square, giving the crowds surrounding the many street performers as wide a berth as possible. Bright neon lights and giant billboards cast vibrant reflections on the wet pavement as they walked. Reed kept glancing around, clearly puzzled by their sudden change of route.

"What's going on?" she asked, struggling to keep up as Beckett ducked into a side street.

"Trust me, this way is better."

They emerged onto 42nd Street to a sea of marquees and awnings announcing the latest Broadway shows. Here the crowds thinned out slightly, but Beckett wasn't looking for space. He turned into a narrower street lined with small shops and cafés, the air filled with the mingling scents of coffee and spicy food.

"Why are we in a hurry?" Reed asked.

"Just trying to avoid the crowds." He glanced back, frustration tightening his jaw as he spotted the two men cutting through the crowds with determined speed. They were closing in, and after all the detours Beckett had no doubt they were coming for them.

"Beckett, what's really going on?" Reed urged.

He grabbed her arm and pulled her into a narrow backstreet lined with the rear ends of restaurants, complete with industrial dumpsters and the pungent stench of rotting food. He kept hold of Reed's arm, steering her forward at a brisk pace while she hissed and grumbled her displeasure. At the end of the alley he turned right into another backstreet, deserted except for a stray tabby cat that darted away as they approached.

"All right," he said. "Look back. What do you see?"

Reed glanced over her shoulder. "Umm... Two men. Mid-thirties. Fit. Determined... No! They're following us."

"I noticed them as we left the station but my guess is they've been on us since the park. We can't lead them to the hotel. We're going to deal with them."

Reed's eyes widened. "Ah, shit."

"You said it."

He guided her into a narrow alleyway, the sounds of the city fading behind them. The alley was dim, with rusty fire escapes clinging to the walls and a couple of dumpsters at the far end. The ground was littered with discarded cardboard and shards of broken glass. He couldn't have brought her to a nicer place.

Reed pulled her arm free. "This is crazy," she hissed. "I'm a CIA officer, not some street brawler. I'm usually behind a desk."

"Don't worry," Beckett said, slowing to a stop and turning around. "Let me do the talking."

"You're going to talk to them?"

He shrugged. "All right... let me do the fighting."

As if on cue, the men appeared at the end of the alley, their expressions hardening as they spotted Beckett and Reed waiting for them. They seemed confident, unhurried, the one in the jean jacket even had a slight smirk on his face as they approached. They were the kind of men who did this sort of thing on daily basis without breaking a sweat. But whilst confidence was important for success, it could also lead to one's downfall.

"I'm a government officer," Reed announced. "I need to know who you are and what you're doing here."

The men said nothing. Just continued their slow, deliberate approach.

"I mean it. My name is Erica Reed. You need to turn around."

Harrington sniffed. Jean Jacket casually cracked his knuckles.

"They don't seem too big on conversation," Beckett said. "We might have to do this my way."

The men lunged forward. Beckett pushed Reed behind him and met the attack head-on. Jean Jacket got to him first, swinging a heavy fist. Beckett deflected it with his forearm and delivered a sharp jab to the man's ribs, followed by an elbow to the jaw. The man staggered back, dazed, blood trickling from his mouth.

Meanwhile, Harrington was circling, trying to flank Beckett. He anticipated the move, and as the man swung at him, Beckett ducked under the punch and stomped down on his knee. A sickening crunch was followed by a sharp scream as Harrington crumpled to the ground, clutching his shattered joint then checking he still had all his vocabulary.

"Shit! Fuck! Bastard!"

Beckett spun back to Jean Jacket, who had recovered enough to charge at him again. Using the momentum of his turn, Beckett drove his fist into the man's solar plexus, knocking the wind out of him. The man's eyes bulged and he doubled over, gasping for air. But Beckett didn't let him get any. Grabbing him by the back of the head, he slammed the man's face into the metal corner of a nearby dumpster. Blood splattered across the dumpster's lid, and the man slid to the ground, taking an early nap.

"Beckett!" Reed called out.

He spun around to see Harrington struggling to stand. "Oh come off it." He shook his head, almost in disbelief at the man's persistence. "Stay down, you fool. It's over."

But Harrington snarled, gritting his teeth as he pushed himself upright. Beckett closed the distance in two steps and delivered a swift kick to the side of the man's head, knocking him out cold. It felt like the noble thing to do. Like putting down an injured stray.

Stepping back, Beckett surveyed the two unconscious

men at his feet. A moment later Reed appeared beside him, looking a little uneasy.

"Should we find out who they work for?" she asked.

Beckett shook his head. "They won't talk."

"You sure?"

"Maybe if I got them into a dark room and had a tray of special tools," he said. "But not here. Best we get away."

"Okay. Right. Good." She looked relieved.

Beckett checked their pockets. He didn't expect to find any ID, but he was happy to relieve them of a hundred and fifteen dollars – an unplanned addition to his go fund. He dusted himself off and did a quick injury assessment as they made their way out of the alley. He was still in one piece, but these encounters were becoming too regular an occurrence for his liking.

As they reached the next street, Reed paused and looked up at him. "Listen, do you want to get a drink instead of heading straight back to the hotel?"

Beckett hesitated for a moment, checked she was serious. It appeared she was, though he sensed it was she who needed the drink more than he did. "Thought you'd never ask," he replied.

Chapter Thirty-Two

It had been a long time since Beckett had sat down in a typical American bar and passed the time over a cold beer. Not that he was doing that now for mere enjoyment – this was more about decompression than relaxation; Reed's as much as his – but it was a welcome respite from the chaos of the past few days. In Beckett's world the small things mattered. He grabbed his moments of contentment when he could.

He was seated at a round table along one side of the bar, the kind that could accommodate four but was better served for two. Reed was in the bathroom – to freshen up, she'd said – but had been gone long enough for him to finish half his beer. It was understandable. Beckett knew she was rattled after the alley attack, even if she tried to hide it. Reed was tough, but everyone had their limits, even CIA officers.

Beckett sipped his beer and glanced around. Louie's Bar and Kitchen was a quaint little spot nestled down a side street near Grand Central. It had a cosy, old-world charm, with dark wood panelling, vintage posters on the walls, and a long, polished bar that gleamed under the dim lighting. A few local drinkers were scattered around the place, on stools and at tables, engaged in quiet conversations. The speakers on the wall played unobtrusive jazz music and the place smelt like real bars should, of wood and leather and liquor. The atmosphere helped ease some of the tension that had been coiled inside Beckett these last five days. But only some.

As he drank, his thoughts drifted once more to Turner and Dr Bader. Something about the situation was nagging at him – a puzzle piece that didn't quite fit. Turner wasn't the man Templeton had made him out to be. But equally, he didn't appear to be an innocent pawn either. He was hiding something, just as Templeton was hiding something, and most likely Reed was hiding something too. Hell, even Beckett was hiding something – for the time being at least, until he could make sense of it himself.

Damn it.

This old espionage game. Who'd have thought it?

He glanced at his knuckles. The skin was red and slightly swollen, but he'd washed out the dirt in the bathroom, and pressing his hand against the cold beer bottle provided some relief. No big deal. He'd suffered worse injuries at the punch bags.

He took another sip of beer as Reed reappeared. She'd washed her face, and it had put a touch of colour in her pale cheeks. Physically she looked more composed, but there was still something in her eyes that concerned Beckett. A flicker of doubt, maybe fear. She was thinking hard about something. As she walked over to the table, her movements were controlled to the point of stiffness. She forced a smile and sat down across from him.

"How are you holding up?" he asked, watching her carefully.

"I'm fine," she replied, taking a sip of her whisky, now diluted by the ice that had melted during her absence. She made a face and set the glass down, her eyes darting around the room before returning to settle on him. "How are you doing?"

"Same as always."

"Just like that, huh? No bother."

"What do you want me to say?"

"You handled those guys well back there."

"It's what I'm trained to do." He smiled. Downplaying things was Beckett's way, a trait he'd inherited from his father, a mix of modesty and that British stiff upper lip. But the truth was, it was getting tiresome. Two run-ins with heavies in the past three days, and he was still no closer to figuring out who was sending them.

"Any ideas who they were?" Reed asked, echoing his thoughts. "Or should we just chalk it up to the perils of walking around New York?"

"No. They weren't street punks," Beckett replied. "Whoever's behind this knows our every move and they're determined to keep us from getting answers."

Reed gulped down another mouthful of whiskey. "Shit. So they want us dead?"

"Or scared enough to back off. Which, in my case, could still mean ending up dead."

Reed scowled. "Templeton would never..." But she trailed off, perhaps deciding she couldn't hold up the pretence. "I can see why he wanted you onboard though, even if he..." Again she hesitated, looking away as if reconsidering her words.

"If he... what?" Beckett asked, leaning in.

"Nothing." She avoided his gaze. "It's all so crazy. Do you think there's one person behind all this?"

"One person, or one organisation."

"Right, yeah." She still didn't look at him. "So… who? The Rosenwald Committee? Turner? Bader? The Russians?"

"All possibilities."

Reed's brow furrowed as she thought it over. "Turner could have hired those thugs to get us off his back. If he knows we're coming for him."

"Not his style," Beckett replied, shaking his head. That was as much as he wanted to say about that for now. On the way back from Lake Pharaoh, he'd mentioned to Reed that he'd spoken with Turner when they were tied up together. She'd reacted strangely – tense and jittery – prompting Beckett to drop the subject. As if maybe she was worried Turner had swayed him, anxious that her first in-field mission would go south.

"But if Turner has defected and is now collaborating with the Russians, they could be behind it. Or the Rosenwald Committee," Reed suggested, more animated. "They let you go so they're in the clear and then send those goons to finish the job, make it look like a mugging gone wrong or something."

Beckett had considered this. "It's possible, but no." He watched Reed as he took another sip of beer. She seemed frantic, grabbing ideas out of the air. Again it was understandable, given what had happened and the looming threat of mission failure, but it made Beckett cautious about what he shared. She was Templeton's charge, after all.

"There's another angle I've been considering," he said, testing the waters. "Another player in the game we've yet to mention."

"Oh? Tell me." She leaned in, eager.

"Not yet. No point in building castles in the air until we know more. First I want to understand exactly what Bader has invented."

Reed's expression hardened, a flicker of annoyance crossing her face. She sat back and folded her arms. "I thought we agreed to forget about Bader. It's Turner we're after."

"Aren't you curious about what happened at the lab?" Beckett asked, keeping his tone even despite Reed's rising tetchiness. "Remember the threats Brandon mentioned. And why is Turner so intent on finding Bader? That's the entire reason he was at the Rosenwald Committee meeting. Hell, from a national security perspective alone, you should care."

"I have a clear directive," she replied. "And so do you. Find the rogue agent and take him out."

Beckett finished his beer. This wasn't how he'd planned the conversation going. Reed was sounding like every other spook he'd met – guarded, combative, too locked into their orders to see the bigger picture.

"Do you trust Templeton?" he asked. "I mean, do you *really* trust him?"

"Of course," she replied, without missing a beat.

"You know he wanted me dead because he thought I was a rogue agent. Same as Turner."

"Weren't you?"

"No. Well... not really. I certainly wouldn't sell intelligence to the Russians."

"But you could."

"I wouldn't."

Beckett leaned back, Reed sipped her drink, neither

willing to meet the other's eyes. Finally Reed let out an exasperated tut and shook her head.

"Typical macho guy. Thinks he knows best. Thinks only he has the answers."

Beckett was genuinely taken aback. "Where did that come from?"

She sneered and looked away.

Damn it. Was she…?

Reed sniffed and wiped away a tear with a quick, angry swipe. Beckett stayed silent as she composed herself and turned back to face him. "I think the job's just getting to me, you know? I want this all to be over."

"Me too," he said, forcing a smile. They sat quietly for a moment. Reed stared at him, her eyes searching for something.

"So you're not going to tell me what you're thinking about – this other player in the game?"

"Not until I've looked into a few more things," Beckett replied, holding her gaze.

"What makes you think they're involved?"

"They're involved in a lot of things. But there's something else that's been bothering me. I recognised one of the guys from the Rosenwald Committee when I was taken to the lodge. It's been bugging me ever since. I know his face, but I can't think of his name or where I know him from."

"What did he look like?"

"Late thirties. Short sandy hair and big orange glasses. Kind of like a Hollywood version of Elton John in his heyday."

She laughed, the tension easing a bit. "Okay. But no, sorry, doesn't ring any bells. Why does it matter?"

"I don't like leaving loose ends, especially when we're working with so few leads." He closed his eyes, trying to force the memory of the man to the surface, but got nothing. "He's famous in tech circles, I'm sure of it. Not so much in the mainstream. Damn... what is his name?"

He opened his eyes to see Reed glancing at her watch. "Don't let it bother you," she said.

"Everything bothers me until I know why."

"Would knowing who he is help?"

"It might."

Reed looked troubled suddenly. She checked her watch again and then downed her drink. "Come on, let's make a move," she said, standing and motioning for Beckett to do the same.

He was about to protest but thought better of it. He got to his feet and followed her out.

The late afternoon air was a refreshing change from the bar's stuffiness as they stepped onto the street. They'd only walked a few steps when a large black car pulled up alongside them. It was an official-looking vehicle with tinted windows and sleek, polished bodywork. Beckett stopped, his instincts kicking in. Beside him Reed bristled as the back window rolled down to reveal Xander Templeton's granite features.

"Fancy running into you here."

Beckett's jaw tightened. He turned to Reed, her sheepish expression telling him everything he needed to know. She'd known this was coming. She'd set it up.

Templeton sat back and the door lock clicked. "Get in, Beckett," he said. "We need to talk."

Chapter Thirty-Three

Reed could feel the anger radiating off Beckett as they climbed into the back of Templeton's car. It was a standard CIA ride, a black Chevy Suburban, with plush seats that smelt faintly of new leather and antiseptic. She opted for the seat furthest from the door – and from Beckett – on the bench next to Templeton, with an armrest separating them. Beckett took the fold-down leather seat behind the driver, who was sealed off from them by soundproof glass, ensuring their conversation stayed private.

Templeton gave the driver a nod and they set off. It was rush hour and the streets around Grand Central were jammed, but it didn't matter, they weren't going anywhere in particular.

An awkward silence settled over the car's occupants as they drove, the three of them quietly assessing each other. Reed chewed on the inside of her bottom lip, trying to stay calm. She felt claustrophobic and on edge, though the car's spacious interior had nothing to do with it. In a bid to assert herself, she crossed her legs and stuck out her chest, but it only made her feel more ridiculous and out of place. The faint hum of the engine and the muffled noise of the city outside were the only sounds as they crawled along Madison Avenue. She stole a glance at Beckett. He caught her looking and quickly averted his eyes, but not before she noticed the hardness in them. The muscles between his jaw and cheekbone twitched with tension.

Reed turned away and peered out the window. She'd expected Beckett to be furious, but in truth he had no real reason to be. She was just doing her job. Being a professional. She'd called Templeton from the bar's restroom after he'd messaged her to let her know he was in town. She felt a little pathetic, reaching out to her boss for help, but at this point she just wanted it all to be over. With every passing hour she felt more out of her depth, and she hated that feeling more than anything. She was a good officer, just like she'd been a good soldier, it wasn't her fault the system had failed her. None of this was her fault.

She shifted in her seat, uncrossing and recrossing her legs, trying to shake the familiar sting of resentment that so often overwhelmed her.

Stop this. Now is not the time.

Taking a deep breath, she smothered her emotions and sat up straight, refocusing on the task at hand.

Beckett cleared his throat. "Well as lovely as it is going for a drive in the city, I take it you ambushed me for a reason?"

Templeton let out a low, growling chuckle. "Ambush? That's a bit rich, don't you think?"

Beckett said nothing, just stared at Templeton without blinking. Reed braced herself for another long, awkward silence, but after a few moments Templeton continued.

"All right, what's going on, Beckett?" His voice was calm.

Reed started to speak but Templeton cut her off with a sharp look. It could have pissed her off, but she was used to this now – men in power dismissing her input. Although, it didn't make it any easier to swallow.

Templeton turned back to Beckett. "Why is Turner still alive?"

"How do you know he is?" Beckett fired back, his eyes flicking to Reed.

She felt the weight of his glare and shrugged. "Just doing my job."

"I know." He sounded resigned, and turned his attention back to Templeton. "I tracked Turner to the woods outside Pharaoh Lake. He'd infiltrated the annual Rosenwald Committee meeting. I'd reason to believe he was there on the tail of a scientist. Dr Adram Bader."

Reed noticed Beckett's eyes narrow slightly as he watched for Templeton's reaction. She shifted in her seat, trying to do the same. If Beckett was dropping names to see what Templeton knew, he would be a better interrogator than her if he got anything from it.

But Templeton just shrugged, noncommittal. "Your mission is to take out Saul Turner before he sells information to the Russians."

Beckett smirked. "You're still going with that line?"

"Why wouldn't I be?"

Beckett leaned forward, his irritation evident. "I spoke to Turner face to face. I had him cornered, but the Rosenwald security intervened. They took us to a holding cell, where I managed to ask him a few questions."

Templeton lifted his head. "Oh? And?"

"He swore he was no traitor. Said he was still working a

mission as part of SAC." Templeton remained silent, his face unreadable. Beckett pressed on. "Do you know who this Bader guy is or why Turner might be after him?"

"Didn't your new buddy fill you in?"

"Turner's been tracking him all over," Beckett added, ignoring the comment.

"I've never heard of Dr Adram Bader," Templeton grumbled. "But that doesn't matter. I just want you to take out Turner. None of this other shit interests me."

"Bader is an eminent biologist specialising in biochemistry," Beckett explained, pausing as if to let the significance of that sink in. "He's developed something that a lot of bad actors are after, and it seems there's a tight circle of protection around him. Every time I get close to finding out what's going on, a bunch of heavies show up to stop me."

Reed interjected. "Maybe Turner's been sent to protect Bader, to keep whatever he's invented out of the hands of people like us." Trying to make her voice heard between the two alpha males, she was relieved when it came out steadier than she felt.

"So what do you think this Bader guy has?" Templeton asked, directing the question squarely at Beckett, completely ignoring her comment. Once more she felt that familiar pang of resentment, but remained poker-faced.

Beckett glanced at her briefly. "I'm not sure, but we spoke to one of Bader's former colleagues. The guy was terrified, said he'd been threatened, warned not to talk to anyone. From what little he did share, it sounds like whatever Bader has could be catastrophic."

"Is that so?" Templeton didn't seem convinced. "And if Bader's such a big deal, who's he working for?"

"Himself. That's what it looks like from the limited intel I've seen."

"I see," Templeton growled in response and turned to glare at Reed.

"Don't worry, *boss*," Beckett said. "Reed here is sticking to the party line – still insisting Turner is the enemy. But after speaking with him, I'm not so sure."

Reed sat back, biting down hard on her lip until she tasted blood. Who did this prick think he was? Sure, he was good at what he did, and he had a certain reserved charm, but really he was just like all the rest of them.

She took a deep breath, focusing on her mission. There was no point in clashing with Beckett. Not yet, anyway. And maybe he had a right to be angry. Maybe calling Templeton had been a mistake. She caught the Englishman's eye, trying to convey an apology, though she wasn't sure she fully meant it. The conflict within her was growing stronger, the lines between right and wrong blurring more with each passing moment. She knew this world was full of grey areas and moral dilemmas, but nothing had prepared her for this. The uncertainty twisted her stomach, but she tried to ignore it.

She had her reasons for being here.

She had her purpose.

"Turner has gone rogue," Templeton reiterated. "I've seen the reports."

"Sometimes our intel is wrong," Beckett countered. "You know that. I spoke to Turner firsthand. I believed him when he said he wasn't a traitor. I'm rarely wrong."

Templeton seemed troubled by this, falling silent as he mulled it over. Beckett just stared from their boss to her, his expression neutral but his dark blue eyes as intense as ever.

"You need to remember your mission," Templeton said finally, all traces of joviality gone from his voice. He glared at Beckett, his eyes cold and unblinking. "Turner is a liability. A threat to national security. Forget Bader. Turner is your target."

Beckett shook his head. "I think there's more to this. I want to talk to him again first."

"For God's sake, Beckett!" Templeton snapped, then caught himself and coughed. "You have to kill Turner and then disappear, as we arranged. Or…"

"Or what?"

Templeton's eyes narrowed. "I didn't want it to come to this."

He lifted the lid of the armrest between him and Reed and pulled out a tablet. He tapped it a few times with his thick fingers, the screen illuminating his stern, chiselled features.

"Here." He handed the tablet to Beckett.

Reed felt the knot tighten in her stomach. She knew what was coming. She watched Beckett as he registered what was on the screen. His eyes widened, his face flushing with anger and then twisting with hate as he looked at them both. He lowered the tablet, and Reed caught a glimpse of the image: a teenage girl sitting on a beach under the Mediterranean sun. The photo was a wide shot, taken with a long-range lens, but the girl's face was clear enough to identify – especially if you were her uncle and only living relative.

"That was taken two days ago in Churriana, Spain," Templeton said. "The closest beach resort to Alora. I believe you know the area – and the subject of the photo?"

Beckett couldn't hide his rage; he positively shook with it. "You bastard. If you hurt her, I'll kill you."

Templeton didn't flinch. "Take Turner out, Beckett. Do what we agreed. Or I will have to escalate matters. I don't want to have to do that, but this is a matter of national—"

"Yes, so you keep saying." Beckett's voice was heavy with sarcasm and fury. He looked at the tablet, then at Templeton, and finally at Reed. She forced herself to hold his gaze, despite the turmoil inside her. Beckett tossed the tablet onto Templeton's lap. "Fine. I've got no choice, have I?"

"Good man," Templeton said, a smirk tugging at his lips. "I knew you'd see sense. And Reed was right to call me. You've gone off course, overthinking things that don't concern you. That's not your job, Beckett. You're a weapon, remember that. You have one job: kill Turner. Then everyone's happy. You, me… your niece."

Beckett's gaze bore into Templeton. "I want you to do something for me, though."

Templeton's smirk widened. "What's that?"

"There's a young man called Brandon who works at the Axiom Lab where Bader used to have a facility. He's a good person who got caught up in this, and he's scared. I want you to put protection detail on him, just for a week or two. He has a young family, and he could be in danger."

Templeton grumbled, clearly annoyed by the request. "You're in no position to ask for favours."

"Maybe not," Beckett said. "But I'm appealing to you as a human being."

Templeton glanced at Reed. She gave him a curt nod, which she hoped conveyed her support for the request without seeming too emphatic. Maybe Beckett wasn't such an egotistical prick after all. But she knew better than to let her guard down.

"All right. I'll see what I can do," Templeton said.

"Good." Beckett unclipped his seatbelt. "Now stop this car and let me out so I can finish this damn mission."

Chapter Thirty-Four

Beckett stepped out of the car, fists clenched at his sides. It was uncharacteristic of him to lose his temper, and he was keeping it in check, but one small thing and he might flip. Templeton had dropped them off at the corner of West 44th Street and 6th Avenue, just a block away from their hotel. It was early evening and the last of the October daylight bathed the city in a red glow, casting long shadows across the bustling streets.

He set off walking at a brisk pace, not waiting for Reed. The sidewalks were crowded with people heading home from work. Car horns blared, sirens wailed, the rumble of a subway train echoed up through the grates, but Beckett barely registered any of it. He could hear Reed hurrying to catch up, could sense her eyes on him, but made no effort to slow down or acknowledge her.

"Beckett, wait, please, I—"

"Don't," he cut her off, his voice a low growl. He didn't want her apologies or explanations. He was over a barrel and he hated it. He felt cornered, manipulated. The thought of his niece, innocent and unaware, being used as a pawn in this dangerous game made his blood boil.

He strode on, Reed trailing him a few steps behind. At least she had the sense to keep her distance. But he couldn't shake the image of Amber from his mind. He knew Templeton was an unrepentant prick, but he hadn't expected him to stoop so low. Yet a part of Beckett's anger was also directed at himself. He thought he'd been so careful in placing her where he had. Obviously not careful enough.

His breathing had grown heavy, and he forced himself to slow it down. Losing control wouldn't help anyone. He had to take Templeton at his word, which meant he had no choice but to comply with his demands.

That bastard…

There might be more to the Turner situation than Templeton was letting on, but Amber was Beckett's top priority. It had been good to see a recent photo of her, despite the circumstances. She'd looked healthy and happy, and far more grown-up than he remembered. It had been too long since he'd seen her. He vowed, right then, to visit her as soon as this mission was over. But first, he had to finish it.

He reached the hotel and pushed through the revolving doors without waiting for Reed. The lobby was quiet, with only a few guests milling about. The soft murmur of conversations mingled with the clinking of cutlery from the adjoining restaurant preparing for dinner service. Beckett headed straight for the elevator, Reed following a few steps behind. They rode up in silence. She kept glancing up at him but he stared straight ahead.

When they reached their floor, Beckett exited first and made a beeline for his room, swiping the keycard with more force than necessary. The door clicked open and he stepped inside, hoping for solitude. But Reed caught the door before it closed and followed him in.

"You don't get the message very easily, do you?" he muttered. "You might need to work on your perception skills if you're going to make it as Templeton's little helper."

"All right, I get it. You're pissed at me. And I'm sorry that I called him. But what he said needed saying."

Beckett spun around and glared at her. "And did he need to threaten my niece's life, also?"

Reed looked at the floor. "No. I don't like that he did that," she said quietly.

"Well, we agree on something at least." He felt hot suddenly, there was no damn air in this room. He fumbled with the first few buttons of his shirt before getting annoyed with the tiny fastenings and pulling it off over his head. Balling it up, he tossed it onto the chair by the window, hoping she'd get the message and leave him alone.

"Look, I'm sorry," she said. "But we need to get past this. Your niece... *everyone* will be okay if you just do what Templeton wants—" She cut off abruptly and turned away. Her neck was flushed with colour. Maybe she hadn't expected her boss to stoop so low either.

Beckett sighed. She was right – there was no point in arguing. "I don't appreciate ultimatums," he said, easing off on his tone. "Or dirty tactics."

She sat on the edge of the bed, and when she looked up at him, her eyes were heavy with exhaustion. "The sooner we get this done, the sooner we can all move on with our lives."

"He threatened my niece," Beckett said. "She's the only family I've got."

"I know. But haven't you done or said things just as bad to get the job done?"

Beckett didn't have a good answer to that. Of course he had. For the greater good you do what you have to. But that didn't mean he had to like it.

He sat down next to her. He could put in a few calls, get Amber moved elsewhere temporarily. But was anywhere safe? And hadn't the poor kid had her life disrupted enough; did he really want to put her through anymore of that crap?

"So then…" Reed said. "Here we are." She was trying to ease the tension but Beckett wasn't in the mood to meet her halfway. He was too preoccupied, too bitter. The only things he knew for sure were that he didn't know much and that he could trust no one.

But what was new?

He'd spent enough time in this world of shadows and deception to know that trusting someone was like stepping onto a tightrope above a pit of vipers.

"So where should we start?" Reed asked, offering a timid smile.

He looked her up and down, trying to get a read on her, still unsure of where she stood in all this. One minute she was all business, the next she was floundering and second-guessing herself. Was she just inexperienced, or was there more to it?

"You tell me," he said. "I'm running low on ideas."

She looked at him, her eyes a mix of emotions he couldn't quite decipher. Retrieving her work phone from her pocket, she checked the screen. The device looked more advanced than anything Beckett had seen during his time in Sigma Unit.

She saw him looking. "I didn't take you for a man interested in gadgets."

"I'm not. I prefer to rely on my wits and fists, what I know will get the job done. But I've never seen anything like that before. All-singing, all-dancing, I imagine."

"It's decent enough, with extensive capacity and wide-ranging 5G capabilities," she said. "But as is the way with most tech, it's already behind the times. Apparently, we're getting new kit soon. Pango has developed a new unit specifically for government use."

Beckett leapt up, his mind racing.

Pango. That's it.

The guy from the Rosenwald Committee with the orange glasses. He still couldn't recall the man's name, but now he knew where he'd seen him. He was the new CEO of Pango Inc. Beckett had read about him in a free magazine on the plane. It was definitely him. He turned away from Reed, processing this new information. He was relieved to have made the connection, but now what?

He was about to share his thoughts with Reed when he hesitated. He had another idea. A better one.

But he needed something first.

Beckett rubbed at his chin, considering how best to utilise this new piece of intelligence. Now that he knew which company the man from the Rosenwald Committee was linked to, he could find out his name. Once he had that, he could find out where he lived – or Beaumont could do it for him if he needed a deeper search. But first he needed internet access.

Reed had noticed his change in demeanour and frowned. "What is it? What's wrong?"

He raised a hand, feigning nonchalance while he ran a real-time assessment of the situation. He would keep the discovery to himself. Trust no one, that was his rule now. "I just remembered it's Amber's birthday soon," he said. "She'll be nineteen." This was a lie. She'd already turned nineteen a few months ago. He made another silent vow to buy her something special once all this was over.

"She means a lot to you," Reed said.

"She's all I have."

Reed smiled. It was almost tender. "She'll be fine. Young women are resilient. We have to be."

Beckett returned her smile, but his mind was elsewhere – focused on her phone still clutched in her hand. He needed to get online without Reed knowing, and his best bet was that phone or her government-issued laptop. Failing that, he could go to the library and use the computers there to search for Pango Man, but he doubted he'd get a chance to do that without Reed wanting to come too.

He stood by the bed with his hands on his hips, staring at the carpet as he mulled over his options. Reed seemed genuinely invested in the mission, but he couldn't risk sharing his theories – not yet. Maybe he could trust her, maybe not. But then…

Looking up, he caught Reed's eyes lingering on his bare torso. An idea, unwelcome but potentially effective, began to form. This wasn't the way he'd like this to go, but sometimes you had to bend your principles to get the job done. And it wouldn't be the most unpleasant undercover work he'd ever been involved in. Reed was a good-looking woman. His type for sure. Nice figure, strong. A tough exterior but something softer beneath. Big blue eyes to get lost in.

He stepped closer. "Listen, I'm sorry about before," he said, lowering his voice. "I know you're just doing your job. You're a good officer."

Reed looked up at him, her eyes softening. "Thank you for saying that. I've just got a lot on my mind, I guess," she replied, her tone mirroring his. "This job… it's hard."

"I know."

They stood for a moment, their breaths moving in a steady rhythm, the silence between them sparking with a different kind of tension. Slowly he reached out and touched her arm. A tentative gesture, testing the waters. She didn't pull away. Instead she moved closer. Their eyes met, and Beckett leaned in, his lips brushing against hers.

The kiss began softly, almost hesitant. But quickly it deepened, driven by an urgency that seemed to surprise them both. As the kiss grew more passionate, Beckett wrapped his arms around her, pulling her closer. The weight of her breasts against his naked torso, the curve of her hip bone against his thighs – it was a welcome distraction, one he realised he needed. Not just to lower her defences, but to lower his own, to feel something other than the relentless frustration of this mission and his worry for Amber.

Reed was trembling a little but responded in kind, her hands sliding up to his shoulders, her nails digging into his muscles. They stumbled back onto the bed, Beckett landing beneath her as their movements grew more hurried. He unbuttoned her shirt and she shrugged it off, pressing her warm body against his, her hands roaming over his broad chest. He closed his eyes, inhaling her scent, feeling the heat of her skin. Their breathing grew heavier, more primal. He reached down to unbutton her trousers when, suddenly, she pushed him away and sat upright with a sharp intake of breath.

"What's wrong?" he asked, propping himself up on his elbows. Reed was staring away into the middle distance, her expression hard to read.

"I can't," she said, her voice shaking. "I'm sorry..."

"Oh?" He took a moment to process what had just happened. She looked to be in shock. "Hey, it's okay," he whispered. "We can slow down if you'd prefer. It's just... I thought you wanted this."

She grimaced. "I do... I don't... Shit, I don't know."

When she shuddered, Beckett sat up too, tilting his head to catch her eye. "Erica, it's totally fine. We don't have to do anything. It was probably just a momentary thing. I get it."

She let out a bitter laugh. "No. You really don't."

"Someone back home?" he asked. "A boyfriend?"

"No! God, no!" She got up and paced the room. She looked angry, then frustrated, then embarrassed, then sad – all the things you didn't want to see in someone when you were both half-naked. She grabbed her shirt and quickly put it back on. "I don't have anyone," she admitted. "At all. And it's been a hell of a long time since I... But I just can't. I won't."

Beckett got up from the bed but kept his distance. "Listen, I'm sorry. I misread the situation. No one's making you do this. It's okay."

Reed snorted. "Not *making* me. But..." She stopped pacing and glared at him. Tears glistened in her eyes. "Templeton suggested that I... you know. He said I should be *accommodating* to you if it made you more compliant. But I'm not like that. I mean, you're a good-looking guy, and you've got a lot going for you, but I..."

"I get it." He could have been angry, but he wasn't surprised. "It's a lot to ask of anyone. So what is it? You don't like men?"

Reed opened her mouth and almost said something, then looked away. "I'm not gay, if that's what you mean."

Beckett held his hands up. "Whatever it is, don't worry

about it. The moment's passed. Let's forget it ever happened." He glanced around, wondering how to move forward. Reed scratched her neck like she'd rather be anywhere else.

She sighed. "It's my fault. I'm just really tired. Today has been a lot. I think I'll turn in early. Get up tomorrow and start fresh."

Beckett glanced at the clock – it was just after 7 p.m. Still very early, but that was fine by him.

"Maybe I'll do the same," he said.

Reed stared at him, her eyes lingering on his lips as if she was considering kissing him again.

Talk about mixed messages.

He waited, unsure. But then she met his eyes and forced a smile, nodding to herself as she scooped her phone off the bed and headed for the door to her room.

"Good night, Beckett."

She left, closing the door behind her. Beckett didn't move. This wasn't how he'd expected things to play out, but fair enough. If Reed fell asleep naturally rather than post-coitally, that worked for him too.

He switched off the light and lay on the bed, staring at the ceiling. It was 7:06 p.m. He'd give it another half hour. Maybe a little longer. As the minutes ticked by, his thoughts inevitably circled back to Turner, Bader and Templeton. He couldn't stop theorising, running through every possible connection, every piece of intel that might link them. But the more he thought about it, the more chaotic his thoughts grew. He replayed everything that had happened since meeting Erica Reed – the interrogation room, the flight to New York, his first encounter with Turner, the chase through the park – culminating in his confrontation with Templeton just an hour earlier. But through it all, Amber's face hovered at the edge of his thoughts, tugging at his focus. She'd looked so youthful and innocent in that photo. So carefree.

He had to make this work.

He closed his eyes, visualising Reed in her room – removing her make-up, brushing her teeth, changing into her nightwear. He imagined it all in real-time. She said she was tired and she'd certainly looked it. Once she was in bed, he guessed it would take her about five minutes to fall into a deep sleep. He'd give it ten, just to be sure.

When he was confident enough time had passed, Beckett quietly approached the connecting door and eased it open, careful not to make a sound. The room beyond was dark, with only the faint glow of the city lights filtering through the curtains. He paused, letting his eyes adjust to the dim light before moving further in, scanning the room as he went. Reed was fast asleep, her breathing slow and steady – not yet in REM sleep, but deep enough that he could move around without waking her. He spotted her laptop and phone on the dresser. The laptop would be easier but the phone quicker. He picked it up and carried it to the bed. Lowering it towards Reed's face, he let the facial recognition unlock the phone and he was in.

Moving back to the dresser, he quickly navigated to the search function and typed in *Pango CEO*. The results came up in an instant and there it was: *Dillon Gruett, Venture Capitalist, Real Estate Developer, CEO of Pango Inc.*

Of course. Gruett. It was obvious now he knew.

Gruett's credentials were impressive. He'd inherited a real estate empire from his father, but Pango was all him. It had made him a billionaire before his twenty-seventh birthday. Good going. But no matter how accomplished the guy was, his involvement with the Rosenwald Committee tied him to some very dubious activities.

Beckett continued speed-reading Gruett's Wikipedia page, pausing only when Reed mumbled something that sounded like, "Now you'll listen." He froze, holding the phone screen to his chest. But she was still asleep, and after a few seconds her breathing returned to a steady rhythm.

Returning to his search, he finally found what he was looking for. It was lucky for him Gruett had a flair for publicity. The section on his real estate empire, *The Gruett Organization*, noted that he had built three skyscrapers in Manhattan for commercial use and had recently expanded into residential properties. Famously, he lived in the penthouse of one of his buildings when in town. Another quick search revealed the address.

Got him.

Beckett gently placed the phone back on the dresser, making sure everything was exactly as he'd found it. Then he slipped back into his room, grabbed his balled-up shirt, and got ready to move. Sleep could wait. He had work to do.

Chapter Thirty-Five

Dillon Gruett lay semi-conscious in his custom-made emperor bed, in the master bedroom of his luxury penthouse apartment. It was late, probably after midnight, but he'd awoken for some reason, which annoyed him. He did a quick physical check – he didn't need to pee, but maybe he was thirsty. Regardless, he remained still, refusing to fully wake up, content to linger in that hazy space between sleep and wakefulness, where the consciousness begins to stir but isn't yet troubled by worldly issues. Or indeed the physical world in general.

He sighed deeply, trying to coax himself back to sleep even as his thoughts began to drift.

Bastard. No!

This was not what he needed. If he woke up now and didn't get back to sleep, he'd miss out on his sacred eight hours. His eyelids fluttered beneath his silk eye mask.

Think happy thoughts.
That'll do the trick.

His mind wandered to the deal he had closed two days

earlier – a multi-billion-dollar acquisition of prime property in Ridgewood, perfectly positioned for redevelopment. The terms were airtight: a blend of upfront capital and strategic tech investments, projected to triple in value within five years. The satisfaction of another successful venture seeped through him, warm and gratifying.

But it wasn't enough.

He lifted his head, searching for a more comfortable position on the pillow. The Château Margaux 2009 he and Marissa had shared with supper was now making itself known, throbbing at his temples and behind his eyes. He rolled over, the cool satin sheets sliding over his skin. Marissa wasn't beside him, but that was no surprise. They hardly slept in the same room anymore. Whether it was her way of punishing him or simply because she found him less appealing since he'd put on ten pounds, he couldn't be sure.

He was almost certain she knew about his affairs and his trips to high-end escorts, but they never discussed such things. They'd been in love once, but these days their relationship had been reduced to snide digs across the dining table, held together only by their shared love of the twins, and money.

He rolled back over, hoping to drift off, but was jolted fully awake when his hand brushed against something on the bed. It was hard. Big.

A man?

Shit.

What the hell?

His heart pounded as adrenaline surged through his body forcing him upright. He yanked off his eye mask and fumbled for the lamp cord.

Fuck!

The light snapped on, revealing a man sitting on the

edge of the bed, watching him with an unsettling calmness. Gruett knew him from somewhere.

"What do you..? Who..? Oh, Jesus!"

The words tumbled out as Gruett's mind scrambled to make sense of the situation. Instinctively, his eyes darted around, searching for... what? Help? A weapon? Something he could use to defend himself? He opened his mouth, inhaling sharply.

The man raised a finger. "No. Don't scream. It won't go well for you if you do."

Gruett swallowed hard. The man was English.

Motherfucker.

That was where he knew him from. He was one of the men their security team had apprehended at the Rosenwald meeting, along with that bastard who killed two of their best men. Was he... CIA?

Gruett blinked, a part of him hoping this was just a fever dream. But the man was still there, still staring at him in that same disconcerting way. He was broad-shouldered – broad everything, really – with scruffy sandy-blond hair and dark blue eyes that seemed to pierce straight into Gruett's brain.

"Do you remember me?" the man asked.

Gruett nodded. "What do you want?" He'd tried to sound bold but his voice came out in a pathetic wail. "What are you doing in my bedroom?" He tugged the covers up, suddenly feeling exposed in just his boxers.

The man shushed him again, a finger to his lips. "I want to talk to you. I need some information."

"My wife's in the next room, with my children. Please don't hurt us," Gruett pleaded.

"Why would I hurt you? I only want to talk." The man's tone was almost soothing, which somehow made it worse.

"Talk about what?"

"What do you know about Dr Adram Bader?"

Gruett tensed, trying to mask his reaction. "Who?"

The man leaned in closer. "Don't play dumb with me, Gruett. It's not a good idea. I can tell when you're lying."

Gruett's eyes flickered to the scars on the man's arm, his roughed-up knuckles. It was clear he meant business.

"Everyone in your circle seems to know Bader," the man continued. "Yet no one will tell me where he is or what he's invented. Why is everyone so interested in him? The other man security nabbed at your little get-together – he was looking for Bader. I think you knew that. I want to know why."

Gruett gritted his teeth. This guy was good, but there was no way he could spill what he knew. They'd kill him if he did. That had been made crystal clear to everyone involved. A cold sweat broke out across his forehead.

"I don't know what you're talking about," he lied, trying to sound convincing. "I can't help you."

The man's eyes narrowed, the calm facade slipping. "Don't lie to me. I need to know who Bader is and why everyone cares so much."

"I can't. They'll kill me."

"*I'll* kill you."

Tears welled in Gruett's eyes, something he hadn't experienced since he was a kid. "I don't know anything."

"Fine." The man stood, and for a brief moment Gruett felt a flicker of relief. Maybe he was going to leave. But then the man grabbed him by the hair and yanked him out of bed. Gruett screamed, but the man's rough hand clamped over his mouth, cutting him off as he dragged him across the room.

Gruett struggled, his arms flailing in a desperate attempt

to break free, but it was useless. The man hauled him into the en-suite bathroom and shoved him into the bathtub, his body slamming against the cold porcelain with a jarring thud. Pain shot up his back, but he barely registered it over the terror coursing through his veins. He lay sprawled in the bathtub, gasping for breath as the man loomed over him.

"Tell me what you know about Bader," he said, in a low menacing growl.

"Go to hell," Gruett spat. He was terrified but there was anger there now too. How dare this man invade his home, violate his sanctuary? Didn't he know who he was dealing with? The sheer audacity of it left Gruett reeling.

"What has Bader invented?" the man asked.

"Screw you."

The words came out of Gruett's mouth, but it felt surreal, as if he wasn't the one speaking. He attempted to scramble out of the bathtub, but the man's hand shot out, pinning him down. He was strong. Very strong. Gruett's legs flailed, the deep slippery tub making escape impossible.

"Last chance," the man warned, reaching behind him to grab a face towel off the rail.

"No. Please."

Gruett had seen enough movies to know what was coming. The man turned on the faucet, soaking the towel until it was drenched. Then in one swift motion he slapped the wet towel over Gruett's face. The sudden pressure and wetness made him gasp, his mouth filling with the coarse material. The man raised his hand off Gruett's chest for a moment, only for it to be replaced by his foot, preventing any attempt he might make to sit up. He froze as he heard the shower unit click on. Cold jets of water sprayed over his skin, sending shockwaves through his already frayed nerves. He tried to scream but the towel muffled his cries.

Panic surged as the cold water soaked through the towel, flooding his nose and mouth. His senses were overwhelmed. He was drowning. His body convulsed, his lungs burning for air. He tried to thrash, but the man pressed down harder with his foot, he couldn't get away. Water seeped into his lungs. He couldn't think, he couldn't focus. He just wanted it to stop.

Help! his mind screamed, but he couldn't breathe let alone speak.

After what seemed like forever, the towel was wrenched off his face and the man dragged him upright. He gasped for air, his chest heaving as he screwed his eyes up against the bright light.

"What do you know about Dr Adram Bader?" the man demanded.

Gruett's head was a mess, he couldn't think straight. His entire body was wracked in a flight response.

"Please," he gasped. "You're CIA. You can't do this to me. I pay my taxes."

This was apparently amusing to the man, but he got over it almost immediately. "Tell me what you know."

"I can't." Gruett sobbed, salty tears mingling with the cold water on his face. "They'll kill me." The man slapped the towel over his face. "No! Please!"

His cries fell on deaf ears as he was pushed down harder, the cold water drenching him, filling him with dread. He fought against it, but it was useless. The sensation of drowning consumed him, crushing his mind and body. He was going to die here. He was already dead. He was floating. He was….

"Tell me!"

More harsh lights stung his eyes as the towel was

whipped away. He tried to swallow but couldn't. He just wanted it all to end.

"Okay! Okay! I'll talk." His voice broke, along with his spirit.

The man dropped the showerhead, water still streaming from it. Gruett glanced down, overcome by a new wave of shame as he realised he'd lost control of his bladder and bowel. The disgust and humiliation hit him harder than the stench. He felt like a child, helpless and terrified.

"So talk."

Gruett nodded, resigned to his fate. If they killed him, so be it. At least it would probably be over quickly. This was worse than death.

He took a deep breath, trying to steady his nerves. "I don't know much, I swear. But you're right, Bader has made real waves in certain circles. He's developed a formula for a new nerve agent."

He paused, hoping that would suffice, but the look on the man's face said otherwise. He looked down, then at the wall when faced with his own stinking effluence. "He calls the formula Nerex-9. Or at least that's what people are calling it. It's a super strong chemical mixed with man-made enzymes to make it work faster and more effectively. It's packed into microscopic particles that can penetrate skin, mucous membranes, even protective gear. The real kicker – he's designed it to be undetectable by standard sensors. As you can imagine, a lot of countries want it. A lot of individuals too. And you're right, the other guy at the meeting was on our radar. We were told to watch out for him and get rid of him if he showed up."

"Who told you?"

"I can't say."

The man closed the toilet lid and sat, his eyes never

leaving Gruett. "Has this nerve agent been put into production?"

"Not yet."

"Where's the formula now?"

"Bader still has it."

"Where is he?"

"I don't know. I swear. But word around camp last weekend was that he'd agreed to sell his creation to a man called Nico Vassos. He's pretty high up in—" He caught himself, realising the danger of revealing too much. He could just about handle the thought of his own death, but not the twins. Never the twins. He coughed as if to correct himself. "He's an influential guy."

The man raised an eyebrow. "Why haven't I heard of him?"

"Because he's smart. He has a vast network of loyal operatives who handle his... dirty work."

"Tell me more."

"That's all I know."

The man narrowed his eyes, scrutinising him like a damn human lie detector. "You're lying. Where can I find him?"

"I don't know and I wouldn't tell you if I did. He's a powerful man. He'd kill me when he found out."

The man stood, towering over him. "I'll kill you right now."

Gruett shuddered, tears streaming down his face. "I don't know where he lives, I swear. He was at the Rosenwald meeting. I imagine he's got a place nearby. Everyone has places in New York, right?"

The man didn't reply. He just stared at him.

"Please," Gruett sobbed. "Leave me alone now. You found me. You'll find him."

The man still didn't move, his gaze piercing and relentless. Then, after what felt like an eternity, he nodded. "Okay," he said, then pulled a face. "You might want to clean yourself up, seeing as you're already in the shower."

Gruett looked down, feeling the full weight of his humiliation crash down on him as the man strolled out of the room.

"Ah, crap."

He picked up the shower head and began to hose himself down.

Chapter Thirty-Six

Beckett left Gruett's apartment as quietly as he had entered, careful not to wake his wife and children. The door closed behind him with a soft click, and he paused momentarily in the low-lit hallway, listening for sounds from within. Satisfied no one had stirred, he headed to the elevator, pressed the button, and waited. As the doors slid open he stepped inside, pushing the ground floor button and leaning back against the wall, his mind already processing the intel he'd extracted from the Pango CEO. Some of it confirmed what he'd already suspected; some of it was new.

It had been a valuable trip, coming here tonight. Though breaking into Gruett's place had been no small feat. With cameras in every corner and a guard stationed at the front desk, Beckett had to rely on stealth rather than just waltzing in through the front entrance.

Fortunately, a narrow alley ran alongside the building, with a fire escape visible from the street. Timing his approach, Beckett had waited until the security guard left the front desk to do his rounds and slipped into the alley.

The fire escape ladder hung nine feet above the ground, just out of easy reach. Beckett took a running start, leapt, and grabbed the bottom rung, pulling himself up with minimal noise. He scaled the side of the building quickly, checking each floor for a way in. On the fifth floor he found a window slightly ajar. He pried it open further and got inside, landing softly on the vinyl-covered floor of a storage room.

There he paused, listening for signs of movement. Silence. All good. The storage room was flanked by metal shelving units, cluttered with tattered boxes, cleaning supplies, old paint cans, and tubs of screws and replacement door handles. He rifled through a few boxes, finding an old security guard ID badge, which he pocketed before easing the door open.

Certain the coast was clear, he left the storage room and hurried up seven more flights to the twelfth floor, where a separate set of stairs led to the penthouse.

Floor thirteen – unlucky for some.

Unlucky for Dillon Gruett, as it turned out.

The top of the last stairwell opened out onto a wide landing area with huge rubber plants in each corner that added a touch of greenery. Beckett had removed the ID card he'd found in the storage room from his pocket and moved over to the apartment door to examine the lock. It was a sleek, modern electronic model, not something you'd normally pick with just a card. But the slight gap between the door and the frame caught his attention – there to accommodate intumescent strips to meet fire regulations. Just enough space to work with.

Crouching, he'd slid the old ID badge into the gap, angling it carefully. He wasn't relying on luck; he knew these doors often had a flaw in how the latch connected with the strike plate. If he could just hit the right spot...

The card pressed against the latch mechanism and Beckett shifted his weight slightly, applying steady pressure. A second later the latch clicked back and he felt the door give. Rising, he carefully eased it open and stepped inside. Almost there. In the hallway he'd clocked the alarm panel on the wall and froze. But a quick inspection told him what he needed to know: the system wasn't armed. Someone was home, but they weren't expecting trouble. Good.

He moved through the apartment, clocking the empty wine bottle on the kitchen counter. A glance into a side room revealed a woman – Gruett's wife, no doubt – snoring softly beside two cribs, both housing identical sleeping children. He continued to the end of the hallway and found Gruett alone in what was clearly the master bedroom. Standing in the doorway, Beckett allowed himself a brief moment of relief. Everything had fallen into place perfectly. After that, getting what he needed from Gruett was straightforward. The entire operation took less than fifteen minutes.

Back on street level, Beckett strode through the still empty lobby and hit the door release button, stepping outside. The cool night air greeted him as he exited the building. It was half past one in the morning, and a light mist that could almost be a fine drizzle hung in the air, coating the streets with a slick sheen. Beckett crossed the street and paused, surveying his surroundings. Hudson Yards was one of Manhattan's most exclusive neighbourhoods, and thus eerily quiet at this hour. The tall buildings loomed overhead, their large windows dark, their wealthy inhabitants asleep. The only sounds were the distant hum of traffic and the gentle wash of water from the nearby river.

Beckett headed that way. A wide boardwalk overlooked the Hudson, lined with temporary fencing around a construction site that was yet to get going – nothing more than a pile of sand under a blue tarpaulin and a stack of slate tiles for now. Streetlights cast halos of light in the fog above him. He turned to look up at Gruett's window. The light was still on, but that didn't concern him. The guy was terrified, and just deep enough in this mess that calling the cops wasn't an option.

Beckett considered heading back to the hotel, but dismissed the idea. Sleep was out of the question right now and he needed space to think. Instead, he continued toward the river's edge. His shirt clung to his back, damp with sweat and rain, but he barely noticed the chill. He never did.

The area was deserted, and he soaked in the solitude as he approached the railing and looked out over the river to where the lights of New Jersey twinkled faintly, their reflections shimmering on the dark surface of the water. He leaned against the cold metal and took a deep breath, filling his lungs with the cool, damp air.

He considered what he knew.

If Bader had intentionally created the nerve agent, then he was clearly the enemy, and no doubt purposefully elusive rather than simply hard to pin down. He also held all the cards, with a lot of powerful people vying for what he had. That made him a target as much as a prize. No wonder he was hard to find. Beckett now understood why so many people had tried to stand in his way or scare him off from digging deeper. A bioweapon like the one Gruett described would be a game changer – and in the wrong hands, devastating.

But who was pulling the strings? He doubted it was Bader himself, so it had to be someone with a vested interest in keeping him alive. Those eager to get their hands on the formula.

He thought back to Gruett's hesitation earlier. Beckett had picked up on it immediately but hadn't pushed further. Gruett had been on the verge of breaking, and that hesitation alone was enough to tell Beckett his hunch was correct. No one hesitated in those situations unless the truth was worse than being waterboarded. Gruett's fear was more telling than any confession.

Beckett's grip tightened on the railing as he stared out across the Hudson. The low moan of a distant foghorn broke the silence, its mournful tone echoing through the mist.

"Nico Vassos," he muttered to himself, trying the name out loud.

He hadn't heard of the guy, which wasn't too surprising given how long he'd been out of the loop. But he also knew that the most dangerous players in this game operated in the shadows, never seen and rarely heard.

He needed to find Vassos, and fast. From what Gruett had said, Vassos hadn't yet secured the formula from Bader. That gave Beckett a narrow window to intercept one of them before their paths crossed and the deal went through. But there was still Turner to consider, and Templeton's orders, making everything more complicated.

"What a bloody mess."

He sighed, the river's dark expanse mirroring his turbulent thoughts, frustration battling for dominance against his misgivings. If these things were all connected as he suspected, then Templeton had to be aware of it.

So why hadn't he given Beckett the full picture? And did Reed know more than she'd been letting on?

The lack of transparency only fuelled his distrust. Still, it was getting late, and he should get back to the hotel before Reed woke.

He was about to start walking when a noise behind him caught his attention. He spun around, senses on high alert. The mist made it difficult to discern shapes and movements. He cast his attention wide, straining to hear anything beyond the usual nighttime sounds. Probably just the wind. Or a cat.

He turned back around. Then he felt it. A hard object pressing into the back of his neck. He froze.

"Hello again," a voice said, calm and familiar.

Beckett raised his hands slowly. "Mr Turner. You found me."

"We need to talk."

Beckett nodded, turning his head just enough to catch a glimpse of the elusive American out of the corner of his eye. "I was hoping you'd say that."

Chapter Thirty-Seven

Turner kept the gun trained on the back of the Englishman's neck, his grip steady and precise, each finger perfectly aligned.

"I'm currently aiming a SIG Sauer P226 with a SilencerCo Osprey 9 suppressor at your occipital region," he said. "It's loaded with 124-grain Speer Gold Dot hollow points. The kind that expands on impact, causing maximum internal damage. If I pull the trigger, the bullet will penetrate the base of your skull, fragmenting on entry and causing hydrostatic shock and extensive cavitation. It'll sever your spinal cord, shred your brain, and leave an exit wound just under your nose. That will all happen in a tenth of a second. You'll be dead before you hit the ground."

"Thank heaven for small mercies," the Englishman replied.

Sarcasm. It wasn't lost on Turner; he just didn't find anything funny about it.

"But I get it," the Englishman added, his voice steady. "Don't worry, I'm not going to try anything. You want to talk. So do I. I've been wanting to talk to you for the last week. I had hoped our conversation in the cabin the other night would be more enlightening, but you didn't seem too open to the idea."

Turner remained silent, listening closely not just to the words but the way they were delivered. The man was relaxed, confident. There was sincerity in his tone and steadiness in his stance. He noted the lack of tension in the man's shoulders and the evenness of his breath. He was on the level.

Turner lowered the gun slightly, keeping it trained on the man's stomach as he stepped around the side of him. It was a tactical compromise. A shot now would be enough to incapacitate, but not lethal. "Let's go," he said, nodding for the man to move.

They walked along West 33rd Street, with Turner a step behind the whole time, his pistol never wavering. The mist hung low, muting the usual city sounds and lending a stillness to the night he found relaxing. The distant hum of traffic was still there, but it was mostly quiet.

They took a left and walked half a block up Hudson Boulevard East until they reached Bella Abzug Park.

"In here, away from the street," Turner ordered.

The park stretched between the towering buildings of Hudson Yards, its rain-slicked pathways gleaming under the streetlights. It was a modern space, dotted with art installations that cast small pools of light in the surrounding shadows. The innovative water fountains, designed to adjust to wind speeds, were now silent, their jets stilled by the weather. Off to one side, a playground featured a domed rope climbing frame. Turner glanced around, taking in every detail, every possible hiding place. The pathways, lined with trees, formed dark tunnels that disappeared into the mist.

"Sit," he said, pointing to one of the steel benches near the fountains.

The Englishman chose the middle bench, the one furthest from the road and obscured from view by a row of trees. It was the same bench Turner would have picked. He took the opposite end, leaving about twenty inches between them. The bench was cold and slightly damp. Turner kept his weapon raised.

They sat in silence for a few moments, Turner staring straight ahead as he counted the streetlights in his line of sight – six; and the trash cans in the park – three. He flexed his fingers on the gun handle, solidifying his grip.

"I've been looking into you," he said, once he was ready.

The Englishman turned his head slightly. "That makes two of us. Not so easy, is it?"

More humour, his attempt at connection. Turner ignored it.

"I had a micro camera hidden in my button at the Rosenwald Committee meeting the other night," he continued. "It got a clear shot of you, which I later ran through facial recognition software."

"Did you get anywhere?"

"Eventually. Although you weren't on the usual databases. I had to dig deeper. Three clearance levels deeper, in fact." Turner cricked his neck. He was holding himself stiff, for some reason. "You're a hard man to find, but nothing's impossible in this brave new world. Though I'm sure I don't have to tell you that, John Beckett, once of Sigma Unit, the most covert intelligence wing of the British Secret Service."

Beckett didn't flinch, his training evident in his calm

demeanour. "I knew you were good," he said. "But I'm surprised there's still a file of me somewhere."

"Who sent you after me?" Turner asked.

"Xander Templeton. A CIA section chief, mostly based in London, though he's got his fingers in a lot of pies." Beckett's voice was steady, but Turner detected an undercurrent of frustration.

"I've never heard of him."

"I believe you," Beckett replied. "He told me you went rogue, that he was tasked with dealing with you, and that the SAC wanted it kept under wraps."

Turner fell silent, processing the information. He hadn't checked in with his handler for over six months, but there was good reason for that. They knew what he was working on. They wouldn't have given an order like that without just cause.

"I'm still a paramilitary officer with the Special Activities Center," he said. "I haven't *gone rogue*. You've got the wrong man."

Beckett shrugged. "Maybe."

Turner studied him as he stared at the buildings in front of them. The man was hard to read, but there was something off in his expression. "What is it?" Turner asked.

Beckett turned to make eye contact. "I'm a nobody these days," he said. "A ghost. I've been pulled into this mission against my will. But if I don't do what Templeton says – if I don't kill you – they'll kill my niece. He claims you're a threat to national security."

"That's not true. I'm on the right side of this," Turner replied.

Beckett shrugged again, more resigned this time, as if he'd heard it all before. "Being on the right side of things –

that's a very murky and grey area in our line of work, my friend."

"My role hasn't changed," Turner said. "I'm to eliminate Dr Adram Bader before he can sell his formula to the highest bidder."

Beckett nodded, staring out across the park. "How's that going?"

"He's slippery. I thought I had him in Stuttgart, but he's got a lot of people protecting him."

Beckett chuckled humourlessly. "I'm aware. But I just heard about this formula, and only briefly. Care to fill in the blanks?"

Turner cleared his throat. "It's a nerve agent. Nerex-9. Based on an advanced organophosphate, combined with synthetic enzymes that enhance its potency and delivery. What makes it so dangerous is that the nerve agent is composed of original synthetic analogues. Without getting hold of a sample to work on, any traditional spectrometric or chromatographic methods are useless."

"So it's undetectable."

"Exactly. Nerex-9 isn't just another nerve agent, it's a new class of threat. It kills within seconds, no chance for first aid, and it's completely invisible to current tech. Imagine a vapour – a simple touch – and you're gone. The psychological impact alone would be catastrophic. Governments would collapse under the weight of paranoia. Economies would tank as people avoided public places, and faith in security services would vanish. In a military context, the implications are even more severe, entire units could be wiped out in moments. Whoever controls this 'doomsday formula' – as SAC insiders call it – holds the ultimate trump card."

Beckett nodded, taking it all in without showing much

reaction. He was good. Very good. Turner wasn't one to warm to others easily, but he respected competence, and this Englishman had earned his regard.

"I assume you're also familiar with Nico Vassos?" Beckett asked.

"Of course. Word is he's put in the highest bid for the formula, a billion dollars no less, and Bader's preparing to sell. I intend to take him out before that happens."

"Can you tell me more about Vassos?"

Turner sized him up, weighing the risks of sharing more. "Why do you want to know?"

"I'm a curious person. And maybe I can help?"

Turner decided it was worth the risk; after all, he was the one holding the gun. "Nico Vassos. Born in Athens, Greece, to a modest family in the mid-eighties. He had a natural talent for finance and technology from a young age and used those skills to build a powerful empire in the early 2000s. He rode the dot-com boom and later made strategic investments in emerging markets and cryptocurrencies."

"Yet he remains elusive? The name's new to me, and I thought I knew every shadowy billionaire out there."

"Vassos is an enigma to the public and most authorities," Turner said. "But not to someone like me. He built his fortune through a series of high-stakes ventures – tech startups, arms deals, and the manipulation of global stock markets. His knack for predicting market trends and his ruthless business tactics helped him amass billions in just a few years. Yet despite his vast wealth he remains under the radar, protected by a web of shell companies and offshore accounts. He uses intermediaries to handle his business deals and employs state-of-the-art cybersecurity measures to shield his identity."

"And now he wants to be the proud owner of the

doomsday formula. Sounds like a great guy. Do we know why he wants it?"

Turner frowned. "Isn't it obvious? Whoever has that formula controls... everything."

"But he's not working alone."

Turner shot him a look, impressed. "Correct. Vassos is also a key figure in The Consortium, a global neo-liberal organisation that—"

Beckett raised a hand. "No need to explain. I'm well acquainted with The Consortium. They're part of the reason I'm persona non grata at MI6 and SIS. Them, and Templeton. He thought I'd gone rogue, and put a target on my back too."

Turner noted the bitterness in Beckett's tone. "So you appreciate the extent of my mission. It's why I had to go dark. The Consortium has its tentacles in every level of government. I couldn't trust anyone. But I'm no traitor."

Beckett stared off into the distance, silent for a moment. Turner gripped the handle of the SIG. He knew what was coming. He didn't like it, he didn't understand it, but he knew.

"That all makes sense," Beckett said after a long pause. "And I believe you. You have my word that I'll find Bader and I'll stop him before he can sell the formula. But I can't let you complete your mission." He sucked in a deep breath. "If I don't do what Templeton asks, they'll kill my niece. They've shown me proof – pictures. If I don't follow through with his orders, she's dead. I can't take that risk. It's you or her, and I can't choose you. I'm sorry."

As the words left Beckett's mouth, Turner was already raising his gun. But Beckett had anticipated the move. He grabbed the silencer, twisting it sharply as he drove his fist into Turner's wrist with his other hand. Turner's grip slackened but he recovered quickly. As Beckett yanked the gun away, Turner knocked it from his grasp with a swift upward strike.

The gun skidded out of reach. Beckett lunged after it, but Turner rammed his shoulder into him, sending them both crashing off the bench. They hit the ground hard, each trying to gain the upper hand as they rolled across the rubberised surface of the playground. Turner drove an elbow into Beckett's ribs. Beckett countered with a knee to Turner's kidneys, sending a sharp jolt up his spine.

Seeing an opening, Beckett dove for the gun, but Turner grabbed his leg, pulling him back. Beckett kicked out, connecting with Turner's chest, and scrambled towards the gun again. This time he reached it but Turner was already on him, knocking the weapon out of his hand once more.

They scrambled to their feet, both gasping for breath. Turner swung again, but Beckett dodged and tackled him to the ground. They rolled, fists flying, each man fighting for control. Turner managed to pin Beckett, but the Englishman freed a hand and struck him across the side of the head, blurring his vision momentarily. Turner reeled back before what felt like a freight train slammed into his jaw. For a second the world flipped – up was down, black was white. Then he hit the ground with a thud that knocked all the air out of his lungs. Somewhere nearby a siren screamed, getting closer.

No. Get up.

He pushed himself upright, struggling to stay alert. But as he regained his balance, Beckett was already fleeing across the park. Turner snatched up the gun and fired, but Beckett ducked out of sight behind a cluster of trees.

"Damn it."

Turner stood and brushed himself down. There was no

point giving chase, Beckett already had a thirty-yard lead, and Turner was still a little unsteady. At the edge of the park a couple of windows in nearby houses lit up as residents opened them, shouting into the night about the noise. The leaves on the trees flickered with the approaching red, white and blue of the NYPD.

Turner holstered the SIG and took off in the opposite direction. This wasn't how he'd intended tonight to unfold, but at least now he knew where he stood. As always, he was on his own. Just him against the world he was trying to save.

Chapter Thirty-Eight

Xander Templeton stood in the middle of the room staring at his feet. When that grew tedious, he examined his hands front and back, noting his nails needed trimming. Letting out a deep sigh, he leaned his head back to take in the ceiling, trying to keep his composure, looking anywhere but at his reflection in the mirrored wall in front of him.

The black box room in the basement of The Consortium's secluded country estate felt especially stifling this morning. It was just after eight, and he should be on his way to the London office right now, tackling the assignment Director Collins had laterally shunted his way. But as soon as he'd touched down at Heathrow an hour ago, the call had come in – a robotic female voice summoning him here. Needless to say, he could do without this detour.

He rolled his neck, trying to ease the tension in his muscles. He shifted his stance, transferring his weight from one foot to the other. Finally, his gaze drifted to the mirror.

Well, shit.

He looked like hell. His eyes were bloodshot, his shoulders slightly hunched. He straightened up, puffing out his barrel chest in a show of confidence.

What the hell was going on?

He glanced at his watch. Five minutes he'd been standing here. The silence was oppressive, broken only by the tick of a clock he couldn't see. They were making him sweat today.

"Are we keeping you from something?" crackled a voice over hidden speakers. It was a woman again, but not the one who'd called earlier. It was always a different voice.

Templeton sniffed, staring straight ahead. "No. All good." He smoothed his hair, raising his chin to a more complimentary angle. "What is it you want this time?"

The woman clicked her tongue. "Why is Saul Turner still alive and running around New York? And why did one of our contacts receive an unwanted visit from someone matching John Beckett's description? You assured us you had this under control, Mr Templeton."

Templeton bristled, fists clenching at his sides. "It is under control!"

"Is it?"

He tensed his jaw, holding eye contact with his reflection, determined not to show any weakness. "Beckett knows what he has to do, and I've upped the stakes just to make sure he complies. He won't let me down. Turner will be eliminated, and you, I, and the agency will all have complete deniability. As agreed, nothing will touch us. Same as always."

The woman chuckled, a condescending echo that filled the room. "We don't concern ourselves with such trivialities, Mr Templeton. You know as well as we do that nothing can touch us. We are omnipotent, everywhere and nowhere all at once. That's why you're here. That's why you want to remain an associate of ours. We understand. And we're happy to collaborate with the CIA. Just as long as it's to our benefit."

Templeton nodded. "Of course."

"We need Turner taken out immediately, so our man can meet with the scientist without fear for his life."

Templeton cleared his throat. "And when you get the formula, I need your assurance it won't be used."

"That's an awfully vague request, Mr Templeton," the woman replied. "We won't deploy it, but we may leak information and evidence regarding its existence to certain organisations, certain world leaders. Knowledge of its undetectable nature and rapid lethality makes it a potent psychological weapon. But no, we won't use it the way you mean. In that respect we're doing the world a favour – keeping it out of the hands of less benevolent sources."

Templeton nodded. He'd thought as much but it didn't ease the knot in his gut. The world was just a game of chess to these people and he was fast realising he was more of a pawn than a knight in their scheme of things.

"You're going to use it to control people, governments, countries."

"That's a rather crude way of putting it, but something like that, yes," the woman replied, almost breezily. "But don't get your damn knickers in a twist about it, Templeton. It's nothing new – just the next evolution of the nuclear threat."

Templeton grumbled inwardly. As far as he was concerned, the old threat was plenty. But he didn't say this. No point. He had no leverage here.

Just a pawn. Fuck.

The woman seemed to sense his turmoil. "Don't worry,

Mr Templeton. Everything will work out perfectly for all of us. You and the CIA included."

"And you'll keep me informed of any pertinent information, share intelligence when necessary and beneficial?"

"As always. Just so long as you follow our requests. You do your thing; we'll do ours."

Templeton nodded, swallowing his frustration. "Anything else?"

"No. Leave now. But next time we meet we want to be celebrating the death of Saul Turner. Understood?"

Templeton stared into the reflection of his tired, red-ringed eyes and gave a final nod. "Loud and clear."

Chapter Thirty-Nine

The hotel staff barely noticed Beckett as he walked through the lobby and headed for the stairwell. A glance their way confirmed they were still the night crew, their hair and uniforms having the lived-in appearance of a long shift, their eyes glazed with boredom. This was New York City, after all. It would take more than a man soaked through with rain to stir their interest.

He took the stairs two at a time, eager to get to his room and grab a few hours of rest before Reed woke up. The corridor was quiet as he moved silently along, no sounds coming from any of the rooms. He paused outside his door, listening for signs of movement from within. Satisfied that all was still, he slid the keycard into the lock and stepped inside.

Once in his room, Beckett unbuttoned his shirt and draped it over the radiator beneath the window. He followed with his jeans, turning them inside out to speed up drying, then removed his socks and boxers also. The October chill had prompted the hotel to turn up the radiators, filling the room with a damp warmth as his clothes began to dry. Moving into the bathroom, he selected the largest towel from the heated rail, rubbing it briskly through his hair before wrapping it around his waist.

Dry enough, he approached the connecting door to Reed's room. He stood for a moment with his head close to the wood, allowing his awareness to drift through the room beyond. It wasn't just sounds he was alert for, but any sense of movement that might prickle his senses. But there was nothing. Carefully, he eased the door open, the only noise a soft swoosh as the bottom of the door made contact with the thick carpet.

The room was dark, lit only by the faint glow of predawn New York filtering through a gap in the curtains. Beckett paused in the doorway, letting his eyes adjust to the gloom before stepping inside. Reed was still in bed, her breathing deep and even, the steady rise and fall of her chest the only sign of life. The air carried the faint scent of her perfume, which wasn't at all unpleasant. He scanned the room for signs of disturbance or trouble but it was just as it should be, everything in its place, untouched. Satisfied, he retreated into his own room, closing the door silently behind him, feeling the latch click softly into place.

He removed the towel, draped it over the back of the dresser chair and lay on the bed. His body craved sleep but his mind was eager to keep going, thoughts coming at him thick and fast. He closed his eyes and tried to unwind, focusing on relaxing each muscle group in turn – starting with his face, then moving to his shoulders, chest, and arms. But by the time he reached his lower torso he knew it was pointless. Next he took a deep breath, holding it for a count of seven before slowly exhaling for a count of eight. This technique usually slowed his heart rate, easing him into sleep within minutes, but tonight it wasn't working.

His eyes snapped open, staring at the ceiling above. Part of him wanted to run, to grab Amber before Templeton's goons could get to her, and disappear. The thought wouldn't leave him, growing more tempting by the second. If he left right now he could be at JFK in an hour. He'd retrieve his credit card and passport from the safe deposit box and be on a flight to Spain before anyone knew he was gone. At the airport, he'd also call Santos and explain the situation, ensure he got Amber and his family out of Alora immediately. They'd arrange a safe rendezvous point for a few days later. Beckett had trusted Santos with his niece's care for a reason – he knew his old friend would act fast and keep her safe.

Damn it.

What to do?

The prospect of The Consortium getting their hands on the doomsday formula weighed heavily on Beckett's mind. He suspected their primary goal was psychological warfare, using the threat to instil fear and tighten their grip on power. But the possibility of them unleashing something even more cataclysmic couldn't be ignored. Then there was Saul Turner to consider. Beckett had no doubt Templeton was setting him up, positioning him as the perfect scapegoat whilst eliminating Turner in the process. It was a calculated move, exactly what he'd expect from Templeton, and it made his blood boil.

So maybe it's time to call Mr Templeton's bluff.

He was on the verge of jumping up, gearing up, and getting out, but something held him back. It wasn't fear or concern for Amber's safety – it would be a tight extraction mission and the logistics alone were daunting, but he had full confidence in his ability to pull it off. It was about his principles.

He thought of his father, a man who had instilled in him the values of honour and duty. He thought of Jacob Beaumont, who had stood by him through thick and thin. They wouldn't run when the chips were down. They would face the danger head-on. And so would he. He'd do the right thing, even if he wasn't yet sure how that would play out. It was that damned grey area again – where right and wrong blurred, where every decision felt like a gamble.

Decision made, it was clear that this indecision alone had been keeping him awake. Now that it was just a matter of figuring out the 'how' rather than wrestling with doubts and uncertainties, a fresh wave of fatigue washed over him. He trusted the answer to 'how' would come, and experience had taught him that his mind worked best when rested, not clogged with a thousand other thoughts.

He glanced at his watch: 3:20 a.m. His eyes felt heavy suddenly. It had been a long day. He lay back, the pillow beneath his head soft and warm. His eyelids drooped as he slipped into sleep, the chaotic thoughts fading to a dull murmur at last.

Calm...

Benign nothingness...

His eyes snapped open. He blinked, disoriented, and looked at his watch: 6:32 a.m. He'd been asleep for over three hours, but it felt like nothing.

Had something woken him?

A threat?

Sitting up, alert, he peered into the gloom. The room around him was silent and still. There was no one else here. Rolling his head from side to side, he stretched his neck muscles. It seemed his subconscious wasn't going to let him rest for too long. Swinging his legs off the bed, he planted his feet on the carpet, already fully awake. The short nap had reset his mind just enough to power on through. Probably for the best – there was no time to waste.

He got up and dressed in his backup outfit, identical to the one drying on the radiator. The clothes were a bit wrinkled and overdue for a wash, but he smoothed them out as best he could. In the bathroom, he masked any lingering mustiness with a quick spray of deodorant and slicked his hair into a neat side parting using water from the tap. Back in the main room, he put on his boots, then paused, organising his thoughts.

He needed to use Reed's phone again but it was tricky now. Morning had broken and she could wake at any moment. He moved to the door and listened. Silence. He nudged the door open slightly and peered through the gap. Reed was still sleeping soundly, making little puffing noises with each out-breath. He watched her for a moment to make sure she wasn't about to wake, then confirmed the phone was still where he'd left it on the dresser.

He slipped into the room and retrieved the device. Holding his breath, he moved to Reed's bedside and carefully held the phone to her face. The screen unlocked, flashing to life and illuminating her peaceful features. Exhaling slowly, he retraced his steps and quietly shut the door behind him.

Back in his room he sat on the edge of the bed and opened the search engine app, typing *Nico Vassos* into the input field. The results appeared instantly but offered only what he'd expected – very little. No Wikipedia page, no significant articles. A short AI-generated piece on a site called *Watching The One Percent* provided only basic details – date of birth, country of residence, estimated net worth –

but nothing of substance. He clicked through a few more links, searching for something of value, but all the information was the same. Vague, unverified, and ultimately uninformative.

Closing the search engine he noticed another app on the phone desktop titled simply, *Database*. He opened it and saw it provided access to government records, but conducting a search required passwords and double verification. Any attempt to access it would raise red flags and the risk was too high. He leaned back, the phone still glowing in his hand, a galling reminder of his limited options.

The time was approaching 7 a.m. He rubbed his eyes. Okay, another way. He had a phone – why not use it for its original purpose? The idea seemed almost novel in this digital age, but he didn't have many other options. He also didn't know many numbers by heart, but there was one he still remembered. After a quick time conversion, he clicked on the keypad and tapped out the number. Then he hit call. Then he waited.

Chapter Forty

Jacob Beaumont stood in the guest bedroom of his Crystal Palace home, getting ready for an afternoon of gardening. He was already wearing an old t-shirt and a pair of frayed cords, but with the cold creeping in outside he knew he'd need another layer. He slid open the fitted wardrobe that stretched along the back wall – the only piece of furniture in the room since they'd decided having people to stay over was a thing of the past – and grabbed his favourite bottle-green jumper. The front was spattered with white paint from countless decorating jobs, but he couldn't bring himself to part with it, even if Martha rolled her eyes at his refusal to throw it out.

He put it on and took a moment to stretch. It was just after noon, but on his days off he liked to ease into things slowly. The skies were clear despite the cold, and it was probably his last chance to do some weeding before winter set in. Gardening had become one of his favourite pastimes since he went part-time. He'd never really seen the appeal before, but after losing two fingers he'd been forced to slow down and reassess his outlook on life. Gardening allowed him to get out of his head and focus on something in front of him rather than unseen threats and potential catastrophes. He hadn't turned into some sort of mindfulness nut, but he did appreciate the benefits of taking things at a steadier pace.

Busy hands, quiet mind.

That's what Martha would always say whenever he asked why she spent all her spare time knitting, sewing or baking. But these days it made perfect sense to him.

Having just finished a hearty lunch of kippers, potatoes and salad, accompanied by two slices of buttered brown bread, Beaumont felt ready to tackle the rest of the day. Once he was finished in the garden, he and Martha planned to take a walk up to the local park. It was a pleasant contrast to his old life, but even during his time with Sigma Unit he'd always fiercely guarded his downtime. His home life was important. Martha was important.

He headed downstairs and into the hallway, the smell of buttery fish still lingering in the air. Moving into the porch, he found his padded green gilet on the rack and slipped it on.

"I'm heading outside," he called out. "Shouldn't be too long."

"Okay, love," Martha replied. "Have fun."

Fun. He smiled to himself. Now there was a novelty.

He grabbed his gardening gloves from the small table near the door and shoved them in his pocket. Just as he was about to leave, he heard Martha saying something.

He craned his neck. "What was that, love?"

He shuffled into the front room as his wife looked up from her book. Her glasses sat low on her nose and she pushed them up with a finger. "I was just saying, don't forget to deadhead the roses. And trim some of them back if you get a chance. They're getting wild."

"Got it." He was about to head out when the metallic buzz of a phone vibrating stopped him. "Shit. Sorry. Where is that thing?"

He scanned the room until Martha sighed and pointed to the coffee table. "There. Where it always is."

Beaumont walked over and squinted at the screen as it continued to vibrate. He rarely received calls these days, so his first instinct was to ignore it. "Says ID Unknown," he grumbled.

"It's probably someone selling something," Martha said.

"Yeah, probably," he agreed, turning to leave again. But the phone kept ringing, and something made him pause. He picked it up and looked at it.

"Either answer it or switch it off, will you?"

He hesitated, his finger hovering over the answer button. Martha watched him, her expression shifting from curiosity to mild concern. Finally, he answered it. "Jacob Beaumont here."

"Hey. It's me."

Beaumont recognised the voice instantly. Beckett's tone was rougher than the last time they'd spoken but still unmistakable. A rush of emotions surged through Beaumont — relief, concern, curiosity — all at once.

"Good to hear your voice, son. How's it going? Did my info help?"

"Yes, it did. But now I need a little more. That's if you've got time and it doesn't put you in an awkward or dangerous position."

Beaumont glanced at Martha, who was now watching him intently. Awkward and dangerous were relative concepts. Her brow furrowed slightly and she mouthed, *Who is it?*

"I'm at home right now, my day off," Beaumont told Beckett. "But I have my work laptop and can connect to the system remotely. Hang on a second."

Martha wasn't letting up. She put her book down, her full attention on him now. "What's going on?" she whispered.

Beaumont covered the receiver. "It's John. He needs my help."

Martha's eyes widened, though he couldn't tell if it was from surprise or indignation – maybe a bit of both. He shuffled out of the front room and headed for his office at the back of the house, feeling the weight of her gaze on his back. He knew she had questions, but now wasn't the time to answer them.

Beaumont's home office was in more of a state than his office at Nightingale House. It was only on days like today, however, when he was jolted into full alertness, that he truly noticed the mess. He liked to think it was familiar chaos, though Martha didn't see it that way. She let it slide since he was the only one who ever came back here, but even he had to admit his office was a disorderly outlier in their otherwise immaculate home. Papers were strewn across the desk, old notepads and correspondence interspersed with gardening catalogues. The faint smell of stale coffee lingered in the air, no doubt coming from the army of empty coffee cups, some of them containing weeks' worth of mould. An old, worn-out chair sat in the corner, draped with a random assortment of jackets and bags.

He navigated through the clutter, shifting a stack of newspapers off the chair before sitting down. He dragged his laptop in front of him, the screen flickering to life as it woke from sleep.

"What do you need, son?" he asked, cradling the phone between his chin and shoulder as he logged into his desktop.

"How about a miracle," came the reply.

"That bad, eh?" Beaumont leaned forward, his remaining fingers hovering over the keyboard. "Why don't you fill me in as best you can?"

Beckett cleared his throat before launching into a concise rundown of his week. He began with his encounter with Erica Reed, followed by Templeton's ambush, then moved on to what he had uncovered – and what he suspected – about Turner and Bader. Lastly, he explained the situation with the doomsday formula and the roles of The Consortium and Nico Vassos.

Beckett spoke quickly, sticking to the essentials. Beaumont struggled to take it all in, and when Beckett finished, he leaned back in his chair, running a hand through his hair as he tried to make sense of the situation. He was quiet for a long time.

"Beaumont? You still there?"

The question pulled him from his thoughts. "Yeah, I'm here, John." He took a deep breath, trying to steady himself. "You know, for someone who's supposed to be out of the game, you sound like you're in pretty deep."

"I was forced out. Then I was forced back in," Beckett replied. "Not much I can do about it now. If I don't do what Templeton says, he'll have Amber killed."

"You really think he'd go that far?" Beaumont asked.

"I have to assume he would."

Beaumont shook his head. He didn't envy Beckett's position. He didn't have kids, but he had nephews, nieces, and of course Martha. In the same situation, he knew he'd do whatever it took.

"So you're going to kill this Turner guy, even though he's in a similar boat to you?" he asked, playing devil's advocate, hoping it might help his friend solidify his thoughts. "Even though Templeton is throwing him under the bus too?"

"We don't know that for certain," Beckett said.

"No. But it sure sounds like it."

"Yes. It does."

Beaumont nodded to himself as his eyes drifted to the door. He knew he was stepping into dangerous territory by helping Beckett, especially now that he understood the full extent of the situation. Even though he was only working part-time at Sigma Unit, in what was essentially a glorified admin role, he still had to answer to his superiors. Templeton was still in and out of Nightingale House on a semi-regular basis. But he couldn't abandon his friend, not now, not when he needed him the most. The risk was high, but like so many times in their shared careers, the cost of inaction was even higher. And that was before they factored in this damned doomsday formula.

He adjusted his laptop screen. "All right, whatever you need me to do," he said, pre-empting Beckett's request by clicking on the icon to establish a remote connection to the SIS database. "Just keep in mind, my activity will be logged as usual."

"But no one will check the logs unless there's a reason to?" Beckett asked.

"Correct," Beaumont confirmed, inputting his credentials and scanning the familiar interface as it loaded. "As long as we don't trigger any red flags."

"I just need any information you can give me on Nico

Vassos," Beckett said. "There's nothing of any use available online."

"Well, if he's part of The Consortium, that makes sense," Beaumont replied as he navigated through the system's menus. "Those guys must have spent a fortune on the best tech team around to scrub any trace of them from the web."

"Do we have anything in PIMS?" Beckett asked, referring to the Personal Identity Management System – the intelligence service's database for profiling individuals of interest.

"Let's find out," Beaumont said, typing *Nico Vassos* into the search bar. The old laptop whirred as the remote system processed his request. "Come on, come on," he muttered, scrolling through the preliminary results. He bypassed a few irrelevant entries, filtering out the noise until he hit on something substantial. "Yes! Got him."

Beckett breathed in sharply. "Tell me."

Beaumont's eyes flicked across the text as he speed-read the most pertinent points, reciting them aloud. "Nico Vassos, billionaire, born in Athens, yada yada... Finance and tech whiz... Made his fortune during the dot-com boom... Heavy investor in emerging markets and crypto. Operates through shell companies and offshore accounts." He paused, absorbing the information. "And you're right. We've got him flagged as a potential member of The Consortium, linked to three other key players already identified. Looks like he's a serious operator. Unfortunately."

He leaned back, picking at a callus on his palm as he processed the details. "So this guy is buying the doomsday formula and plans to hand it over to The Consortium?"

"That's what Turner believes, and I'm inclined to agree," Beckett replied.

Beaumont swallowed hard, his thoughts drifting to his wife in the front room. "What's their endgame here?"

"Absolute best-case scenario? They use it as a leverage tool. But even that isn't worth thinking about. They'd have the entire world over a barrel."

Beaumont nodded. "That they would." He hesitated, not wanting to voice his next thought but knowing it was necessary. "And this supposed rogue SAC officer, Turner – he told you he's been ordered to take out Bader before the sale can happen?"

"Yes."

"But Templeton wants you to—"

"Correct."

"So can we assume Templeton is working for The Consortium?" The silence on the line was answer enough.

"He's involved with them in some capacity," Beckett added. "But we already suspected that."

"Yeah. Though I've never been able to dig up anything concrete on him," Beaumont said. "And not for lack of trying, either. But if Templeton's the double agent, you can't kill Turner."

"And if I don't, Amber's dead," Beckett replied.

"Shit."

They both fell silent, the impossible dilemma hanging between them like an unexploded bomb.

"Listen, thanks for your help, Jacob," Beckett said. "I appreciate it, and I'm sorry for dumping all this on you. You don't need this. I'd better go—"

"Wait," Beaumont interrupted, spotting a new pop-up at the bottom of his screen. He clicked on the link, which opened to reveal a memo. He narrowed his eyes, reading as he spoke. "Whoa. Looks like Vassos's passport just pinged at JFK an hour ago. PIMS flagged it during routine cross-checks with immigration records. He was on a flight from Casablanca, Morocco, where he's also got a home."

"Do you trust that intel?" Beckett asked.

"It's the system we've always used. It's rarely wrong."

"He's in town," Beckett muttered. "Anything else?"

Beaumont cast his eyes down the screen. "Yes, actually. The residential address listed on his flight details is in Montauk. He must have a place there, probably where he's headed now. Do you have a pen for the address?"

"I'll remember it," Beckett said.

Beaumont relayed the information. "Be careful now, son. I mean it."

"I'll do what I always do," Beckett replied. "But it looks like the trade is happening today. I have to move. Thanks, Jacob."

"Good luck," Beaumont said, but the line was already dead. He sat back, staring at the screen for a moment before glancing out the window. Then he looked down at his scruffy attire. His garden was calling him. Time to prune those roses.

Chapter Forty-One

Beckett had known the sale of Bader's formula to Vassos was imminent, but discovering it was likely to happen within the next twenty-four hours sent a fresh jolt of urgency through him. Still holding the phone, he opened the maps app and entered the address Beaumont had provided. There was no property listed, but the drop-pin marked a coastal area high up on Culloden Point overlooking the ocean.

Interesting.

He glanced at the clock, calculating the logistics. It was almost 7:30 a.m. Vassos had landed at JFK an hour earlier. Even with a driver waiting at the kerb to whisk him away, the journey to Montauk would still take a couple of hours. Vassos wouldn't reach his destination until at least nine. But the real question – was he planning to get straight to business as soon as he arrived?

It was possible, but Beckett's instincts said otherwise. A deal of this magnitude wouldn't go down first thing in the morning, especially not after an eight-hour flight. Vassos would likely want to rest and freshen up before diving into business. Beckett figured the earliest he'd meet Bader would be that afternoon, most likely in the evening after they'd secured the meeting site. That gave Beckett six or seven hours to get there. First though he needed fresh air to clear his head. The room suddenly felt suffocating.

After returning Reed's phone to her room, he grabbed his keycard and left the hotel, slipping past the morning staff at the front desk without being noticed. The early morning air was crisp as he stepped outside and the chill bit through the thin linen of his shirt. He really should have bought a jacket at the store when he had the chance, but the last thing he felt like doing now was wasting time in stuffy shops, and besides, the cool air would keep him alert.

For Times Square, the streets were unusually quiet — just a handful of commuters, with the usual tourist hustle nowhere to be seen at this hour. Neon lights still flashed their advertisements, but the sidewalks were easy to navigate. He walked past the closed shops and darkened theatres, stopping at a small coffee cart on the edge of Broadway.

The owner, an attractive young woman with dark brown hair shaved on one side, looked up and smiled as he approached. "What can I get ya?" she asked in a broad New York accent.

He clicked his teeth. There was no menu on show. "Just the strongest coffee you have, please."

"Ah, English. Nice." She pursed her lips. "How about a double-shot espresso? I can top it up with hot milk if that works?"

"That works perfectly. And a Danish too," he added, noticing the tray of iced pastries.

"Coming right up." The woman got to work making the

coffee, too engrossed to make small talk. Either that or she'd picked up on his mood and decided to keep quiet, which he appreciated. Once done, she handed him a steaming cup and a small paper bag with the Danish inside. He thanked her and gave her ten dollars from the money he'd accumulated.

Sitting on a nearby bench, Beckett placed the Danish beside him and removed the lid from his coffee. The first sip was hot and bitter but it delivered the bump he needed. As he drank, he let his awareness spread, taking in the city as it came back to life, the early morning sunlight stretching across the sky.

Beaumont had only confirmed what Beckett already suspected – Templeton was up to his neck in this mess. But just how involved he was, and what his true motives were, remained unclear.

That conniving, two-faced bastard.

Beckett unwrapped the Danish and took a bite, enjoying the flaky pastry and sweet filling. It was going to be a long day, he knew that much, and he'd need the sustenance.

The idea of killing Turner weighed heavily on him. With what he now knew, and what he suspected, he was more conflicted than ever about whether he could go through with it.

He looked down at his hands, flexing his fingers. Physically and mentally, he knew he had what it took to kill Turner, and he'd do anything required of him to protect Amber. But morally? On a humanitarian level? The certainty of what needed to be done clashed with the weight of the act itself. His mind was a storm, each choice leading to consequences he wasn't sure he could live with. He needed another way out, but the path ahead felt impossibly narrow.

Above all, he had to ensure Vassos never got his hands on the doomsday formula. The potential fallout was unthinkable. If an organisation as powerful and far-reaching as The Consortium acquired something that dangerous, it could trigger a global meltdown.

He took another sip of his coffee and glanced at his watch. Just after 8 a.m. Time was ticking away, and he needed to move. He decided it was best to get back to the hotel before Reed woke and wondered where he was. Finishing his Danish, he crumpled the bag and tossed it into a nearby trash can, taking the coffee with him.

The sun was peeking between the high-rises and the cool morning air felt good against his face. As he walked, he considered the conversation he needed to have with Reed. He had to reach Montauk as soon as possible, and the decision to go alone wasn't one he could take lightly. Then there was the bigger question – could he trust her? His gut said no. But the situation was complicated; he might need her. Relying on someone he couldn't fully trust made him uneasy, but it wasn't new territory for him. Often in Beckett's line of work it wasn't about who you could trust but who would do the least harm. He shook his head. Back to that murky grey area that he'd once called his life.

But who was he kidding? It was *still* his life. Trouble and John Beckett went hand in hand.

Back at the hotel, he took the stairs and slipped into his room without a sound. A quick sweep confirmed everything was just as he'd left it, and his thoughts shifted back to Reed. He needed to see her, needed that face-to-face. Once he looked her in the eyes and laid out his plans, he'd have a clearer sense of how to proceed. This job was all about taking chances and adapting on the fly.

He pressed his ear to the door connecting the two

rooms. Silence. He cautiously eased the door open and peered inside.

Shit.

The lights were on, and the bed was unmade, but no Reed. He checked the bathroom. Empty – the air cool and with no hint of steam or recent shower activity. He looked for signs of a struggle. Apart from the tangled sheets, there was no indication of disturbance. But if a professional had taken her, they wouldn't have left any obvious traces. He checked under the bed, in the closets. Nothing. Reed was nowhere to be seen.

So where was she?

Beckett stood in the middle of the room, weighing his options. Should he wait here? Search the hotel for her? Decision made, he turned to head out when he heard a noise behind him. He spun around, muscles tensed, every sense on high alert. There was no one there. But then he heard the beep of a keycard, and he braced himself as the door opened.

Chapter Forty-Two

As Reed's door creaked open, Beckett shifted his weight onto the balls of his feet, his muscles primed to react at a moment's notice. A second later Reed walked in, carrying two large cardboard cups. She was dressed in leggings and an oversized black hoodie that was so big it could almost double as a dress. Her hair was pulled back in a ponytail, and she wore minimal make-up. She looked good, natural. But when her eyes landed on him, her mouth dropped and her eyebrows drew into sharp, downturned lines.

"What the hell are you doing in my room?"

Beckett hesitated. No matter how he explained it, being found alone in a woman's private space was never a good look. Reed stepped forward, letting the door click shut behind her as she surveyed the room. Almost simultaneously their eyes landed on a pair of lace panties near Beckett's foot. Reed let out a huff of displeasure, before shifting her attention to the dresser. Her phone and laptop were exactly where she'd left them, but even though Beckett had been careful, it didn't help his current situation.

Reed turned back and glared at him. "Well?"

"I knocked a couple of times but there was no answer," he said. "I was worried about you."

"Right, well, I was getting coffee." She held up the cups. "As a way of saying sorry... you know, for what happened last night. Or rather... what didn't."

He nodded, the awkwardness only deepening as he was reminded of the car crash of their last encounter. "No need to apologise. We were both tired. Signs were misread. It won't happen again." He smiled, trying to defuse the tension. But something was off.

Reed stayed near the door, her expression unreadable. She was acting edgy but not in the way he would have expected. She didn't look disappointed or embarrassed, more like unsettled. And this didn't feel like typical morning-after awkwardness. Something else was wrong.

He kept his eyes on her. Had she checked on him earlier? Had she noticed he wasn't there?

"You were up early," he said, trying to shift the conversation.

"I had some calls to make." She came forward and handed him one of the coffees. "You just wake up?"

"Yes. Well, about ten minutes ago. Just enough time to shower and get dressed."

Reed nodded, a half-smile tugging at her lips, suspicion in her eyes. He smiled back and took a sip of the coffee, glad he'd already finished his first cup on the way back and tossed it in the trash downstairs. This one was weaker, not quite as good. The cups were identical, but that didn't mean much, the vendors around here probably bought from the same wholesalers. He forced himself to relax. If their paths had crossed, he would have seen her.

"Sleep well?" she asked.

He shrugged and grinned. "Think so, I was asleep." When in doubt, play it cool. But she didn't smile back. "Listen, if I came on too strong last night, I apologise. I can be a real oaf sometimes and I—"

"It's gone. Let's move on, okay?" She shot him a brittle smile and moved further into the room, taking a seat in front of the dresser. Beckett nodded and filed the experience away in the part of his brain labelled *Never think of this again.* He sipped his coffee, letting the warmth and bitterness ground him for a moment. He'd tried to be a gentleman about it, but now he needed to focus on the doomsday formula and the implications of Vassos's arrival in New York this morning.

His mind wandered back to what Beaumont had told him about Vassos and the very real implications of his arrival in New York this morning. He thought about Bader and Turner, and the mission he was tasked with. Templeton was still a concern. The guy was as slippery as they came, and Beckett was all but convinced he was involved in this somehow. And what about his temporary partner? Did she know more than she was letting on? He barely knew the woman, but he got the sense there were more layers beneath her outer shell than she knew what to do with.

He watched her sip her coffee, noting the tension at the corners of her eyes and the rigid set of her shoulders. She'd been hyperalert since they arrived in New York, but without a baseline he couldn't tell if this was just her natural state or if something specific was causing it. Maybe it was the mission or her drive to succeed, but she didn't strike him as a people-pleaser. Clearly she could be agreeable when needed, but it didn't come naturally to her.

"Everything okay?" she asked, noticing him looking.

"Not really." He walked over to her and stopped as she turned in the chair to face him. "We've got a problem."

"Oh?"

"I did a little research last night after you went to bed," he said, choosing his words carefully. "I called up an old colleague and asked him to do some digging on my behalf."

Reed frowned, apparently not thrilled about him pulling in outside help, but she didn't argue the point. "And?"

"Bader has invented what they're calling a doomsday formula, and he's trying to sell it for a billion dollars. That's why everyone's so eager to keep us away from him."

He observed her intently, assessing how much of this she already knew, but her face gave nothing away. "From what we can presume, a man called Nico Vassos is putting up the cash. He's part of a wider network, acting on behalf of The Consortium."

Reed looked down at the lid of her coffee cup. "That's a hell of a lot of information from your old colleague."

"What can I say, he's a well-informed guy." He didn't see the point in giving her the full story right now. He just needed to know where he stood.

"Beckett, what the hell is going on?" she asked, looking up, irritation creeping into her voice. "What are you getting at?"

Either she was keeping her cards close to her chest, or she genuinely had no clue what he was talking about – and he didn't have time to figure out which. Time was ticking away, and he no longer had a choice. He had to trust her. For starters he needed to get to Montauk, and she was the one with the rental car.

"Okay, here's what I know." He sat on the edge of the bed across from her and laid it all out, telling her everything he'd uncovered in the last twelve hours. He filled her in on

Gruett and about running into Turner again. He relayed what he knew about Bader and Vassos, and the urgent need to get to Montauk before the trade went down. As he spoke, he watched her for any tells or micro-expressions. By the time he finished, she'd turned a few shades paler.

"Thoughts?" he said, when she remained silent.

Reed opened her mouth, then shut it. Tried again. "I... umm... I think that's good work. I think we've got a lot to think about."

"We don't have time to think, Reed. We need to act."

"Or maybe we need to cool off first," she suggested, setting her coffee down on the table, her fingers drumming lightly on the lid.

"No," he said. "We have to stop that trade. And I have to kill Turner. Or have you forgotten that your boss threatened to kill my niece if I don't?" He kept his gaze locked on her as she stiffened slightly.

"I had nothing to do with that. I swear."

Beckett dismissed the comment. Not the time.

"But... you are going to kill Turner," she added, more a statement than a question.

"I have to," Beckett snapped, noticing a slight, almost imperceptible curl at the corners of her mouth. It was subtle, but for someone like him it spoke volumes.

She folded her arms across her chest. "So what now?"

"The meeting between Vassos and Bader is going to happen sometime in the next twenty-four hours. I'm betting Turner knows that too, which means he's already on his way to Montauk to try to stop it."

"But he's still our target."

"Yes. But if that trade goes down it's bad for everyone. And if Turner takes Bader out before we get there, Turner's gone too. In the wind. Either way we need to get there before anything happens."

"But we don't know where this Nico Vassos lives."

"Yes. We do."

She looked perturbed. Maybe this was too much information all at once. Her eyes darted around the room as if she were searching for an escape. When her attention landed back on him she asked, "Can we intercept Turner before he acts?"

"Why?" Beckett countered. "Might be better to let him do the hit. Then we'll see what happens with…" He trailed off as an idea formed. It was a long shot, dependent on too many variables to be certain, but it was an idea nonetheless.

"What about your niece?" Reed asked. "You said it yourself, if we let Turner take Bader out, he could run. Then what?"

"I won't let that happen," he said firmly.

She nodded but didn't seem convinced. "Are you sure this is a good idea?"

"No, it's a terrible idea," Beckett admitted. "But we have to see it through. We can't let The Consortium get that formula."

Reed didn't answer, just went quiet. He noticed the conflict in her eyes before she looked away and reminded himself this was her first intelligence mission and she'd be wanting to impress her boss.

"We can do this," he said. "It'll be fine."

"Maybe." She shook her head as if to clear the doubt away. "I guess I'm just feeling a little out of my depth. I don't want to screw this up."

Beckett dropped his elbows on his knees and leaned forward. "I know it's a lot to take in. But that's usually how these things go. Nothing happens and then everything happens all at once."

He offered her a reassuring smile but that was all she was getting. It was time to get to work.

"Okay, let's do it," she said, all business again. "What do you need from me?"

"Get yourself and the car ready," Beckett said, deciding to take a chance, adapting on the fly. "We need to beat Turner to Vassos's place. My guess is he'll try to take them both out, belts and braces. It's what I'd do, catch them while their guard's down. So we need to arrive first and be ready for him."

She looked up as he moved towards the door. "Where are you going?"

"I need to pick up a few supplies. Can I use the credit card?"

She didn't look thrilled about it, but then reached for her bag and handed it over. "Don't go crazy."

"We'll need darker clothes, something low profile." He took the card, pausing as she got to her feet. The last thing he wanted was her tagging along. He pointed to the laptop. "In the meantime I need you to use the CIA's database and dig up anything you can on Nico Vassos." He nodded towards the equipment bag under the desk. "Check the weapons too. Make sure everything's in working order. We'll need pistols, ammo. Maybe the rifle, though I doubt I'll get a chance to use it. Vassos's place looks to be on a cliff edge overlooking the sea, no good elevation points for a sniper hit."

"I'm on it."

"Good. I'll be back soon." He gave her a quick nod then was out the door, moving fast down to the lobby. There was a lot to get done, and now he had the outline of a plan. He just hoped time and luck were still on his side.

Chapter Forty-Three

Beckett exited the hotel and retraced his steps to Times Square, using the landmark as a starting point. He knew time was short, but he had a feeling he'd already spotted what he was after. He headed north up 7th Avenue, scanning each storefront he passed and assessing what they had to offer. The morning air was still crisp, and the white-noise drone of a working city filled his ears – horns blaring, people shouting, the clatter from a nearby construction site – yet he felt strangely peaceful, his focus laser-sharp on the task at hand. He sidestepped a woman pushing a stroller, dodged a delivery cyclist, and pressed on, letting his instincts guide him as he continued up 7th Avenue.

At the corner, he turned onto West 46th Street and glanced at his watch. It was 9:15 a.m. He had to speed this up. Every second was critical. He had a destination in mind, though it was more of a feeling than a certainty. Weaving through the crowd of commuters and tourists, his awareness constantly shifted, assessing and recalculating with each step. At the intersection with 8th Avenue, he paused briefly to get his bearings.

And there it was – an Army and Navy store across the street. His subconscious must have logged it sometime in the last few days, possibly when he was heading to Axiom Labs. He crossed over the road and headed straight for the entrance. The awning read *M*A*S*H Military Surplus Store*, styled after the TV show, complete with asterisks. The name was stencilled in white spray paint on army-issue green tarp. A nice touch, he felt.

Stepping inside, Beckett was immediately struck by the familiar smells of oil and canvas. He found the scents strangely comforting, anchoring him to a past that still felt very present. Except for him and the clerk, the store was empty, the silence almost oppressive. A welcome reprieve from the chaos outside its front doors. It was like walking through a favourite museum or art gallery, except here the exhibits were all shades of olive and khaki. A home no matter where he was in the world. A moment of calm before the coming storm.

Long shelves were stacked with boots and camping equipment, and opposite them, surplus military hardware lined the wall, from canteens to night vision goggles. Beckett moved down an aisle, his fingers brushing against the sturdy fabrics. He paused by a shelf of tactical gloves and picked up a pair. They were well made – reinforced knuckles, weather-resistant fabric, designed for the harshest conditions – but he had no need for them. He placed them back.

As he ventured further into the store, he noticed the clerk watching him. The man looked to be in his mid-forties. He was tall and skinny, with greying hair that nearly matched his skin tone and gave him a washed-out look, almost like a blob of beige if you squinted. He wore a green military jumper complete with epaulettes and elbow patches. His posture was relaxed but attentive. A veteran, Beckett assumed. He could feel the man's eyes on him as he moved along the racks of camouflage, and met his gaze with a brief, respectful nod before turning back to the clothing. He picked up a pair of sturdy boots, feeling their weight and flexibility, before setting them back down. Next he came to the jackets, feeling the well-worn leather and canvas, appreciating the durability and craftsmanship. But again, not what he was after.

Reminding himself why he was here, he headed for a display of black cargo trousers. He selected a pair he knew would fit him, and another pair he hoped would work for Reed. She looked to be a medium, though the sizing in military gear could be inconsistent; it was better to judge by eye. Slinging the two pairs over his shoulder, he also grabbed two black tops that looked about right. They were long-sleeved, made of lightweight yet durable material – ideal for the kind of work they had ahead.

Beckett crossed to the far side of the store, where a wide array of backpacks hung from slatwall panels. He chose two in dark charcoal, the nearest colour to black, and with plenty of compartments. Bundling the items in his arms, he headed to the register, his mind already shifting to his next steps. He knew he needed more but wasn't entirely sure what it was. Then, as he approached the counter, something on a high shelf caught his eye.

Of course.

He stopped and squinted up at the item. He'd never seen anything like it, but it was almost perfect, and suddenly his plan began to take real shape. The beige man noticed his interest and grinned, a hint of pride in his eyes.

"Cool, huh?" he said. "We just got those in. They're

brand new. Apparently the inventor just won some kind of design award."

Beckett pulled an impressed face. "Mind if I take a closer look?"

The clerk clambered up a small stepladder behind the counter and took down the box, placing it on the counter in front of Beckett. "Good piece of kit by all accounts."

"How small does it go?" Beckett asked, opening the box to examine the contents.

"Pretty small. Fits right into one of those backpacks you picked up," the clerk replied confidently.

Beckett leaned in to get a better look. "How much?"

"Only $500."

"*Only*," Beckett repeated. But he didn't hesitate. He had Reed's credit card and knew this was a necessary investment. "I'll take it," he said, handing over the card. He noticed a carousel of maps on the counter and pulled out the one covering Montauk, tossing it on top of the clothes. "This too."

"No worries. That everything?"

Beckett twisted his mouth to one side as if his next question was just an afterthought. "Actually, do you have any TraumaMend, or anything similar?"

The guy turned and perused a lower shelf, returning with a packet of the advanced wound dressing. "One? Two?"

"Make it two," Beckett said. "Can't be too careful, right?"

As the guy rang up the sale, Beckett unboxed his new purchase and stuffed it into one of the backpacks. It fit perfectly and he handed the packaging back to the clerk for disposal.

"Do you know how to use something like that?" the guy asked.

"I'll figure it out," Beckett replied, waving away the offered receipt. "Thanks a lot."

"No problem. You take care now."

Beckett raised a hand in farewell as he made his way out. He felt a bit more together now, his mind clearer. He had a plan. One that might just work. It was still a hell of a long shot, but it was something to hold onto. And for this mission, that was as good as it was going to get.

Chapter Forty-Four

Montauk sits at the easternmost tip of Long Island, a blend of rugged natural beauty and coastal charm. Known for its windswept beaches, dramatic cliffs, and historic lighthouse, it offers those who can afford holiday homes there a serene escape from the hustle and bustle of city life. Surrounded by the North Atlantic Ocean, the air is briny and bracing, carrying in summertime the fresh scents of wildflowers and pine. Fishing boats dot the harbour, a nod to the town's maritime heritage, while upscale resorts and quaint cottages provide a haven for vacationers seeking tranquillity.

The drive to Montauk from New York City usually took a little over three hours, though Beckett was hoping they could shave off some time since it was a weekday afternoon. It was gone midday, and they'd been on the road for about an hour, having just passed the turnoff for Plainview on the Long Island Expressway. He settled into the passenger seat, watching as the urban sprawl gradually gave way to stretches of rolling farmland and dense woodland, the horizon brushed with autumn's oranges and reds. Trees lined the highway, their leaves rustling gently in the breeze. Every so often, clusters of buildings interrupted the greenery, and billboards advertising local attractions and restaurants stood out in vivid colours against the grey sky.

In contrast to the expansive view outside, the Taurus's interior was simple and functional. It wasn't the most luxurious option in the rental brochure, but it wasn't the cheapest either. The dashboard was modern and sleek, displaying an array of gauges and controls, most of which he vaguely understood. The speedometer, however, he knew well, the needle hovering just above the speed limit as Reed kept a steady foot on the accelerator. He silently urged her to push it harder, but held his tongue.

Reed's hands were firm on the wheel, her eyes locked on the road ahead. They hadn't spoken much since setting off, but that was as much Beckett's doing as hers. Now, as he studied her, he wondered what she was thinking about. They both had plenty to deal with, but Reed seemed more troubled than ever. Her brow was furrowed and her lips were pressed into a thin hard line. It seemed to Beckett there was a storm brewing inside her, and she was struggling to deal with it.

Was it just the mission that had her so preoccupied?

Or was something else bothering her?

Beckett had hoped his suspicions about Reed were off, but with every passing minute he became more certain he was right.

Both of them were dressed in the black tactical gear he'd picked up earlier. His top fit almost too snugly around his biceps and chest, but overall he'd chosen well. Reed looked good in her outfit. On the backseat were the two backpacks, one for him and one as a backup, both containing a Glock and plenty of ammo. Beckett's pack was also stuffed with the rest of the equipment he'd need. He hadn't mentioned the purchase to Reed, for obvious reasons, but it folded down so small she hadn't even noticed.

The sniper rifle was in the trunk, along with some extra ammunition. The rifle might have been useful if Beckett planned to play this a different way, but as it stood, he doubted it would see any action. From the map he'd purchased, it was clear that the terrain around Vassos's mansion wasn't suited for long-range sniping. This also meant Turner would have to get close to take out Bader, a scenario that would make the mission even messier and more chaotic than it already was. But that suited Beckett just fine. Chaos was what he needed. His plan hinged on shock and confusion, not precision.

He just hoped he could pull it off.

They drove on, passing vineyards and farm stands offering fresh produce and homemade pies. As the cityscape faded into the background, the patchy skies began to clear, and the sun broke fully through the clouds. It was shaping up to be a bright afternoon – another factor to consider in his ever-evolving plan.

Beckett closed his eyes, pretending to sleep. The rhythmic hum of the car and the steady vibration of the road beneath the tyres created a backdrop that allowed him to relax, at least outwardly. He thought he heard Reed tutting beside him, but he might have been mistaken. Either way he ignored it. If she was tense and nervous, that was helpful. Nervous people were easier to predict, their anxiety often betraying their next move. He'd rather have her noticeably on edge than closed up. This way it would make her actions more transparent and her loyalty clear.

He kept his eyes closed as the miles and minutes passed. An hour drifted into two. He remained still, his breathing deep and steady, almost falling into a meditative state but not quite. His senses were finely tuned to the environment around him. The map in his head told him they were getting closer; another twenty minutes, give or take, and they'd be there.

The rest of the journey was spent mentally running through scenario analyses, preparing for every potential outcome. This process had become second nature to him over the years, ingrained through countless missions and high-stakes operations. For Beckett, survival wasn't just about reacting in the moment, it was about meticulous preparation and strategic foresight.

He contemplated every possible scenario, categorising them into best, worst, and most likely outcomes. Best-case scenario, he'd infiltrate Vassos's mansion, neutralise Turner as planned, secure the formula, and get out without attracting undue attention. However, he knew that hoping for the best wasn't enough. It was just as crucial to consider the worst-case scenarios and mentally prepare for setbacks.

He envisioned unexpected ambushes, interference from unknown players, equipment failures. In his mind he saw Turner slipping away for good, and Vassos's security teams proving to be more extensive and highly trained than anticipated. This wasn't pessimism but a necessary exercise in realism. By mapping out the full range of possibilities he could devise contingency plans, ensuring that even in the worst situations he had an exit strategy. Each imagined disaster had a countermeasure, a way to pivot and adapt.

The most likely scenario was just that – what ultimately he aimed to navigate. It was what he hoped to achieve with a bit of luck and the wind at his back. There was a lot to consider, but in these contemplative moments he found a semblance of control amidst the chaos. This was how

Beckett turned uncertainty into a tactical advantage. These mental exercises gave him a sense of readiness, a preparedness for whatever lay ahead.

Once finished, he realigned his focus but kept his eyes closed. He could sense Reed's tension in the quickened pace of her breathing, the way she shifted in her seat every few seconds. He opened his eyes and straightened up, taking in the surroundings. The landscape had changed again, with the ocean now visible to his left and, ahead of him, a sweep of green dotted with secluded, upscale residences.

"Good sleep?" Reed asked curtly.

Beckett cleared his throat. "I wasn't asleep, just thinking."

"Well, we're almost there."

As they neared the address, a grand mansion came into view, visible from over a mile away. Perched on Culloden Point on the north side of the peninsula, it was remote, high above sea level, and difficult to approach without being seen. The location had no doubt been chosen by Vassos for these exact reasons. It told Beckett that the Greek was a savvy operator. But of course he already knew that. He was part of The Consortium after all.

"Stop here," Beckett said, indicating a small turnaround at the end of a long road.

Reed hit the brakes, bringing the car to a stop in front of a row of tall trees. "No place else to go anyway," she said. "Looks like it's all private land from here."

Beckett pulled out the map, studying it briefly before looking out across the landscape. Two houses stood in view, their white facades gleaming in the afternoon sun. Both had large bay windows and were surrounded by wide lawns and neatly trimmed hedges. Beyond them, the beach stretched out to meet the choppy waters of the North Atlantic. In the distance, Beckett could still see the top of Vassos's mansion perched on the cliff edge, about half a mile north. Part of the property and garden jutted out over the sea before the land dropped sharply to the water below. That worked in his favour. Following the shoreline and then scaling the cliff would keep him out of sight for most of the approach.

Reed cut the engine. "Vassos will have armed guards up there," she said.

"I'm counting on it. That's why we've got the guns."

"But is it smart to go up there now?" she asked. "Wouldn't it be better to wait here for Turner to show? We could intercept him and…" She trailed off as Beckett narrowed his eyes at the cliff edge.

"I need to get up there. I need to see what's going on."

Reed shifted around to take in the backpacks on the rear seat. "I should come with you."

"Do you want to?"

She glanced at the mansion, then back at the gear. "My orders are to make sure you kill Turner," she murmured, as if reminding herself.

Beckett leaned in closer. "I know. And that's exactly what I'm going to do. I'll take out Turner, Templeton will back off, Amber and I will be left alone, and you'll get a pat on the back. Everyone wins."

Reed nodded, but her expression remained tense. "And Vassos? The formula? What happens with that?"

Beckett paused before answering. "What does Templeton want to happen, Erica?"

She didn't blink, her eyes locked onto his with a fresh intensity. "I don't know."

"Don't you?"

"No. I imagine he wants it secured by the US, by the agency, so their enemies can't get their hands on it."

Beckett nodded slowly, letting the silence linger as he studied her face. "Then that's what will happen."

He had more to say, a lot more, but Bader could show up any minute and there was no time for it now.

"Wait for me here in the car. Don't move," Beckett instructed. "Vassos's place is half a mile from here. I'm going in and out on foot, so keep that in mind. Also from this point on things could get messy. If you hear gunshots, stay put. All being well, that's me dealing with Turner. When that happens, be ready to get us out of here. Fast."

A subtle smile tugged at Reed's lips. "Okay. On it."

Beckett stepped out of the car, the cool coastal air hitting him as he slung his backpack over one shoulder. Without looking back, he set off towards the cliffs.

The surrounding area was still, the only sounds the distant crash of waves and the occasional cry of a seabird. He walked in a straight line for a few hundred yards before veering off behind the first of the two white houses. Once he was out of sight he altered his course, angling towards the water. A glance back confirmed Reed no longer would be able to see him. Good. He didn't want her – or her bosses – knowing of his pre-game preparations.

As he neared the cliffs, Beckett glanced up at the overhang where the mansion loomed, dark and imposing against the sky. From down here it seemed even higher. A thin veil of mist clung to his skin and clothes, the tang of brine filling his nostrils and sharpening his senses. He slowed his pace, carefully picking his way across loose rocks and avoiding the slippery seaweed underfoot. Below, the sea was deep and choppy, waves smashing violently against the jagged rocks.

At the base of the cliff he spotted a rocky alcove slightly above water level. Gripping the rock, he crawled laterally towards it as the sea crashed around him, sending up sprays of saltwater that stung his eyes. Once inside the alcove, he shrugged off his backpack and retrieved the Glock and three magazines, stuffing them into his cargo trousers. He stashed the backpack and its remaining contents deep in a crevice, high enough that any rising tide couldn't get to it. Shoving the Glock into the back of his waistband, he crawled back to drier ground and looked up at the towering cliff face.

Now he was ready.

His plan was risky as hell and could fall apart at any moment. It also relied heavily on luck, which was far from reassuring. But if it worked, it would solve everything. He took a deep breath and rolled his shoulders, feeling the tension ease as he mentally braced himself.

He allowed himself only a moment to think of Amber.

Then he began to climb.

Chapter Forty-Five

Nico Vassos's mansion was a striking modern structure of glass and steel that dominated the landscape, looking down – both literally and figuratively – on the neighbouring properties of the affluent peninsula. Local residents had opposed its construction when he first commissioned it, but as always money and intimidation spoke louder than a group of envious old bastards. Vassos had paid off the relevant officials and got his way. The mansion was built.

Reinforced glass walls on four of the six sides of the house reflected the sun and the vast expanse of the Atlantic Ocean below. The main entrance was flanked by two grand pillars, each intricately carved with scenes from Greek mythology, a nod to the owner's heritage. Inside, every square foot of flooring was made of natural stone, the most expensive choice due to the high costs of excavation, transportation, and installation. The walls were adorned with bold, contemporary paintings in striking colours, and the entire house was filled with custom-made high-end furniture, regardless of whether one piece matched the next.

The cavernous kitchen-diner boasted a double-height ceiling with expansive skylights that bathed the room in natural light. A Sub-Zero refrigerator, a Wolf range with dual ovens, and a sleek Miele dishwasher were flawlessly integrated into custom-built cabinetry. At the centre of the room stood a long, polished mahogany dining table, capable of seating twelve. Above it, exotic pendant lights added a touch of elegance and warmth to the modern, airy space.

On the far side of the open-plan property, a vast lounge stretched out before the floor-to-ceiling glass walls, offering an uninterrupted view of the ocean. Plush leather sofas were arranged around a central fireplace, and a grand piano stood in one corner, although it had never been played or the keys even tinkled.

Two armed guards stood watch on either side of the room, though the mansion's full security detail numbered four. Each man had been handpicked for their loyalty, experience and ruthlessness. Two were former Mossad operatives, another was a Russian who'd been an enforcer for the Vorovskoy crime family, and the last was a Greek named Dimitris, who'd spent his entire career in protection. Dimitris had been with Vassos the longest, serving as both his right-hand man and head of security. His presence was formidable, and his loyalty to Vassos unwavering. He made Vassos feel both safe and powerful in equal measures, not an easy feat to pull off.

Nico Vassos himself was sitting on the edge of the bed in the master bedroom. He was freshly showered, wearing only a towel, but the scent of the local woman who had just left lingered on the sheets. Juliette Foster. She was a married diamond heiress worth a fortune, and an esteemed figure of high society – yet the things he'd had her do this morning still made his skin prickle with excitement as he thought of it.

He finished drying himself and tossed the towel on the floor for the maids before striding into his huge walk-in wardrobe. He liked it in here. Despite its size, the acoustics were clipped and close, offering a rare moment of peace and quiet. He dressed in a pair of tight white boxers, admiring the way they complemented his swarthy skin in the full-length mirror, before picking his favourite zebra-print socks.

But what else to wear for this momentous occasion?

After a moment's thought, he selected a light crimson Armani suit and paired it with a brand-new white t-shirt. Vassos liked to think of himself as a man of contradictions, balancing the formality of his suits with casual touches – like the zebra-print socks, like the plain t-shirt. It signalled to the world that he was confident in himself, and didn't play by the rules. That he was his own man.

And wouldn't they all realise that soon enough?

Opening the top drawer of the built-in dresser, he selected a few pieces from his extensive jewellery collection. A Rolex, an 18-karat Byzantine bracelet for his wrists, and two gold rings – one embedded with a huge ruby for his left hand, and the other with a cluster of diamonds and tiger's eye for his right. He completed his look with a pair of purple velvet Ralph Lauren Alonzo Bullion slippers. Once dressed, he sprayed on a generous amount of cologne and stood in front of the mirror, ensuring everything was perfect.

He ran his hand through his jet-black hair. It had been recently cut short and was already dry from the shower, as was his freshly trimmed beard, sculpted into sharp angles by his personal barber to highlight his features. Despite being forty, Vassos looked a decade younger. His skin was smooth, and his features were sharp and well-defined, a tribute to both good genetics and the dedication of one of the best plastic surgeons Turkey had to offer. He examined his reflection with satisfaction, pleased with the result. He looked good. Sexy and dangerous, the perfect combination. Checking his Rolex, he noted the scientist was due to arrive any minute. A grin spread across his face, his white teeth gleaming.

Showtime, baby!

He left his room and walked into the main living area, where his men were stationed. Dimitris was near the large glass doors leading outside, and approached him immediately.

"Bader's chopper entered our airspace five minutes ago, sir. He should be touching down any moment."

"Thank you." Vassos patted him on the shoulder and, as if on cue, heard the distant thrum of helicopter blades. "Okay everyone, get ready."

The formula was close.

It was happening at last.

He walked over to the bar and poured himself a glass of Macallan 18-year-old whisky. The amber liquid swirled in the glass as he lifted it to his lips, savouring the first sip of the expensive liquor. He drank slowly, imagining himself on a movie screen, relishing the moment. He could have been an actor. He certainly had the looks for it.

At the window he looked out over his vast lawn, spanning the entire north and east sides of the building. The grass was impeccably maintained, a vibrant green blanket extending two hundred feet from the house before ending abruptly at the cliff's edge. A step or two further and you'd be heading swiftly for the ocean or dashed against the rocks below. He could have installed railings, but he preferred the raw proximity to nature, the danger. People talked about coastline erosion due to global warming, but he had time – two hundred feet worth of time, to be precise.

The property's helipad was situated on the east side, a flat, circular area visible from the air but free of the usual markings. Vassos found the standard 'H' rather gauche and incongruent with the ambience of his coastal estate. If the pilot couldn't see where to land, he deserved to end up in the damn sea.

Vassos moved closer to the window, watching as the helicopter crested the horizon and his guards instinctively took their positions. The sight of the approaching chopper sparked a surge of anticipation within him. Bader and his formula were on board, the key to everything. Securing the much-coveted bioweapon would finally give Vassos the leverage he needed to take control of The Consortium. Despite the party line that they were a co-operative network with no leader, everyone knew that was horse shit, and in Vasso's view it was high time for a regime change. The current leadership had grown complacent, sinking too much time, energy and capital into property, casinos, and other semi-legitimate ventures. If nothing changed, the once dynamic and innovative organisation would soon become bloated and obsolete. The heads were too obsessed with money and not power. But what was the point of money without power? Vassos intended to correct that imbalance and restore The Consortium to its roots of dominance and influence.

As the helicopter touched down, Dimitris slid open the large bi-fold doors and Vassos stepped outside. Despite the excitement buzzing beneath the surface, he maintained a stern, neutral expression as the rotors whipped the air around him. He halted a few feet from the chopper as the engine powered down and a slim man wearing designer glasses emerged, clutching a metal briefcase.

"Mr Vassos," the man said, extending his hand. "We meet at last."

"Dr Bader, welcome," Vassos said, shaking his hand with a bit more enthusiasm than intended. "Let us go inside." He gestured to his security team, who flanked them as they entered the mansion. The presence of the guards was more for show than actual protection. Vassos always felt secure up here on the cliff edge – but in order to tempt the mouse to the cheese, so to speak, and put an end to all this dithering and delaying, he had given Bader his word that extra measures would be taken. He wouldn't normally conduct business at home, but needs must, and the assurances that his home was his fortress had at last brought them both here, moments from sealing the deal.

They walked into the main space and stopped, exchanging nods and polite smiles as they sized each other up. Bader wasn't what Vassos had expected. He seemed slightly on edge, but he was far from the nerdy, socially awkward scientist he'd imagined. Instead, Dr Bader was surprisingly suave and hippy chic, dressed in lightly flaring cream trousers and a black turtleneck, a silver chain around his neck, the pendant of which featured an intricate design of a stylised sun and moon. On his feet were a pair of sandals, more Jesus Loves You than biological warfare. But who was Vassos to judge? Each to his own.

"So… you have it?" Vassos asked, his greedy eyes drifting to the briefcase.

"Of course. As arranged." Bader's eyes darted around the room, sharp and vigilant, as if committing every detail to memory.

Vassos offered a reassuring smile. "Relax, my friend. We're up high and well-protected by my team. Everything is good."

Bader nodded, but his grip on the briefcase tightened. "I know I'm a target," he admitted, a slight tremor in his voice. "I've hired a team of mercenaries to watch my back, as have your people, I'm told. But this… this is hot property. It's world-changing."

Vassos made a deliberate show of relaxing his posture, resisting the urge to snatch the briefcase right then and there. Knowing he was this close to the formula was almost intoxicating.

"Come," he said, guiding the scientist over to the bar. "We'll have a drink, then we can talk business."

He glanced at Dimitris, a silent message passing between them. Vassos had originally planned to strong-arm Bader into lowering the price, but seeing how sharp and guarded the man was, he realised that approach might backfire. Despite the getup, Bader didn't seem easily intimidated, and his reticence suggested he knew exactly how valuable the formula was.

Sure, Vassos could have his men snatch the briefcase and dispose of Bader in the sea, but he was a businessman first and foremost and that wasn't how these things worked. Besides, Bader might have more valuable inventions up his sleeve, and what was a billion dollars between future allies? He could certainly afford it, and the potential of what this formula could bring was worth every cent. With it, he wouldn't just control The Consortium – he'd have the entire world at his feet. Governments, countries, entire continents, they would all bow to their new leader: Nico Vassos.

Yes, he reassured himself, as he reached for the bottle of Macallan, it was more than worth it.

Chapter Forty-Six

Beckett crouched low in the undergrowth bordering the south side of Vassos's estate. The tall grass and leafy canopy provided adequate cover, but he remained perfectly still, knowing even the slightest movement could betray his position. Leaves brushed against his face as he settled into a comfortable crouch. From this vantage point he had a clear line of sight to the glass-fronted interior, the late afternoon sun reflected off the pristine windows, obscuring much of what was going on inside. He'd counted four armed guards so far, but knew there could be more out of sight.

A well-kept, simple garden bordered the north side of the property; beyond which the land dropped off sharply, a sheer cliff that jutted out over the ocean – the same overhang he'd observed from below. The distant sounds of birds and crashing waves were just audible beneath the rhythmic hum of helicopter blades winding down.

Up close, Vassos's summer house looked even more out of place, its sleek design and modern architecture clashing with the surrounding natural beauty. Despite its fortress-like appearance – albeit a fortress of luxury – the expansive open spaces and glass walls posed significant security vulnerabilities. Vulnerabilities Beckett hoped to exploit.

He was on high alert now, in full-on soldier mode, feeling not thinking, every sense heightened, instincts razor-sharp. His attention flicked from the armed men in the front room to the mansion's entrance, to the garden, then to the helipad stationed precariously near the cliff's edge. Each man was analysed, and every exit and entrance point catalogued. His mind was quiet, his body relaxed, yet ready to spring into action at a moment's notice. This was his prime operating mode, where every detail mattered and every second counted. He took slow, measured breaths, keeping his heart rate steady. There would be no room for mistakes.

Security was tight, as expected. Two of the guards had now moved out into the garden, leaving one inside and another whose whereabouts was currently unknown – possibly stationed at the front entrance. They each had an assault rifle slung over their shoulders and held at waist height, relaxed but alert.

The guards took up positions on either side of a set of bi-fold glass doors. Moments later, two men emerged from the house. Beckett hadn't seen photos of Nico Vassos, but he assumed the man in the crimson suit was him. The other, dressed sharply in black and cream, was unmistakably Dr Adram Bader.

Both men were sipping from heavy-bottomed tumblers and appeared relaxed – confident, even. But then it was easy to feel that way with an armed security team hovering nearby. Beckett observed the two men closely. Vassos and Bader were acting like old friends shooting the breeze rather than criminal masterminds plotting the potential demise of civilisation. The sight made his stomach churn, but he shoved the feeling aside. This wasn't the time for emotion, only action. But not yet. Not until everything was in place.

The chopper had fallen silent, its blades gradually slowing to a stop. From his vantage point, Beckett could only see the tail, but he assumed the pilot was still on board. Something to keep in mind. The pilot might be part of Vassos's crew, but he could just as easily be an innocent local hire, unaware of what he'd just set in motion by bringing Bader here.

Beckett stayed put, his attention shifting from one zone to another, from one face to the next, maintaining sharp situational awareness as he pieced together a comprehensive picture of his surroundings. Bader and Vassos were still talking, with Vassos laughing zealously at something Bader had said. Beckett slowly rolled his neck from side to side, stretching the tendons to keep them from stiffening. Then he froze. Movement. To his left, on the northwest side of the property, in a patch of tall grass. He squinted, focusing, not surprised but not relieved either when he recognised Saul Turner. Turner was hidden from view of those in the garden, crouched behind a three-foot ha-ha wall that formed a boundary line on the west side of the property. He was carrying a rifle but hadn't yet lined up a clear shot.

Beckett tensed, waiting.

First nothing happens. Then everything happens all at once.

Every muscle in his body was coiled with anticipation as he watched Turner rise up on one knee, staying concealed behind the wall as he prepped his shot, the rifle snug against his shoulder.

Then, all at once Turner froze. He'd sensed something, perhaps a flicker of motion in his peripheral vision. Beckett stayed perfectly still as Turner slowly turned his head and locked eyes with him. Neither of them moved, but their expressions spoke volumes, a silent acknowledgement passing between them, a shared understanding.

Or so Beckett thought, until Turner shifted his aim directly at him.

Okay...

Beckett lowered his chin, meeting Turner's gaze through the scope. He remained still. He didn't blink.

Don't do it, Turner.

Think of your mission.

Seconds passed that felt like hours before Turner lowered the rifle and returned his attention to Bader. Beckett released the breath he'd been holding and did the same. Vassos and the scientist had moved to the far edge of the property and were now partially obscured by foliage. Turner adjusted his scope, rising slightly to get a better angle. The top of his head was now visible to the security team. He was taking a big risk.

Beckett held his nerve, knowing he had to play this just right. Three things needed to happen, but they had to happen in the right order. The problem was, the first move wasn't his to make.

He waited, his focus shifting between Bader and Turner, alert for the slightest hint of movement. His breathing was controlled, his gaze unwavering. The margin between success and failure was razor-thin, and while Beckett wasn't much of a gambler, he hoped today Lady Luck was on his side.

Vassos and Bader circled back around the house, stopping in the centre of the garden in front of the bi-fold doors. Beckett's instincts told him they were about to head inside. He tensed, shifting his attention back to Turner, who was now ready to take his shot. Beckett rocked forward slightly, reaching back to ease the Glock from his waistband.

Time slowed to a crawl, then seemed to stop altogether. Turner held his position. Everything was still. The noise of the world faded away, leaving only the tunnel vision of his focus.

This was it.

Five, four, three...

He reached two before a sonic crack split the air and Bader's head snapped to the side in a burst of red mist. It felt as if it happened in slow motion, the scene unfolding with surreal clarity. Then everything sped up. Then all hell broke loose.

First nothing happens. Then everything happens all at once.

Chapter Forty-Seven

Beckett watched as Bader's body collapsed against Vassos before crumpling to the ground. For a moment the Greek just stood there, eyes wide, struggling to make sense of this sudden, violent disruption. Then he peered down at the blood and brain matter splattered across his white top. Then he screamed.

Instantly his security team snapped into action, their casual postures vanishing in a flurry of coordinated movement. Barked commands cut through the chaos, panic lacing their voices as two of the guards rushed forward, unleashing a hail of gunfire towards the shooter. Turner, now shielded behind the ha-ha wall, drew his pistol and returned fire.

Meanwhile, the other two guards closed ranks around Vassos, forming a protective huddle. They moved quickly, scanning the vicinity for additional threats as they hustled him inside the mansion.

Good. That's what Beckett had hoped would happen.

Seizing the opportunity he sprang to his feet, staying low

as he moved along the perimeter, using the chaos around him as cover. His eyes darted across the scene, assessing the guards' positions and Turner's line of fire. He had to close the distance and find a vantage point where he could effectively engage Turner without exposing himself.

Vassos's once tranquil country estate had transformed into a warzone, the coastal calm shattered by gunfire and violence. Turner and the remaining guards continued to trade bullets as Beckett inched nearer. A single precise headshot from Turner dropped one of the guards, but it only made his comrade more determined as he stepped forward, unleashing a wild spray of bullets over Turner's head.

Keeping his head down, Turner hurried along the edge of the ha-ha wall, then sprang up ten feet to the guard's left, dropping him with another well-placed headshot. Now Turner saw his chance to escape. But up here his options were limited – a steep drop to one side and Beckett closing in fast from the other. His only other option was to move closer to the house and escape via the garden.

At least, that was what Beckett was counting on.

He stayed on Turner's heels, firing a few wide shots to keep the American off balance. Turner stumbled but kept moving, firing blindly over his shoulder. Beckett ducked behind a tree as the bullets zipped past but they were wild and desperate, not even close to being a real threat. He took a moment to steady his aim, then fired again – this time with precision – not to hit Turner, but to drive him towards the garden. As Turner veered right, two shots ricocheted off the perimeter wall forcing him left. Beckett closed the gap as Turner ran, but the cliff's edge loomed ahead. Turner was out of options. Beckett glanced at Bader's lifeless body sprawled on the grass, the suitcase still clutched in his hand.

It was all still to play for. But now it was time to play his trump card.

With nowhere to go, the American turned and raised his gun. Beckett stopped and mirrored him, keeping his aim high. They were now just forty feet apart.

"Drop it!" Beckett hissed.

"You drop it!"

"Come on, Turner. It's over."

"You idiot. You're the damn traitor."

Beckett shrugged. "They've got my niece. I'm sorry. But I can make it okay. Just don't shoot."

It was a classic Mexican standoff. Both men with their fingers tight on their triggers, hearts pounding. The air was electric, tension crackling between them. Beckett was all in now, betting everything on these next few moments. He just had to hope it paid off.

"I'll kill you," Turner spat.

"You think you're faster than me?"

"Let's find out."

Neither of them moved.

"Then what?" Beckett asked.

"Then I'll retrieve the formula," Turner replied, his eyes narrowing with determination. "I'll complete my mission."

"No. It's over. But I can help you."

"I don't need your help," Turner growled, his trigger finger twitching.

Hold your ground, John.

The world around him faded, leaving only the two of them. He tightened his grip on the pistol, shifting his aim ever so slightly. Then he waited.

Suddenly shouts erupted from the direction of the mansion, followed by gunshots. Beckett didn't flinch, but the noise drew Turner's attention. It was only for a split second.

Less than that. But it was all Beckett needed. In that brief moment of distraction, he squeezed the trigger. The shot rang out, the echo numbing his senses as blood burst from Turner's chest. He staggered, trying to aim, but Beckett fired again, the second shot tearing into the American's right shoulder. Turner stumbled backwards, his eyes widening with panic as his feet lost their grip on the cliff's edge. He flailed desperately, trying to regain balance, but it was no use. He cried out, grabbing at the air.

Then he disappeared over the side of the cliff.

Chapter Forty-Eight

Beckett stood facing the ocean, raising his hands as Vassos's security team closed in, their boots pounding the grassy terrain behind him.

"Drop your weapon!"

"Turn around – slow!"

One of the guards yanked the gun from his hand and roughly spun him around, shoving a rifle muzzle in his face.

"Don't shoot. I'm an ally." Beckett kept his hands up, his expression calm and open.

"Who the hell are you?"

Only two guards remained, both with their guns trained on him. One had a shaved head and pale blue eyes. The other was tall, with dark skin and hair, and could have been Greek, like Vassos. Both were mean-looking. Beckett kept his hands up, palms facing outward in a calm show of surrender. He could see the guards were wired and full of adrenaline, just itching for a reason to take him down. He glanced past them as Vassos approached, moving once more with the assurance of someone used to being in control. Easy enough when you had two armed guards flanking you.

"Who are you?" Vassos demanded as he got closer. "And who was that man you killed?"

"They're working together," one of the guards spat.

"No. We're not," Beckett shot back, eyes fixed on Vassos. "I eliminated him. I saved your life. That's why I'm here."

Vassos frowned. "You saved my life? Why? I don't know you."

"I work for the same people as you," Beckett said.

"I don't work for anyone!"

Shit. Bad choice of words.

"Apologies. What I mean is, there are certain... people who want this trade to go down without a hitch. They hired me."

Vassos stared at Beckett as his guards adjusted their weapons, awaiting their boss's signal.

"What do you mean?" Vassos asked. "Who hired you?"

"I'm a mercenary," Beckett replied. "A hired gun. The man I just shot was a CIA operative named Saul Turner. My mission was to kill him before he got to Dr Bader." He lowered his head, adopting a grave expression. "I'm sorry, Mr Vassos, sir. I failed you in that. But he's dead, and you're still alive. In that I succeeded."

Vassos's eyes narrowed. The conflict playing out across his face moved from anger and confusion to worry, then reluctant understanding. Beckett knew his story made sense, now he needed Vassos to believe it. He had to sell it hard.

"That man was prepared to do anything to stop you from getting Bader's formula," he continued. "I apologise you weren't in the loop, that you didn't know about him or me. That was an oversight. But he's no longer a threat to you."

"No one is a threat to me," Vassos boomed. "Not some CIA prick. Not you."

He was putting on a front, but the bravado barely masked the uncertainty in his eyes. One of his men leaned in and whispered something in his ear, glaring suspiciously at Beckett as he did. The other guard remained on edge, finger tense on the trigger of his AM-17.

Beckett held his nerve, keeping his expression neutral. "Call Xander Templeton," he said.

"Who?"

"Your colleagues will know him. He's their man on the inside. The Consortium's mole in the CIA."

At the mention of both C-words, something clicked for Vassos. His stance relaxed slightly and he stepped forward, studying Beckett up close. Beside him the guards shifted uneasily, their attention flicking between the two men. Seconds ticked by. No one spoke. Beckett was getting pins and needles in his hands from holding them up.

"All right. Let's go inside," Vassos said finally, jerking his chin towards the house. "Looks like we've got some shit to work out."

The guards tightened their formation around Beckett, weapons still trained on him as they moved across the grass in a tight unit. Things had gone his way so far but Beckett remained hyperalert, already planning his next move and the one after that. There were still too many variables in play, but he was confident he could steer this his way once they got inside and Vassos lowered his defences a bit more.

Except they didn't make it to the house. Halfway across the lawn Vassos paused beside Bader's fallen body, prompting one of the guards to grab Beckett's arm, yanking him to a stop. He looked down at the dead scientist. Turner's hit had been textbook – a headshot right in the T-zone, the bullet entering through the philtrum beneath the nose. A .308 Winchester round would have shattered the upper jaw and obliterated the brainstem. Instant kill. Blood pooled around Bader's skull, soaking into the once vibrant green grass, turning it the same deep red as Vassos's suit.

"I should have acted sooner," Beckett said. "He should never have been allowed to take that shot."

Vassos turned on him, jabbing a finger in his face. "You were hired by someone in my network?"

Beckett held his gaze. "Yes. To protect you. To guarantee the trade."

"I can make a call," Vassos said. "Find out for sure."

Beckett didn't flinch. "Please, go ahead. Ask them what you need to do now. Let's get this sorted."

Vassos glared at him for a few more seconds, then a grin spread across his face. "No. It's fine. I get it."

Beckett raised his head, allowing himself a moment of relief.

Ask them what you need to do now. Those words had been carefully chosen, subtly implying that Vassos needed to ask permission, that he wasn't his own man. It was a gamble, one that played on the billionaire's ego, and it had paid off.

"What's your name?" Vassos asked.

"Michael Day," Beckett replied without missing a beat. He kept his head up, not allowing himself to become complacent. He might have bought himself some time, but the situation was still precarious, and he was unsure where the chips would fall.

"Well, it is good to meet you, Day," Vassos said, letting out a rough laugh, the kind shaped by too many cigars and too much liquor. "You might've just saved me a billion dollars, you know that?" He gestured at Bader's briefcase.

Beckett nodded, mentally spinning plates as he tried to fit all the moving parts together. If Vassos got his hands on the doomsday formula, everything Beckett had done would be for nothing. He hesitated, an idea coming to him.

"Well done, sir," he said, adopting an admiring, almost subservient tone. "You did it. You got the formula."

He glanced around. The guards still had their rifles aimed his way, but Vassos wasn't making any move to claim the briefcase. Beckett pointed at it. "Would you allow me?"

Vassos stuck out his lip and nodded. Beckett knelt beside Bader, leaning over the dead man for a moment as if inspecting him closely.

"This prick's been a tricky bastard to find, but I guess it worked out okay in the end," he said, shifting to a gruffer tone now, mimicking the countless mercenaries he'd encountered over the years. It was wrong, even dangerous, to generalise, but most of them shared that same brusque, detached way of speaking, devoid of humour. "Some crazy scientist, huh? But we got what we needed from him." He patted Bader's chest, then picked up the briefcase, wrestling it from the dead man's grip.

"Here you go." He stood and handed the briefcase to Vassos.

"Excellent." Vassos held up the metal case, eyeing it greedily, almost salivating. "And without spending a dollar," he said, as if this was the ultimate win. He looked at Beckett. "Do you do a lot of this sort of work?"

"I do what I'm paid to do. And I'm very good at it."

Vassos raised his eyebrows. "You want a job? A real job? I'm being serious. I'm a couple of men down, as you can see, and I pay well."

Beckett smiled, though his instincts were screaming at him, red flags going up all over the place. He'd caught something out of the corner of his eye – movement inside the house. Vassos, oblivious to the shift in atmosphere, gave him a hearty slap on the back.

"Think about it," he said. "But for now let's get a drink and celebrate."

The guards began to lower their weapons, ready to move. But as they turned they stopped abruptly, and so did Beckett.

Reed stood in the doorway, Glock aimed squarely at Vassos's head. Beckett faced her, trying to meet her eye, but she refused to look at him.

"Give me the formula," she said. "Now. Or I'll kill you all."

Chapter Forty-Nine

The security guards instinctively raised their rifles. But due to their proximity to Vassos and their at-ease stance, they had to step aside and twist their bodies to get a clear shot. This movement took them all of half a second. In that brief window Reed flicked her aim left and right, dropping them both with precise headshots. They were dead before they realised what had happened.

Beckett watched, stunned. He had no idea Reed could shoot like that. But something told him there were a lot of things he didn't know about Erica Reed.

"What the fuck?!" Vassos yelled, trying to dance out of the way as his men fell around him. His suit and white t-shirt were now covered in blood – though at this point, his dry cleaning bill was the least of his worries. His eyes darted wildly as he struggled to process the sudden turn of events. His hands trembled as he wiped the blood from his eyes.

"Who the hell do you think you are?" he snarled, terror quickly giving way to anger. "Do you not know who I am? Who my associates are? You'll never get away with this—"

Another gunshot cut his rant short. Beckett felt the warm spray on his face, and a second later Vassos collapsed beside his men, the back of his head blown out in a grisly mess of blood and bone.

"Idiot," Reed spat, shifting her aim to Beckett as she advanced.

He said nothing. Just slowly raised his hands. No sudden movements.

"So here we are," she said. "Just me, you, and the formula."

"So it appears," Beckett replied. "And what a lovely setting for it."

She sneered at his attempt at humour, then frowned. "You don't look shocked."

"I'm not. I was expecting this. Almost counting on it."

She tilted her head slightly. "You were expecting it?"

"I was about eighty percent sure. Not at first, but as time went on it became clear there were other factors at play. You covered your tracks well. Nothing obvious, nothing specific. All I had was hunches. But in my world, hunches pay off. Then in the car earlier you slipped up. You said *their* enemies, talking about the agency and the US like you weren't part of it all. A loyal officer – a real patriot – would've said *our* enemies."

Reed flinched; at her own mistake, perhaps. "So why didn't you do something?"

"Because I was expecting it to play out a little differently. And because I wasn't fully convinced they'd got to you, still had that twenty percent doubt. But now... here we are. You're working for them, I presume. The Consortium."

Reed curled her lip, her features sharpening, her expression growing colder. "I'm working for myself," she said. "But yes, they're paying me."

Beckett kept his hands up as she circled him, the Glock steady in her grip. "But it's not about the money, is it?" he said. "For you this is about revenge."

She stopped in front of him, her eyebrows lifting slightly, a hint of surprise on her face. "You're good."

"I wouldn't still be breathing if I wasn't."

She knelt to run a hand down his calves, the gun in her other hand never wavering.

"Don't worry, I'm unarmed," he said. "You're the one holding all the cards."

She stood and shook her head. "You think you know me? You think you really know what's going on here?"

"I'm guessing something happened in the Marines," Beckett continued. "That's why you left. Someone hurt you. Maybe… worse. And your unit looked after themselves instead of you."

Her shoulders stiffened.

So he was close.

She glared at him, her eyes hard as steel. "I hate this country. I hate its government and its military – every last one of them. I want them to pay for what they did to me. They used me and tossed me aside like a rag doll."

A single angry tear threatened, but she made no move to wipe it away. Her jaw clenched, her grip on the gun tightened as she fought to stay in control.

"But those bastards are going to pay. All of them."

"If you give The Consortium that formula, then it's over," Beckett said. "The world will change overnight – and not for the better. Even if they don't use it to annihilate their enemies – or wipe out entire countries they feel are a drain on resources – just having it will make them untouchable. We won't be able to stop them, contain them, or even negotiate with them."

He waited for her to respond but she just glared at him.

"Is that what you want, Erica?" he asked gently. "Because I don't think it is. It wasn't right or fair what happened to you. But you're a good person. I see it. You don't have to do this. I'll vouch for you. We'll get the formula to the right people who can safeguard it. No one has to—"

"Enough!" she screamed, tears streaming now down her face, her voice on the edge of hysteria. "Enough with the talking, Beckett. My mind's made up. I'm doing this."

She pressed the gun against his forehead, her teeth clenched in fierce determination. Beckett remained still, watching her intently, studying every twitch. Would she pull the trigger? His instincts said no, but a little more reassurance wouldn't hurt.

The seconds stretched out, the tension between them straining to breaking point. Then with a frustrated scream Reed stepped back, keeping the gun on him as she reached down to snatch the briefcase from Vassos.

"Don't follow me," she said. "I know you think you can save the world – men like you always do – but it's over. Let it go."

Beckett didn't reply. Just watched her as she backed away.

"I mean it," she yelled. "Don't do anything stupid. Just walk away. Live your life."

She moved towards the helicopter, and they both noticed at the same moment that the pilot had vanished. That settled the question of his involvement. If he was just an innocent bystander, who could blame the guy for getting out while he could? They both hesitated, but then Reed continued on her way, climbing into the cockpit and firing up the engine. As the rotor blades began to spin, she looked up and locked eyes with him.

Of course.

She'd mentioned when they first met that she'd flown UH-1Ys – Venom utility helicopters, used for transport, reconnaissance, and close air support.

Beckett lowered his hands, eyeing the array of guns scattered across the lawn. He could try to take her out, but this way there was still a chance it could play out in his favour. Another big gamble, but what else was new? His entire plan had been one long shot after another.

He stood his ground as the chopper lifted off, the rotors whipping the air into a furious downdraft. Reed manoeuvred over the ocean, holding the helicopter steady about ten feet in front of him as they stared at each other, neither willing to break eye contact. Reed looked like she wanted to smile but didn't. Beckett didn't either. Then she banked away from the property and accelerated away.

Beckett didn't move, watching until the chopper vanished from sight. Then he walked to the cliff's edge. Reed had shown her hand, and now he was ready to play the ace up his sleeve. He took a deep breath, the salty air filling his lungs.

It was time to finish this.

Chapter Fifty

Beckett raced down the side of the cliff as fast as the terrain would allow. The ground was loose and treacherous, with rocks shifting beneath his feet, threatening to send him plummeting into the ocean below. He nearly lost his footing twice but managed to recover, grabbing onto jutting rocks and clumps of coarse mountain grass to steady himself. It had taken him close to twenty minutes to scale the cliff earlier, but now he was already halfway down, the descent feeling like it had taken no time at all. He navigated around jagged rocks and scuffed down a sharp incline, dropping onto his haunches for balance as he scanned the landscape below. He just hoped this part of the plan had gone off as intended.

Reaching the bottom he paused, taking in his surroundings. The sea was choppy, with waves angrily smacking against the rocks. He cast his awareness further, searching for a sign, for anything at all. But there was nothing. His heart sank. Had he screwed up? He moved further along the jagged shoreline, stepping tentatively on rocks slick with seawater as he scanned the horizon for signs of life.

Just as despair began to take hold, he spotted something in the water – a dark shape, a figure floating just beyond the rocks. Without hesitation he dove in, the icy water jolting his senses but invigorating him as he swam towards what he hoped was... Yes. As he got closer he saw it was Turner. Even better, he was alive and conscious, but only barely by the looks of it.

"Turner, it's me. Hang on, I've got you."

Beckett circled behind the American, securing him in a rescue hold – one arm hooked under his armpit and across his chest, the other cradling his head. Battling the relentless waves and surging currents, he swam them both back to the relative safety of the alcove he'd discovered earlier.

Once there, Beckett dragged Turner onto a rocky ledge just big enough for the two of them. Turner instinctively tried to lie flat, but Beckett propped him up, ensuring he was stable before checking him over.

"We're good," Beckett assured him. "That was a hell of a fall, but you're okay. You'll live."

"You shot me," Turner groaned. "You tried to kill me."

"If I wanted you dead we wouldn't be having this conversation," Beckett replied, relieved to find two clean exit wounds as he inspected Turner's injuries. "And I had good reason to shoot you."

"Huh?"

Beckett gently guided Turner onto his back. "I need to take a closer look at you," he told him.

Turner's shirt was already torn at the collar, so Beckett used the tear to rip it open, exposing two almost perfect circles of singed, puckered flesh – one in the upper chest, the other in the shoulder. Neither shot was fatal, just as Beckett had intended.

"Good thing you're a lousy shot," Turner muttered.

Beckett allowed himself a brief grin. The American was disoriented and would need proper medical attention in the coming days, but he was alive. It had been touch and go up there, but Beckett was confident he'd staged the shooting convincingly enough to fool any onlookers. He'd done what Templeton asked of him. Amber was safe.

Turner lifted his head, his breaths shallow and laboured as he took in the sight of his torn and bruised torso.

"You're going to be fine," Beckett said. "The seawater's already done a decent job of cleaning the wounds. Now I'll patch you up enough to get you out of here."

Turner studied his injuries, then nodded in agreement. Beckett stepped away for a moment, scaling the side of the alcove to retrieve the backpack he'd stashed in a crevice. Returning to Turner's side, he unzipped the top compartment, pulling out the two packs of TraumaMend dressing. Ripping one open, he quickly unravelled the contents and set to work on Turner's wounds.

Beckett had used TraumaMend countless times before, though mostly on himself. Designed for managing severe bleeding, it was also effective on deep lacerations and puncture wounds. The dressing contained blood clotting agents and an integrated pressure bandage to control bleeding, perfect for men like him and Turner who lived the lives they did.

Beckett worked quickly, applying the dressing to the wounds and pressing down until the bleeding slowed and the pressure bandage took hold. Once finished, he helped Turner sit up before retrieving a bottle of water from his backpack's side pocket and handing it to him. Turner drank deeply, then let out a soft belch, momentarily shedding his hard, robotic demeanour.

"What happened after I fell?" he asked.

Beckett filled him in on events, detailing Vassos's death and Reed's betrayal. Turner listened in silence, absorbing everything, his expression shifting between anger and reluctant acceptance. When Beckett finished, Turner was quiet for a long time, sipping water and muttering under his breath. The anger was there, but it was a cold, focused rage, the kind that simmered deep, directed inward at what he saw as his own failure.

Beckett stared out to sea, mentally calculating the tide, current, and roughness of the water.

"So what now?" Turner asked. "What about The Consortium, the doomsday formula?"

"Don't worry about any of that," Beckett replied. "I'll handle it. Your priority is to disappear; otherwise, all of this would be for nothing."

"What do you mean?"

"I mean Reed and The Consortium believe you're dead. They won't be coming after you." Beckett smiled. "You're free."

"Oh yeah?" Turner's lips twitched. It might have been a smile. "Free like you are?"

Beckett shrugged. "Yeah, just like me." But Turner had a point. Maybe there was no such thing as freedom for people like them.

"And how do I get away?" Turner asked. "I can't just stroll back into town. These people have eyes everywhere. If I'm seen, all this is still for nothing."

"Agreed," Beckett said. "But I've already thought of that."

He opened the main body of the backpack and pulled

out the foldable canoe he'd picked up from the Army and Navy store. "Pretty good, huh?" he said.

Turner looked sceptical.

"Well, the clerk was more excited than that," Beckett continued. "It's cutting edge. Nothing else like it on the market. MI6 has been testing prototypes of something similar, but this is the first time I've seen anything like it available to the public."

Turner looked out across the sea, the plan dawning on him. But he didn't seem fazed.

"It only weighs nine pounds," Beckett added, as he began to assemble it, keeping Turner engaged and alert. "The frame is carbon fibre, and the hull's made from aramid – the same stuff they use in bike tyres and body armour. The main structure is built from these telescopic poles, and the paddle is made from two more of the same. The seat hangs from a cross brace."

Turner didn't respond, just watched with calm detachment as Beckett fitted the pieces together. It took less than five minutes to assemble, though it would've been much quicker if he weren't knee-deep in surf, bracing himself against slippery, jagged rocks. When he finished, he stepped back to admire his handiwork. The canoe looked sturdy enough and even pretty comfortable.

"If you want to stay dead, this is how we do it," Beckett said, handing Turner the paddle. "It'll take you about six hours to row north-west to Orient Point, maybe seven given your injuries and this paddle. But the current and wind are in your favour, so you'll be fine. Lie low for a few hours, then catch the first Cross Sound Ferry to New London in the morning."

"Right," Turner said, sounding only a little daunted.

"And take this." Beckett handed him the backpack.

"There's a compass, two hundred dollars and some supplies inside. It's not much, but it'll get you started. A resourceful chap like you, you'll manage." He smiled. It was going to be a tough couple of days for the American, but he was a tough customer and this was their best option.

Turner knew it too. "I guess I should get going then," he said.

"No time like the present." Beckett squinted up at the cliff top. "The Consortium will be sending a clean-up crew once they find out what happened. We both need to be long gone by then."

Turner nodded, glancing out to sea. "Looks pretty rough out there."

"That works in your favour too. They'll think the current swept you out to sea and won't waste time looking for a body."

"What about you?" Turner asked.

"I'll keep my head down," he replied, glancing in the direction of New York. "I'll wade up the coast for a mile or so then make my way back to the city."

"Okay, so..." Turner cleared his throat. "Thank you, I guess."

They stared at each other, nodding awkwardly. No smiles, just a mutual understanding.

Beckett helped Turner push the canoe into open water and climb aboard. He winced slightly as he settled into the seat, but otherwise he was ready to go.

"What do I do next?" he called out, as Beckett made his way back to the rocks. "When I get to New London, I mean. Who am I? Where do I go?"

"Speaking from experience," Beckett called back, "I'd say don't overthink it. Deal with things as they come. One day at a time." He cringed inwardly at the banality of his advice, but Turner seemed to take some comfort in it.

"And no going back," Turner said, almost to himself.

Beckett forced a smile. "In this life sometimes you have to take a bullet to the past. But that paves the way for something new." And from what he'd seen, Turner didn't have much of a past worth holding onto. No family. No loved ones. An odd guy. But a good one, in the end.

The sea buffeted the canoe, pushing it further out, but Turner used the paddle to steady himself. "And the formula?" he asked. "Can you guarantee it's safe?"

"Don't worry," Beckett replied. "It's taken care of."

"For certain?"

"You have my word. I'll handle it."

Beckett watched as Turner paddled away, waiting until he was nothing more than a speck on the horizon before turning towards the shore. It was time for him to get out of here too. There was still unfinished business that needed his attention.

Chapter Fifty-One

The warehouse basement was as cold and unwelcoming as the steel that encased it. Thick brushed metal panels covered every surface, with large rivets punctuating the sheets, giving the space a grim industrial feel. A faint breeze whispered through the room, carrying with it the low hum of machinery. Yet all Reed could see was the metal table in front of her as she stood alone in the centre of the room.

She'd flown directly from Montauk to this desolate warehouse at the edge of Breezy Point, Queens, touching down on a patch of grass near Rockaway Point and hurrying the rest of the way on foot. Despite being summoned here, there had been no one to meet her. There was just an intercom, a heavy steel door that opened on her approach, a dark corridor, and a stairwell leading down. The isolation and lack of human contact only heightened her anxiety. Every sound was amplified, leaving her nerves frayed and her senses razor-sharp as she waited.

Suddenly a voice boomed out from an unseen speaker,

echoing through the space. "Ms Reed, welcome. Do you have the formula?"

She placed the briefcase on the table with a sense of finality. "It's in here. I haven't been able to get it open yet. It's a special fastening, and I thought you'd want to do the honours." She forced a smile as she shoved the briefcase forward. A slight tremor in her hand betrayed her, but she quickly steadied it. These were dangerous people, and this was her first assignment with them. The last thing she wanted was to show weakness.

The voice crackled over the speaker. "Is the SAC operative Saul Turner dead?"

"Yes," Reed replied. She'd been in Vassos's front room when it happened, after letting herself in using a set of skeleton keys. She'd seen Beckett pull the trigger and watched Turner fall. "He's no longer a problem."

"Very good. We are pleased."

The voice was different from the one she was used to – her handler, who had gone by the name Zed, or just Z. From what she knew of these people, there was likely an A, and a B – and a whole alphabet of operatives – acting as disembodied voices in spaces like this all across the globe. Always with the theatrics, always referring to themselves with the royal 'we'.

Standing alone in the cold metallic room, Reed felt a wave of self-consciousness wash over her. Talking to a faceless voice made the situation feel even more incongruous – as if she were part of a live-action video game with no clear objective but the highest of stakes. Yet despite the strangeness of it all, she felt a swell of pride. She had accomplished what she set out to do.

Hadn't she?

She'd got her revenge on a world that had wronged her. She'd shown America's military-industrial complex that they couldn't just discard people when they became inconvenient.

Hadn't she?

"Is there a problem, Ms Reed?" the voice asked, cutting through her thoughts.

She straightened, adopting a stern expression. "Not at all," she replied. "So what now? I did everything you asked of me."

The Consortium had anticipated Vassos's betrayal, knowing he intended to keep the formula for himself and seize control. Hence they'd maintained close contact with Reed since her initial recruitment and had summoned her multiple times over the past week. Each time, it was just a text message with a single letter: Z; her cue to call in on the secure phone they'd provided.

It seemed almost absurd now, thinking back to how it had all started with a random email to her personal account. She'd been recruited by these people, risked her life and career for them, yet she'd never met a single member of The Consortium in the flesh. There was Vassos, of course, but by the time she came on board he was already a traitor – a persona non grata. Now, here she was, speaking to yet another faceless voice in a bare, steel room. The whole situation was surreal, but none of that mattered anymore. She'd done what needed to be done. She'd exacted her revenge on a world that had taken so much from her.

Yet so far the satisfaction felt a little hollow, to say the least. Still, it was something. A temporary bandage for old wounds that might some day eradicate the scars,

"What about John Beckett?" the voice asked.

Reed stiffened, her mind racing. *What to tell them?* "He got away, I'm afraid. But I'm confident he's no longer a problem, either. We won't hear from him again."

Not killing Beckett had been a mistake perhaps, but in the moment she couldn't bring herself to pull the trigger. He wasn't a monster. The men who'd attacked her were the monsters. Beckett was different. He was a good man in a bad world. He knew, or at least had an idea, of what she'd endured, and she hoped that would work to her advantage. He wouldn't come after her, and if he had any sense he'd disappear for good.

The door behind her swung open. Reed spun around as two men entered the room, both over six feet tall, their broad shoulders and muscular builds accentuated by impeccably tailored black suits. The first man had close-cropped blond hair, icy blue eyes, and a square jaw that gave him a stern, almost Germanic appearance. The second man, slightly shorter but equally imposing, had black hair slicked back, dark piercing eyes, and a rugged, chiselled face. Their expressions were blank, radiating cold professionalism.

They didn't acknowledge Reed, but something told her they weren't part of the inner circle – just hired muscle. They carried specialised tools, including what looked like a compact laser cutter, and a set of precision screwdrivers. She stepped back as they set about the lock with the efficiency of men who had done this a thousand times. In under a minute the briefcase was open. The blond one lifted it off the table and silently presented the contents to the wall.

"What is this?" the voice boomed. "Reed?"

She circled the table, her heart pounding, and peered

into the briefcase. Her stomach dropped. Inside were two protein bars and a phone charger. No formula, no documents – nothing of value.

Panic surged. "What? Where's the..." she stammered, her mind a tangle of thoughts, none of them useful, most of them dark. "But I saw... He..."

"Ms Reed, is this a joke?" the voice asked, colder now, with a sharp edge to it.

"No, no joke," she replied, her voice shaking. "Bader was carrying it. He was..."

She snatched the briefcase from the man and placed it back on the table, her hands trembling uncontrollably. Frantic, she tore through the contents, lifting out the protein bars and phone charger, desperately feeling for a false bottom or hidden compartments. There were none. The briefcase was empty. "What the fuck!"

"You have failed us, Ms Reed. This will not do. This will not do at all," the voice boomed, each word like a hammer to her guts.

She turned and faced the wall, eyes wide with fear. "Please, no," she pleaded. "There must be some mistake. I did everything you asked. Please give me another chance." Her voice wavered, the icy grip of fear tightening around her throat. Her thoughts were a chaotic, frenzied swirl.

"Take her away," the voice ordered.

The men moved in, grabbing her arms with their unyielding grip. She screamed at their touch, memories flooding back, but this wasn't the same as before. This was worse. Or if not worse, it was more final. The realisation hit her like a tidal wave. She felt sick, faint, utterly powerless. It wasn't fair.

This wasn't fair.

She continued to scream, thrashing against the men's grip, but they were too strong. As they dragged her towards the door she was overwhelmed with regret, fear, shame – all the usual feelings, but magnified a thousand times.

She'd messed up. She'd failed in her mission.

And now she was going to pay the price.

Chapter Fifty-Two

Templeton climbed out of the back of the black Chevy Suburban, giving the driver a curt nod in lieu of thanks.

"I'm taking a personal day tomorrow. I'll see you later," he said, before shutting the door and tapping his knuckles gently on the roof. He stood there for a moment, watching the vehicle disappear around the corner, his breath misting in the cold Manhattan night air. It had been one hell of a day.

One hell of a week.

He rubbed his temples, thinking about the glass of scotch he'd help himself to once he got up to his apartment. Just as he turned to his building, his phone rang. He glanced at his watch – 2:30 a.m.

"Who the hell is calling at this—" He cut himself off, realising exactly who would be calling him at this hour. "Shit."

He pulled the phone from his jacket pocket, eyes narrowing at the screen. No caller ID, as usual. He composed himself for a moment then answered. "Xander Templeton here."

"We know, Mr Templeton. We called you." The voice on the other end was calm but there was an edge to it. Templeton's grip tightened on the phone. "Where is the formula, Mr Templeton?"

"What? I don't know. Retrieving the formula wasn't my assignment." He heard a deep breath on the other end of the line, a rare show of emotion for them. "Don't you have it?"

"No, we don't. Something has gone wrong."

Templeton leaned against the front door. "I see." He paused, weighing his next words. "Does Turner have it?"

The line went dead for a moment. It wasn't uncommon; they often played these games. He waited, the seconds dragging on. At last the voice returned. "No."

Templeton stepped back and lifted his head. The night sky stretched endlessly above him, a vast, cold expanse. He exhaled slowly, feeling the tightness in his chest ease just a bit.

"Is Turner dead?" he asked.

More silence, then a single clipped word. "Yes."

"Then I did my part."

He wanted to ask about Reed but held back. They had no idea he was aware of her betrayal, and it was better to keep it that way. Finally a voice spoke, a different one from before. That wasn't uncommon, either. "No matter, Mr Templeton. We move on. We reset the game. We go again. This isn't what we anticipated, but time is on our side, as always. Good evening, Mr Templeton. Until next time."

The line went dead. He switched off his phone and slid it back into his pocket. "Yeah, until next time."

He sniffed and shook his head. Funny. In the end, The

Consortium didn't give a damn. To them it was all just a game, and people were nothing more than pawns on their chessboard. But what could he do about it? He was just one man. He scanned the dark, empty street before unlocking his front door and stepping inside.

In the lobby he called the elevator and rode it up to the eighth floor. There were only two apartments on this level – his, and one belonging to an elderly woman named Louisa who rarely ventured out. He reached his door and unlocked it, more eager than ever for that glass of scotch.

The security alarm was off. *Strange.* Had he set it? Maybe not. His mind had been all over the place these last few days. He shrugged off his jacket, hung it in the hall, and moved into the front room, flicking on the light.

"Shit!"

John Beckett was sitting in Templeton's favourite chair, right in front of the fireplace. He was dressed head to toe in black, his hair slicked back. In his hand he held a Glock 19, aimed directly at Templeton.

"How the hell did you—?" He stopped himself. He didn't need to ask how Beckett found him or how he got in. This was John Beckett. That was all the answer he needed.

Beckett looked around the room, taking in the bespoke Italian leather couch, the antique Persian rug, the custom-built walnut bookcases. "Nice place," he said. "What does an apartment in the Flatiron District overlooking Madison Square Park go for these days? Two, three million?"

Templeton said nothing.

"After twenty years of service I imagine you're pulling in, what, a hundred, a hundred and twenty grand a year? Good money, Templeton. But there's no way you can afford this place, plus your listed residences in Washington and London, on a government salary."

"It's family money. I inherited it."

Beckett's expression remained cold. "Of course you did."

He stepped further into the room, gesturing at the chair opposite Beckett. "May I?"

Beckett flicked the gun in response.

Sitting down, he took a moment to gather his thoughts. "Well, son. Looks like you're holding all the cards. What do you want?"

"What do I want?" Beckett's eyes narrowed. "You bastard. The Consortium? Really? I had my suspicions you were flirting with them, but now you're outright in bed with them."

Templeton smirked. "You think you know it all, huh, Mr High and Mighty? Well, you don't."

Beckett jutted his chin. "So… enlighten me."

"Reed acted alone. I had nothing to do with what she pulled."

His visitor didn't respond immediately, but the skin around his eyes tightened as he absorbed the information. "Did you know she was working for The Consortium?"

Templeton shrugged. "I had my suspicions. Putting her on this assignment was as much about testing her loyalty as anything else. It looks like she failed."

Beckett's eyes flickered with understanding, maybe even a hint of resignation. "I'd say so," he muttered. "Is she dead?"

"I don't know."

A brief flash of sadness crossed Beckett's face before vanishing behind his mask of professional detachment. Templeton watched him closely, trying to gauge just how much he knew. The Consortium didn't have the formula.

Templeton didn't have it. Nobody knew where it was. What a fucking waste of time.

Or... was it?

"I should kill you right now," Beckett growled, keeping the Glock steady, aimed squarely at Templeton's chest. "I can't let this lie. If one of us doesn't die, then you'll keep coming for me."

Templeton let out a bitter laugh. "Is that what you think of me?"

"It's what I know."

He shook his head. "No. No, son. You've got it all wrong." He watched Beckett's expression, waiting for it to crack. "How is our friend Mr Turner?" he asked, but Beckett didn't flinch. They stared at each other like rival poker players for several seconds until at last Beckett relented.

"He's safe. How did you know?"

Templeton allowed himself a small, triumphant smile. "Because that's how I wanted it to go, son."

Beckett's eyebrows twitched, and his grip on the Glock loosened slightly. Then his gaze sharpened as he got it. "Explain."

Templeton leaned back in his chair. "I knew it would turn out this way. Or at least I did everything in my power to steer it in this direction. I know what you're like, John. I knew you'd dig up the truth and pull something like this. That's why I coerced you into taking the mission. It had to be you." He paused, letting his words sink in before continuing. "The Consortium wanted Turner dead as soon as they learned he was assigned to take out Bader. I had to figure out how to save his life without losing my standing with them."

"I see," Beckett said. "And what about my niece?"

Templeton raised his hand. "Leverage. But you have my word I would never have hurt her." He placed his hand on his heart. "I just needed to focus your attention – so you'd figure out how to make it look like you'd killed Turner without actually going through with it."

"Big risk for you."

"Aren't our entire lives big risks, son?"

Beckett curled his lip. "The Consortium have you well under their thumb, don't they?"

"No. It's not like that." He shook his head firmly. "The Consortium are ruthless bastards, but they're powerful. It's in everyone's best interests that I keep them onside, for now."

"Coward."

He chuckled. "Not at all. I'm just keeping my hand in as many pies as I can, like any good operative in this seedy world we call intelligence."

Beckett scoffed, but Templeton noticed a glint of respect in his eyes. Just for a second.

"You know what they say, son. Don't ever underestimate an old man in a profession where men die young."

Beckett almost smiled. "So this all played out the way you wanted it? You fancy yourself as a real puppet master."

"Not entirely – in either sense," Templeton replied. "The formula is still in the wind. We don't know what happened to Reed."

Beckett's face darkened. "She's probably dead. Like you said, she took the briefcase but failed to secure the formula. I doubt her paymasters will let that slide."

"Where is the formula?"

"I don't know."

They stared at each other for what seemed like an eternity. Finally Templeton cleared his throat. "Well, it seems we've come to an impasse. A stalemate."

Beckett got to his feet and walked over to him, pressing the cold barrel of the gun against his forehead. Templeton tensed. Another eternity passed. Then Beckett lowered the gun and spun it around, offering him the handle.

Templeton hesitated, then took it.

"It's one of yours anyway," Beckett said.

Templeton placed the gun on the chair arm, immediately sensing by its weight that Beckett had removed the magazine.

"Don't get up," Beckett said. "I'll see myself out."

As Beckett walked to the door, Templeton leaned forward and lifted his trouser leg just enough to reach the Ruger LCP II in his ankle holster. The gun was compact and lightweight but effective enough at this range.

"Hey, Beckett."

Beckett turned, his eyes narrowing as he noticed the gun in Templeton's hand and realised it wasn't the Glock he'd handed over.

"Sorry, son. I'm going to need that pendant," Templeton said.

Beckett paused, then snorted softly, a smirk tugging at the corner of his mouth. He reached into his back pocket and pulled out a silver chain and pendant – the one Bader wore around his neck.

"Did you check it?" Templeton asked him, and Beckett shook his head.

"But if the formula isn't on there, I don't know where it is. The pendant's a USB drive, as I'm sure you already know."

"How did you figure it out?" Templeton asked.

Beckett shrugged. "Intuition, experience. How did you?"

Templeton tapped his temple with the muzzle of his gun. "Great minds and all that. Was it hard to recover?"

"Not really. Vassos and his crew – even Reed – were all too eager to get their hands on the briefcase to consider it might be a decoy."

Templeton stood and walked towards him, holding out his hand. Beckett let the pendant dangle from the chain for a moment before flicking it back into his fist. "What are you going to do with it?" he asked, then handed it over.

"I'm not sure yet. But don't worry, it won't fall into the wrong hands. I'm one of the good guys, remember?"

Beckett didn't reply.

"And you and I are done," he added. "I'm not going to come for you anymore. If… you can say the same."

Beckett hesitated, then nodded. "I suppose so. But Turner's out there somewhere. You turned him into a ghost. He might come looking for payback."

Templeton grinned. "I'll be ready. I always am."

Beckett walked to the door and paused, gripping the handle. "So this is it?" he asked, turning his head slightly. "We're good?"

Templeton shrugged. "We're good."

"Okay then. I suppose I'll see you around." Beckett opened the door and stepped into the corridor, leaving it ajar for a moment before pulling it shut behind him without looking back.

Templeton remained still, listening as Beckett's footsteps faded away. Only when he was certain he was gone did he lower his gun.

I suppose I'll see you around.

"Yes, more than likely, Mr Beckett," Templeton muttered under his breath. "More than likely."

Chapter Fifty-Three

Three days later, Beckett found himself back in Costa Rica. The last few days had been a blur of travel, sleep and recuperation. But now, feeling a little more grounded, he was back at the Casa Selva hotel to tie up loose ends and say goodbye.

It felt a little absurd – retrieving a safely stored passport just to collect another one in a different name. But for Beckett, wrapping up details like this was second nature. More than that, he wanted to leave the place he'd called home for months without raising too many eyebrows.

He kept things simple, exchanging a few polite words with the staff, stripping his room of his belongings and any trace he'd ever been there. He'd decided to take Templeton on his word, but for a man like John Beckett the instinct to vanish quickly and completely was ingrained. No matter what he said, or what had happened to him these last few years, the truth was he'd always be a ghost. That was his life. That was who he was.

Señor Morales had looked genuinely dismayed when

Beckett handed over his keys and explained it was his final day. The manager had even pleaded with him to reconsider, baffled by the abrupt departure of his handyman. But Beckett had no real answer for him except for the one he gave everyone: it was time to move on. Simple as that.

As he stepped out of the cool lobby into the midday heat, a voice called his name from the bar. He turned to see Isabella sitting alone, enjoying a glass of wine in the lunchtime sun. She looked good. Petite, confident, attractive in a way that didn't need much effort. She waved him over with a smile that suggested there was still something unresolved between them. Beckett paused, then turned in her direction.

"No goodbye?" she said, in her husky Spanish accent.

"Word travels fast." He nodded at her drink. "Enjoying yourself?"

"Day off." She raised her glass. "Drink with me?"

He hesitated. There was a flight he could catch tonight, but another half hour wouldn't change anything. He caught the bartender's eye and raised a finger; mouthed, *una cerveza*.

Isabella looked pleased as he slid into the seat across from her. "I also hear you leave forever," she said, sticking her bottom lip out in a playful pout. "That is sad. Where will you go?"

Beckett offered a small smile in return. "Not sure yet. Phoenix, for now. Then maybe Spain. I have family there."

Isabella's expression shifted, clearly expecting more, but Beckett left it at that. Simple, direct. She didn't need to know the rest. She wouldn't understand it anyway. That when he'd first arrived in Costa Rica he'd thought it could be a place to lie low for a while. Maybe even settle for a stretch. But that was just wishful thinking.

He'd already called Beaumont to thank him and let him

know things were wrapped up on this end. He didn't tell him everything, just enough to ease any lingering concerns. And he'd made sure to warn him about keeping a close eye on Templeton. Not that his old handler needed the heads-up. Beaumont had been in this game long enough to know how to deal with someone like Templeton.

"Maybe I should come with you," Isabella said, flicking her eyebrows. "A holiday. Company. Do you think?"

Beckett's beer arrived, and he took a slow sip, using the moment to ease the tension. As the waiter strolled away, he smiled and shook his head, pretending to take Isabella's offer as a joke. "You'd get bored with me quickly. Or irritated. I'm not the best company, I can assure you." His tone was light-hearted, but there was truth in his words, he knew.

The conversation drifted into casual, lazy banter. Isabella tossed out questions, teasing him for details, but Beckett kept his answers vague, giving her only what he could afford to reveal and no more. She didn't seem to mind. They were just passing the time, after all.

"You will work?" she asked.

"Eventually. But I've got the inheritance from my father," he replied, sticking to the story he'd told everyone. "Gives me some breathing room."

In reality, what came next was her guess as good as his. A part of him wondered about returning to London for a while. It'd be good to see Beaumont in person, maybe visit his father's grave. But even with Templeton's assurances, Beckett wasn't convinced where he stood with Sigma Unit or MI6. He didn't want to press Beaumont for answers – it wasn't the old man's decision to make, and he probably didn't have the clearance to know. Best to play it safe for now. Keep moving, stay off the radar.

"Another drink?" Isabella asked, her voice dropping as

she added, "Or... I have tequila. In my room." Her eyes and smile left no doubt regarding the subtext of her offer.

But before Beckett could respond, Señor Morales appeared at the side of the seating area, calling out to Isabella in rapid Spanish. Beckett caught the gist – something about a lost key and needing her help *urgentemente*.

Isabella groaned and stood, finishing the last of her wine in one quick gulp. "I will be quick," she said. "You'll stay a while?"

Beckett smiled, holding her gaze for a moment before she turned to help her boss. He watched her walk away, her thick, dark hair swaying with each step. Her intentions were clear, and for a moment he entertained the idea. But as he leaned back in his chair the moment was already fading.

He took another sip of his beer, thinking again about what came next. Spain, probably. He had to see Amber. That decision was made and now it was time to follow through. It would be nice to spend some quality time with her, make up for lost ground. But maybe he'd make a stop along the way, see the Grand Canyon. He'd always wanted to visit but had never had the chance. An endless expanse of hard rock, shaped by relentless forces that refused to let it rest. The metaphor was almost too relatable.

His thoughts shifted to Erica Reed. He still didn't know the full story of what had happened to her, and he wasn't sure he wanted to. She'd taken the wrong path, like so many others. When the world tries to break someone, they usually respond one of two ways: either they dedicate themselves to helping others who are hurting, or they try to burn everything to the ground. Reed had chosen the latter. He felt bad about what happened to her, but there was nothing he could do now. She'd made her choices.

He looked over to the open doorway at the side of the

hotel where Isabella had disappeared. Her voice carried faintly through the air. She'd be back in a few minutes. He could stay, let himself fall into the easy rhythm of Costa Rica for a while longer. But that wasn't his life. It never had been. He understood that now better than ever.

He set his beer down, still half full, and got to his feet. He took one last look at the bay, the hotel, the life he could have had if things had been different. Then, without a second thought, he turned and walked away. Best to leave now, before he got too comfortable. Men like Beckett and Turner didn't get to stay anywhere for too long.

That was just the way it was.

Next in The John Beckett Series

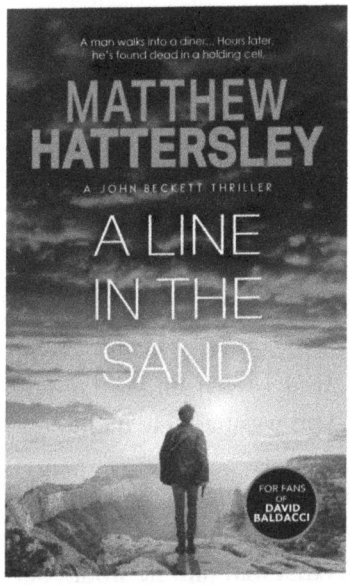

vinci-books.com/LineintheSand

A man walks into a diner, bleeding and armed. He claims he's being hunted. Hours later, he's found dead in a holding cell.

John Beckett doesn't buy the suicide story. When the evidence vanishes and questions are brushed aside, he starts digging. His search leads to a missing device everyone wants but won't admit exists. The closer he gets to the truth, the more others want him silenced. Without backup, resources, and time running out, Beckett faces a threat that could bring down all he's fought to protect.

Turn the page for a free preview…

A Line in the Sand: Chapter One

Evan felt as if he'd been running for hours but was still nowhere at all. This was bad. He had to find safety. Sanctuary. He had to get away.

But even as this realisation hit, darker thoughts were already creeping in, tightening around his mind like a noose. Thoughts that told him he would never find safety in this world. Not now. Not after what he'd done.

Pushing these ideas aside, he gritted his teeth and pressed on. His side was burning with a stitch and his hair was wet with sweat, but stopping wasn't an option. Not now. Not with everything behind him. He had to keep moving.

His lungs burned with every breath, sharp and hot like someone had shoved a knife between his ribs. His legs were weak, threatening to buckle with every step, but he forced them forward, one after the other.

He ran as fast he could, running for his life, running until he couldn't run any more and had to stop, gasping for air. Leaning against a rock, he wiped his face with the back of his hand, smearing sweat and dirt into the streaks of blood already drying on his skin. It wasn't his blood, but he didn't have time to think about where it had come from. Not now.

It was early afternoon and the Vegas sun beat down hard, the higher than average October temperatures turning the desert into a furnace, the kind of heat that pressed down on you, made you feel small. He licked his cracked lips. What he wouldn't give for a cold beer right now. Hell, even a glass of water would do.

He'd lived in Las Vegas his whole life and the city had never been good to him. But it had been his world, and now he couldn't ever go back. He'd screwed that up, just like everything else he touched. His chest tightened at the thought but he pushed it aside. He couldn't afford to feel sorry for himself.

He glanced down at the sweat-darkened front of his shirt. His arms and shoulders ached, and his side still felt like someone had driven a spike into it, but rest was a luxury that he couldn't afford. They would be coming soon enough, and he had to get out of Dodge before they found him.

He set off again, pressing his hand against his ribs, breathing through his teeth as the pain flared. He'd only travelled a few metres when every muscle screamed for him to stop again. For good. To drop right there on the gravel and let it all catch up to him. But he didn't. He couldn't. His daddy had taught him to keep moving even when it hurts.

Especially when it hurts.

He stumbled, nearly going down, but caught himself just in time. Swiping at his face, he tried to steady his thoughts, though the heat made his head spin. The highway stretched endlessly ahead, a jagged strip of cracked blacktop slicing through the barren desert. He glanced over his shoulder, checking to see if anyone was following. That's when he spotted the gas station in the distance.

Shit.

What the hell had he done?

In the last ten minutes things had gone from bad to worse, from chaos to catastrophe. And no matter how fast he ran, some part of him knew he couldn't outrun it. He hadn't planned to stop there. He hadn't planned any of this. But his truck's gas needle had dipped into the red and there was nothing but open desert for miles. He'd pulled in because he had no choice, the old Buick coasting to a sputtering halt beside the first of the two pumps. At least he could fill up and get some water.

Or so he'd thought.

He'd stepped inside, hoping for a break, a chance to figure this out. Instead, he got some shitty kid behind the counter smirking at him like he'd seen it all before. He'd fumbled for his wallet, patting his jeans pockets as the sinking feeling took hold. He had the device. But no wallet. He could picture it on his dresser back home. He'd left in such a rush that he'd...

Fuck.

And of course, the kid didn't care.

"No money, no gas."

As he'd stepped away from the counter, he'd felt the hard steel of the revolver stuffed down the back of his jeans. His daddy's old Smith and Wesson. Could he? Should he?

The kid was behind reinforced glass, but maybe if he caused enough of a scene he'd turn on the pump. But before he even drew, the kid reached for the phone.

"You want me to call the cops?"

He'd turned and bolted outside, desperate. That's when the man came out of nowhere. Evan couldn't remember his face; he hadn't really looked. But he could still feel the grip on his arm. He'd tried to twist away but the man wouldn't let go, kept telling him to calm down.

Evan's hand had gone to his waistband before he'd realised what he was doing. He could still hear the shot that followed.

The memory of it made him stumble, but he caught himself and kept going, wiping a hand across his forehead to clear the sweat dripping into his eyes. He hadn't meant to shoot anyone, it just happened. One moment the man was pulling him back, and the next he was—

But he shouldn't have damn well tried to stop him! That was his fault, not Evan's. He'd panicked.

He hadn't even checked if the guy was dead. He couldn't. He'd taken one look at the body lying on the concrete, blood pooling beneath him, and his legs had taken over.

Run.

He could hear sirens now, faint but getting closer. The kid must have called them.

Cursing under his breath, Evan pushed himself to move faster. As he ran, he tapped his jacket pocket, checking for the device, needing the reassurance that it was still there.

It was. The thing that had set him on this hopeless path. Some kind of tablet but smaller, more like a phone, used in the warehouse for logging deliveries. And, as he'd discovered, so much more.

Why the hell had he taken it?

It had felt like the right thing to do at the time. Later it became insurance – a way out of the mess he'd made. Now it felt like a curse. He was running because of it. Hunted because of it.

A murderer because of it.

It was all Jen's fault. Or it was his feelings for her, at least. She made him want to be a better man, like old Jack Nicholson said in that movie. She made him want to do good. So he'd taken it, thinking it might stop the ones using it for bad things. Instead all he'd done was paint a target on his back.

And now he might never see Jen again.

His stomach twisted at the thought. She'd been the one bright spot in his life, the only person who had ever believed in him. She'd seen something in him that no one else had. Maybe something that wasn't even there. Shit, would they go after her too? He didn't think they would. Hoped they wouldn't. But hope didn't mean much these days.

He should have gone to the cops with the device the moment he realised he was being followed. That had been the plan, hadn't it? Do the right thing for once in his life. Walk into a police station, hand over the device, and tell them everything. A clean slate. Maybe even redemption.

But he hadn't done that.

He'd spotted the black SUV parked at the end of his street, seen the men watching him from the corner, and any plan he'd had evaporated in an instant. Panic took over, overriding reason, shoving aside whatever good intentions he'd started with.

Now he was running. From them, from the cops, from everything.

He swallowed hard, tasting dust and sweat on his tongue. He wasn't built for this. He wasn't clever enough, wasn't strong enough. He'd thought he could make Jen proud, thought he could make a difference. But he was just another idiot who'd gotten in over his head.

Paranoia kept him glancing over his shoulder, scanning the empty highway. It was still just him, the endless stretch of asphalt, and the heat waves rippling off the road. But they'd come. He knew they'd come.

Up ahead something broke through the shimmering haze. At first he thought it was a mirage, some cruel trick of the sun. But as he squinted, raising a hand to shield his eyes from the glare, a diner came into focus. One of those old-fashioned places that looked like it had been dropped on the side of the road fifty years ago and hadn't seen a lick of paint since.

He slowed his pace, weighing his options. Out here he was a sitting duck, a lone figure on an empty highway with nothing but endless desert on either side. The diner didn't seem much safer. It was too open. Too exposed. And if someone inside started asking questions, things could spiral fast. But it was something, and something was better than nothing.

He felt for the device. Still there. Felt for his revolver. Ditto. Neither felt like they'd save him, but the sirens were getting louder now. If the people he'd stolen from didn't catch him, the cops would. Staying put was asking for trouble, and he couldn't run for much longer. He needed cover.

Casting one last look down the highway, he took a deep breath and headed for the diner.

A Line in the Sand: Chapter Two

Beckett clocked the guy the second he walked through the door. Other people in the diner saw him too, but most just looked up briefly before returning to their meals or conversations.

Beckett didn't.

There was nothing overtly wrong with the guy. He was in his early thirties, medium build, average looks, he carried no visible weapon. The kind of guy you'd pass on the street most days without a second glance. But Beckett didn't miss details. The man's clothes were streaked with dirt and sweat like he'd been on the move for hours. His hair clung to his forehead in damp curls.

But it was how the man moved that held Beckett's attention. His steps were jerky and hesitant, like he didn't know what he was doing here. Most guys walking into a diner have one thing on their mind – maybe two if the waitress is a looker – but this guy wasn't eyeing the menu or the female servers. He was looking for something. Or hiding from it.

His eyes darted around the room as he headed to the

counter, scanning every face without letting his gaze settle, like he was assessing threats and tracking exits. That was the giveaway.

A man who moved like that wasn't hungry or overheated.

He was scared.

Beckett didn't look away, but he didn't stare either. He just sipped his coffee and watched. From his seat in the far corner of the diner, he had the wall at his back and a clear view of the entire room. He'd chosen the spot instinctively, as he always did, even if it meant sitting apart from his fellow travellers. They'd been here twenty minutes, waiting out the heat and the delay caused by their broken-down coach.

The diner was small and run-down, barely holding itself together, the kind of place that survived on passing truckers and the occasional stranded tourist like himself. The walls were cluttered with old licence plates and tin signs advertising long-dead brands. A jukebox sat in the corner, but the lights were off and there was no music to drown out the clatter of plates and low murmur of conversation.

The waitress – a hard-faced woman in her fifties – worked the room with brisk indifference, her faded blue uniform straining at the seams as she dropped off plates and refilled mugs, not paying attention to anything she didn't have to. But Beckett was paying enough attention for everyone. He watched as the new guy leaned against the counter, rubbing at the side of his face, then patting at his pockets as if worried he'd lost something. He wasn't looking for a place to sit or for someone he knew. He didn't want to be here.

Beckett understood that feeling. He hadn't wanted to be here either. The difference was, he didn't have a choice.

Four hours earlier he'd been standing at the edge of the

Grand Canyon, staring out into the kind of vastness that made people insignificant. And it had felt like balance. A reminder of forces that had shaped the Earth over millennia, forces that didn't care about lines or boundaries or consequences.

Not that standing beside something of such epic grandeur hadn't given him cause to reflect on his own life. As usual when faced with such things, John Beckett's thoughts went to his past. To the things he'd done. The lines he'd crossed – and, more specifically, the ones he hadn't. He'd lived his life dancing on the edge of those lines, never fully crossing but never stepping back either. Looking down into the rocky abyss was a brutal reminder that nature was in effect its own line in the sand. The kind he respected but never fully obeyed. For a fleeting moment, though, he'd felt free. As free as a man like him could ever feel.

But the trip to the Grand Canyon was only meant to be brief, just a way to kill a few hours before his flight that evening. His passport and luggage were stashed at Harry Reid International Airport, and he was booked on a 7 p.m. flight to Germany, with a connection to Spain to finally see his niece, Amber, who he hadn't seen since both their lives had been thrown into chaos. She'd been staying with an old friend of his, a man Beckett trusted to keep her safe from the kind of danger that always seemed too close to his door. But with the CIA's Xander Templeton off his back – at least for now – it felt like the right time for a visit. Nearly two years had passed since he'd last seen her. She'd already turned nineteen a few months ago. A young woman. The thought of reconnecting with her stirred something in him that felt almost like hope. But there was also guilt there too, as well as a little unease.

He had hoped to work through his unrest during the

space, fresh air, and peace and quiet of the canyon trip, but his tight schedule had forced him to join a tour group instead. It wasn't ideal – too many people, too much chatter – but it had been the only option. And in the end it was worth it. The canyon hit him harder than he'd expected. The size. The emptiness. It was a worthy reminder that some things were bigger than him, a feeling that stayed with him even on the ride back to Vegas.

When the bus overheated outside Arrolime, he and the other passengers had filed out onto the highway under the blazing sun. Some grumbled quietly to themselves, others directed their frustration at the tour guide, but no one was happy. The diner had been their only option while they waited for a replacement bus.

So now here he was, sitting in a corner booth, irritated by the delay and watchful of the clock. He had six hours until his flight, ample time as long as nothing else went wrong. Which was why the man who had just walked in had his full attention. Beckett didn't like problems, and this guy looked a lot like one.

He kept his eyes on him, watching the way the man's hands twitched like he couldn't decide what to do with them, and the way his eyes darted to the window every few seconds. The atmosphere in the diner felt different now, charged, like the other customers were starting to pick up on something even if they weren't consciously aware of it yet. Beckett didn't move, his hand still resting lightly on the table. His instincts told him to stay ready.

"Hey, sugar, what can I get ya?"

Beckett glanced at the waitress who appeared at his table. He hadn't seen this one earlier, possibly she was on her break when he came in. She couldn't have been more than twenty-five, her blonde ponytail bouncing as she tilted her head, giving him a once-over.

"We got a fresh pot of coffee on, or the eggs are good," she added, with a flirtatious wink.

He returned a polite smile. "Eggs sound good. I'll take them scrambled, with toast if you have it. And a coffee."

"Good choice."

She lingered for a moment, her smile turning a shade more playful, but Beckett didn't bite. After a second she walked off, swaying her hips as she went, and he turned his attention back to the man at the counter.

The guy was now talking to the older waitress, who was wiping her hands on her apron and shaking her head. She looked worn out, like she'd been on her feet for decades. There was no warmth in her expression, no hint of a smile. What he was saying clearly didn't sit right with her. She shook her head again, more emphatic this time. Whatever he wanted, the answer was still no.

"I need you to fucking listen to me!" the man yelled, slamming his fist on the counter, hard enough to make a row of ketchup bottles jump.

Someone yelped. But the waitress held her ground, raising her hands in a plea for calm. "All right, sir. Take it easy. We don't need to make a scene."

But the man wasn't interested. He looked like a cornered animal. No plan, just panic. Beckett grabbed the edge of the table but he didn't move. Not yet.

"I need a car," the man was saying. "I need to get out of here."

"That's a big ask, sir." The waitress shook her head. "I can't help with that."

The guy was spiralling now, his entire body tense and jittery. He wasn't hearing her. He wasn't hearing anything.

His eyes darted to the door, then back to the counter, his jaw clenching and unclenching like he was chewing a scream.

Beckett rolled his shoulders back, steadying himself as he waited for the moment to break. He knew it was coming.

The guy cried out and reached around his back. Beckett tightened his grip on the table edge as a revolver was whipped out and pointed at the waitress.

The room froze.

For a split second everything was still. The waitress, already holding her hands up, looked more shocked than frightened as she stared at the gun. The man stood there, chest heaving, the revolver shaking in his grip.

Then all hell broke loose.

Someone screamed. A baby wailed. A chair screeched across the floor as it was shoved back hard. Diners scrambled under tables, overturning drinks and plates in their desperate bid for safety.

The man grew frantic, shouting at people to stay down as he swung the gun in a wide arc. His hand was trembling so badly that if he fired it could hit anything. Or anyone.

Beckett still hadn't moved and the guy hadn't noticed him yet. That was a good thing. But then Beckett heard it.

Sirens.

They were faint at first, but growing louder by the second. The man heard them too, his head snapping towards the window. Outside it was still just desert and empty road, but any minute now police cars would come screeching to a halt at the door, kicking up dust and commotion. Two, at least, judging by the sound.

The man gritted his teeth and turned back to the room, his eyes wide, panicked.

"Nobody move!" he shouted, waving the gun around as if he'd already lost whatever game he was playing.

Not good. Not good at all.

Beckett stayed where he was, his fingers resting on the handle of a fork for a moment before he dismissed the idea. Too risky. The man was scared and erratic, still pointing the gun at the terrified diners. It wouldn't take anything at all for him to pull the trigger, and then a fork wouldn't change a damn thing.

The sirens were almost on top of them now, closing in fast.

"Everyone shut the hell up," the man yelled, shouting for calm like that would do any good. "I need to think! Goddamnit!"

Beckett released a long, steady breath. The cops were almost here and the guy was running out of options. It wasn't time to move yet. But it would be.

Any second now.

Get your copy...
vinci-books.com/LineintheSand

About the Author

Over the last twenty years Matthew Hattersley has toured Europe in rock 'n' roll bands, trained as a professional actor and founded a theatre and media company. He's also had a lot of dead end jobs…

Now he writes high-octane pulp action thrillers and crime fiction.

He lives with his wife and daughter in Derbyshire, UK, and doesn't feel that comfortable writing about himself in the third person.